The Broken Cross

A Cameron Ballack mystery

Luke H. Davis

Permission to quote in critical reviews with citation:
The Broken Cross
By Luke H. Davis

ISBN 978-0-9884613-8-3

DUNROBIN
PUBLISHING

www.dunrobin.us

To Joshua and Lindsay,
for their hope and determination
in the midst of life's brokenness.

And in memory of our sweet little Jordan,
who already enjoys everlasting peace and wholeness,
and who waits for us.

AUTHOR'S NOTE

The world of detective fiction, while a product of the writer's imagination, nonetheless intersects with the warp and woof of gritty reality. When that world is the cloistered structure of the Christian religion, such fiction can breed an understandable amount of backlash. Part of this is due to certain expectations, namely that the Church at large should be a safe haven from harm rather than a perpetrator of it. Yet my experiences, coupled with the historic Christian teaching on humankind's moral corruption, keep driving me toward a picture of the Church as a beautiful yet profoundly stained entity. If one doesn't see this, then I would surmise one's eyes are not fully open.

Despite this actuality, readers should not interpret *The Broken Cross* as a punchy diatribe against the Catholic Church. An institution of more than one billion followers will have ample faults among its leadership and lay members. To its credit, the Vatican has owned up to a number of its failings. The issue of other organizations and lay movements under the Catholic umbrella can be a good bit thornier. Such activities are represented herein by the fictional portrayal of Father Joseph Quinn, Corpus Sancti, the Barons of St. Paul, and the Barons' founder Antoine Levesque. This is done for the sake of the plot, not to deepen further sadness or depression amongst those affected by such horrific malevolence in their lives. If you are among those afflicted by clergy sexual abuse (or sexual abuse of any provenance, from any denomination), rest assured that you—part of a wider host of victims—are in my prayers for your recovery and healing.

I would also hope that the character of Cameron Ballack has opened and will continue to open the minds and hearts of others, thus making them willing to see the physically disabled as handi-capable and not handicapped. While Ballack is a fictional character, his neuromuscular disorder is all too real. X-linked myotubular myopathy (and its cousin, centronuclear myopathy) stalks its victims even as progress is being made toward a hoped-for cure. Our oldest child Joshua and our late son Jordan are among the afflicted. If the one thing that comes out of this series is a growing awareness of myotubular myopathy and a dedication toward a cure, such blessings will be satisfaction enough. You can find out more details through our friends and colleagues in hope, Paul and Alison Frase, at www.joshuafrase.org.

Once again, I would be wrong to bypass those who have been a part of this project as it moved toward completion. Heartfelt thanks must go to my immediate and extended family for their support and encouragement, not to mention my parents' pecuniary generosity with the efforts of bringing this volume to publication. Mark Sutherland of Dunrobin Publishing continues to be both a refreshing encouragement and an honest soul. Shannon Hathaway deserves perpetual gratitude for her feedback, watchful critique, and editorial eye. Lester Stuckmeyer and John Bauer provided much insight into the details of courtroom life.

Natives of St. Louis will find I have altered some locations to fit settings within the story. However, I trust such readers will find landmarks such as the Cathedral Basilica, the Drury Plaza at the Arch and its surroundings, Smugala's Pizza, and the popular Fast Eddie's

Bon Air are laid out with rigorous precision and care. A number of locations in the novel are obviously contrived, among them being Harvest Capital & Mortgage, the law office of Lance Stubblefield, and the firm of Gillette, Wales & Alexander. I would again emphasize that the characters and activities of this story are fictitious and exist either in the terrain of my imagination or are a matter of coincidence.

The tragedy of murder is that it happens. The heartbreak of this story is that it strikes within the secure hallows of a church. The ongoing reality is that faith communities will sometimes let us down. But the beauty of justice is that, even in meager ways, healing might begin. And perhaps that means some of us can come to grips with faith in a new and better way.

Ash Wednesday 2015

"God bless us, every one.

We're a broken people living under loaded gun,

And it can't be outfought, it can't be outdone,

It can't be outmatched, it can't be outrun, no...

God save us, every one.

Will we burn inside the fires of a thousand suns

For the sins of our hands, the sins of our tongues,

The sins of our fathers, the sins of our young?"

(Linkin Park, "The Catalyst")

Then Peter went up to him and said, "Lord, how often must I forgive

my brother if he wrongs me? Up to seven times?"

Jesus answered, "Not seven, I tell you, but seventy-seven times."

(The Gospel of St. Matthew 18:20-22)

"Force may subdue, but love gains,

and he that forgives first wins the laurel."

(William Penn)

PROLOGUE
"I absolve you"

(Five years ago)

Philippe navigated his way through the north cloister behind the chapel. A cool breeze caused his loose shirt to billow as he walked. The words of Father Joseph's homily scalded his ears. It was as if he could visualize the guilty verdict materializing from the chaplain's hands as he gesticulated, directing his words toward Philippe and those assembled in the church. He knew, thought Philippe, but of course he knew. Like a small bear in a hunter's trap, he was caught with nowhere to go. Whatever integrity he brought to this place, whatever shred of rectitude he hoped to retain, all of it was gone. The words he had read at Mass just two hours before pierced his soul like a javelin.

"Hear my cry, O God, listen to my prayer; from the end of the earth I call to you when my heart is faint. Lead me to the rock that is higher than I, for you have been my refuge, a strong tower against the enemy."

How his voice had trembled at the reader's lectern. How Father Joseph's glance, though discreet, had burned through him. And how the words seemed so empty, so void, so hopeless. No confidence was there that his yearning would be known, that deliverance could come. He continued to read to the end of the Psalm, but his voice was wooden, carrying no assurance of the ancient truths on the sacred page.

"Let me dwell in your tent forever! Let me take refuge under the shelter of your wings! For you, O God, have heard my vows; you have given me the heritage of those who fear your name."

He stood there, clutching the lectern, sensing he would topple into his gorge of despondency. *Who fear your name,* he thought to

1

himself. *Who fear your name.* He had looked out at the sea of faces in the chapel. *And fear is all I have.*

The rest of the Mass had gone on without disturbance, and now the least he could hope for was a quiet dinner in the dining hall. But his brooding thoughts were broken by Father Joseph again. The strong hands with perfectly trimmed fingernails set the tray of rosemary chicken, potatoes and broccoli across from him. Father Joseph permitted nothing on his person to be out of place. His blond hair seemed more carved than styled. His perfectly spaced, pale blue eyes seemed to burrow into the soul of everyone he met. Even the white collar peeking through the top of his robe was placed rigorously in the middle of his neck, as if to bless his whole being with unimpeachable symmetry. He gave Philippe a curt nod and a slight smile as he took his seat.

Today, however, Father Joseph was not alone. Joining him at table was a shorter, darker priest who looked as if he'd spent the last two days straight under a tanning bed. His wiry black hair matched his thin goatee that danced around his chin. A pleasant, inviting smile played on his lips and he greeted Philippe kindly.

"Good evening, young man."

"Good evening, Father," replied Philippe, pleased to have company other than Father Joseph for this meal.

"I'm sorry to you both," interjected Father Joseph with a minimal smile, "I should have introduced you. Robert, this is Philippe, one of our most outstanding community members. We've been trying to convince him to think about university and seminary after some time here. He has the gifts, and I've tried to encourage him toward the priesthood, but to no avail. He's certainly the most gifted person I have here."

Philippe stayed silent but reached across to offer his hand to the visiting priest. As always, something in Father Joseph's voice carried both an invitation and a threat. Every time he conversed with his mentor over a meal, the lights of the dining hall seemed to dim. Philippe put such thoughts out of his mind in order to greet the visitor, who warmly took his grip.

"Hello, Philippe. I'm Father Robert DeFazio, here on a consulting visit from California. Very good to meet you."

"Did you just arrive today, Father?" asked Philippe, aware of the glint in Father Joseph's eyes.

"I did, actually. Flew from San Francisco to Chicago, then took a rental car the rest of the way here."

"California's a long way away and a very different territory from here," Philippe said, aware of—yet ignoring—the disapproving gaze of Father Joseph. "What brings you here to our little family?"

"Some administrative … shall we say, opportunities. It actually doesn't touch upon Corpus Sancti, but rather other details. I was charged with starting Immaculate Conception Apostolic School out near Sacramento a few years ago, so I am aware of the sacrifices and growing pains of a new school. I was invited here to head up a venture to think through some visionary aspects of the coming years for the community here."

"Sounds like a decent challenge," said Philippe, all but ignoring Father Joseph by now.

"It was when we got Immaculate Conception up and running," said Father Robert, "and there are features of my work here this week that will be likewise. In truth, it is a bit out of my element. I have normally worked with youth and young adults. I was chaplain at a school in Scranton, Pennsylvania, for a couple years, have led retreats in Wisconsin, and I've stayed on as dean of discipline in California. Personally, I've enjoyed the ministry side of things so much more, and I'm looking to get back into chaplaincy with young adults."

Philippe, suddenly bold, piped up. "Like the role Father Joseph has here?"

"Father Robert," interrupted Father Joseph. "I don't think you've seen the campus in its totality and there are only a few moments of daylight remaining. Perhaps we can continue this conversation another time? Philippe, I seem to remember you have some reading to finish before it's due for report? Victor will come speak with you about that later this evening, I believe."

And with that discharge, every shred of Philippe's bravado disintegrated. He bowed to Father Robert, mumbled his goodbyes and picked up his tray, heading for the rear of the dining hall.

Ten o'clock came slowly, and if Philippe had thought there was any chance of escape he would have done so. He sat in his spartan room, peering at his book rather than reading it. It was never an exercise in devotion. It was always a ticket to despair, to the arena of his sheer temerity and cruelty. He cursed his slight frame and timorous spirit. All hopes of serving Christ had been laid waste and dismembered. *No*, thought Philippe, *it will end tonight.* When he illuminated the story behind these walls, that penetrating truth would bring justice. No one would ever bother him again. If Philippe could not break through and conquer the demons, neither could the demons reach him where he was going.

Again the knock on the door. Victor. Simple, pure-hearted Victor, who had no idea of the sheer hell that went on. He was only an innocent messenger boy in whom Father Joseph found no promise. Philippe sighed. How ironic. Being eschewed because of lack of potential, and that could be liberating. He had no idea. Victor had not a clue.

"Father Joseph wanted me to let you know he wanted to see you," Victor said. "He also said bring the book as usual. He would exchange it for your next assignment."

"Thank you, Victor," replied Philippe. "I'll get over there shortly. Good night."

Victor nodded and backed out. Philippe picked up his worn copy of St. Anthony of Padua's *Sermones de Tempore*. He had not read a word. He never had. He never would. His heart was incapable of such glory. He had no idea what book Father Joseph would have tried to give him tonight. All he knew was that it all had to end, one way or another. The path he would take now was his only option.

He desperately wanted out. He had for some time. The walls continued to press in from all sides. He could serve God and continue to submit himself to a private hell. He could attempt to run away, but that was impossible as well. He remembered when Jeremy tried to escape. It had all the ambiance of a prison break, and priests and administrators alike strategized in hushed tones. The call went out to the archdiocese. Philippe wasn't privy to the inner circle of conversations, but he had good enough ears to pick up snippets around corners and through thin walls. The common refrain was "Chicago will cover it" or "O'Brien sent out his men." Sure enough, Jeremy returned two nights later, submissive as a chastised puppy. And the terrors kept repeating themselves. For Jeremy. For Philippe. And for heaven knew who else was caught in the web of tortured hearts and shattered souls.

Philippe knew this much: He could not face the boys from Chicago. He wanted to run away but he knew the rough treatment he'd receive once the word went out. He wanted to escape this life, but he feared this would make him the scourge of God's kingdom. He had sworn a vow to serve Christ and to run was turning his back on that vow. Most of all, he wanted to be free from the preying tentacles he knew awaited him in the next buiding. He had tried for eighteen months to work himself loose and had no reserves left.

It was when he walked past the chapel a few days ago that he experienced both a collapse of hope and a resignation to act. Knowing no one would be in there, he opened the doors and marched straight up the middle aisle of the nave. Sliding into the third pew from the front on the right hand side, he looked up at the crucifix that dominated the apse. Slowing his breathing, Philippe began to pray. It was not a prayer of belief; this was resignation.

Remember me, Lord, that I might come into your kingdom, in spite of what your Church would teach otherwise. May I find my rest in you, because I will never receive it from them.

He trod down the hallway toward Jeremy's room. Philippe was not expecting to find his friend there, and thankfully he found the room empty. He wouldn't have been able to bear the pain in his friend's face, anyway. He had said what was required. Jeremy would know what to do with the letter. The precise instructions would guarantee that. The only question was getting it outside these walls. But that was Jeremy's mission, not his.

He passed Victor on the way down the hall, nodding to him as they drew near.

"Have a good night, Victor," he said, smiling ever so slightly.

Victor looked at his friend, who had eighteen minutes to live, and nodded politely before continuing.

The chapel, as he knew it would be, was unlocked. The priests believed that the students' desire to pray could be piously spontaneous. Philippe reflected how this idiotic over-estimation of their relative holiness was his ticket to freedom tonight.

He went to the side door in the narthex and opened it, revealing the small elevator that led up the tower to the carillon above. No church he knew of retained a manually ringing bell. Everything here was done by remote. Yet maintenance still needed to have access to

7

the tower for any cleaning or repair. Philippe was amazed that every element of his escape was coming together tonight. No one ever locked this door.

In less than a minute he had ascended to the zenith of the tower. Even in the darkness, he could see the three-foot ledge running along the tower walls. He moved around the bell, there only for decoration, and maneuvered his way to the side opposite the elevator shaft. The metal grille was securely in place, but Philippe had brought a bag of tools to rectify that. He had been up here three weeks before and had noticed the precise sizes and heads of the screws and bolts. In no time, he had unfastened the grille and set it aside. Then he reached into his other bag, pulling out the materials needed. He had swiped them after the picnic two months ago. He reached outward, finally grasping the iron bar running across the opening into the inky blackness of the night.

As the swirling breeze enveloped him, he sat there for a minute. He looked out over the campus that he thought would reflect all the promise of following Christ. All he saw now were the flames of judgment tearing at his soul. He saw the faces of the past that never smiled except when he had let them down. He saw a priest who never cared except to satisfy his selfish desires. For the last time in his life, tears welled in his eyes. All he could hope was that at the end of this, God would care. For some time, it seemed he hadn't. Otherwise, why was there the neglect and horror of days past?

He shifted forward, dressed in his cassock set aside for special occasions. Closing his eyes, he let out a groan that carried with it one last prayer.

"Father, I cast myself toward your grasp. Please catch me. I can do this no longer. Just don't be disappointed with me."

He knew the spectacle of what would follow would be an unsightly shock come morning. Yet it was the only way the truth could come out. He opened his eyes once more as he breathed deeply. He looked into the distance at the slivered moon. Through glazed eyes he swore it changed shape, from an austere, pocked curviture into the warm, adoring face of God. And this God was smiling and reaching out his hand.

LUKE H. DAVIS

BOOK ONE
"In the name of the Father"

(September 15-22)

LUKE H. DAVIS

12

1

Toby Zweig shifted nervously in his chair, quietly taking notes on his legal pad. He wiped a film of sweat from his forehead as he looked at the orchid-colored paper. He remembered the days long past when his eyes would blur with disorientation over a yellow pad, and the softer tones of the paper he used now had saved him from much ocular suffering. That wasn't reducing the warmth in the courtroom, however. Zweig privately wondered if the St. Louis County Courthouse was behind on its electric bill. The final moments in this trial—the conspiracy case of *10:21 Alliance v. Harvest Capital & Mortgage and the Archdiocese of St. Louis*—were proceeding at full throttle in this stifling venue. His counterpart, Lance Stubblefield, clicked his pen twice, a superstition that was always a precursor to his cross-examination. Stubblefield's client, 10:21 Alliance director Pat Fishwick, sat smugly in the front row behind the prosecutor's desk. Zweig immediately thought of several reasons why he would love to leap across the row and choke the life out of Fishwick. Returning his thoughts to the home stretch of the case, he watched as Stubblefield—rival, tennis chum, and sometimes partner over a glass of Shiner Bock—approached the witness box.

With a plethora of index cards in his hand, Stubblefield looked directly into the eyes of Jerome McPadden. The chief executive officer of Harvest Capital & Mortgage had given crisp, lucid answers during direct examination. Zweig had led him through a bevy of questions, focusing on the legitimacy of Church property transactions and the absence of canon law to prevent such a temporary shift of ownership. At stake was the highly unusual maneuver by the Archdiocese of St.

13

Louis to transfer possession of property to thirty parishes and eight schools in the greater St. Louis region. The overt explanation given by the Church and Harvest Capital—and what was found on nearly every document of significance—was that these individual churches and schools required a streamlined process of budgeting and stewardship. Transfer of property ownership from the diocese to the particular institutions—said Zweig in his clients' defense—would assist in these matters. Besides, even though the Church technically owned all ecclesiastical property, Zweig had deftly argued in his opening statement that nothing in canon law explicitly prevented this maneuver.

Stubblefield had been on the offensive all three days of this trial, seizing upon the concept of "maneuver" and re-reading it as "manipulation of reality." At the center of the storm was a popular uprising among several parochial schools that included allegations of sexual abuse. There were several priests named, but the key figure was Father Joseph Quinn, who had come to the area only three years before. Formerly the chaplain at Santa Maria Academy in Wildwood, Father Joseph had been moved to *in absentia* director of development of the school prior to its closing. The accusations had gained such force that Stubblefield—representing the watchdog 10:21 Alliance in this case—easily put two and two together. It was clear to him what this pecuniary sleight-of-hand was all about.

Abruptly, Stubblefield slapped the card cluster into his left hand, startling McPadden before the cross-examination began. The attorney was practically salivating at this chance. He could have, he mused, called McPadden as a witness when the prosecution made its case. Either way, under direct or cross examination, McPadden would have been a gamble. But he confidently believed he could nail the executive here and now, in the latter stages of this trial. Stubblefield valued the importance of the final witness, the last fresh testimony the jurors would hear. If there was a time before the closing statement to push the defense over the edge, it was now.

"Mr. McPadden, would you describe yourself as a faithful Catholic?"

The question startled the executive for a second, but he gathered himself and replied calmly, "I am not sure of what your definition of a faithful Catholic would be, but on balance I would say yes."

Stubblefield took a single step in McPadden's direction. "Faithful enough to know some basics about canon law?"

"Objection, your Honor," called Toby Zweig, "Relevance? This is a civil court and Church law is not on trial."

"And yet the defense willingly hides behind its ambiguities to make its own case, your Honor," retorted Stubblefield. "My question is part of a larger fabric that gets to the heart of the conspiracy question."

Judge Dave Valle peered over his gavel with icy, silvery eyes. His gaze went from Stubblefield to Zweig, and then to McPadden for some odd reason. "Overruled."

Stubblefield lifted the stack of cards and pretended to scratch his left temple with it. Zweig was the only person in the courtroom to notice his counterpart give him the finger before continuing.

McPadden said, "I know a bit of canon law. Certainly the average amount that any garden-variety Catholic would know."

"Wasn't it your contention that canon law should be ignored in this matter so that Harvest Capital and the Archdiocese could conspire to unload their assets?"

"That's not how I put it, nor would I."

"Really?" asked Stubblefield with a tinge of a sneer in his voice. He retrieved a sheet of paper from the prosecution's desk. "According to a statement made by the Duchesne High School board vice president, the—and I quote—'manipulations of Harvest Capital & Mortgage to direct this unloading of assets is highly unusual and finds no warrant in Catholic church law. We are being told to accept a financial reality without regard to its timeline or the reasons behind it.' That was…" Stubblefield's finger went down the page and found the name he was looking for, "one Frank DeCesare voicing a pretty strong objection, if we are to take these minutes of their March 16, 2010, board meeting at face value."

"I'm not sure," said McPadden, "that I would qualify that as a strong objection any more than the straightforward stating of an opinion."

"That's an interesting remark considering I never asked you a question. But you seem confused by that. You don't recall that remark?"

"I don't see how I could."

"What do you mean, Mr. McPadden?"

"You give me a quote from a meeting of a school when I'm not even a member of the board, and you expect me to tell you my

16

memory of it?" McPadden said tersely. "Why would I be at a board meeting of Duchesne High School?"

A triumphant smile played at the corners of Stubblefield's mouth. He knew of McPadden's Irish temper from other situations, and it was his firm conviction that the simmering emotions and quick mouth would hand him an opening sooner or later.

"Thanks for the inroad, sir. That leads me to my next question. Are you saying that you were not present at a Duchesne board meeting on March 16th, 2010?"

McPadden hesitated, aware he had overstepped on his last remark. "I'm just asking why they'd need me there."

"Well, Jer, either they wanted you there or you wormed your way in. Your Honor, I'd like to approach the witness and show him this document I hold in my hand. Now, Jer, if you would..."

"Objection, sir," barked Toby Zweig as he jumped to his feet from the defense side. "While Mr. Stubblefield may delude himself into thinking he has this sequence well in hand, he can at least show my client some proper respect and address him as 'Sir' or 'Mr. McPadden'."

"Mr. Zweig, I think we can do without the objection, and the jury will ignore the objection," said the judge. "However, Mr. Stubblefield, I will ask you to put an ice pack on your rancor and proceed with some respect for the witness."

Slightly miffed, Stubblefield nodded, "Yes, your Honor."

Zweig sat down, satisfied. While the objection had been technically ignored, he had gotten the judge to straight-arm

Stubblefield a bit. Right now, throwing the prosecutor off-stride might be his best bet.

"Mr. McPadden, if you would read the top line of the first page of this document out loud for the court."

The mortgage executive looked at the sheet like it was a rotting turnip but found his voice for the answer nonetheless. "The minutes of the Duchesne High School board of directors for its stated meeting of March 16, 2010."

"Yes sir, yes sir," whispered the extremely confident Stubblefield. "And the first paragraph, right here where it lists the attendees. Could you, um, read that aloud for us?"

McPadden was growing more dour by the second, but he dutifully read through several names before he came to the implicating evidence. "Mr. Jerome McPadden, chief executive officer and president of Harvest Capital & Mortgage and lead director for the proposed asset redirection under discussion this evening, was an *ad hoc* visitor for this meeting and agenda discussion."

Stubblefield folded the document and handed it in. "Your Honor, I'd like this entered into evidence. I've made a copy for myself. Okay, Mr. McPadden, I guess we can return to *your* original question: Why would you be at a Duchesne board meeting?"

"As a visitor. No more."

"Yes. It had nothing to do with the fact that, as one Frank DeCesare would say, to badger people into accepting this deal of self-ownership of property so the Archdiocese of St. Louis could cut down its assets for a strategic reason?"

"Objection, your Honor!" thundered Zweig. "Speculation!"

18

"Sir," said Stubblefield, "I'm only noting what Mr. DeCesare wondered in those minutes. As such, there's no speculation, just taking the man at his word."

The Honorable Matthew Valle, growing weary with the thick spite in the air, said "Overruled. Get on with this, counselor."

"Yes, your Honor. I'd also like to enter in evidence the following minutes from the following board meetings: St. Louis Priory School on March 25th of last year. Chaminade on March 29th. St. Dominic High School's special called board meeting of March 30th. Bishop DuBourg's on April 1st. And finally, John F. Kennedy High School held one on April 5th. Now, Mr. McPadden, we can do this either way. Your choice. We can go through each one of these documents before I turn them in and have you read the list of attendees. Or you can just let us know if you were at each one."

Jerome McPadden sat in silence, weighing his options. Behind the defense desk, in the courtroom audience, sat Father Joseph Quinn, along with the Cathedral rector, Monsignor Peter Grenier, and Harvest's chief financial officer Julian Webber. It looked as if they were weighing the options for him as well.

"I was."

Stubblefield nodded to no one in particular. "Wow," he said sarcastically, "Seems like there was a great need for you to show up at a wide variety of schools over a significant geographical area in such a short amount of time. What could that need be?"

"As we have stated throughout this case, it would grant a streamlined process of budgeting and remove a layer that might be otherwise inhibiting for these schools."

"Inhibiting?" asked Stubblefield. "Hmmm, interesting word choice. Almost as interesting as what was roiling in the water at these schools."

Stubblefield returned to his desk, snatched an envelope and walked back to the witness box.

"Why just these schools, Mr. McPadden? What was the archdiocese's reasoning? Why the thirty churches and eight schools mentioned in the course of this trial? If this is such a good idea, why not give every parish a shot at this? Why not give all archdiocesan schools a chance at this independence?"

McPadden was obviously uncomfortable as the questions piled on, but he didn't waste time with his reply. "The archdiocese is under no obligation to provide these means to anyone. This was a trial run to see how well this program might work, and Harvest suggested to the archdiocesan leadership that extending this on a limited basis at first would help us gauge the success of the endeavor for the future."

Oh, Mother of mercy, thought Zweig, his eyes blazing a hole through his client in the witness box. *Why don't you just shut up and say what you need to and no more? Is that so difficult?*

"Trial run, huh?" asked Stubblefield. "That word *trial* is rather ironic. It's interesting that these churches and schools had one thing in common. They all had individuals in them who had recently transferred to these schools from the Santa Maria Academy in Wildwood, Missouri. Are you aware of that?"

"No, I wasn't."

"Well, are you aware of who used to be the chaplain at Santa Maria Academy?"

20

McPadden, flat-footed, knew there was no way out of this question. "I assume you mean Father Joseph Quinn."

"Yeah, Father Joseph. Um, and why did these students leave? I'm sure in making the rounds to these board meetings you would know."

"I do not. I guess they left because they wanted to go elsewhere?"

"Oh, come on, Mr. McPadden. You do know what sort of school Santa Maria is, don't you?"

Trying to delay things with a touch of sarcasm, McPadden said, "A Catholic school?"

Stubblefield leaned on the front edge of the witness box. "I'll bypass that little childish display and get to the point. You are aware the Barons of St. Paul had primary academic and spiritual authority at that school."

"Yes."

"Now, I'm not Catholic, but this I do know: Nobody just ups and leaves a Baron school. Unless … you know, there have been things going on under the radar?"

"Objection! Speculation!" snapped Toby Zweig, "Your Honor, Mr. Stubblefield knows that rhetoric does not an argument make. Unless he has evidence, which as prosecutor he is required to bring, he has no basis."

"Withdrawn, your Honor," said Stubblefield, who had expected Zweig's interjection. "But here's the one thing that I'd like to draw to everyone's attention." He returned to the table to retrieve several printed e-mails and letters. "You might recall some of the testimony during the prosecution's case from several board members at these schools, furious about the lack of transparency from the archdiocese on these financial matters and issues of sex abuse allegations. I have taken a list of the students who left Santa Maria Academy for other schools. Mr. McPadden, could you look at this list and tell me what pattern you notice when you look at the schools where they transferred?"

He waved the paper in front of McPadden. Fourteen feet away, Toby Zweig blankly stared forward as his heart went into his shoes. He knew where his rival was going with this.

Stubblefield grew impatient with the witness' silence. "They all transferred to schools which are involved in this transfer of property by the archdiocese. And … let's look at this column over here that identifies the church membership of each student. Do you notice anything interesting about this list of parishes?"

McPadden groused for a quick second, then quietly said, "They are all on the list of churches involved in the property transfer."

Stubblefield allowed the quiet gasps in the courtroom to subside before continuing. "And one more thing, Mr. McPadden, would you look at the names on this correspondence regarding claims of sexual impropriety at Santa Maria Academy from late 2008 through the spring of 2010? Do you see any relation between the names of the families on this document and that of the students on the previous document?"

Again the pained pause. Zweig fell the case was slipping away, yet to voice any objection, even for badgering, would paint him with a very bad brush.

"Yes."

"Let's be more specific, sir," snapped Stubblefield, "Would you say there's a general correlation or an exact match?"

"Fine. An exact match."

"Indeed, Mr. McPadden. An exact match. And given this final bit of correspondence which I will bring to the attention of the court, maybe we can pull the final threads together. Your Honor, one of the pertinent bits of recent history we must note is what went on a few years back in the Diocese of Nashville, Tennessee. In August 2005, the diocese was faced with a sixty-eight million dollar sex abuse lawsuit. Before that case could go to trial, the diocese shifted ownership of eight churches and one school to the individual institutions. Church officials pled that it was a legitimate maneuver, stating it was part of an effort for property deeds to reflect their true owners, and there was nothing verboten about the tactic within canon law. Lawyers for the alleged victims in this Nashville suit said this was part of a scheme to reduce the diocese's value; throwing the game, so to speak. They were ditching some assets, creating some financial hardship, trying to lower the dollar amount they'd have to pay if they lost the trial."

Looking the mortgage patriarch full in the face, Stubblefield asked, "Were you aware of this past history, sir?"

"No."

"All right. Eight churches and one school for Nashville corresponding to sixty-eight million dollars. Here, we have thirty churches and eight schools. I can only imagine the dollar amount now."

Zweig wasn't going to let this proceed unmolested. "Objection! Assuming facts not in evidence!"

"Sustained," growled Judge Valle. "Watch your step, Counselor."

Stubblefield ignored the rebuke. "My point is this. Such action requires the services of a mortgage company for this herculean task. A mortgage company that would know the ins and outs of this situation and might have people on the inside colluding with the archdiocese."

Zweig snarled again, "Your Honor, objection. If Mr. Stubblefield wants to win a gold medal in speculation, I'm prepared to award him the prize now."

"Sustained," said the judge. "Mr. Stubblefield, if you want the court to recall what it is you're arguing, I'd suggest you stay on track."

"Yes, your Honor. I was referring to this piece of correspondence that we have entered into evidence. Do you recognize the signatures at the bottom of this document? Right there."

"It would appear to be mine and Mr. Webber's," said McPadden.

"Exactly, sir. Please the court that this letter, which was given to us jointly by Harvest and the law firm of Gillette, Wales, and Alexander …"

McPadden burned him with a look that could have destroyed Nagasaki. Stubblefield smiled and went on.

"Given to us by the archdiocesan law firm, no less, when we requested papers. Why? You can't seriously be surprised by this? Hadn't we made your team aware? I am somewhat chagrined by the fact that in this letter to the law firm and the archdiocese, signed by you and drafted by Mr. Webber, we have reference to the Nashville situation. We also have these words: *Given the same activity in the diocese of Nashville, we might need to consider options of similar reaction. Since there are more rumors of lawsuits here, we may want to explore the chances of shifting the property resources of strategic places to those institutions. The question of returning the property at a lowered price could provide the 'safety net' we discussed previously. We are not ignoring justice, but seeking an alternative for the Church to provide it for those in need."*

Stubblefield handed the letter in with a flourish and asked the witness, "Returning the property at a lowered price? Safety net? The Church provide justice? For a lawsuit that hasn't even happened? Mind telling me what this means?"

Now McPadden was quick to reply. "It means we were looking at legitimate, future legal options and found no need to formulate them in the span of one letter."

Zweig didn't know whether to cheer or vomit. McPadden at least spoke the truth and had given nothing away. Whether or not that would convince the jury was another matter. He groaned inwardly. Twelve people and they were only able to get two Catholics on the jury.

"Of course not, Mr. McPadden," said Stubblefield gently. "Because why formulate the end game in a letter when we can connect the dots for ourselves? Property ownership shifted to others so the archdiocese can cry financial uncle. Act as if it's an official sale, then when it comes to buying the properties back, you do so at a mysteriously lower price. The churches and school pocket the change

25

to channel to those who have been wounded by men like Father Joseph, like in other locations. No need for a lawsuit as long as you have laundered funds running below the radar."

McPadden glared at Stubblefield with a look that pled for the attorney's fiery death. "That's a nice conspiracy theory, but this was a business deal for the good of budgeting and stewardship. Plain and simple."

Stubblefield leaned onto the front of the witness box, so close to McPadden that he could smell the meatball sub the executive had for lunch.

"Not a conspiracy theory, Mr. McPadden. That is the legal definition of conspiracy—as you would say, plain and simple."

He looked at the judge and said, "No more need for this witness." And he returned to his seat.

Like a flash, Toby Zweig was up out of his chair before Valle could ask if he wanted to re-direct. "Mr. McPadden, you have given testimony. You have been at the center of these completely legal negotiations from day one. Yet one question has not been asked of you. It reveals a theory at the heart of the prosecution's case which they have not been able to prove, so in fairness, let's make this simple. Was the reason for this shift in property ownership for reasons of individual parish and school budgeting, or was it for the conspiracy theory described in vivid yet desperate detail by Mr. Stubblefield?"

"I'm not even going to waste my breath objecting to his smearing use of the term *desperate*, your Honor," chuckled Stubblefield.

"Then I would suggest you not waste your breath at all, Counselor," Valle shot back, with a firm grip on his gavel.

With a cocky grin on his face, Zweig turned to his witness. "Mr. McPadden?"

Jerome McPadden sat straight and oddly confident in his seat. "The first reason. As we've always demonstrated and maintained, Mr. Stubblefield's words have no merit."

Backing away slowly, Zweig stopped when he reached the desk and sat on its top. He nodded kindly twice, looked at Judge Valle, and spread his arms wide.

"Your Honor, the defense rests."

2

One hour later, three men positioned themselves around a 2008 Honda Odyssey in the west parking lot of the Cathedral Basilica at Lindell and Newstead. The ramp began its short journey into an upright position before the van door would close after it. The warm breeze and inviting sunlight was making this a glorious Indian summer day. The door clicked just as one of the men asked, "And does our fourth know to meet us here?"

"He should, considering I just told him this morning," said Martin Ballack, letting go of the door switch once it clicked shut. "And as a matter of fact …" he gestured toward a bright yellow Cooper Mini cruising to a stop ten yards away, "there he is."

Cameron Ballack whirled around in his power wheelchair and took measure of their fellow visitor. "Keeping Owen away from a cathedral is like restraining a beaver from soft wood. He majored in architecture at the University of Virginia. Summa cum laude. He'll be a better tour guide than any of the docents the Cathedral has."

A slightly built fifty-something man with a kind face, dressed in a dark blue button-down shirt, jeans, and Birkenstocks approached their group, his right hand extended toward Cameron's father and his left holding a bulky paper bag.

"Martin, thanks for asking me to come," he said.

"Owen, it's been a while," smiled Martin, clasping Owen's hand in a sincere handshake and giving him a quick chest bump, a tradition between the two friends. "You remember Cameron, of course."

"I do indeed. Good to see you again, and I understand congratulations are in order for your promotion."

"Well, not exactly," replied the younger Ballack. "It's a provisional appointment to the Division for specific cases. It could be a great opportunity or a train wreck." He raised his eyebrows. "Or a bit of both."

In truth, Cameron Ballack had no way of knowing. However, he couldn't deny his pleasure at his nomination to the Special Investigative Division of Metro St. Louis. After five years on the St. Charles Police Detective Bureau, he and partner Tori Vaughan had taken on a case of multiple murders at St. Basil's Seminary just seven months before. The courageous and dramatic way they had solved the case opened the path for their chance to serve on the Special Investigative Division. Of course, now they had to wait around before getting an actual case. Easier said than done, he thought, especially since he wasn't convinced the Division would hand a hot case to a crippled detective.

"Well, nonetheless, I'm extremely happy for you," said Owen.

"Thanks, man," replied Ballack. "And I don't think you've met my friend here. Graham Whittaker. We've known each other for over twenty years. Our dads taught together at King's Prep and then Westminster. Graham, this is Owen Stams. Used to be the associate pastor at Memorial Presbyterian Church until Pastor Stuart retired. Now Owen's the one with the laser vision from God."

"Nice to meet you, Owen," said Graham. "You're not planning on replacing the Communion wine in there, are you?" He gestured to the bag.

"This? No," said Owen turning towards the elder Ballack. "This is actually for you, Martin. A belated birthday gift since I missed yours at the end of August."

Martin took the bag, looked within, and said with a smile, "Ah, Owen. I owe you a debt I can never repay. Thanks, brother!"

He pulled out a large bottle of Jim Beam bourbon whiskey with a grateful look on his face.

Owen slapped him on the back. "I thought you might like having the 'other friend of sinners' as a gift."

Graham cocked his head. "Thought you'd prefer Jack Daniels."

"Not a chance," growled Martin, as if Graham had just offered him a wasps' nest. "Only the good Kentucky stuff for me. I don't go in for that Tennessee sewage."

He placed the bottle reverently on the van seat, closed the door, and the four walked toward the side door to the cathedral.

"Gentlemen," said Owen, "prepare for rapture."

The Cathedral Basilica of St. Louis—known locally as the New Cathedral, or more simply the Cathedral—was completed in 1914 and designated as a basilica in April 1997 by Pope John Paul II. The greatest architectural legacy of the Neo-Byzantine structure is its forty-one million tessarae that comprise one of the largest collections of mosaics at any cathedral in the world. The glass pieces cover eighty-three thousand square feet in more than seven thousand colors and took seventy-four years for full installation. The exterior is made of solid granite, while brick and marble cover the interior. The

Cathedral's dimly lit nave takes nothing away from the breathtaking majesty of the three domes running south to north. Despite his skeptical worldview, Detective Ballack loved taking in the sights of religious architecture and he never turned down a chance to see this edifice. Upon their entry, he wheeled from the side door near the west transept and went toward the rear of the church to make his way up the center aisle. He tilted his chair to view the first dome in the historic bay. The great seal of the Archdiocese of St. Louis was set on a midnight blue background, surrounded by stars. He zipped up the pathway and then looked upward again toward the central dome, which towered one hundred forty-three feet above. His eyes scanned the mosaics counter-clockwise starting from the east. Ezekiel the prophet receiving the Word of God. The mysterious representation of the Holy Trinity. Elijah being carried to heaven in the chariot of fire. And the woman of John's Apocalypse. Surrounding the edge of the dome were depictions of angels, keeping watch over the various arches of the biblical story. God the Father creating. Jesus' triumphant salvation. The Holy Spirit's sin-defying war. And the chilling Last Judgment. Slowing his breathing to a minimum, Ballack was momentarily overwhelmed by such beauty. He knew that was not the entire story. He wished one particular person were here to share this with him.

Since his last case closed, he and Dana Witten had slowly grown closer together. Ballack's work at the St. Basil's case had thrust him into Dana's world in the midst of tragedy. Dana's husband, Dieter, a student at St. Basil's, had been one of the individuals caught in the crosshairs of a tragic long weekend. Ballack knew there was no doubt that he was profoundly attracted to Dana. For whatever reason, she seemed to be strongly drawn toward Ballack. They had been able to cram a couple of outings into Ballack's busy schedule before Dana began her teaching load at Whitfield School. It was enough to make Ballack know he wanted to see more of her. There were moments when he drew back with questions of his own: *Could she really love someone who can't walk? Is my job a hindrance to any traction in this relationship?* And always there were the other questions he often considered but never spoke: *Does she like me because I can't stray from her like her husband did? Is it the emotion of the tragedy that brought us together, and nothing more? Can we go forward on more than just that?*

Ballack tore himself away from his brooding. He stifled a cough and opened his portable suction pack. His affliction of myotubular myopathy had not only consigned him to a wheelchair years before it also brought on other adversities as well. His neuromuscular disorder consistently compromised his respiratory function, and this meant Ballack required nebulizer breathing treatments every day to keep his bronchioles opened. Even then, his low muscle tone meant he had less than a productive cough, and during these times when he had difficulty clearing his lungs, he had to have his suction pump close by. Expertly, he turned it on and placed the small Neosucker into his trach positioned in his throat. A few seconds passed, and the mucus cleared from his airway. *It never ends,* mused Ballack, *but at least I'm alive and doing what I love.*

Graham was approaching him from the side, having checked out the confession booth in the west transept. "Having fun?"

Ballack came back to the present and nodded. "While Owen is bending Dad's ear up front at the sanctuary dome, I can show you the chapels. We can start back here."

The two friends headed toward the rear of the nave and the southeast corner of the church. An open door off the narthex led toward the Mosaic Museum and the lower crypt. Ballack wheeled his way into the All Souls Chapel and stopped at the tomb on the floor. Of all areas in the Cathedral, this had become his favorite. He loved the Viennese Reconstructionist style, but even more than that, there was the marble. Black marble to signify death; white marble for the resurrection to eternal life. He wasn't sure if such a hope existed, but he liked to think it might.

"You like this place," whispered Graham next to him.

"I like the simplicity of it," replied Ballack. "Clear cut. Black and white. Sharp distinctions. Darkness and light. And I like the respect for tradition. You have Cardinal Glennon, Cardinal Ritter, and others buried here, as if they are still watching over their friends. There's something honorable about that."

"You feel that way about Christopher, don't you? That he's watching you."

Ballack went silent. His late brother was still his delight even though he had died nineteen years before. Despite Ballack's agnosticism, it was because of Christopher that he hoped that eternal life just might be true. Tearing himself away from the memory, he said, "C'mon, let's go. I think I saw Owen and Dad head toward that chapel up near the front."

The two friends began their lengthy trek up the right side of the nave. Though the final Mass for the day had finished more than four hours ago, several people were scattered throughout the pews in silent prayer and meditation. Ballack tried to squeeze between a column and the end of one pew and was unsuccessful, clipping the armrest and disturbing a kneeling figure deep in prayer.

"Sorry," mumbled Ballack, looking briefly into the thoughtful eyes of a black man dressed in hospital scrubs and a hunter green windbreaker. He looked at Ballack's wheelchair, then the detective and—as if he understood that it had been an innocent mistake—nodded his absolution.

They finally reached Martin and Owen in the northwest corner, at the Blessed Virgin's Chapel. The two clergymen were looking at the picture of Pope John Paul II's visit to the Cathedral and his time of prayer in that sacred space.

"Nice depictions," said Martin, turning to his son and Graham as they approached.

"But no chance of my getting up those steps," remarked Ballack. "I'd need the ramp out of the Sprinter to climb that mountain."

"Let's check out the transepts and the baptismal font," said Owen. "Some interesting stories behind these things. Follow me."

Ballack followed him, figuring there was no point lingering in that spot. *Not like there'll ever be a reason to go into that chapel anyway.*

In one week, he'd realize just how wrong that thought would be.

3

The closing arguments for each side came and went. The decision had been in the jury's hands since midday Friday, and now Monday morning brought on more of the waiting game. Toby Zweig sat in the attorney's lounge on the second floor of the circuit court building. The team from Harvest had gone out for an early working lunch. They clearly had other business matters to attend to, and Zweig had no desire to sit in on that. He had brought some celery stalks, carrot sticks, and several cuts of Colby cheese in a Tupperware container for what would pass for his lunch. The Cathedral would send over a representative from the clergy the moment it was announced the jury had made up their minds. There was nothing to do now except linger and daydream.

With no word on how much longer it would be, Zweig figured a midday reverie might be just the thing. No one else from his legal team was here to interrupt his wandering thoughts. He had the whole room to himself. He stretched out on the sofa and closed his eyes.

One trial winding up, he thought, and yet there was another on the horizon. After the flames of this judgment abated, he would be expected to pick up the baton to defend Father Joseph for what looked like a nasty sex abuse case. Thank God the archdiocese paid well for such unpleasant work—for the task of creating reasonable doubt even when Zweig knew the man had to be guilty as Richard Nixon after Watergate. But that was his role. Put out one fire only to be handed the water for the next blaze. Such was his life.

At least that was the way his marriage seemed to run for some time. Up and down. Hot and cold. Financial success mixed with relational meltdown that settled into an uneasy slough of functional workability. He and Monica had married twenty years ago, having met in a bar during separate celebrations—his for passing the bar exam, hers for finishing her residency. The brief, passionate courtship led to a rushed marriage, with the certainty their professional lives would provide for their personal desires. The marriage bed produced a daughter, Serena, but no lasting amorous bliss. His increased workload with the archdiocese kept him away from the women in his home. Monica's devotion to her clients in her private psychiatry practice—the most successful one in the city of St. Louis—helped with the mortgage payments of their University City home but drew her more into the souls of others who sensed her compassion. Zweig said nothing about her relationships—partly because to blow the whistle on such a breach of professionalism would destroy her practice and halve their income, but mainly because he was no model of chastity himself.

His three-year entanglement with his personal assistant was the stuff of cheap romantic fiction, and he wavered back and forth between feeding and cursing his fallen nature. But with the questioning eyes of his firm's partners increasing in their intensity, Zweig knew even he couldn't keep this up forever. As if on cue, the accident that nearly took Serena's life—a drunk driver careened into her on the eve of Thanksgiving the year before—brought he and Monica back together. His steady and disciplined control of the situation with the doctors, nurses, and friends awakened a new admiration within his bride. It was on Christmas Eve when, seated on the floor in front of a crackling fireplace at home, she confessed her past and renewed her faithfulness to her husband forever. It was the man before her that she wanted. He smiled and forgave her, never admitting his own unfaithfulness with Tabitha. Putting her off, when she wished the liaison would proceed, was becoming yeoman's work. There were still powerful currents of passion that ran deep, and their times together were occasionally laced with knowing looks and piercing remembrances. But his intensity toward his assistant had waned noticeably over the past few months, and he was determined to honor the wife of his youth.

Honor. That word took him back, years prior to his birth. He always associated the word *honor* with his aged grandfather, who passed away quietly on New Years' Eve, just days after his wife's confession. His grandfather the trial lawyer, who was absolutely determined that the downtrodden receive justice. The one who took less money from the Irish, the Italians, the union workers, the blacks, and—in a massive show of forgiveness—working class Germans in order to bring hope out of blight. The attorney well known by the residents of the Hill, Dogtown and Bevo Mill. The man who worked for survivors because he had survived the greatest fight of all. Zweig had heard his grandfather tell various parts of his story. It moved him by its savage adversity, by its sheer tenacity and by its spiritual triumph. It inspired him through his own darkest moments, for if his grandfather would never give in, neither would he.

1938. The *Anschluss* had brought the Nazi Wehrmacht across the Austrian border on toward Vienna. Stefan Zweig was a young, popular and well-respected history professor at the University of Vienna. Bright, articulate and witty, he enjoyed the intellectual atmosphere at school and he enjoyed his wife Marta and children

Rainer and Anna when at home. But an admired intellectual among fellow Austrians automatically became a target for Hitler's regime. With only hours to spare, Stefan was able to get their children off to stay with his brother and sister-in-law in Linz. A good thing, too, because they would not have survived the ordeal that was Mauthausen.

The most dreaded concentration camp in Austria nearly took away Stefan Zweig's faith. Sadly, the Nazis did succeed in taking away his dear Marta, first starved, then bludgeoned and left to freeze outside on Valentine's Day 1940. Stefan willed himself through the months ahead, gutting his way through half-rations and skirting the tuberculosis that affected a number of other prisoners. When the Nazi guards realized they could not break him with lack of food, they tried psychological torture. For a solid month, his duties consisted of the most nihilistic motions—first moving a pile of rubbish from one end of the camp to the other in the morning, and then reversing the process in the afternoon. Fellow prisoners, forced into this routine along with Stefan, had breakdowns from the meaninglessness of it all. Stefan masked his despair, aware of something else his captors had in mind for him, a most recent arrival.

In 1940, a gas chamber was constructed at Mauthausen, a way of ridding the camp of the excess baggage of worn-out souls. While the Nazis were undeniably cruel, they weren't subtle, and Stefan noticed when his fellow prisoners were in line for the final solution. He also noticed that there was one massive difference between he and them. He, for the sake of his children, wanted to live.

The process was always the same. Targeted prisoners were pointed out in the afternoon and given a beating late at night in a private corner of the camp, along the northwest barrier. Two guards would single out those who had run their course of usefulness and assign them for beatings. When the battered ranks had been swelled, then cleaned accordingly, they were led to the chamber *en masse*, never to be seen again. Stefan knew this was meant to be his end the afternoon of November 16, 1940, when Sergeant von Beck pointed to him before the dinner line-up. The hushed conversation two hours later was meant to be private, but Stefan didn't need good ears.

"But Stimmel isn't available to help. You remember he's had fever for a week. We're running short on personnel as it is."

"Shut up, Krause. You're whining worse than that professor will after you've bloodied him. Take him to the corner yard and do it yourself."

That was why much later—ten o'clock at night, to be exact—that Krause dutifully dragged Stefan to the area cheerlessly called *Tal von Knochen*, the Valley of Bones. The beating began with fists and kicks, which Stefan didn't mind at first. But when Krause began to use the butt of his rifle, smashing his jaw, the pride and anger welled up to levels heretofore unknown. Another strike, then another. He tasted blood. He touched his nose with his pinky finger and was chagrined to find his digit could go through another hole. Krause had given him a third nostril.

And then, his eyes sweeping the yard, Stefan noticed two things Krause didn't. One, a dagger lay visibly on the ground, well within Stefan's reach, likely fallen from Krause's belt. The other thing was that mysteriously—and serendipitously—there were no guards within two hundred feet.

Krause, a left-hander, brought the rifle down for another assault, but Stefan slapped the gun on the downward stroke, knocking the guard off balance. With a lightning-quick grab, Stefan scooped the dagger into his hand, grabbed Krause by the hair of his head, and slammed the blade through the underside of the Nazi's mouth, sending it up through the tongue and skewering the upper palate. Krause fell back soundlessly except for a low grunt, blood spurting from his lifeless form.

Not even believing himself what he had just done, Stefan quickly looked around. No shouts, no reaction, no one near. He pulled the dagger from Krause and began checking the wall for openings of any kind. Although he hadn't prayed in three years, he sent pleonasms of supplication heavenward. He was sure no God was listening until he found it—a trap door near the wall, designed for the guards to direct the sludge and human waste of the prisoners underneath the walls and outward, toward a cesspool beyond the fence. Beyond the fence, thought Stefan, as he tucked the dagger inside his worksuit.

It took several minutes to clear the fence and dredge himself out of the filth just beyond the Erinnerungstrasse. Even then he knew he had to be on the run immediately, for fear of pursuit. He told Toby often that he finally got to Linz, found his children, and left immediately, the three of them snaking the back roads and friendly farms on the way to neutral Switzerland. He was less forthcoming in details about the post-camp jaunt, and Toby figured there was some level of shame in the way he managed it. Probably stole a wagon from a farmer, bread from a baker or money from an unsuspecting merchant. Whatever was needed to survive until the next step. Even

Switzerland was no option to stay for good. Many Swiss weren't welcoming to an Austrian professor, even one who hated the Nazis.

So Rainer and Anna tagged along with their father on a long and winding path that eventually led to America. Philadelphia was where they began, but jobs in academia were not forthcoming. More sojourning finally brought them to their permanent home, St. Louis. Eschewing the teaching profession, Stefan Zweig managed to enter law school. More for strategic than religious reasons, the family attended the Cathedral for services. Noting Stefan's drive and determination, the Cathedral provided funds to help him complete his schooling. He graduated with high honors and showed a remarkable penchant for picking up both the nuances of English and the company of the less fortunate. It was this throng that he would represent well for years to come.

Stefan Zweig never remarried, instead allowing his joy to increase as his children settled down and began families of their own. Many granddaughters followed, making him wonder if the Zweig name would continue on American shores. But those fears were allayed when Rainer called him from St. Mary's Hospital in late autumn 1963. Stefan had been glued to the television, obsessed with the horrific news of President Kennedy's assassination just fifty minutes before. That sadness was washed away with Rainer's words, *"Poppa, you have a grandson. A grandson at last ... Tobias Stefan Zweig!"*

Tobias, also known as Toby. For years he grew up as the apple of his grandfather's eye, digesting the stories and mimicking his qualities. He knew the pride that swelled within the man with each of

41

his achievements. And he remembered the moment at Christmas nearly thirty years ago when—over the first glass of whiskey they ever shared—he told his loving grandpa he was going to be an attorney just like him.

How he remembered the joyful twinkle in his grandfather's eyes at that private announcement. And how the delight and awe was his the next day as the whole family opened their gifts. From his grandpa, he received the ultimate token of affection, the beacon of survival from that darkest night years ago. It was a dagger, gleaming in the candlelight, graced with the insignia of the overcome Reich. Toby smiled and brushed tears away from his eyes as he hugged his grandfather. Not a word passed between them in this sacred moment. He knew from where this gift had come.

It was as tears welled in his eyes in the present that he heard a knock on the lounge door, and his clerk put his head in the room, saying the words he knew would be spoken.

"They've reached a verdict."

4

Julian Webber and Jerome McPadden took forty minutes to return to the courtroom, mumbling something about the difficulty in getting out of the parking garage at Maggiano's. Ten minutes after their arrival, Father Jim Behringer quietly sat directly behind Zweig. Evidently, Monsignor Peter Grenier was not coming and—given the lightning-rod nature of his presence—Father Joseph Quinn would be taking the day off as well. Zweig turned to his right, locking eyes respectfully with Lance Stubblefield and sending a half-hearted salute in his direction.

"Loser buys Shiners?" asked Zweig as Pat Fishwick sat behind the prosecutor.

"Yes, you will," chuckled Stubblefield. Despite the intensity of the trial, they couldn't help but joke around before the verdict.

"All rise," called the bailiff, and for the next three minutes, the process of judge and jury entrance took center stage. Zweig crumpled his notes and tossed them on the table before him, then whispered to his clerk out the side of his mouth. "Mark!"

"Sir?" replied his timorous aide.

"Remember, they can't kill us. Underneath those trendy clothes and all that vested authority, they're just twelve idiots, just like us."

Mark tried to suppress a smile, but failed. Zweig's pre-verdict humor never ceased to amaze him.

Judge Valle looked to his left. "Members of the jury, have you reached a verdict?"

"We have, your Honor," said the foreman, a stocky individual whose face—except for a well-trimmed beard—looked eerily similar to former St. Louis Rams quarterback Sam Bradford.

Zweig always focused on his wedding band whenever the verdict was handed in. He wished this would wrap up. He could hear Father Behringer breathing heavily behind him, the inhalation trekking noisily through the bushy nose hair the cleric obstinately refused to trim. Judge Valle asked both the prosecution and defense teams to stand. Zweig got to his feet slowly; Stubblefield practically bounced out of his chair.

The judge cleared his throat. "As to the count of joint conspiracy between Harvest Capital & Mortgage and the Archdiocese of St. Louis, how do you find the defendants?"

With a deep, firm voice, the foreman said, "We find the defendants not guilty, your Honor."

Zweig exhaled ferociously, and out of the corner of his eye he could see Stubblefield accept the ruling with reserve and dignity. That was in marked contrast to Pat Fishwick, whose face went bright red and his eyes flashed darts in Zweig's direction. The 10:21 director couldn't have thought a guilty verdict was a slam-dunk, thought Zweig, although he knew it was no fault of Stubblefield's. The prosecutor had brought every weapon in the game and fallen just short.

"Congratulations, sir," said Mark, pressing his hand and slapping him harder on the arm than normal. The lesser counts were dealt with in rapid fashion, and Zweig was still beaming when he turned to the row behind him after the gavel fell. Father Behringer gave him a thumbs-up and wrung his hand. They got the one vindication they needed.

"Thank you, thank you sir," he whispered. "You did beautifully."

"You're entirely welcome, Father, but don't smile too much. You haven't gotten my fee," Zweig winked as he patted the priest on the shoulder. Father Behringer was already pulling out his cell phone to text the monsignor the results. Zweig turned to Webber and McPadden. The CEO offered his hand.

"I suppose we should refrain from smiling, too?" said McPadden.

Zweig leaned in close to the mortgage officers and lowered his voice where no one else could pick up on its bitterness.

"Listen, Jerry. Given what a fool you looked like on the stand last week, you'd better buy plenty of ChapStick because you need to start kissing my rear end right now. Harvest's reputation was at stake as well as that of the archdiocese, and you survived because I blew enough smoke around this room to keep people from seeing what went on. So the first words out of your mouth should have been dripping with honey-like courtesy and gratitude."

"Thanks and congratulations, Counselor," growled McPadden after a brief pause. "Is that good enough for you?"

Before Zweig could answer him, Julian Webber intervened and held out a stiff forearm between the two men. "Seriously, Toby. Thanks for everything," he said. "We are just a little drained from all this. You did a fantastic job, but maybe what we all need is some time apart. You know, familiarity breeding contempt and all."

Mark was waiting for Zweig, all the documents scooped up and placed in a briefcase. Noting that Pat Fishwick was immersed in conversation with several couples by the side of the courtroom, Zweig's initial thought was to make a break for it and avoid the acerbic words he knew would be coming. But he couldn't walk out without speaking with Stubblefield. The prosecutor turned, hand outstretched, as he approached.

"Looks like I'll be buying, Toby. How about Wednesday evening?" he muttered with a tired grin. "Congratulations, buddy, by the way."

"Wednesday it is, Lance. And no congratulations are necessary. You're a prince to even take up this case. We both know conspiracy is the greased pig of all charges."

"It's my Boy Scout moment of the year. Now I can get back to the usual slew of cases and make THF Realty one big happy family."

"Well, thanks for smiling after all this is over."

"I'm glad you can when your boys were guilty as sin. Sleep well, Toby."

Zweig hustled down the center aisle, his eyes fixed on the hallway that was his deliverance from the individual he was trying to avoid most. He thought that rescue was at hand as he started toward the pedestrian bridge, when he heard a threatening growl behind him: "Zweig!"

He turned, slowly, until he was facing into the stony glare of Pat Fishwick.

"Pat," he said, "I know what you're going to say, and even though I've plodded through this trial for over a week, that doesn't mean I have any patience for your victimized spew. So save it."

Fishwick smirked. "You sellout. You'd rather pad your bank account through a soiled Church than use your skills to reform it."

"I believe the phrase that matters," replied Zweig, as he saw McPadden, Webber, and Father Behringer approaching from behind, "is 'innocent until proven guilty'."

With an audience gathering, Fishwick couldn't resist ending with a flourish. "To win this case doesn't make your clients innocent. Don't think this is the end of it, and don't think we won't continue to dog you."

Having had enough of this grandstanding, Zweig set himself where his face was four inches from Fishwick's. With a surge of pride and a touch of spite, he snapped, "I don't care if you want to dog me straight to kingdom come. You lost, Pat. Just deal with it like a man. At least your attorney is. If you want to speak to me like a gentleman, come by my office. If you want to add to my list of sins, you can find me confessing to Monsignor Grenier every Thursday at four o'clock at the Cathedral. Whichever path you choose, I really don't care."

Fishwick looked as if he wanted to get a nasty last word in, but the sight of journalists and photographers pressing in made him think otherwise. He smiled broadly and stuck out his right hand, shaking Zweig's warmly.

"Thursday at four?" he growled. "Why not?" He released the attorney's hand and began moving toward the elevators, the press corps nipping at his heels.

47

5

"That's it. Great game, everyone. Two lines and let's have a final shake before getting off the floor. We still have the championship game to go."

Ballack exhaled with complete satisfaction, pumping his left fist in the air as he wheeled his chair toward the post-game lines. Following the referee's instructions, he gave and received muted acknowledgments before turning toward the south bleachers. His part in the open invitational was over and the St. Charles Storm had just claimed victory in this Tuesday's third-place game. He smiled broadly as his defensive play and first-half assist had been significant contributions to the win. He zipped to the end of the bleachers in the community college gym; his father and mother sat there along with Tori Vaughan and another figure: his lieutenant Scotty Bosco.

"Hi, boss," winked Ballack. "Glad you could see the tail end of this."

"Hi yourself, Cameron. I can see why you took off work today for this. Gets out the aggression that must build within you working for me."

Ballack couldn't help but laugh. "If you want, I can meet you and Tori in the front alcove by the concession stand. This won't take but a second."

"Nah, we'll wait," said Bosco. "We have time."

"Really, it won't take long," said Martin Ballack, and he was right. In no time, he had lifted his son from his game wheelchair to his regular power device. "You all have a good time while Marie and I head out."

"Making mischief?" asked the younger Ballack.

"You don't need mischief for an evening out with your beloved," said Marie. "Since your dad has tomorrow off, we thought about hitting the buffet at Ameristar before seeing the play at Lindenwood."

"A play?" asked Tori. "You're going from a casino munchdown to high culture?"

"Not sure how high it'll be," replied Martin. "It's called *Thanes and Flames*. A satire of *Beowulf*. I'm guessing it'll be much worse than the poem and much better than that CGI movie version."

"That's right, and if we don't hustle we'll miss it," said Marie, grabbing her husband's hand. "We'll see you later tonight, Cam."

The detectives headed in the direction of the alcove as Tori watched the Ballacks head out the gymnasium door. "There are many days when I really wish I had that."

"What's that?" asked Ballack.

"What your folks have. A functioning marriage. Where they enjoy each other and don't stop at just tolerating one another. I think about what Eddie and I had—or the lack thereof—and then I look at your parents. Do you ever think what you've had as a family is a miracle?"

Ballack hadn't thought about the intricacies of his parents' marriage for some time and couldn't put it into mellifluous wordage on the spot, but he knew silence wasn't an appropriate rejoinder. "I think even they'd see it as a miracle. Anyone who knows us knows it's been an uphill battle. What happened to Christopher. My health. Even Jill never had it easy. I guess Mom and Dad had this joint reaction that it's better to gut it out and find some way to enjoy the life you have rather than bemoan the one you didn't get."

He paused, then added, "Maybe they got to the place where they realized nothing mattered but faith and family. And each other. Sometimes when there's nothing else, you recognize how lucky you might truly be. And about your situation—even though you and Eddie split up, you've got a pretty good kid in Paula as part of what used to be."

"Can't say I disagree with you there," she agreed.

"Beautiful, Shakespeare," said Bosco, clearly wanting to redirect the conversation. "Now that we're seated, I just wanted to have a check-up on where we are with the SID assignments. First of all, here are your IDs. Keep them with your regular identification cards. When you're called in for a Special Investigative case, you'll need to present these as proof you can operate in other jurisdictions."

"If we're called in on a case," said Ballack dryly.

"Don't be so cynical," responded Bosco. "It's a provisional appointment, and a targeted one. You would be called in for what would be cases of a clear religious and spiritual nature. Your primary caseload will still be in St. Charles County unless called in for an SID case."

"We kind of knew this going in, Scotty," said Tori. "Why this repeated pep talk? What's the catch?"

"Now who's the cynic?" laughed Ballack.

"A few things just to give you the lay of the land. First, whoever is over you, whether it be yours truly, the SID commander for the case, or whoever, report directly and often. Don't leave anyone in the dark. Those St. Louis boys can get funny about that. No news isn't good news. It's a disaster."

"Next," said Ballack.

"Second, it seems the consensus of others that when you two get a case, then by virtue of your past work and expertise in this area, you would be the lead detective team. Cameron, that means being the senior, you would be number-one on the ground."

"Over the whole team?" asked Ballack. "How much personnel are we talking about?"

"That leads me to number three on my list. In these situations, there might be some potential blowback in public opinion. It's important to the SID that these matters be handled with, shall we say, a considerable amount of discretion."

"That's odd for us," said Tori, "Considering neither of us is the model of political correctness."

"Well, it's not about re-wiring your personalities. Even if I wanted to change you both, I wouldn't. Who you are makes possible what you do."

"My ears couldn't have heard that correctly," said Ballack in mock joy. "It sounded like Scotty … actually … appreciates us!" He grabbed a napkin and sarcastically used it to dab his eyes.

"Shut up," growled Bosco. "The discretion angle is the third thing. Sensitive religious matters, involving churches or clergy, would actually mean smaller squads on the case. The Division doesn't want a ton of people investigating when it could stir up the media and compromise things."

"Sounds like the powers-that-be making rules so tight-fisted that we might never get a shot," said Tori sharply. "C'mon, Scotty. St. Louis is predominantly a Catholic and Lutheran city. We're pussyfooting around issues relating to those groups with limited help because we're afraid of pissing off influential powerbrokers, right?"

"So what you're saying," Ballack thought out loud, "is that we get explosive cases with fewer weapons to take the hill, or we're sending out the Red Army after a Baptist youth pastor sacrifices the church organist to Zufandu the Unholy Fire God?"

"Oooh, that was creative, partner," laughed Tori.

Scotty was done with his detectives' rising sarcasm. "Can we get back to the point? My final thing is a warning wrapped in a compliment. You guys got this chance because you earned it. It's not a gender-equity thing," he looked at Tori, "and it's not an ADA mandate," he continued, glancing at Ballack. "You both got this opportunity because you clawed your way up the ladder, thought on your feet, went outside the box when needed and always got the job done."

Neither detective spoke. Neither sarcasm nor jocularity was required now.

"But," continued the lieutenant, "not everyone across the Missouri River will see it that way. Whoever gets attached to your team, when you're in the lead, might not be the most appreciative of your generalship. I'm just telling you to be aware of that. And don't throw fire back in anyone's face. You don't need to make any problems worse than they are."

And then Scotty Bosco leaned in close for the coup de grace.

"But don't take any crap from them, either. Do your jobs, lead well, and stand your ground. You'll be fine from the moment you get your first case."

Ballack couldn't leave that alone. "Again, *if* we get our first case."

Bosco rose to leave. "You never know. It might happen sooner than you think."

6

The darkening twilight surrounded the offices of Gillette, Wales, and Alexander as six men gathered in the conference room on the first floor. The prestigious group, well known for being the archdiocese's official law firm, was located on Pershing Avenue just northwest of the Cathedral Basilica. The few blocks' distance meant the clergy involved could walk to this rendezvous on this cool September evening. Monsignor Grenier opened the door of the conference room and allowed Joseph Quinn and Jim Behringer to enter before him.

"Welcome, Fathers," called Toby Zweig, "Have a seat. What can I get you? We have champagne for victory or brandy for reflection or whiskey for both."

"I'll have a brandy, Toby," said the monsignor. "And I'll allow my fellow shepherds to choose for themselves. Julian, Jerome! Hello." And he went across the room to greet the Harvest executives.

Zweig watched the monsignor drift across to the other party. Apprehensively, he turned the other two priests. "Is Peter okay? He's acting unnaturally distant."

"More like tired," replied Father Behringer. "The archbishop is at that conference in San Antonio and won't be back until Saturday night. When the general is away, we seem to get hit with the pastoral needs. Hospital visitation, more people at confession this past weekend than we've had in a while, plus this trial took its toll. Thanks to His Excellency not being here, the Monsignor and I had to handle the media blitz. I think he just wants it to go away."

"Well, it won't. That's the point," replied Zweig. "That's what we're here to discuss. The Santa Maria transfer and Father Joseph's defense. One immediate and the other on the horizon. We'll need Harvest to oversee the finances of the transfer. That's why they're here."

"I hope that's all it is," said Father Behringer.

Zweig's brow scrunched. "What do you mean by that?"

"Just …" the young priest's voice trailed off. "Ah, forget it. I have no idea what I was saying. Um, I'll get some champagne." And he brushed past them.

Zweig watched him move to the other end of the table. "Father Joseph," he said, not looking at the older priest. "What did Jim mean by that?"

"I'm out of whatever inner circle might be drawn here, son," Father Joseph replied. "I would have no idea. Thank you, by the way, for agreeing in advance to my defense."

"Toby," called the monsignor. "Maybe we should begin?"

"Of course," said Zweig, and he gestured for all to be seated. The room had a classic look about it. The dark walnut table with plush chairs made for a comfortable environment for discussion. The walls were painted a rich Chinese red, with beautiful white crown molding and chair rails accenting the color. Zweig grabbed his glass of whiskey and sat at the head of the table and began.

"My motive for calling this meeting was twofold. The first thing I want to say is thank you. Everyone here banded together in both major and minor ways when we had to take on the 10:21 Alliance and our vindication was the result. Whether you were on the witness

55

stand or involved in passing along information and evidence and counter-evidence … or if you were just on the sidelines praying, thank you all. That chapter is closed.

"The second item regards moving forward. We still have to draw up the contract regarding the sale of some of the Santa Maria property, and so Jerome and Julian, we'll need documentation as we proceed there. The other matter is that we might expect a backlash from 10:21 and S.N.A.P. over this case, and we need to start working toward a possible defense for Father Joseph and anyone else in the region regarding any abuse charges. For that, we'll need insight from you, Monsignor, and the rest of the archdiocesan staff."

Zweig expected some feedback on which case they should discuss first. What he did not expect, however, was the reaction he got.

Jerome McPadden leaned in and placed his fingertips gently on the tabletop. "As a matter of courtesy, I will be the first to say thank you, Toby, for all the work you put in defending us. However, I would also say that regarding the Santa Maria transfer … well, I believe this is a matter handled directly by Harvest and the archdiocese. I know that on contracts like this the archdiocese has always used this firm, but perhaps we can leave the lawyers out of this one."

Before Zweig could reply, McPadden continued, "And Toby, I want you to hear me on this. We didn't win because of your expertise, but because Pat Fishwick and his gang tried for too much. I know the fathers like you and all, but this is a big money deal. If we have you on it, I don't feel comfortable. Surely we can do something without you."

Zweig was incredulous, not because McPadden's words dripped of acid, but because he brought up this feelings in front of everyone else.

"Are you nuts?" he said. "You were lost on the witness stand if it wasn't for me. You nearly gave the whole case away when Stubblefield cross-examined you! And here you go swearing me off the Santa Maria contract? You never checked with the monsignor or the archbishop!"

"Neither did you," barked McPadden.

"Look," interjected Julian Webber. "Maybe we're getting ahead of ourselves here. No one is suggesting you are sub-standard, Toby. Maybe this property transfer doesn't need you like you think it does. But if I might also step out of my zone, I'd suggest you might need a break from church matters for a time. Let someone else take the case for Father Joseph. Or settle."

"Settle?!" cried the three priests and Zweig at once.

"Yeah, settle," said Webber. "With all these names here coming out of the woodwork, Father Joseph, can you maintain your complete innocence?"

"That is outrageous!" snapped Father Joseph.

"Is that a denial?" smirked McPadden, clearly trying to antagonize.

"Enough!" shouted Monsignor Grenier above the fray. "Perhaps what everyone here should recall is this: The archdiocese, not the firm, and not Harvest, decides on legal representation. That's the way it's done. How about this: Jerome, you and myself, along with the archbishop when he gets back, can sit down with the leadership at

57

Santa Maria and draw up the new contracts ourselves. Then, Toby, at the end of that process you can look it over for revisions."

"I really don't think …" began Zweig.

"Toby, please, you do need a break, and you'll get one."

"Excuse me, Monsignor?"

"*After* the matter of Father Joseph has run its course, and you will have your hands on the wheel for the entire ride there."

"Mother of …!" Jerome McPadden exploded. "Are you ever going to consider anything we say?"

"If you want any business from us on this, Jerome," said Grenier gravely, "perhaps you'll go along on this decision. Because quite frankly, there are other mortgage companies around to choose from!"

"You wouldn't," hissed McPadden.

"I must have missed the letter that said we were obligated to Harvest. Just because we've done business long-term doesn't mean it always must be so. The same would go for this firm, and for you, Toby. You have done excellent work, but does it always need to be you front and center? That's a question that will take much reflection and prayer. You need rest. I can see that clearly myself."

Nobody spoke. It was as if the monsignor had let the air out of everyone's balloon.

"Well, Toby, if you don't mind, I'll declare this little pow-wow over," smiled Grenier. "And now I think I'll stroll on back to the rectory."

7

Toby Zweig slid through the back door of his large brick house on Yale Avenue in University City. The stereo volume was low, permitting a soft throb of Rachmaninoff's *Prelude in C Sharp Minor* throughout the home. The music indicated Monica was home. More than that, the open bottle of cabernet sauvingnon gave away her presence. He stretched his neck and closed his eyes, exhausted from the day's twists and turns, and when he opened his eyes again, Monica stood before him, corking the wine.

"Wow," he said. "You are one quiet vixen."

"I thought you liked me that way, dear," she responded, deftly putting away the wine and several other groceries with the graceful movements of a ballet dancer. "How did the conference go with everyone?"

"Finished well even though it smelled bad."

Monica shut the refrigerator door with force, turning around and asking, "What's that supposed to mean?"

"McPadden—and Webber to a lesser extent—wanted me off the Santa Maria transfer, and they even tried to get Monsignor Grenier to remove me from the Father Joseph defense!"

His wife's eyes bulged, "But they can't do that! After all you did during this trial? And why are they barking about the Father Joseph case? Why is that any interest of theirs?"

"I don't know, I don't know," said Zweig, already weary of the memory. "The monsignor intervened and stopped them. It's ... ah, forget it. My brain is full and I just need to lay down for awhile."

"You look like you need to do more than lie down, dear. Listen, I have to run and get Serena. She went to Ellie's house after tennis practice tonight, where they are allegedly studying for their history test."

"She'd do Grandpa proud."

"Um, hum. Anyway, we can talk more when I get back. There's ham in the fridge, some salad, and there are some crescent rolls you can warm up. Try to stay awake. You look bushed. I don't want you going to bed with this weight on your mind."

She walked over to him, slipping her hands around his neck. He smelled the perfume. White Aoud. He sniffed at her shiny, blond hair and got a whiff of strawberries and cream. The senses were building, layer upon layer. He wanted her to stay, even if she said nothing. Let Serena stay out. But he decided against it. Worrisome emptiness was driving him elsewhere.

"I won't," he said, his thoughts clearing. And with a smile, Monica headed through the side door toward her cream Acura.

The ham was smoky and to his liking, the salad crisp, and the rolls hot. But after a few bites he felt something gnawing at him, a craving he had not felt in some time. It would also satisfy his need to know from the inside. How convenient Monica had just left the house. He pulled his cell phone from his belt holster and punched a few keys, waiting out the rings.

"Hello."

"I need to see you tomorrow afternoon," said Zweig. "Where would be a good time and place?"

"I thought I had the day off, Toby."

"You do. This would be after I go into the office for a few hours."

"You sound desperate."

"I need information."

"It sounds like you need more than that, Toby."

Zweig was losing patience with this unruffled playfulness. "Just name the time and name the place."

Six miles south of where Zweig was standing, Tabitha Stowe slowed traced her tongue over her pouty lips before pressing her mouth to the phone. "Four-thirty. My house. See you there, honey." And with that, she hung up.

8

With a firm knock that disguised the tremulous beating of his heart, Zweig rapped on the door of Tabitha Stowe's gray, two-story house on the far eastern edge of Webster Groves. He had turned off Laclede Station Road and left the car at Lockwood Park to minimize any suspicion. He had taken a circuitous route there, partly for fresh air and partly to calm his nerves. He hadn't been to Tabitha's house since last Thanksgiving weekend. He trudged westward on Amelia Avenue, turning left onto Fairlawn. He glanced sideways at the quaint yet tastefully magnificent structure of Old Orchard Church, a stone building that seemed to be the neighborhood beacon of peace and calm. But it couldn't assuage his inner turmoil, he thought, as he went eastward on Elmwood and went to the familiar house on the left with the wraparound porch.

The same front door opened, and Zweig gritted his teeth immediately. Her stonewashed jeans were practically painted on, and she wore a black top with a scissored neckline that revealed what she wanted to display and what Zweig was trying to avoid.

"Come on in," she smiled, following him to the sofa.

Zweig had his head in his hands, more to avoid looking directly at Tabitha than to do some serious thinking. "Like I said, I need some information. It's related to the Harvest case with Santa Maria and to the Father Joseph defense."

"Ask away," his personal assistant said breathily, leaning closer and sliding her bare toes under his left thigh.

He didn't mean to, but he recoiled from the touch. "Tabitha, please! I came to talk. I need help."

"Fine," she cooed. "What do you need, since I'm of no other use to you?"

"Harvest wanted me off both cases," he said. "The archdiocese went to bat for me, but not like in the past. Something nasty is in the water and I need to know if someone at the firm is after my caseload."

She looked stunned. "What? What did you say?"

"You heard me. I'm right here."

"*That's* what you needed to ask me?" Tabitha screeched. "You come all the way down to my house, in my den, to ask me that?" She pushed him violently to the side, nearly knocking him off the sofa.

Zweig pulled himself up, angry at her but expecting these games. "You could have just answered the question. Especially since *you* nearly blew the case yourself with that letter you handed over for evidence!"

"No!" she hissed, standing up and facing him. "For three years we had each other. You needed me, and I needed you. Now you've gone back to her and I'm left cleaning up these scraps! This is what I'm worth to you? Finding out some middle school-type gossip?" She turned away, her body shaking lightly.

Zweig knew it had been a mistake to come. He wasn't getting anything from her. He stood to go. "I'm sorry, Tabitha. I've made a mess of this. I'll go."

He hesitated. He felt he needed to apologize with more than words. He was also afraid what that might do. But before he knew it, he had walked around her and enfolded her in his arms. "I'm sorry," he said, lightly kissing the top of her head.

63

She pressed against him more firmly, and before he could stop her she was in his ear. "I'm sorry, too, baby. Listen, I do know. I can tell you. I know you need it. But I need something, too. It's been ten months now. I can tell you everything you need, but please give me what I need."

The last word was squelched as her lips mashed against his. For the second time in the past few minutes, he recoiled.

"Tabitha, I can't. I won't! If that's the only way you'll help me, forget it!"

"You jerk! Get out of here, then!" she screamed, eyes flashing, grabbing the television remote and sending it whizzing past his head. "What came over you? You nearly lose your daughter and you think that's justification for remaining faithful to Monica?! What if I called her right now and told her you're here? Where would you go then, Toby?"

The bitterness coming from her was palpable, thought Zweig, coming off her like cheap perfume. For a second he thought she was capable of picking up the phone and blowing his cover to Monica right then and there. But just as suddenly, Zweig had a rush of clarity. *Enough of living in fear*, he thought. *Enough of hiding, of piling on the hidden evils to be wiped away later.*

"Go ahead."

The statement was so bold, so other-worldly, that for a second Zweig looked around to seek the genesis of the voice, and then suddenly he realized it was he who had thrown down the gauntlet.

"What?" asked Tabitha.

"Go right ahead," Zweig said, more confidently this time. "I'm telling her anyway. I won't have a half-honest marriage on my end any longer, no matter what her reaction might be. But as for you, Tabitha … well, I'm disappointed. I thought you'd be more tactful that to trade information for lust."

"You self-righteous ba …" she stopped herself. "Oh this is beautiful, you accusing me of offering myself, of playing the office hooker. Don't you think for a second that the rest of the firm will believe you! And you can go to your little booth with Grenier tomorrow for your special little appointment and confess it all away, but it won't mean anything to me! So make up your mind now, Toby Zweig: Either make your peace with God, or make your peace with me. But not both. Choose!"

Zweig had reached the door and looked back at his beautiful yet troubled assistant. He swallowed hard and stepped past the point of no return.

"I've made my choice, Tabitha. And you know what it is. And as for the rest of the firm: Well, they'll have a more difficult time believing something from the lips of a disgruntled ex-employee."

The shock of it all hit her like an Alpine avalanche. "You wouldn't!"

"I'll put through the paperwork on Friday. You can serve till then, but when the weekend hits, you're officially fired."

9

The smell of roast beef sandwiches along with fish and chips hit Lance Stubblefield as soon as he entered Smugala's Pizza on Watson Road in Sunset Hills. He left his briefcase in his BMW; no drink with his friend Toby Zweig was a working affair. This would be strictly a celebration of friendship maintained even after the stress of a trial. He pressed through the crowd waiting to be seated, gesturing to the hostess that his party was already here. He avoided bumping a waitress juggling dinner for a family of five, said hello to a client munching on a cheeseburger just two tables away, and then finally slid into the booth across from Zweig.

"I'm coming from Webster Groves and you're coming from practically down the street," chuckled Zweig, "and you're ten minutes later than me."

"Sorry," replied Stubblefield. "Vicki called and kept me longer than usual. Had to tell me every detail of the day's activities."

"She and the kids having fun in Little Rock?"

"Other than the fact that it's hotter there today than here during August, and that's saying a lot. You haven't ordered your beer yet, have you?"

"You're paying, so I was waiting for you."

A fresh-faced waitress, likely a college student and wearing a nametag labeled 'CATHEY', approached their table.

"Shiner Bock in the house tonight, sweetheart?" asked Stubblefield.

She shook her head. "Been out of it for a week now."

Stubblefield cursed under his breath and quickly browsed the beer menu for an alternative. "Warsteiner Pilsner for me. A twelve-inch chicken tomato basil pie for both of us to share and whatever he wants to drink. It's on me."

Zweig looked up from the list and said, "Stella Artois."

Cathey left the table, upon which Stubblefield looked at his friend. "Belgium again, huh? Still won't get a German beer."

"Not now, not ever. On principle. I'm not as forgiving as my grandfather."

They swapped small talk and office complaints until the beer came. They raised their glasses to each other and said, "To the bench," taking their first sips before placing the beers on the lime green tabletop.

Stubblefield couldn't place it, but something was a tad askew about Zweig. "Toby, what's going on?"

"You know me well, don't ya, Lance?" said Zweig in between sips of his beer.

"You can't look me in the eye and you've come here direct from Webster Groves. I think that amounts to something. Why were you over in Webster?"

Silence, then Zweig sighed.

"Oh man," moaned Stubblefield. "Don't tell me. Not her again. I thought you'd told her no, that you and Monica were together."

"It's not what you think," replied Zweig, "so shut up about that. I was fishing for something else. I'm being targeted by Harvest and I'm not sure the entire diocese is behind me on upcoming cases."

"What for? I thought your assignments were a done deal. The archbishop loves you. I'm sure the rest of the clergy is grateful for you, as well. So what if Harvest wants you out of any upcoming contract deals? I'd be happy not to see their faces."

"Well, you don't get it, Lance. I'm worried someone is smelling out my plans."

"Plans? What plans? You've got two things coming up, one for sure and one in the works." Stubblefield tilted his Warsteiner to his mouth for another gulp before going on. "You're making me paranoid. If you've told me this much, you need to open the door a little wider." He noticed his friend's flushed, pasty expression. "Come on, Toby! I've never seen you look like this. We may be on opposite sides of the courtroom, but I'm your friend here. What's going on?"

Zweig leaned closer. "Okay. The 10:21 case, the Santa Maria transfer. What would you say if I told you those were part of a bigger picture for the sex abuse case?"

"You'd better scatter those clouds because I'm not seeing where you're taking me. Start making more sense."

Zweig nodded. "Okay. I realize this is going to violate every code of conduct, not to mention undermine any confidence certain people would have in me. Please, Lance. You need to take this to your grave."

And he began to tell him the entire story.

10

At precisely twenty minutes until four o'clock Thursday afternoon—one week after Toby Zweig told Judge Valle the defense rested—a figure wearing full clerical garb with collar stepped out of his car on the north side of West Pine Street. He stood for a moment, wistfully looking eastward at St. Louis University's Museum of Contemporary Religious Art and—beyond that in the distance—to the Gateway Arch. Without dropping his eyes, he reached into the back seat on the driver side, lifting out a extra large padded manila envelope. Locking the car, he broke into a brisk walk until he reached Boyle Avenue, turning right and heading more slowly toward the majestic structure before him.

He was proud he never missed a confession while he was in town. While others had to fit their absolution into weekday mornings or between Masses on the weekend, Toby Zweig was grateful for a standing special dispensation. Monsignor Grenier had been his confessor for seven years now, faithfully listening to the attorney through the years of lukewarm marriage and extramarital trifles. The priest had remarked recently with much gratitude that Zweig's lists of sins had grown shorter and their quality had reduced from mortal to venial to boring. But, thought Zweig, he could only judge what he heard. Today he resolved to give Grenier the complete picture.

He approached the confessionals in the west transept, briefly arrested by the bold images of Jesus' baptism and ascension and the dual descent of the Holy Spirit as a dove. Mightily, the creature rushed downward, first to bless the Savior of mankind and then again to embolden the disciples to go and declare the Gospel. The calm resolve depicted upon the faces of Christ and his friends was one Zweig admitted he'd been seeking for so long. He turned his eyes away from the brilliant swaths of blue, red and violet and made for the third confessional. Ever since he was a little boy, he remembered the smell of the wood, the cushion, the rasping slide of the lattice screen. The tearful admission to having cheated on the algebra test in ninth grade. The time when he dropped everything while helping the sexton vacuum the crypt stairway because he remembered lying to his father about taking the twenty-dollar bill. The confessional had been a harbor of cleansing for as long as he could recall.

But it wasn't Father Grenier who greeted him through the lattice.

"Bless me, Father, for I have si- … ah, Father Behringer. Um, hi," said the startled Zweig.

The young priest smiled through the grille. "Hello, Toby. The monsignor had to beg off and ask me to take your shift this week. The fourth-grade teacher next door had a stroke during a geography lesson and had to be taken directly to Barnes. The monsignor felt he should go and see her immediately and so he asked if I would hear your confession. I'm sorry. This just came up and we had no chance to let you know."

"No, no. That's fine, Father. Let's go ahead and begin. Is she okay?"

"Yes, for now. The monsignor will let us know later on. We can go ahead. Tell me your sins, my son."

70

"Sorry for being so frazzled by this, Father."

"Oh, that's no sin," laughed Father Behringer.

Zweig smiled and remained silent for a few seconds. So much weighed on his mind and heart. He was torn, standing on a swaying bridge of wooden slats over a deep ravine, between two imposing bluffs. He wanted the reconciliation offered for sins dutifully confessed. Yet he also wanted a true clean slate regardless of whether he was washed clean or not. He wanted to come clean with Monica even if she refused to forgive him. He desired to live more simply and not make his life a rabid push for possessions and comfort. Above all, he wanted his profession to be more than just winning the case. He craved the chance, one chance to bring true justice to those wronged, even if that outed him from the position he held, even if that meant less pay, even if that meant survival rather than opulence. Like Grandpa.

"I have sinned against the Lord Jesus Christ in thought, word and deed, Father. But those words seem so wooden. I have committed grievous sins of which I would be ashamed. I have neglected to do good when I had opportunity. I am ashamed that I can't open my mouth and fully disclose those sins. To be honest, Father, I don't even know how I would define a sin."

"Maybe it depends on how you would define your life, Toby."

"Excuse me, Father?"

"Well, sometimes we think of sin as missing the mark, not living accurately. Perhaps we do this because we envision our lives as dartboards and the whole point is to hit that bulls-eye. The darts that hit the center are clearly good actions. You know, Mother Teresa

71

ministering in Calcutta, that sort of stuff. The darts falling elsewhere on or off the dartboard are sins, and the further they are from the center, the nastier they are."

"On the other hand," Father Behringer continued, "what if there's a better picture of life? What if it's not a static item like a dartboard, but a dynamic one, like a journey or quest? We want to get to our destination, to our true purpose, and enjoy our travels. But circumstances arise that slow us down or cloud our appreciation of our travels. In that sense, anything that wrecks us *or slows us down* is sin."

"What's your point, Father?"

"I'm saying that if life is a journey, that is much more exciting than being a dartboard. But it means we take our faults and shortcomings more seriously. Anything could slow us down from the life God wants us to have. And if that's the case, we don't just pay attention to the big sins: the extramarital affairs, the fits of rage, and the vileness of our language. We critique our motives, our hidden idolatries, our secret enchantments. Perhaps what you need, Toby, is to confess the greater sins. Not the ones the world says are bad. The ones that can shatter and deface your soul, one cut at a time."

Father Behringer didn't need to go on. Zweig had made up his mind.

"I want to confess my true sins for the first time, Father."

"Go ahead, Toby."

The attorney began with the typical recitation, but over the course of the entire half-hour set aside, he began to realize such utterings fell woefully short. Father Behringer's challenge rang true, and with an emotional quaver in his voice, Zweig confessed as tears streamed forth.

"I have exalted greed when I should have desired sacrifice and seeking the true needs of others. I have sought my comfort and selfishness rather than truly listening to my wife. I have pursued what is temporary rather than looking for lasting spiritual treasure. I have taken pride in raw acquisition of victory and not thought of the anguish of the oppressed. And most of all, I have functionally come into this booth for ritual and tradition rather than falling before God pleading for change and restoration."

Father Behringer listened with his jaw open. Toby Zweig had broken down in sobs on the other side of the lattice. Never before had the priest heard a confession this powerful and authentic.

"Toby … Toby. I … I don't know what to say. You have taught me much with those few words. I must ask. Are there others in your life you must share these things with?"

Zweig swallowed and catalogued everyone he implicated in his confession. "Yes, Father. My wife. My daughter. My colleagues. My clients. And my priests. I have much to say."

"Then do this. No 'Hail Marys.' No 'Our Fathers.' Seek all those with whom you need reconciliation. Confess honestly and share your shame. Beg their forgiveness. And if you pursue this path, it is clear that God in his love has forgiven you."

Fifteen minutes later, Zweig walked slowly through the Blessed Virgin Chapel, turning his recent confession over in his mind over and over. When he had spoken with Tabitha the evening before, the statement that he would tell Monica everything had slipped out unthinkingly. But now it seemed to him the most spiritually rational thing he could do. No matter what, he would begin there. And then he would confess to everyone about how he had wronged them. And then he would take on this final case, and he would protect the innocent. For that, he could not confess to the group that would be most betrayed, but perhaps God would not see that as a sin.

A swirl of emotions hit him, and he stumbled past the rows of chairs and toward the chapel's altar, kneeling before the fresco of the Madonna and Child directly in front of him, centered in between six candlesticks. He bowed reverently, confidently, and felt for the first time in his life the assurance that his filth was truly washed away. No longer would he hide. The mask he had presented to the world would be thrown onto the landfill of the past. It felt so right to make this revolution, this repentance, in this place where he had long sought solace, where he could offer this promise alone.

The sound of footsteps behind him, however, told him he was not truly alone. He kept his eyes closed until he felt the presence of his new visitor. Lifting his head, he saw the form of one wearing a clerical shirt with the tab collar. He couldn't identify him at first due to the black robe and hood obscuring the individual's face. A tilt of the head, though, brought the face full into view.

Utterly confused, Zweig whispered, "You? What are you doing here?"

Staring full into the face of the robed guest took Zweig's concentration away from what was in his intruder's right hand, and the lawyer was not fast enough to stop his attacker as he drove his fist toward Zweig's heart. He felt the searing pain and the burning fire that spread throughout his chest. He wanted to scream for help, but the sopping cloth in the assailant's left hand slammed against his face, working its dreadful mission of oblivion to mix with his final seconds. The last sight he had was that of a gleaming dagger rising out of his chest, graced with an evil symbol he knew all too well, and his last word was a plea to the one who had given him that dreadful tool many years ago.

"*Grandpa ...*"

BOOK TWO
"And of the Son"

(September 22-23)

LUKE H. DAVIS

11

Dashing around a slow-moving Pontiac Aztek, Tori Vaughan gunned the Dodge Sprinter down Highway 40 into the heart of St. Louis. Meanwhile, Cameron Ballack sat next to her, simultaneously adjusting his voice amplifier while speaking to Scotty Bosco on his cell phone.

"You got it, boss. Be there in five … What? ... No, we just passed Hampton Avenue. See you in a bit. We'll come in the side door near where you are … Yeah, I know the layout. I was just there a week ago. Later."

Ballack hung up as Vaughan zipped along, Forest Park a virtual blur to their left-hand side.

"Take it easy, Tor. The body isn't going anywhere. Take Kingshighway. No need to double back."

"Well, Cam," Vaughan smiled. "This kind of blew your theory out of the water."

"What do you mean?"

"About it being forever, if ever, that we'd get an SID case."

"Who knew? Humble pie can be just as nourishing."

Vaughan edged off the highway onto the Kingshighway exit, the imposing figure of the Barnes-Jewish medical complex at a cattycorner position from them. "Hey, do you think you might have to give a certain someone a call?"

"Who? What do … oh, man. Just to be safe, I'd better."

He pulled out his cell phone and punched the familiar number. In truth, he hoped to get her voice mail and put the onus on Dana to call him back. He had no desire to shoehorn a conversation on the way to a crime scene, but it wasn't like he had many options.

"Hello?"

"Hi, Dana. It's me."

"Cameron! Where are you calling from? You sound like you're in a World War I dogfight."

"Sorry about that. It's Tori pretending she's Michael Schumacher. And listen, I'm sorry about throwing up this flare, but tomorrow might not work for us to go out."

"Oooh … someone else?" she joked.

"Dana!"

"I'm just kidding. Sorry, that was uncalled for," she repented. Ballack resented any push in that area. Deep down, he understood she knew he was nothing like her philandering late husband. He knew she still struggled with trusting anyone and tossed the resentment aside as soon as it came over him.

"We just got called in. Across the river. SID case and we're likely the lead team. I can't tell you any more, obviously, but given what it's looking like we should probably postpone our celebration to next week when the horizon clears."

"Next week," she repeated in a playful grumble, although it was clear to him that Dana rejoiced in his success. "Okay. Just give me a call sometime tomorrow when you know something more. I'll be at school until six. There's a soccer game I might watch, but I'll have my cell with me."

"Okay," replied Ballack. He hesitated to say what he wanted to. There were certain things that were hard to share with Dana when

80

his partner was hurtling down Lindell Boulevard toward a murder scene, but he didn't feel it would be fair if he signed off without saying it.

"Miss you, Dana," he finally said.

He heard a muffled, gushing sigh on the other end of the line, followed by "I miss you too, Cameron. Be safe."

"Okay. Talk to you later. Bye."

"Going to the chapel and we're gonna get …" began Vaughan.

"Silence your yapper and turn here," Ballack barked, pointing at the sign at Newstead.

Vaughan looked up at the dizzying heights of the Cathedral Basilica as they went around the back. "Can't believe I'm here. It's been ages."

"It's been only a few days for me," growled Ballack. "Turn left, then into that side lot with the handicapped parking. That'll put us smack up next to the chapel where the body is. And grab the portable ramp out of the back. We'll need it."

Vaughan shook her head. "Impressive you recall the layout after only one visit."

"Actually," he said, "I more depressed that this is the reason I have to return."

12

The detectives made their way through the side door, Ballack taking the lead and making a left-hand turn, nearly colliding with Scotty Bosco and another person whom he vaguely recognized.

"Cameron. Tori. You may remember SID Commander Stu Krieger here from the St. Louis police force. Stu, this is Detective Cameron Ballack and Detective Tori Vaughan from the St. Charles Police Detective Bureau."

Kreiger shook Vaughan's hand and cast a hard glance at Ballack, who identified the look immediately. The *Why-is-someone-like-you-doing-something-like-this* glance, the equivalent of acting like he was several ticks above an entry-level beat cop. And yet if I ran over his carcass, thought Ballack, somehow I would be doing wrong.

"Detectives, let me introduce you to the rest of your team," announced Krieger. Four individuals, two men and two women, approached them from the west transept area. "Due to the sensitive nature of this case, it'll be a small team. With me are the detectives, Zane Hull and Missy Crabolli, from the St. Louis force. Next to you are the case medical examiner Marcus Broadnax and crime scene investigator Sheila Grimshaw."

Ballack nodded acknowledgement to the detectives, turned, and shook hands with Broadnax and Grimshaw.

"Glad to have you with us, detective," said Broadnax. He was a black man of athletic build with a solid handshake and confident dispostion. Grimshaw smiled and welcomed Ballack as if they had gathered at a dinner party. Adorned with a bright green blouse and neon yellow slacks, she looked more like a high school drama teacher than a forensics expert.

Ballack's eyes noted a small cluster of folks seated down the west side of the nave. *Wrong place, wrong time,* he thought of the people sequestered until being questioned.

"Are we ready?" asked Bosco.

"I believe so," said Ballack. "What do we have? If it's in the chapel as you say, we'll need to set up my ramp."

"Sounds good. Stu, why don't you give the details?"

Krieger stood in front of the barrier of yellow police tape, cleared his throat and began. "Victim is Toby Zweig. He's an attorney at the law firm of Gillette, Wales, and Alexander, which handles many of the legal matters for the Archdiocese of St. Louis. Father Jim Behringer discovered him at twelve minutes before five here in the Blessed Virgin Chapel. The odd thing was Zweig had just finished a private confession with Behringer just fifteen minutes before. He's stabbed through the chest, or so the story goes. We made sure everyone in the church at the time, which amounts to about eight people, stayed until we get them checked out."

"Next of kin notified?" asked Ballack.

"Of course."

"Was this regular confession time for everyone, Commander?" asked Ballack. "Or was this private confession a matter of special appointment?"

"I don't know, Detective," said Krieger, not even looking up from his notes.

"Is this Behringer his regular confessor?" pressed Ballack.

"Detective," Krieger replied, looking up, "I don't know. You can ask him yourself." Krieger's face was large for a man with such a tall and slender frame. His dark brown hair swept across the top of his head, and it seemed to be thinning. He wore a bushy mustache that carried some wiry gray strands—a bad match for his green eyes. And his reaction to Ballack seemed to carry equal parts aloofness and annoyance.

"Okey-dokey," Ballack said, shrugging his shoulders. He peeked over at Tori who was smiling and holding four fingers to her chin. *He's a seasoned veteran and has little patience with pressure. Tread carefully. He'll hate you no matter what,* interpreted Ballack. He relied on his partner's ability to read other people and was always grateful for this gift.

Krieger looked around as if the Cathedral was wired and the Pope himself was listening in from the Vatican. "The remainder, you guys can get as part of your investigation. We'll let you begin."

Scotty and Tori worked at putting Ballack's ramp in position to give him a smooth incline into the chapel. Hull and Crabolli gathered with Krieger and spoke in hushed tones. Impatient to get started, Ballack looked up at Broadnax and Grimshaw.

"Did you get a cursory look yet?"

"Just from the steps," replied Broadnax. "Looks like a knife or dagger plunged into his chest. He's on his back in front of the altar. We'll get in there in a second. Strange this happened in a church, especially this one. It's freaky. Just like the first murder victim I ever saw."

"Was that in a church, too?"

84

"No, in a locker room in Lynchburg, Virginia. Fifteen years ago. I should explain. I was drafted by the Pirates and played in their system for a few years."

"Pittsburgh? Really. Wow," said Ballack.

"Yeah, I got up to double-A before fizzling out. Anyhow, this happened when I was in single-A ball and I arrived at the ballpark for some early batting practice. My bats were misplaced and I went off to find the equipment manager. He was in his storage room and had been stabbed through the heart and stuffed into one of his lockers. I never got over that."

"My gosh, neither would I. So I imagine there's quite a story from the transition from minor league ball to being an M.E."

"You have no idea. If we get time at some point, I'll give you the short version."

Grimshaw interjected. "I assume you and Vaughan are the lead guys?"

"That's the plan," said Ballack. "Is there simmering resistance afoot?"

"Was it that transparent?" she said, raising her eyes in a friendly manner. "Don't worry about Krieger. Just keep him in the loop. Chances are he'll barely give you the time of day—not to be unfriendly. He's juggling too many cases at once. The other two might need some tender loving care, but they're not bad. They'll take a day to warm up."

"Tender loving care. A quality I'm not well known for," said Ballack. "Looks like the path is clear. Let's go, everybody."

They started toward the ramp, where Vaughan stood in a white oversuit clutching her camera. Hull and Crabolli were getting dressed. Ballack scaled the ramp, flipped open his laptop, and turned on his Dragon NaturallySpeaking software that would automatically type his observations as he spoke them. Everyone gathered around in silence, waiting for a go-ahead. Ballack suddenly, and rather proudly, realized they were waiting on his starting pistol.

"Let's go. Marcus and Sheila, do your things. Tori, pictures. Zane and Missy, look for footprints, smudges, anything. Maybe one of you should check with the crowd in the nave and get times of their arrivals here. Anything could be helpful."

"Which one for which job?" asked Crabolli. Her straight blond hair fell past her shoulder and lay comfortably over the collar of her green cotton blouse. Ballack took one look at her hard stare and figured he had a battle on his hands already.

"I don't care. Choose. This is the first time we've worked together so you should have a clearer idea who would be better at what." He turned away toward the nave to roll his eyes at Crabolli out of her line of sight. And that's when he saw him. Previously obscured by a pillar, now plain as day.

Black as coal.

Hospital scrubs.

And that hunter green windbreaker jacket.

Very nice, my friend, thought Ballack. You came back here. The question for us is why.

"Cameron?"

Ballack averted his eyes from the distant crowd and turned to face his partner. "Broadnax wants you," Tori said.

As Ballack wheeled in the direction of the medical examiner, Broadnax was just cleaning his thermometer.

"Seems like it happened ninety minutes ago," he said without looking up. "A full exam won't be telling us any more. This wound is quite fresh. Once we remove it, we'll be able to tell the depth, of course. Whatever struggle he might have mounted was cut short by this …" He motioned to Grimshaw, who held out a massive wad of gauze. "It was still wet. Smells like chloroform, but maybe with secondary materials added. We'll know more in the lab."

"Odd that he was hit in the front," said Ballack. "A swifter and cleaner attack might be from behind. Unless that is, the perpetrator wanted to do so from the front."

"That way the perp could keep his eyes on the outside, make sure no one was present or watching, provided he was positioned that way." said Grimshaw. "Sorry, though. You probably figured that already."

"Don't apologize for a second, either of you," said Tori. "If there's one thing we expect, it's input from all sides."

"And if there's one thing we can't stand," added Ballack, "it's silence. Everyone has a contribution to make. If you sense or know something and don't share it, that jeopardizes the entire case."

"That's a refreshing attitude," remarked Broadnax, checking the rigor mortis of Zweig's body.

"We St. Charles folks can be quite generous when you get to know us," Ballack chimed. He nodded toward the body. "Rigor mortis confirm or change your diagnosis on time of death?"

"Confirm. Sheila, why don't we get the knife out? That way I can look at the depth of the wound and you guys can look at the weapon itself."

"Tori," called Ballack. "Can you swing over here with your shutterbox?"

Zane Hull approached from the rear of the chapel. "Shoe smudge by the steps," he said in a flat voice. "Maybe the perp getting away, maybe not."

"Thanks, Zane," said Ballack. "Tor, can you take care of that first? I'll be glad when we can give this instigator a name."

Hull wrinkled his forehead as Tori went with him to the spot.

"Ready, Detective?" asked Broadnax.

"Go ahead, slugger."

Broadnax put on another clean pair of gloves and took hold of the weapon lodged in Toby Zweig's chest. It resisted his initial tug, but after fifteen seconds it gave way and came sliding out, slick with blood. The three stared in amazement.

"That," said Grimshaw at last, "is one wickedly long blade."

"What is it?" asked Broadnax. "I've never seen anything of its sort."

"That, friends," said Ballack, "is a World War II-era Nazi officer's dagger. Look," he said, growing noticeably intrigued, "there's the German eagle at the top of the handle, Nazi swastika obscured somewhat by all that blood. Handle looks ivory almost, with brass gilt fittings in a wraparound fashion."

"Look at the length of that blade," exclaimed Tori, who had returned from her scuff photo session.

"At least nine inches, probably closer to a foot," said Broadnax. "And the entire blade is completely soaked in blood."

"There's some engraving on the blade," said Ballack, completely lost in the wonder of this historical find. "Probably the original owner putting his ID on it."

"How do you know so much about this?" asked Grimshaw.

"The benefits of being a history minor in college, combined with my German heritage," said Ballack.

"Seriously," added Tori, "I learn new stuff about this guy every day. If there's something he can obsess over that the rest of the world knows nothing about, trust me—he'll find it."

"She finds my interest in Canadian football disconcerting," deadpanned Ballack.

"Anyhow," Broadnax said, bringing the conversation back to the blade, "the path of the thrust looks diagonal. Entered between the sternum and the right nipple, that way bypassing the sternum and nailing the heart. Only way to explain this much blood."

"But if most of the blade is submerged," said Grimshaw, taking out a tape measure to get an exterior check on the approximate depth of the wound, "that means it came pretty close to going all the way through and coming out the back."

"No wonder we had difficulty getting it out at first," Broadnax thought out loud. "It had to have gone through enough muscle, or the heart sac, maybe even a rib or two."

"What's that?" Tori asked, pointing to Zweig's beltline. "That paper, stuffed in there down his pants."

From between Zweig's trousers and boxers, Broadnax pulled an enclosed quart-sized Ziploc bag that held a sheet of paper. It bore a message, crudely put together with words clipped from magazines, taped to the page. The medical examiner handed it to Grimshaw, who showed it to Ballack.

"Lovely," he muttered.

Tori looked at the sheet of paper, which spelled out the words *TO PROTECT THE INNOCENT.*

"And what's that with it?" she asked.

Grimshaw was handling a wooden crucifix, no larger than her hand, which had rested near the entry wound. The cross was painted, although it seemed to have faded to an olive color. The Christ figure was intact, brass-plated, and hung in the traditional Roman fashion. Broadnax noted the oddity in the object as the others stared at the front.

"That's kooky. The upright post is cut, and I'd say deliberately. Not broken manually, but precisely, like with wire cutters."

Grimshaw turned it over and then Ballack saw it for himself. The vertical beam was snipped in the area of Jesus' kidneys.

Ballack rubbed his temples. *Bizarre.* He needed to pop a couple Excedrin before the next step.

"Seems like someone was pissed about the esteemed counselor for some reason," he said. "We'll let you two finish up in here. We'll get together with everyone else." Tori got to the steps and applied pressure to the top of the ramp to hold it in place. Ballack rolled downward and approached Bosco and Krieger.

"Mrs. Zweig is on her way," said Bosco, "but she'll be awhile. The monsignor of the cathedral, Father Peter Grenier, was at Barnes and he just got here."

"That's fine," said Ballack. "We'll start questioning now. Zane and Missy, if you could question the monsignor. Tori, take Father Behringer since he was Zweig's confessor. Missy, how far did you get with everyone in the crowd?"

Crabolli leveled Ballack with a stern look. "Got names, times of arrival, and all claim they saw nothing."

"That quickly?" Ballack responded, glancing at her notes.

"I got it done. That's what you asked."

Ballack nearly opened his fire hose of sarcasm but thought better of it. "Okay, you two grab the monsignor. Tori, I'll join you with Father Behringer when I'm done."

"With what?"

"Not what … whom." He rolled down the west aisle and parked next to the man in the green windbreaker, whose tremulous eyes appraised him warily.

"Hello again, sir. Remember me?"

13

Following Ballack's directive, the windbreaker-clad individual came to an oak bench on the right side of All Saints Chapel, located in the southwest corner of the Cathedral. The detective maneuvered in front of the bench as he checked his laptop.

"Have a seat, sir," Ballack motioned to the man, who lowered himself uneasily, as if palpably wounded. "I assume you realize why I've pulled you aside."

The dark brown eyes peered at Ballack with considerable trepidation. "You remember me from a week ago. I was sitting across the way when you bumped into the pew where I was sitting."

"That's right. Sorry again for interrupting your meditation then, and I apologize that this is necessary."

"Don't worry about that, although it would be nice to know what this is about."

"Nobody's told you?"

"Father Behringer said no one could leave because there had just been a bad accident."

"Interesting way of putting it. Can I have your name first?"

He hesitated. "It's Varner. Greg Varner."

Ballack made a note of the name, but his eyes strayed toward Varner's wrists. A considerable amount of scar tissue lay on the underside of each one, arranged in horizontal lines.

"Mr. Varner, I'll let you know why I'm speaking with you right now. Exactly one week ago I saw you sitting over there," he pointed across the nave, "and today I see you here again. What has just happened today is that someone was murdered at the front of the church, in the Blessed Virgin Chapel. Since you've been here before, and because—according to the notations of one of the other detectives—you were here before the murder took place today, I need to pose you a few questions."

Varner looked shaken. "I understand."

Ballack adjusted his voice amplifier. "First, some rudimentary matters. I have your name. Do you come to the Cathedral often? Is this close to home? On the way to or from work?"

Varner swept his right hand through his hair, which was knotted in a series of short braids. "I've been coming by here after work each day, and I attend Mass every Sunday evening. The times after work are just to sit, pray, and think."

"And where do you work? I'm assuming with the scrubs it's something in the medical field."

Varner nodded. "I'm a phlebotomy assistant at Barnes. Draw blood. Stuff like that. I work the day shift, so I come here when I get off."

"Do you walk? Bike? Drive?"

"On nice days like today I walk. Occasionally, I'll bike. I have a car, but I use it only when I absolutely need to."

"And you live where?"

"In an apartment on Euclid a couple blocks north of Lindell. Not far."

"The detective that was questioning you all earlier, Detective Crabolli—she noted that you said you arrived here at 4:05."

"That's right. I stopped by the cafeteria at Barnes to get a candy bar and started walking this way. The bells for four o'clock were ringing when I was a couple of blocks from the church."

"When you got here, where were you sitting?"

"Same side as when you saw me last week, just up a few rows. I never stay in the same pew twice in a row."

Ballack nodded. "Did you go into the Blessed Virgin Chapel at any point while you were here today?"

"No, never did."

"Have you ever been in there?"

"Actually, no. I normally don't use the chapels for prayer. The few times I have I've stuck—ironically—with this one here."

"Did you happen to be here for confession today?"

"Confession? No. Why would I?"

Varner's tone of voice wasn't mocking, but Ballack nonetheless countered, "Um, to confess your sins? Isn't that what usually happens during the sacrament of reconciliation?"

"No," Varner involuntarily expelled a nervous laugh. "I know what it's for. When I asked why would I, it was because this isn't the time when confessions occur."

"What? Then why would ..." Ballack caught himself. "When are confessional times scheduled?"

"They have a bulletin listing them, but I think it's 7:30 to 8 every weekday morning. Then you have 3:30 in the afternoon on Saturday up until five o'clock Mass, plus an hour each before the ten o'clock and noon Masses on Sunday."

Ballack was troubled. Why was Toby Zweig here? How private was this confession, if that was indeed what it happened to be?

"Sir?" asked Varner. "Is something wrong?"

"No, nothing," said Ballack. "Did you happen to know a Mr. Toby Zweig?"

Varner slowly shook his head. "Never have."

"I'll be blunt with you, Mr. Varner. He's the murder victim. Are you absolutely certain you don't know him or anything about him? Think hard."

Varner looked upward, closed his eyes, then opened them before looking at Ballack. "Nothing. Sorry."

"So then my next question, if you knew why someone would wish him harm, is a moot one."

"I can't imagine anyone wishing someone harm in a place of prayer."

Ballack thought back to the image of murder victims at St. Basil's—in the guest house, in the library, in the chapel—but decided not to tell Varner how naïve he was.

"Let me ask you this, Mr. Varner. You're a regular visitor here. Six times a week. Has there been anything unusual or strange going on during your times of prayer and meditation? It doesn't matter how small. Can you think of anything?"

Varner shook his head again. "No. When I come, there aren't many here. Usually just people snooping around and touring the cathedral. Like you and your friend last week. I never notice any repeat visitors. That would seem out of whack."

95

"Then did you notice anything today, happening up near the front of the church? Near the Blessed Virgin Chapel? Think sometime between 4:30 and 4:45."

Varner pursed his lips, betraying his weariness, but then he had a flicker of recognition. "Well, it's not that I saw anyone's face, but …"

"Go ahead," said Ballack, grateful for any sort of break.

"I heard something at 4:40. I remember because my eyes were shut and when I opened them the first thing I saw was my watch. The sound was a loud squeak. Could have been someone sliding on the floor, skidding, whatever. Could have been anything. When I looked up, I did see someone moving toward the side door, the handicapped one on this side. Whoever it was, his back was toward me, so I didn't get a look at the face."

"Anything about the clothing?"

"Looked like a priest from behind. Black cloak, but whoever this was, he had a hood pulled over his head. I heard the door open and close."

Ballack—glad for the lead but disappointed it took this long—said, "Mr. Varner, I think that would qualify as something unusual. Why didn't you remember before?"

"I wasn't told what the nature of this case was, detective. I guess memory can depend on the situation."

Ballack rubbed his right cheek with his index finger. "Well, in this case I think that will be enough." He took a business card out of the rail pack on his wheelchair. "If anything else comes to mind, don't hesitate to call me."

"Thank you. I'll be sure to do so."

Varner got up to leave, but Ballack had one more query. "Mr. Varner, you come here six days a week. There are thousands of other things one could be doing in St. Louis at this time. Why set aside this time to pray over and over again? Are you trying to find God? Or are you paying him back for something you feel He's done? What I'm trying to ask is, why be so devout?"

Varner smiled wearily and shook his head, scattering his braids for a few seconds. "All of the above, detective. I discover and re-discover God every day when I come here, so yes, I'm trying to find the God who has already found me. And to your second question, I do owe God big."

"How so?"

"I used to play basketball at SIU-Edwardsville. Shooting guard. Leading scorer. But final year I got undercut on a lay-up and broke my wrist upon landing. Navicular bone. Worst one. Sometimes those breaks never properly heal. I couldn't get used to the idea of life after basketball. I barely skated by with a C average anyway. I got depressed that winter, got into alcohol and drugs, mainly cocaine. One night I got so ripped I went to my coach's house. Didn't even know why I did so, but I blamed him for everything and beat him to within an inch of his life. Cops came and led me away. Don't know if you were living here. You might have seen it on the news about seventeen years ago."

Ballack hadn't. Varner continued, "I spent time in prison. Eighteen months. Never graduated with my class. Got expelled from school, as a matter of fact. That's where these came from." He displayed the slash marks on his wrists. "Didn't want to go on. Prison guards stuffed towels over them and kept me from dying, even though I wanted out of life. But then Coach came to see me in prison one day. Said if he was in the same bind, he couldn't be sure he wouldn't do the same. I broke down crying and he forgave me. I didn't even apologize, and he forgave me for everything. Asked what I needed most of all and I said I wanted my dignity, I wanted my self-respect. He told me I needed to seek out God. Then Coach went about getting me back in school, community college, so I could earn a degree. That's how I ended up working toward being a phlebotomy assistant. Got on with a clinic for four years until the clinic closed. Now working at Barnes. Plus, I'm taking classes two nights a week at UMSL. Sales and marketing. I want to go into medical equipment and technology sales, whenever that ship leaves the harbor."

Ballack had to admit, if anyone had a reason to be that faithful, it was Greg Varner. "Well, that's a good answer. Thanks, Mr. Varner. I hope you find what you're looking for. Good evening."

"And what about you, detective?"

"What about me?"

"Are you looking for God, too?"

The question caught Ballack unaware and unwilling. "Honestly, Greg," he said, using Varner's Christian name for the first time. "Looking for God hasn't been my forte. If there's going to be any discovery, He's going to have to look for me. I will say I'm quite impressed by your faith, if for no other reason that I'm a lousy pilgrim myself."

14

Ballack rolled toward the front of the Cathedral and found Tori seated with Father Behringer near the confessional booths in the east transept. His hunch that Varner might have something to do with, or be helpful in solving, the murder had been dashed. He deplored wasted time and hated even more that he had done so right out the gate.

Tori sensed his simmering self-loathing as he drove up, but decided to keep going. She nodded toward him and looked at Father Behringer, saying, "This is Detective Ballack, the lead investigator for this case." Ballack felt a tinge of anger at those words. He resolved to make no more slip-ups.

Father Behringer introduced himself and Tori gave a quick recap of the interview so far. The time spent in the confession booth was unusually long, about a half-hour. No, he wasn't Zweig's usual confessor. Monsignor Grenier had a standing appointment with Zweig every Thursday at four o'clock, but he couldn't be here today. Zweig had left the booth after confession and wasn't seen again until the priest went into the chapel and saw his body. Ballack listened intently, but he was intrigued why Behringer chose the priesthood. He had well-chiseled features, blue eyes, closely cropped straw-colored hair and a smile that put people at ease. He would have been a real charmer with the ladies, Ballack thought, if he hadn't chosen the celibate road. And if not for that ostentatious nose hair.

When Tori's digest was over, Ballack flexed his fingers.

"Father Behringer, did Mr. Zweig have a tendency to go to that chapel very often after confession?"

"Not to my knowledge, but then again, I was not his usual confessor. The monsignor would be able to give better clarity on that."

"Was there anything or anyone unusual you noticed between the time Mr. Zweig finished in the confessional and when you discovered his body?"

"Nothing out of the ordinary. I was going to check on the elements for tomorrow morning's Mass, so I left the booth and went toward the Bishops' Hall behind the altar. As I went past the chapel, I noticed someone lying down. I figured it was someone at prayer, but I thought I should check to make sure. It was Toby. What a … what a shock."

Tori asked the next question. "Father, we were going to get to this when my partner arrived, but do you know of anyone who might have wished him harm?"

"I can't think of anyone. Toby was the primary attorney for any litigation or financial matters involving the Archdiocese. He always did a superb job, and he had just finished a case in our favor three days ago. It was a huge victory."

"What was the case?"

"It was a conspiracy trial. A watchdog organization sued the Archdiocese and our mortgage company, accusing us of working the system in a transfer of property from us to individual churches and schools. There was no truth in it, but it kept the *Post-Dispatch* and the news channels busy for a few days."

"Name of the watchdog?"

"The 10:21 Alliance. The director is Pat Fishwick. I think he might still be in town, though I'm not sure where he's staying."

Ballack cut in. "Father, I know this is a difficult thing to hear, but I have to ask. Is there any chance Mr. Zweig might have expressed any unusual sense of fear or anxiety? I know Detective Vaughan has asked about people wishing him harm, but did he seem to think something bad might happen to him?"

Behringer looked shocked. "Something bad? Anxiety? I should say not!"

"I was just asking, Father. Had he let on about anything that might make him want to give up?"

"First of all, Detective, if he had shared anything with me in the confessional, that falls under the priest-penitent privilege."

"True, unless he told you he had molested a harem of eleven-year old girls." Both Ballack and Tori, of course, were well aware of Missouri state law on child abuse.

"My larger point is this: No. Nothing. Nada. Zilch."

"Then I think I should ask this," said Ballack, his temper beginning to percolate like fresh coffee. "Was there anyone who would have known about his movements today, that he would be coming to confession at this time?"

"Why do you ask, Detective?"

"Because I happen to know this is outside of your usual confession schedule. The clergy here would likely know Zweig was a regular visitor at four o'clock every Thursday. That makes every member of the Cathedral staff a person of interest. It could mean members of his law firm fall into that category. So, was there anyone else you know of who would know Mr. Zweig would be here today?"

Father Behringer composed himself and seemed to be thinking backwards in time. "There was one moment after the trial. A number of us were in the hallway outside the courtroom when Pat Fishwick came up and confronted Toby about the decision. Walked right up to him with our whole team around ... myself, Julian Webber and Jerome McPadden. Those last two men work for Harvest Capital, which is our mortgage company. Pat and Toby got into a bit of a verbal scrap, after which Toby told Pat that if he wanted to add to his list of sins, he could come here on Thursday at four when he went to confession. Pat seemed rather interested and said why not. Then he walked off."

"And did Fishwick look like he wanted to hurt Zweig?" asked Tori.

"I couldn't discern his motives from that confrontation," said the priest, "but he wasn't angling for a friendly post-trial cup of tea."

"And the other two gentlemen were within earshot?" asked Ballack.

"Webber and McPadden? Of course. But, bless me, Detective, there's no way you'll be considering them as suspects. He had just won the trial for them. They are upstanding members of their communities and well-known businessmen. Surely you're not adding them to the list."

"Just getting the big picture, Father," said Ballack. "I think that should be all for now. I see my partner has given you her card. Please contact us if anything additional comes to light."

"Are you going to be here much longer, Detectives? I could arrange for some sandwiches for dinner."

"I think we'll work straight through, Father. We have to connect with our fellow detectives and compare notes."

Tori craned her neck and noticed an attractive yet melancholy figure near the west entrance. "And Mrs. Zweig has just seen her husband's body."

15

Monica Zweig was seated in the front pew, breathing unsteadily with several tear-streaks running through her lightly applied makeup. As Ballack approached, he took measure of the newly widowed psychiatrist. She wore a black Ann Klein one-button blazer over a white linen blouse, along with a matching pencil skirt. Her hair was up and held with a tortoise shell clip. Her nose twitched as if she was holding back more tears. She had taken care with her appearance, thought Ballack. Tastefully mournful, arguably fastidious, but not overdone.

"Tori," he said as they came to Hull and Crabolli, "Why don't you and Zane go back into the chapel and see if our friends have dug up anything else. Missy and I will interview Mrs. Zweig for now."

"You sure?" asked Tori, barely masking her incredulity.

"Yeah. Go ahead," he replied, before mouthing to his partner the words *Trust me.* She turned and motioned Hull to follow, which, after a glance at his partner, he did.

Ballack motioned for Crabolli to sit in the pew next to Mrs. Zweig. He wheeled in front of her and said, "Mrs. Zweig, I am Detective Cameron Ballack of the Special Investigative Division of Greater St. Louis. With me is Detective Missy Crabolli. I know this must be a shock to you, and I am deeply sorry for your loss. I just spoke with Father Behringer and he has the highest regard for your husband."

The words that tumbled from his mouth, no matter how sincere, always seemed to ring hollow. He knew they must be simultaneously kind and empty from Monica Zweig's perspective. It was the same, he remembered, at Christopher's death and more recently after Michelle—his former girlfriend—took her own life nearly four years ago.

"Thank you, Detective. I just can't fathom this. For the life of me, what could be the reason for my Toby's death?"

"That's what we need to discuss with you, Mrs. Zweig," interrupted Crabolli. "We know this is a difficult moment for you, but it would help us greatly if you could answer a few questions."

Monica Zweig looked at Crabolli with a confused visage and grew eerily quiet. Ballack had no intention of the conversation turning frosty and spoke gently to the widow, "We obviously do have much to cover, and yes—the initial hours and days after a suspicious death are critical. But we do want to be sensitive to what you're going through. Would you be more comfortable speaking in a different locale? Or do you need some time before we would pose any questions?"

Mrs. Zweig seemed more at ease with Ballack's question, and there seemed to be a quieter, more trusting manner about her. "No. Thank you for asking, Detective Ballack. I think perhaps I can try to speak with you here. I don't want to delay your investigation."

She pulled out a tissue and dabbed at her eyes. As she looked downward, Ballack shot a hard, disgusted glare at Crabolli and quickly drew his thumb across his throat in a slashing gesture. Stunned, she returned his look with one that could have burned a Kansas wheat field.

"How did my husband die, Detective? The people in the chapel did not say."

105

"There was a knife wound deep in his chest," said Ballack. "The weapon was an unusual one, and perhaps you can tell us something of it. It was a World War II-era dagger, one that would have belonged to a Nazi officer."

Mrs. Zweig gasped. "His grandfather's?"

"I'm sorry. You said it belonged to his grandfather? Was he the officer?"

"Yes and no. It was a gift from his grandpa, but he wasn't a Nazi. He was a concentration camp survivor in World War II. Mauthausen. It was in Austria. Toby's grandfather had been a professor in Vienna, and he was a victim of the Nazi roundup of official opposition. Intellectuals were in that group. Toby's grandmother died in the camp, but Grandpa managed to escape. The dagger was part of that."

"He used it to escape?" asked Ballack. "Did he cut through the fence or something?"

"No. A guard was beating him savagely. It was preparation for the gas chamber. Stefan—that was his name—was near the fence one night, getting clobbered by the guard when he realized there were no other Nazis around. He grabbed the guard's dagger and stabbed him to death. Stefan escaped through the underground sewage system and ran to freedom."

It seemed to Ballack like a scene out of *The Shawshank Redemption*, with Andy Dufresne stabbing Warden Norton as a bonus. "You're saying the dagger was his?"

"It was. But this is getting disturbing. When we had dinner late last night, he was very shaky and haggard. He hasn't been himself this week, and when I asked him what was wrong, he said he couldn't find his glass case where he had the dagger mounted."

"Did he have this at home or in the office?" pressed Crabolli, anxious to butt in and not let Ballack totally control the interview.

"At the office. It usually sat on the corner table. He didn't keep it front and center, you know, because of the swastika on it. But if someone asked about it, he'd be more than proud and delighted to give the back story."

"Did either of you file a police report," asked Ballack, "claiming it had been stolen?"

"He had been having some things moved around and hoped it was just lost in the shuffle and would reappear. When I called him this afternoon, the case had reappeared behind his office door, but the dagger was still missing. He said he put the case back on the table, but he was still in quite a temper about it. He told me he was going to confession because he really needed it."

Ballack listened silently, thinking carefully. "Mrs. Zweig, did anyone else know about your husband's private confessional appointments on Thursday afternoons?"

"No, Detective. Not to my knowledge."

"Did he have any enemies? Anyone who would wish him harm?"

"He wasn't the type to broadcast his problems, but no. He did tell me a couple days ago that he was worried the mortgage company and the archdiocese were considering pulling him off some upcoming cases. But that hardly seems like a matter that would end up like … like this." She began to weep again.

Ballack gave her some time to compose herself and then asked gently. "I'm sorry to have to ask this, but was he under a tremendous amount of stress? More so than usual? Had he developed any bizarre tendencies? Were there any recent incidents that might have caused emotional distress?"

"Are you asking if this was suicide? Are you asking if Toby killed himself?"

Ballack held up a hand. "I'm not saying that, Mrs. Zweig. From all vantage points, this has all the hallmarks of murder, not suicide. But I do need to get the widest picture possible and at least see if I can rule it out. I'm sorry. I should have done a better job of prefacing that question. Did he seem scared?"

Monica Zweig shook her head. "That's completely forgiveable, Detective. I see now why you said what you did. But no, Toby wasn't exhibiting any emotion that I believe would be problematic or fearful. He had just won a major court case. Our marriage has been on an upward swing and we've experienced a lot of healing. Of course, I don't know who would want to murder Toby, and I can't think of anyone he was wary of either."

She had just volunteered more information than Ballack had asked for and he pressed her on it. "You said your marriage had been improving and healing. What did you mean by that?"

She paused as if calculating how much more to share. Looking down, she began, "Our relationship hasn't been ideal for the longest time. We have one daughter, Serena. She's a junior at Nerinx Hall. This is going to devastate her. But for many years we've been emotionally detached. Totally absorbed in our professions. My private practice grew and I became more soulfully adept with my patients than with Toby. It led to several affairs. I'm sure Toby suspected but he said nothing. I am certain that for some time he was cheating on me with his secretary. At the very least, it was an emotional affair, where he went deeper with her than he would with me. But that changed last year. Serena was nearly killed in an accident and that brought us together. I told him about my infidelity and told him I needed to and would change. He never said anything about a relationship with Tabitha—that's his secretary, Tabitha Stowe—but I didn't push him on it. As it was, the fire came back and he was the old romantic again."

"Would Tabitha or his partners in the law firm have access to his office? Could they have pilfered the dagger for themselves?"

She looked crestfallen. "I'm sure they could but …" and a confused look crept into her eyes. "No! I can't believe it would have been a co-worker! That's absurd!"

"It might be," said Ballack in a calming voice, "but again, we have to check out every possibility. We will be speaking to everyone at Gillette, Wales, & Alexander anyway. One more question. Just for information. Your whereabouts between four and five this afternoon?"

"I was at my office in Clayton. Here's a card with the address and contact information. You can call my personal assistant or my billing manager. Either can confirm. My other two members in our practice were gone. One is on vacation and the other had an emergency dental appointment."

Ballack looked at the card and handed it to Crabolli, who took it without looking at him. "Thank you, Mrs. Zweig. We'll contact you if there's anything else we require. Would there be any problem with one of us coming by later to take a brief look through your husband's office at home? It's not to pry; anything could be a helpful clue and I'm sure you want this case solved as we do. Probably more."

"I don't think I'd object. But if you could give me a call on my cell phone first—it's on the card—that would be helpful. I could let you in. If you don't mind, I have to pick up our daughter from her tennis match and give her this news. Good evening, detectives." She stood to leave.

Ballack was going to give a quick good-bye when a thought struck him. "Mrs. Zweig, again I am deeply sorry. And I know the road ahead will be difficult for you and your daughter. It's just that … well, if you require any help, or if your daughter needs it … I lost my little brother at an early age and I know what this can feel like to an extent. I'm sure you know some quality counselors and that you are more than qualified as a doctor and mother to help your daughter. But if you need any additional resources, I'd be glad to recommend any."

A look of resigned peace flooded Monica Zweig's face. "Thank you, Detective. I will, if it comes to that. You've been very helpful." She gathered her purse and keys and, with a nod, headed toward the door.

Ballack could feel resentment steaming out of Crabolli like a pot of over-boiled water. Before she could snap at him, he wheeled around and addressed her.

"First of all, Missy, I am the lead detective. I realize we haven't worked together before, so you won't recognize what I want immediately. But I've got two beefs with you. First, you ought to know that when someone has just suffered a horrific trauma like this, you need to coax information out of them, not demand it!"

"What are you talking about?"

"That whole *Sorry about what's happened, but we need to talk to you sooner rather than later*. Never approach the bereaved like that again! I have no problem letting them know we need to advance the investigation, but you say that first, and then put how they want to be interviewed in their lap. The last thing you need to be is overbearing! Second, never—and I mean never!—allow your anger and resentment to affect how you approach an interview. You asked only one question that whole time because you got chapped over my dirty look. You need to be part of this. I expect input from all sides. I'd try to interview a blade of grass if it could give me a lead on a case. So don't take yourself out of the game because you're pissed off at me! Got it?"

"You're not exactly the easiest person to work with, you know," Crabolli responded. "You're out of your league on this one."

"Get to know me before you judge how far my league extends," Ballack shot back. "Come on. Our partners are coming this way."

Vaughan and Hull had checked out the chapel again with Broadnax and Grimshaw, but other than the shoe mark, it was a spotless crime scene. Not even a fingerprint of note. Hull had called the law firm to set up interviews with all there. The managing partner told him that would be no problem, except that Tabitha Stowe had left the office with a severe headache around three-thirty and said she needed to go home for the day.

Hull looked at Ballack. "Your call."

Ballack wagged his head from side to side, trying to loosen his neck. "An affair, a missing dagger and a secretary who checks out before her boss goes to confession," he muttered to himself. He turned to Hull. "How many lawyers there now?"

"Three. Andra Alexander—whom I spoke with—is the managing partner, plus there's Steve Santori and Tom Taylor."

"Okay. You two take the law firm. We'll chase the PA, if indeed she's gone home. Does the firm have her home phone number?"

"Got it already. In fact, they said they'd call her and let her know about his death. Here's the number and address. It's in Webster Groves near the intersection of Laclede Station and Big Bend."

"Can't be too bad of a drive this time of night," Ballack said as he looked out at the darkness. "Tor, make sure they have your cell number. Here's my card with my cell and email. Call us when you're done and we'll figure out a place to meet up. Let's go."

"One more thing, Detective Ballack," said Hull. "Something you should know. Mrs. Alexander told me something that Mr. Zweig had requested earlier today. Tabitha Stowe was to be fired, effective tomorrow."

16

It was a frustrating evening for Missy Crabolli and Zane Hull as they briskly worked their way around Toby Zweig's office at the law offices of Gillette, Wales, and Alexander. In Crabolli's case, she was still frosted over Ballack's dressing down just twenty minutes before. Hull had unspoken questions about how a wheelchair-bound detective eight years his junior could be the lead detective on an SID murder case. Both left their simmering anger unmentioned and decided independently that getting to work was a more productive course. Waiting to speak to the office personnel, they cased out Zweig's office.

"Find anything?" asked Hull.

Crabolli shook her head. "Not that anything'll jump out at us or fall from heaven. I'm guessing we're taking the attorneys one-on-one rather than together?"

"More efficient use of time."

"I can't see this crew doing anything."

Hull straightened up. "Maybe. But I doubt our leader would say the same thing."

"Krieger?"

"Him, too. I was thinking about Ballack."

"I'd rather not."

"You don't have a say in the matter. A lot like me."

"And that didn't piss you off, either?"

Hull looked at his partner. It was one thing to stew over any professional slights. It was another for another to keep fanning those embers in flame. Regardless, they had work to do. It was when he turned away from Crabolli that he noticed what he should have upon entering the room.

"So this is the display case?" said Hull.

Crabolli followed his finger. "The one on the corner table? Yeah."

Hull looked closely at it. "Does anything seem strange about it? Other than the missing dagger?"

"Like what?"

He pointed. "Does it even look forced open?"

Crabolli used a tissue on her hands to protect any prints. The case swung open freely. "Looks to be unlocked."

"Then we have to wonder about this little problem,' Hull said, pointing at a skinny drawer at Zweig's desk. Crabolli came around and joined him.

"The lock?" she asked when she saw the awful truth.

"Badly carved up, as if forced open," Hull agreed, sliding the desk open and finding a pair of small keys. Taking them from the drawer, he crossed the room, slipped the key into the case lock, and found it to be an exact match.

17

At eight forty-five, Vaughan pulled the Dodge Sprinter into the driveway at Tabitha Stowe's house where Toby Zweig had come one last time the day before. Ballack rolled down the Sprinter's ramp near the two-car detached garage when Tabitha came around to the west side of the porch. Her voice was husky, as if she'd been crying, and her posture and gait were noticeably shaky.

"I'm sorry, Detective, but my house isn't really equipped for access. Would you need me to come down?"

"Not really," said Ballack with a smirk, as Vaughan pulled the portable ramp out of the van for him, as well as a smaller ramp for negotiating his eventually entry through the front door. He noticed a bright yellow Honda Fit in the garage, with a pink frame bordering the license plate.

"I assume we can set these up over the porch steps and at the front door and then go from there?" asked Vaughan.

Tabitha nodded. "Come on in the house. We can talk in there. Can I get you anything to drink? I have Coke, Sprite and iced tea."

"Coke for my partner, that much I know," said Ballack. "I'll be fine."

The three of them entered Tabitha's den. The contemporary furniture, complete with matching glass coffee and end tables, contrasted with the older, more traditional exterior of the house. Ballack waited while Tabitha went to get Tori's drink. Slowly wheeling around the den, he looked at the bookcases bracketing the fireplace, then peeked into an office just off the main room. Tabitha

115

came out with Tori's Coke as Ballack sneaked into the kitchen behind her. He looked at the refrigerator and swept his eyes over the counter.

"Officer Ballack?" Tabitha called. "We're back in here."

Ballack smiled. He returned to the den.

Tabitha was seated in an easy chair. Her blond, tightly curled hair fell past her shoulders. Her pink button-down sleeveless top and short black skirt covered what Ballack judged to be a knockout figure on her petite frame. Her shirt was strategically unbuttoned one notch too far, he thought. It was difficult to believe this could be the person who drove a Nazi dagger through Toby Zweig's torso, but there could be a multitude of reasons, especially if they had been tangled in a soured affair. Her voice was soft, feminine, and it called Ballack back to the present.

"When I heard the news, I couldn't believe it. Toby was such a great boss and an excellent lawyer. I've worked there for six years and now it's going to be hard going back." She paused, then put her head in her hands, sobbing quietly.

Either a heartfelt catharsis, thought Ballack, or one of the best cover-ups ever.

"You said six years, Miss Stowe?" asked Tori. Ballack had told her on the way over to take the lead with the questioning.

"Yes. I had worked before at a law firm in Brentwood for three years. I came to Gillette, Wales, & Alexander in the summer of 2005. I worked temporarily for Steve Santori and then when Toby's PA quit—her husband took a job out of state—I was offered that position."

"What was Mr. Zweig like?"

116

"Hard-working. Honest. Loved his family. Diligent and thoughtful. Put other people first. The type of lawyer anyone would want to have."

Ballack groaned inwardly.

Tori continued. "Given his admirability factor, were there still any people that might have had problems with him, who might want to harm him?"

"Harm him? No, he was so respected and well-liked."

"I get that, Miss Stowe, but I wasn't asking you about him. I asked if he had any enemies. There are still some sickos out there."

"Same answer as before. No."

"Were there any issues that were causing problems at work? Any competition? Any cases that happened to be especially problematic?"

"He was a lawyer. Every case is problematic until you win it. But there were no problems at the firm that I knew of. And I would have an idea if there were. A small firm like that, you'd know if someone down the hall sneezed differently."

Ballack spoke for the first time. "What were you doing this afternoon between three and five, Miss Stowe?"

"I thought the firm would have told you if you checked with them. I developed a horrible headache that felt like a migraine coming on. I hadn't brought my Imitrex, so I checked out early. It wasn't like Toby would be staying longer. He always leaves early on Thursdays."

"And you went where?" asked Ballack, his voice more clipped this time.

"Straight home. I got here around three fifty-five."

117

"Could anyone confirm this?"

"Yes, my neighbor across the street. Mrs. Dorfmann."

"She saw you?"

"When I pulled in, and then she waved when I walked in my door."

"And how long was the affair between you and Mr. Zweig?"

Tabitha flinched, hit broadside by Ballack's sudden question out of nowhere. Tori turned away, smiling at her partner's ability to shock.

"Affair? What are you talking …" The migraine had obviously disappeared.

"Miss Stowe," interjected Ballack, holding up his index finger. "Save it. I have an extremely low tolerance for what you're shoveling right now. No personal assistant flying completely solo has pictures of her boss littering her house. You have two on the bookcases behind me. You have a snapshot of you and him at some New Years' shindig gracing your refrigerator and another of Mr. Zweig on the beach. Then there's your office, the eight-by-ten of the two of you in a hot tub together."

Tabitha Stowe was floored, speechless. It was all Tori could do to keep from letting loose a piercing cackle.

"Beautiful frame, by the way, on the one in the office," Ballack remarked. "Did you pick that out yourself or did Monica give you some pointers?"

"All right!" shouted Tabitha. "So we had an affair. It didn't last long."

"My phony alarm just went DefCon 1, Miss Stowe. I think if you're going to be of service to this investigation, and if justice is going to be done, you need to level with us. That means going into deep, hidden areas, and confessing things that might not put you in the best light."

"Fine," she spat. "We were together for three years, give or take a few months."

"See?" Ballack replied sarcastically. "It's not hard."

Tabitha glared at him but went on. "As you can see from the pictures, a good bit of it was outside St. Louis, but we managed to sneak around locally. He was very discreet. He was lonely, for heaven's sake! His wife was cheating on him! What was he supposed to do?"

"Yes," broke in Tori. "We covered that already with Mrs. Zweig. But it seems like they had re-captured the heat between them again. Would you say that's correct?"

Tabitha looked down at her nails. "After January rolled around, Toby told me the affair had to stop. I wasn't about to let him go without a fight, but by Valentine's Day it was clear everything was over. He had always been very affectionate and he was the first man I can say I ever truly loved. But he's had nothing to do with me since April. Gone cold fish on me. Guess he couldn't bear to keep bringing that up in the confession booth."

The initial notes of Motorhead's "The Game" interrupted Tabitha's discourse.

"Sorry," said Ballack. "Email coming in. That's my signal." He opened his account and saw, much to his surprise, that Zane Hull had

119

just sent him an attachment from the law firm. He opened it and smiled at the picture staring back at him.

Tori returned to Tabitha's last statement. "You knew about his regular private confession appointments?"

"I did. I imagine a number of his supposed sins revolved around me."

"Any of them involve the sin of unemployment, Miss Stowe?" asked Ballack, a little more forcefully than he intended.

"What? What is that supposed to mean?" replied the suddenly defensive Tabitha Stowe.

"When we asked earlier if anyone would want to do harm, could you be in that 'anyone' category?"

"What?! No! Why would I want to kill Toby?"

"I don't know. Revenge over a ruined fling. Jealousy. Or there's always the popular kill-the-boss-who-was-firing-you." He waved both ladies toward his wheelchair and pointed to the image on the screen. There, in living color, was the paperwork Zweig had written up to terminate Tabitha's employment.

"A severely angered ex-employee," whistled Tori, playing the game along with Ballack. "That is indeed one serious motive for murder."

"Stop it!" screamed Tabitha. "I didn't kill him! I told you that! I was here! You can check with my neighbor!"

"Are you denying or admitting that you were getting the ax?" inquired Ballack.

"Okay. We had a fight yesterday! He came over and said he needed to know if someone was sabatoging his chances of future cases with the archdiocese."

"How, pray tell, did that escalate into an ex-lovers' battle royal?"

Tabitha walked slowly over to the sofa and sat down. "I wanted one last shot at him in exchange for the information. In truth, I knew nothing. I was so desperate. I was going to make something up that seemed reasonable to satisfy his curiosity."

"You were going to lie as part of your inquiry-for-love exchange? That's hardly trustworthy."

"He rejected that notion. Refused me. I blew a gasket and threw him out. Told him I'd tell Monica and the whole firm about our past. But he didn't care. Said he was going to tell her anyway. What upset me more was how calm he was. He didn't react angrily. Just told me that the firm wouldn't believe a fired PA. Said I would finish out the week and then be gone."

Ballack leaned forward and said, "And that's not a motive for murder?"

"No, because I thought he was over-reacting. I thought he would calm down and change his mind later! Plus, I told you," she glowered toward him. "I came home this afternoon. Got here at three fifty-five!"

"With plenty of time to sneak back out after the neighbor saw you come in," replied Tori. "Even with a ten minute turnaround, you could have left at five after four and made it to the Cathedral in time to kill your boss."

121

"I was here the whole time!"

"But we can't confirm that," said Ballack with a thinly-veiled sneer. "How do we know you hadn't come here to throw off suspicion, then headed up to the Cathedral and waited near the crypt stairwell with the syringe full of strychnine and jammed it into his spinal cord?"

And now Tabitha was alive with terror, casting aside any meticulous insouciance she kept in reserve. The cords in her neck strained and her eyes flashed with fear.

"Good Lord, Detective! You can't be serious! I've never used poison on anyone or anything, let alone use a syringe on anyone, even myself! I couldn't kill a soul! I can't believe you'd suggest it!"

She jumped off the sofa and paced, finally facing the detectives. "Please, ask Mrs. Dorfmann. She's out in her front yard nearly every afternoon. She would have seen if anyone on the street left their home."

Ballack, however, knew that would be unnecessary, for this was one suspect they could undoubtedly scratch from the list. Unless she was hiding something extremely well, Tabitha Stowe had no idea how her boss had been killed.

"We'll leave on that note, Miss Stowe," said Ballack. "We'll take the liberty of asking Mrs. Dorfmann about your whereabouts, as well as the latitude to check in with you again."

In three minutes, Tori placed the portable ramp back in the Sprinter as Ballack dialed Hull to thank him for the email.

"How did the questioning go at the firm?" he asked.

"Hard to say," replied Hull. "We did make an interesting discovery. Maybe we should get together and debrief for the night.

122

What happened to Missy? Ever since you and she worked over the widow, she's been in a nasty mood."

"Don't worry about her, Zane. Where would be a good place? Can we pop in somewhere between our locations?"

"How about the county sheriff's office in Clayton? Right near the courthouse on Carondelet."

"Will do. See you in fifteen minutes."

18

"You what?!" snapped Tori.

"Settle down, why don't you?" Missy Crabolli retorted. "We got the job done, interviewed all three people there, and left. So what's your complaint?"

"My complaint is that slipshod interviews piss me off!" yelled Ballack. "All you asked them was about their movements, their alibis, and out the door you went? At least Zane noticed the picked lock and damage to the desk. What are you looking for? You think they'll just volunteer information and drop it in your lap?"

"I went through my entire checklist of questions, Detective."

"Wow, that must've been as extensive a tome as *Peruvian Goaltenders in the National Hockey League*," sneered Ballack.

"Detective Ballack … Missy," pleaded Zane Hull, "Can we please get back on track? We've had a brutal few hours and we really need to assess tonight and plan for tomorrow."

Ballack paused and gathered himself, still looking at Crabolli, "I admire your honesty, Detective, but you did nothing in the last couple hours to help us. Start moving forward and join the game or get left behind."

"And you've never made a mistake yourself?" Her voice was positively reeking of pain and venom.

"I did today," said Ballack in a more even tone of voice. "I recognized one person in the crowd from last week, so I jumped at the chance to interview him first. It led nowhere and I chewed myself out silently for minutes afterward, but I wasn't about to let that affect my next sequence. I don't have a problem with mistakes being part of the game. I do have a problem when you pack it in so quickly on potential suspects."

He looked around at the others. "That goes for all of us, myself included. Now let's talk about the case itself. First, we need a nickname for our murderer, given that we're quite sure it is murder. What are we going to call him?" He stopped. "Or her."

"Name? Excuse me, Detective, but what's the point?" asked Hull. "Can we maintain some impersonal, professional detachment?"

"We're not detached, Zane. We're people. People get murdered. People solve murders," replied Tori, coming to her partner's defense. "Every murder case is personal. We give each perp a name, and we see no reason to amend our little tradition. Whether or not you think it's stupid, we find it helpful."

"Doesn't matter much what we think, I guess," sulked Crabolli. "We've got enough weirdness right at this table with people's names." She was looking at Ballack when she spoke.

"Ballack?" he said. "You think my last name lacks some class?"

"That's pure comedy, Missy," said Tori. "Someone named Crabolli thinks Ballack sounds funny?"

"And what's wrong with that?" Crabolli answered back.

"Just that my name happens to be an old German one," said Ballack, "while yours sounds like moldy pasta."

Crabolli jumped to her feet when Hull intervened again. "Everyone, calm down! We're getting nowhere!"

"Then let's get somewhere," said Ballack. He took two deep, even breaths before continuing. "Let's go over our findings. What did you two find out from the monsignor? Details, please."

"According to him, he was at Barnes on a hospital visit," said Hull. "Left at two-thirty, actually, and he told Father Behringer he might not be back in time for Zweig's confession. He's the one who normally covers that session. Didn't get back until well after we got to the church."

"Over four hours gone," mused Tori. "Was that the teacher next door?"

"Yes. A certain Mrs. Tinordi, the fourth-grade teacher next door at the Cathedral School, had what turned out to be a stroke. Right in front of the kids. They got the word passed on over to the church and Grenier felt he should leave to be with her. He said she was stable but hardly out of the woods. Left side barely moving and she was squinting even in a dark room."

"I called the ER at Barnes to confirm the story," said Crabolli, still upset but looking for a chance to redeem herself, "and they said a priest was with her the whole time in question. They didn't know the name, but I asked for a description and it matched. So Grenier seems to be out."

"Good thinking, about the ER follow-up I mean," said Ballack quietly. "That hadn't occurred to me."

Tori briefly looked at her partner. She knew perfectly well such a ploy did in fact occur to him, but that wasn't the point. She rarely saw a kinder side of Ballack and this was one of those times. He was overcompensating, offering praise for a perfunctory matter to make up for his blowup earlier. She asked, "Anything else?"

"He seemed devastated about Zweig. Like he lost one of his best friends. Could be faking, but not from what I could tell," said Hull. "Also upset that it happened in the church."

"Probably concerned about how that'll affect the offering over the next week," Ballack wondered aloud cynically. "We've already discussed earlier what you uncovered from the firm and the recent history of their litigation on behalf of the archidiocese."

"Which leaves us with Behringer, Stowe, Monica Zweig, and Mr. Green Windbreaker," said Hull. Tori went right into their notes for those interviews, Ballack filling in the details on his meeting with Greg Varner.

"Behringer is of value in that he discovered the body," said Tori. "Too bad he hadn't left the booth five minutes earlier. Then again, he might have been the victim."

"Doubtful, Tori," reminded Ballack. "The dagger belonged to Zweig and it seems clear to me he was the target from the get-go. Consider the note in his pants … *To protect the innocent.* That plus the broken cross."

"What do you think that means?" The question came from Crabolli.

"Can't figure that one. All we know is the dagger went missing from Zweig's office … let's say stolen, given the popped lock. We could consider that a reasonably decent assumption, as long as it's a fresh attempt. It would have to be someone who normally does have or recently had access to that facility."

"No chance that Tabitha Stowe or Monica Zweig are the culprit?" asked Hull.

"Stowe is out," Tori said. "Cameron tried to swerve her by accusing her of the murder using a different method. It was clear she had no clue how Zweig got whacked."

"What was your fake accusation, Detective?" Hull asked, amazed.

"Syringe full of strychnine near the crypt stairwell," smiled Ballack.

"Nice," said Crabolli quietly, with a hint of a grin.

"The widow was at her office, so she said," continued Ballack. "We need to confirm that. Greg Varner—windbreaker man—was helpful in only one respect. He said he saw a black-robed hooded figure come out of the chapel at twenty minutes before five and make for the west exit. A loud squeak made him look up and see it. Maybe the squeak was what made the scuff on the chapel floor. Who knows?"

"Whoever it was probably ditched the robe," grumbled Hull.

"Most likely," said Tori. "Well, should we discuss assignments for tomorrow?"

"First, what are we going to call this murderer?" stressed Ballack.

"Kurgan, from *Highlander*?" suggested Hull in a jocular fashion. "Except they wouldn't kill on holy ground."

"Panzer," put forth Tori, "Given the Nazi weapon?"

"Tread carefully around my German heritage, Tor," said Ballack, clearly miffed. "The Nazis were an aberration of our proud warrior race."

"It's got to be someone who's killed someone in a church," said Hull.

"Or ordered it done … murder for hire," Crabolli said.

The name suddenly clicked with Ballack. "Henry. It's perfect."

"Henry?" Crabolli asked. "As in one of the kings of England?"

"Henry II had the famously fractured relationship with Thomas Becket, the archbishop of Canterbury," said Ballack, a faraway look in his eyes. "His soldiers misunderstood an offhand remark by the king and murdered Becket in Canterbury Cathedral. We've got another murder in a cathedral here. This might be the best fit."

"It's an attorney, not an archbishop," said Hull, "but I'm for it."

"Henry it is," said Ballack. "Now, about tomorrow. You two should hit Zweig's home office and find anything possible. I doubt his computer would be on, but you never know, and if the widow is in a helpful mood she might share his password if she knows it. I doubt she would refuse your entry, given she's an unlikely suspect, but if you get any pushback, tell her a search warrant will be a cakewalk."

"Is that the first item?" asked Crabolli.

"Possibly, although … were there any other nooks or crannies there at Zweig's office at the firm?"

"Like a safe?" asked Hull. "Or hidden compartments?"

"I was wondering if there was anything else that held some incriminating evidence, on anyone, that might be of use. I apologize. I should have put that in your mind for your first visit instead of making you go over the same ground again."

"We don't mind," replied Crabolli, "so let's add that to the list."

Ballack drummed his finger on his armrest. "Out of respect to his widow, you should call their house before heading over. Missy," he turned to Crabolli, surprising her with the use of her first name, "you still have her cell number she gave us on her card?"

"Got it. We'll go to the firm first and then call Monica from there."

"After that, you and we should probably see the folks at Harvest Capital & Mortgage. In fact, it wouldn't be a bad idea if we could split them up. Two of us take Webber and two take McPadden. Sound do-able?"

"No problem," said Hull.

"Now for the lineup for Tori and I tomorrow. Along with one of the Harvest bigwigs, we'll hit the two people involved in the prosecution in this conspiracy case, the one where Zweig defended the archdiocese and Harvest. That would be Pat Fishwick, the director of this 10:21 Alliance, plus his attorney Lance Stubblefield."

"Andra Alexander at the firm said Zweig and Stubblefield were friends," Crabolli said. "Apparently, they had gotten together yesterday."

"That's an interesting wrinkle. Stubblefield's office is near Sappington. We'll aim for late morning with him."

"Where's Fishwick?" asked Hull.

"According to 10:21 headquarters," replied Tori, "still in St. Louis. They said he's at the Drury Plaza at the Arch. I've tried reaching him. Front desk says he's a guest through Tuesday, but whenever I ring through to his room, no one picks up."

"We'll pop in tomorrow morning," added Ballack. "They have a full breakfast at the hotel, so we'll arrive early and give him some indigestion."

The lineups were complete. Nothing else needed planning for the next day. All four of them stretched, but Ballack realized that—as the leader—he needed to wrap things up and make sure everyone left with cool heads.

"Listen everyone," he said. "I know we didn't have the best start tonight, but we ended well. Keep your heads up and we'll make it. I think we need to keep an open mind, not only about the evidence in this case, but also about each other. Zane and Missy, graciousness extended toward us St. Charles types is more than welcome, but also believe that if you guys make mistakes, I trust they are the exception rather than the rule. Is that fair enough?"

Hull and Crabolli looked at each other as if measuring a communal response. Finally, Hull nodded his head and said, "You got it."

"Good," Ballack said. "Everyone go home and get some rest. Tomorrow's going to be a longer day."

19

Ballack rolled into his parents' St. Charles home, bone-tired and followed Tori through the door. Already his mind was on overload. A murdered attorney in a house of God. A red-hot affair that petered out. A slew of appointments tomorrow that promised excruciating chess matches for his mind. He began to wonder if this promotion was going to sap what little strength his body had. He was looking forward to getting into bed and letting his ventilator refresh him for the night.

He and Tori entered the den and saw his parents watching television. "Hey, you two," said his father. "Solved the case already?"

"Nowhere close," said Tori. "What are you watching?"

"And how did you know about the case?" inquired Ballack.

"Marie was in the mood for *Munich*, but then we got a call from Ben Bowers halfway through the movie. Said there was a murder in the Cathedral, so we wondered if that's the one you got. It's all over the news. A certain Commander Krieger was just on giving a brief statement."

"How could it be all over the news?" exclaimed Ballack. "I still need to let Krieger know what we scooped up this evening."

"I keep forgetting to ask you, Tori, how's Paula doing?" said Marie Ballack.

"Okay, I guess. Has me proud and worried all at once. Typical high school freshman. She's spending tonight with a friend."

"No one at your place then? Listen, if you need to get an early start tomorrow, why don't you just stay in the guest room tonight?

You probably have a ton of extra clean clothes and toiletries in the van for any occasion."

Tori laughed. "If Martin doesn't mind."

"It just means making an extra omelette tomorrow, but I'm prepared to make such sacrifices," said Reverend Ballack, with mock exasperation. He noticed a vexed look on his son's face and nodded in his direction. "What's wrong with you?"

Ballack had been kicking the last few hours around in his head. Behind all the details, he couldn't help thinking there was serious dirt below the surface of this case. "Just thinking. Dad, you don't happen to know anyone wired into the Archdiocese of St. Louis, do you? Or someone who used to be involved in it? We're looking into what could be explosive stuff … I don't know."

Martin thought for a second "Actually, I do. There's a priest— no longer at the Cathedral, but he used to be the associate pastor there—named Doyle. William Doyle. Most people call him Billy. He and I were involved in some CPE instruction on trauma about seven years ago. One of those cooperational alliances between St. Luke's and St. Mary's. He was at the Cathedral until about three years ago when he left—or was graciously removed, depending on which story you believe—and now he's across the river. Serves as the rector of Sts. Peter and Paul Church in Alton. You think someone like him could be helpful on the case?"

"If you don't mind getting his number for me, I'd like to give him a ring. He might be worth a shot. Just a hunch for now."

"Hang on," and Martin Ballack was looking through his contacts in his cell phone. "Here you go. You can use my cell since

133

he'll probably recognize the number," he said, handing the phone to his son, who punched the talk button and left the den to head into the dining room and a sliver of privacy.

"You sure it's no problem to stay?" asked Tori.

"You're fine," replied Marie, "We'll be up early anyway."

"Interfaith Matins at eight o'clock for me," said Martin. "St. Luke's went to a new schedule and I'm heading up Friday services now." The three of them chatted on until they heard Ballack say a good night into the phone. He rolled into the room and tossed the phone to his father.

"We got an audience?" asked Tori.

"Lunch time tomorrow," smiled Ballack. "We're going to him."

"And if you're headed to Alton," Marie Ballack shook her head. "I can just guess where you'll eat."

20

The Drury Plaza Hotel at the Arch is an oft-overlooked jewel of lodging. Tucked away near the Sheraton Inn and the Millennium Hotel, the Drury enjoys a well-deserved reputation for customer service and quality. The breakfast buffet is the hub of early morning activity. The robust, delectable smell of hot scrambled eggs, biscuits and gravy, and pork sausage patties hit Ballack and Vaughan the moment they strolled into the main lobby. They darted toward the reception desk and both fished out their identification. Ballack was still getting used to digging out his new SID badge.

"Detectives Ballack and Vaughan," said Tori to the short, dark-skinned woman behind the desk. "We're wondering if Pat Fishwick is still a guest here at the Drury."

The associate, apparently named Nyah, took a look at Tori's badge and made a few clicks on the computer keyboard. As it turned out, there was no need to do so. A tall, stubble-faced man with wavy brown hair turned toward them. Ballack took in his appearance. Copper button-down shirt, tan sport jacket, blue jeans and loafers. One who looked more like a professor than a rabid protector of ecclesiastical justice. He came to within a foot of Ballack.

"I'm sorry to intrude, but I heard you were wondering about Pat Fishwick. You want me, you have me. What do you need? I was on my way to breakfast."

Ballack showed him his identification for good measure. "Mr. Fishwick, I'm Cameron Ballack and this is my partner Tori Vaughan. We are detectives with the Special Investigative Division of Metro St. Louis. Sorry about this intruding upon your mealtime, but we really

135

need to ask you some questions about an incident from yesterday. Is it possible we could sit down?"

Fishwick looked as if he was in a rush. "It will have to be quick, Detective. I am heading over to SLU for a guest lecture, so it may have to be an express breakfast."

Ballack decided to go for the jugular. "And I'm afraid SLU might have to wait." He lowered his voice. "Toby Zweig. You familiar with the name, I expect?"

"I am. We were on opposing sides during a major local trial that ended earlier this week. But what does this have to do with me?"

"When he's found murdered in the Cathedral just after four-thirty yesterday afternoon," Tori said firmly, "it can have a whole lot to do with you, Mr. Fishwick."

At the mention of the word *murdered*, Fishwick's demeanor clouded and his engaging smile wilted into an ashen frown. Tori thought he had the classic look of a disturbed, guilt-ridden hothead. Whether that guilt applied directly to him remained to be seen. Ballack his grip on his briefcase tightened.

"Perhaps we'd better step over here and chat, if you don't mind doing so over some food," Fishwick said quietly once he found his voice. "If you like, I insist on paying the hotel for your meals."

Ballack thought the offer of interrogation over food was insensitive, but he let it go. He did wonder if Fishwick was using organizational funds for this endeavor, and if so, how legitimate they were.

They took several minutes to plate their food. Fishwick asked one of the servers how to make arrangements for "my detective

136

friends", as he put it. Ballack ended up with a plate of scrambled eggs, a banana, and a biscuit with butter and jelly. Tori had a bagel with cream cheese and a sausage patty. She stuck to orange juice while Ballack drank coffee.

Pat Fishwick sat down with an overloaded plate of protein and calories. Whatever effect their introduction had on him, it had not diminished his appetite.

"You okay there?" asked Tori.

"I'm hungry," replied Fishwick.

"There's hungry, there's starving, and then there's what on that platter in front of you," complained Ballack. "You've grabbed enough sustenance to last the Russian hordes under Alexander Nevsky."

Fishwick shrugged and stared blankly at him. Ballack guessed he wasn't too schooled in the history of medieval warfare against the Teutonic knights.

"Let's start from the beginning," said Tori. "You and Zweig were duking it out on a case. What were the details of that?"

"I should go back to what my specific role is," replied Fishwick. "I'm the director of a national watchdog organization of Catholic laypeople, called the 10:21 Alliance. We are very concerned about unethical activity in dioceses around the nation, whether sexual abuse issues involving priests or financial irregularities or other matters. I oversee the coordination of legal action taken against individuals or organizations, and I attend the trials myself with the prosecutors we've selected. Based in Omaha, Nebraska. That's where I live."

"What's the significance of the name, the 10:21 Alliance?" asked Ballack.

"Taken from the New Testament. First Corinthians chapter ten, verse twenty-one. It says *"You cannot drink the cup of the Lord and also the cup of demons. You cannot partake of the table of the Lord and of the table of demons."*

"Strong words."

"I—that is, we—find them appropriate. We must keep God's work free from greed, selfishness and malice. We try to make that as much a reality as possible by rooting out the glaring sins of the Church and trying to make it a more transparent and pure family."

"While making money doing so?" asked Tori.

"I don't do this for the money, Detective," said Fishwick.

"Do you have attorneys who work for 10:21, or do you utilize local prosecutors?" asked Ballack.

"It depends. Whether on moral issues or financial matters, you still need attorneys who are knowledgable of individual state laws. Our attorneys who try abuse cases are quite proficient. What we need are people better prepared to deal with the nuances of property law and real estate. The trial here in St. Louis was just such a case, and so we went with one of the best real estate attorneys we could find locally."

"Lance Stubblefield, correct?" asked Tori.

"That's right. He came highly recommended and prepared about as well as anyone could, but we were trying to show conspiracy between the Archdiocese and their mortgage company. It was a notoriously difficult burden of proof. The case lasted several days and we had them on the ropes. The jury declared them not guilty on Monday. Seems so long ago."

"Did you speak to Mr. Zweig at all afterward?"

"Just after the trial. I was upset. He was celebrating. I reminded him that a verdict of not guilty does not remove the fact that wrongdoing exists."

"Why the frustration? Why the anger?"

Fishwick stared at Tori. "I'll plead guilty to the frustration factor but not the anger. My anger is organizational, not individual— directed toward the Archdiocese of St. Louis, not Toby Zweig."

Ballack set his fork down and spoke deliberately. "Then how do you explain your post-trial exchange with Mr. Zweig, when you agreed to meet him on Thursday when he went to confession at the Cathedral?"

Fishwick was visibly unsettled now. His face drained of color, and Ballack could sense fear pumping through the man's bloodstream. He tried to speak, but thought better of it and held up his left palm, as if to stem the tide of Ballack's inquiry, warding off the verbal blow.

The detective wasn't deterred. "I'll ask you again, Mr. Fishwick. Were you going to confront Mr. Zweig again at the Cathedral on Thursday afternoon?"

"He told me ..." began Fishwick. "He told me when he had confession, and I acknowledged that."

"Thursday at four ... Why not?" Ballack looked directly at him. "Isn't that what you told him?"

"Mother of ...!" Fishwick stopped himself. "You can't be serious! Either of you! Just because I say that doesn't mean I was in earnest! I never intended to go there. I told you I had no beef with him."

"Those who witnessed the scene after the trial might beg to differ," said Tori.

"Look, this is getting out of hand. I wasn't at the Cathedral yesterday afternoon. I was spending the rest of the week seeing friends and recruiting people for 10:21. Yesterday from four-thirty until quarter till six, I was here having some appetizers and doing some pre-interview stuff with Mark Erwine. He's from Voice of Grace Radio in Chicago and we had arranged to meet then. After that, Father Riordan picked me up here and we went to dinner at Schlafly's. He's a philosophy professor at Fontbonne; I had his brother as a professor in college. We were at Schlafly's from about five till six until seven-forty. I had to get back by eight because Erwine was going to do the radio interview in my room. So by the time we were done wrapping up, it was nine-thirty. I was bushed, so I went to bed soon after. I even unplugged the room phone at eight o'clock so as to take no chance my interview would be interrupted. I guess I never plugged it back in. Never even turned on the television at all that night. Hence my surprise when you told me about Zweig's death." He wrote a couple of phone numbers on a card and gave it to Tori.

Ballack thought the phone disconnection might have been the reason Tori couldn't get through, if Fishwick was telling the truth. "That seems like a precise remembrance of one's steps," he said to Fishwick. "Almost as if you were figuring you'd need that to cover yourself."

140

Fishwick looked hard at Ballack, but then the explosion behind his eyes petered out. "It comes from being conscientious about appointments and having a nervous habit of always looking at my watch."

He drummed his fingers on the top of his head. "Look, I'm due to meet a bunch of people today. Aside from going over to SLU, I have several engagements with some folks who are involved in the potential abuse case against Father Joseph Quinn."

"Quinn? Who's he?" asked Ballack.

Fishwick breathed in deeply, as if he was about to divulge the news break of a lifetime. "Father Joseph is an enigma at best, a cancer at worst. He's the reason why all this came about with the property shift by the Archdiocese. A massive lawsuit is going to hit the fan, and many of those testifying are planning to implicate Father Joseph. The Archdiocese had been shedding their ownership of churches and schools to plead hardship. Fewer assets mean less money on hand to shell out in the likely event they lost the other case."

"The priests at the Cathedral never mentioned that," said Tori.

"Nor would they," replied Fishwick. "And they wouldn't disclose that Father Joseph is an ad hoc member of the Archdiocesan staff right now."

"You're kidding," said Ballack. "How do you know all this?"

"Tracking the movements for over a year before this trial came about. Father Joseph was assigned as a chaplain here in the area a couple years back and recently he was reassigned to a different capacity. It's unclear what role he still has, but I'm sure the

Archdiocese offered him some phony position to keep him around. He's always been a tremendous fundraiser."

"So he's still in the area," said Ballack.

"More than that," said Fishwick. "He's here at the Drury."

"No way," said Tori incredulously. A somewhat idealistic Catholic, she believed in the classic model of the priest who counted the cost and eschewed opulence. "Why is he here instead of at a rectory somewhere?"

"Word is he negotiated with the archbishop and Monsignor Grenier for a hotel room here. He wanted privacy for his work and he didn't want his presence at the Archdiocese to be a lightning rod for controversy."

"I think that controversy might be floating around anyway," sniffed Tori.

"I was just thinking that he was aiming for free dinner, free breakfast, a heated indoor pool, and the weight room here," demurred Ballack.

Fishwick looked at his watch. "Is there anything else you need to know? I really need to be out of here in five minutes or else I run the risk of tardiness."

"Were you planning on leaving the city anytime soon?" asked Tori.

"Tuesday," said Fishwick. "Is there a problem with me leaving then?"

"There will be if your alibis don't check out," said Ballack. "I think you'd know that. But crossing that bridge is for later. I see no reason why you can't go over to SLU now."

142

Fishwick rose from his chair and slipped on his sport jacket, but before he could leave, Ballack had one final question. "Mr. Fishwick, would you call yourself a faithful Catholic of high expectations?"

The question seemed cold, overly direct, but Fishwick returned Ballack's gaze and said, "Yes, I am. It's why I do what I do. Not unreasonable expectations, but high ones. The loyal citizens of a kingdom should have first right to critique those who govern and hold them accountable. I, along with others of like mind, desire a transparent Church. And I think you'll find that I possess a better Catholic pedigree than most. Parochial school from the time I could walk. Graduated from Carroll College in Helena, Montana … Catholic school also. Majored in psychology and communications. Met my wife at Creighton in Omaha while I was picking up an MBA. Five kids later and here we are."

"Five children. I'm impressed," said Tori. "Bunched together or scattered in age?"

And here Fishwick looked thoughtful and sad. "Two daughters in college, both at Creighton. One son a junior in high school. And a daughter in eighth grade."

Ballack guessed there was a difficult story in there, but he asked anyway. "And your fifth child?"

A tear glistened in the corner of Fishwick's left eye, and his lip quivered. "Our oldest. Phil. He died a few years back."

He lingered, as if it was wrong to end on that note and expecting a rejoinder from either detective. Ballack broke the silence among them.

"May I ask how?"

Fishwick gathered his briefcase and pulled himself together.

"Tragically," he said, barely above a whisper. And then he was gone.

21

"I don't like him," declared Tori as she turned south past Busch Stadium on their way toward the interstate. "Talk about low-grade irritation! I get what he says, and I'm all for keeping corruption out of the Church, but Fishwick has a major axe to grind!"

"Which means exactly what when it comes to guilt?" snapped Ballack. "It's nothing concrete, and … watch out!" Tori pulled up quickly enough to avoid slamming into the back end of a Toyota Yaris, which the Sprinter would have crumpled into twisted metal on impact.

"My point is," continued a clearly annoyed Ballack, "that we keep our heads about us. Fishwick is a person of interest until we check his alibi. That's our Occam's Razor, the simplest approach."

"He really got unnerved about his late son," Tori said.

"Anyone with a soul would have been, Tori," he replied. He looked out the window so she wouldn't see the response written on his face. "About this Father Joseph. If he's mixed up with the Archdiocese, and neither Behringer nor Grenier acted like he existed yesterday, that's something to check out. I'm sure Stubblefield will be able to give us the scoop on him. I'd like to know more from the priests, though."

"Or go directly to Father Joseph himself."

"We're crunched for time," Ballack grumbled. "We need to honor our appointment with Stubblefield, and he's way out from here. Hold on."

He dialed a number on his cell and in seconds Zane Hull answered.

"Good morning, Zane. Where are you guys right now?"

"At the station on Jefferson," Hull responded. "Krieger called us in to go over your report from yesterday."

"Why didn't he call me?!" Ballack growled.

"No clue. The guy can border on unreasonable. Expects us to be in five places at once. We just got out of there. He wanted me to tell you to email any reports earlier than nine p.m."

"Then he can tell me that to my face! And he doesn't have to go to bed at that time. Anyhow, I guess Krieger kept you from getting to the firm to search Zweig's office."

"Yeah. We're headed there now."

"Okay, listen. I need you and Missy to swing by the Cathedral at some point today. We're on our way to meet with the attorney who opposed the Archdiocese and then we've got more to do after that. But there's a slight change of plans for you two. I need you to question both Monsignor Grenier or Father Behringer about Father Joseph Quinn's role in the Archdiocese."

"Who's Father Quinn?"

"We stepped into that name during our breakfast with Pat Fishwick this morning. He's meeting with people today, many who claim to be abuse victims at the hands of Father Joseph. Since the priests weren't exactly volunteering that information, you might need to be our crowbar today."

"You got it. Would Quinn be at the Cathedral by chance?"

"Not sure. I wouldn't know what he looks like. Apparently they've been putting him up at the Drury per his request."

"Hmm. Nothing like the sacrificial life of a man of the cloth. Maybe … what?" He stopped, and for a moment Ballack wondered if he'd lost the connection before he heard Hull's voice again. "Hey, I'm putting Missy on with you. She's got a question."

Ballack waited a few seconds before he heard Crabolli's voice—direct and confident, but without the edge he sensed the day before. "This Father Joseph. Is he the one who came here three years ago to a really strict Catholic school out west of town and then got canned last year?"

Ballack had heard nothing of the sort, but that didn't mean it wasn't true. "Can't say for sure. You guys have Internet access? Just Google his name and you might find everything you need. I just want to make sure we're turning over every rock."

"We'll check him out. How far are you from Stubblefield's office?"

"Twenty, thirty minutes."

"See you later. We'll call with an update from the firm."

Ballack signed off and turned to his partner. "Seems like we're all one big happy family now."

"Okay," she said. Ballack barely heard her. He looked forward, then back at her.

"Sorry I snapped at you earlier, Tor," he confessed. "You were just thinking out loud. I can't fault you for that."

"It's okay," she replied. "You did nothing wrong. I'm just stressed out, is all."

"Does it have to do with Eddie or whatever you said earlier this week?"

147

"No, it's something your mom said last night, when she asked about Paula."

"She in trouble?"

"No, just dating a senior. Way too old for her, and she and I don't see eye to eye about him. Just a really horrible vibe."

"About what? Does he sniff glue in public? Or grow marijuana in his horticulture seminar?"

"Would you shut up? Remember Occam's Razor? Simplest explanation is the best. Do the math. She's a freshman. He's a senior. Senior guys who go for freshman girls have only one thing on their minds ..."

"And it's not volunteering at nursing homes. I get it, Tor. But is she pretty determined to stick with him?"

"Unfortunately, yes."

Ballack thought of something comforting to take the sting out of Tori's worry, but nothing popped into his head. "Well, we don't get to choose in those instances. Jill's been dating Ethan for a year and a half, and while he's an okay guy and Jill can't imagine being with anyone else, I always get the impression they don't mesh as well as she thinks they do. It's something intangible, not that I have any hard proof."

"Have you ever talked to Jill about this?"

"Nah. It's not the kind of thing I'd feel right about saying. I've never told her what to do and she knows not to tell me how to live. I mean, I love my sister, but it's an area where I don't feel comfortable going. Not like my own record is stellar, either. Plus, I think if it's not meant to be, something will happen that steers the relationship toward an end. Sometimes that's an instantaneous event, sometimes a relationship dies a slow but conclusive death. But if it's meant to happen, it'll happen."

After a pause, he said, "That's what I've come to believe about Michelle." He looked out the window as he thought back to his former girlfriend. "Anything more serious than what we had at the time would've been a disaster. I see that now. It wouldn't have worked. It's just too bad that suicide had to be her solution."

Tori said nothing, focusing instead on steering off Interstate 55 to Interstate 44. Suddenly, as if on a whim, Ballack pulled out his phone and dialed Dana's number.

The voice mail engaged, and he began. "Hi, it's me. I know you're probably in class or something. We've had a crazy start today, with checks all around the city. Just letting you know. If … ah … we're out in your area, I'd like to stop by. Anyhow, call me if you can. Bye."

He pocketed his cell phone. "That was about the clumsiest phone call I could have concocted. I wish I could reach through the phone and erase that message."

Tori turned left onto Lindell and shook her head. "I wish you could erase your anxiety. There are some things not worth agonizing over. Let's worry about the next step and focus on Stubblefield."

They sped westward on Interstate 44 toward the next turn in their labyrinth. Overhead, the gray clouds gave way to a sun that would not be denied.

22

Crabolli and Hull, drained after their early morning encounter with Krieger, wearily flashed their identification once more at Gillette, Wales, and Alexander. The front receptionist nodded politely before asking how long they would be.

"Can't say for sure," replied Hull, "although an efficient thirty minutes would be our goal."

"We're just making sure in going over our steps," added Crabolli.

"I'm not sure what you expect to find," said Audra Alexander, descending the staircase from above into the narthex, "but I see no reason why you should be prevented. If you have any additional questions, Lana here will be at your service. We only ask that you limit your search to Mr. Zweig's office only. His PA is coming in to clean out her desk—as we spoke of yesterday—and I would think there would be little to interest you there. Besides, I would not like a scene. We are still grappling with our own grief in reaction to Toby's murder. Please tell me you are making progress."

"As much as we are able, Mrs. Alexander," Crabolli assured her. "The first days are critical to our investigation. We'll let you know if there is anything more we require."

After that it was filing cabinets and drawers for the next twenty minutes. Hull had brought their own fingerprinting kit, but the glass dagger case was devoid of any human markings. Crabolli moved toward Zweig's desk and began checking the bookshelf behind it. It was a well-constructed piece of furniture, six feet high and four feet wide with a depth of sixteen inches, solidly built as if hewn by the hands of Amish carpenters and anchored to the wall with two studs. The brown maple wood was stained with a rich tobacco color, and Crabolli paused to take a deep draught of the smell.

"What're you doing over there?" asked Hull. "Convinced he put something in the jacket of one of his books?"

"If you had something controversial, something you wanted to keep hidden, you might lock it up, right?" replied Crabolli.

"Makes the most sense."

"And yet you'd figure that's the place others might choose to look."

"True."

Crabolli's gloved hands danced around the bookshelf. "Zweig had a relationship with Miss Stowe," she whispered, "and to protect himself, what might he do if he had called it quits with her and she wouldn't accept?"

"I'd say be ready for the onslaught."

"An onslaught like … written threats, love letters, or a combination of the two?"

"Perhaps."

"But being a sharp lawyer, you wouldn't toss them."

"You'd use them as evidence against her if things came to a head."

"Yes."

"Or," said Hull, "if the follow-ups were especially enticing, he might keep them. Remain technically faithful to his wife, but enjoy the attention of another while having the control of keeping her at arm's length."

151

"That's a sick idea, Zane."

"How does this explain why you're giving his bookshelf a rubdown?"

"Because a man who played a dangerous game might dare to hide these hypothetical items in broad daylight!" She grasped the side panel of the bookshelf and tugged, and the panel swung free, opening on two nickel-plated hinges.

"You are a magician," Hull gushed, sliding to the other end of the bookshelf and opening the opposite panel. It too revealed a secret vertical compartment, yet like the one Crabolli discovered, it was empty.

"That's disappointing," Hull mused.

"Not for long," said Crabolli, eyeing the base of the shelf. Kneeling, she took hold of the bottom skirt and pulled directly outward.

Hull swallowed. "The mother lode."

Crabolli nodded. "Letters, notes on what seem to be perfume-scented stationery, and," she paused as she gripped several computer-printed pictures, "it seems that Miss Stowe was quite the photographer."

23

"What an ordeal!" Ballack exclaimed as Tori parked outside the offices of Stubblefield and Associates. They had been delayed back in Shrewsbury by a car wreck, the kind of stoppage due to other drivers slowing down and peering at the misfortune of the accident. They looked over the light blue Cape Cod structure just off Tesson Ferry Road. Finally, Tori noticed a ramp running the opposite side of the front door, obscured by a cluster of hedges.

Once inside, they were greeted by a smiling receptionist. Tall with straight blond hair and carefully disguised wrinkles, Ballack judged her to be in her early fifties. Obviously ignoring her desk as a line of demarcation, she swept around and shook both their hands.

"Good morning. It's Detectives Ballack and Vaughan, correct? Mr. Stubblefield is expecting you. Straight back down this hallway and it's the office at the very end. Would either of you care for coffee? I'm about to put on a fresh pot and could bring a mug to you when it's ready."

Both detectives declined the offer and headed down the hall. They entered what must have once been a den converted into a library. Mahogany bookshelves stood floor to ceiling, except for the back wall where a three-foot section rose to the base of a large picture window. A matching mahogany desk was remarkably free from clutter, and from behind it came Lance Stubblefield, pulsating with controlled vigor. His navy blue suit fit his trim frame well. His fingernails were nicely trimmed except for his right thumb, which also bore evidence of a blood blister near the cuticle. His smile was even and sincere, and his pointed nose twitched when he raised his eyebrows as he first addressed the two of them.

"Detective Ballack. Detective Vaughan. Good morning. Hope you didn't have any trouble finding us," he said, shaking each by the hand. "And I assume that Diane has already offered you coffee. We also have soda or Vitamin Water, if you like." He motioned for Tori to sit and for Ballack to take the empty space next to her.

"None for us, thank you, Mr. Stubblefield," said Ballack. "It was kind for you to take time out of your schedule today. And I'm sorry it's under these circumstances. I understand you and Toby Zweig were friends."

Stubblefield sat back in his chair and crossed his legs. "I think that would be a safe label. We weren't overly close. Maybe the best tagline would be 'competitive, yet extremely cordial' if one could say that. We were members at the same health club and would play tennis fairly often, plus we'd grab a beer once every couple months. We'd bounce questions off each other. He wasn't the easiest person to get to know, but it's not as if he was unlikeable. It's hard to imagine I'll never see him again, anywhere."

"You've been practicing law here for some time, Mr. Stubblefield?" asked Ballack, who felt specifics about Zweig could wait until they got him comfortable.

"Locally, for close to eighteen years," the attorney replied. He seemed to relax some. "Classic case of a boy from the Lou going off only to come back. My father was a union electrician and I grew up just north of here in Crestwood."

"High school?" The question came from Tori.

"Well, Dad was able to play his financial cards right to send me to private school. I ended up going to King's Prep."

Ballack raised his eyebrows. "King's Prep, really? My father taught there for a number of years before he left to be a hospital chaplain."

Stubblefield smiled. "How about that. Did you end up there?"

"Nah. That was one of the things that went sour with Dad. We wanted to get me in for my ninth grade year, which would have been the late nineties. I would have needed some allowances regarding writing assignments and the amount of homework, given my lack of fine motor skills. My nurse would have attended with me, so there was nothing medical the school would've needed to provide. But they said no. Not in a vicious manner. It seemed clear they moved slowly on the issue. Dad ran out of patience and never forgave them for that. Come to think of it, neither did I. No offense to your alma mater."

"None taken. Plus, my list of grievances against them might rival yours or your father's. Where did you end up, Detective?"

"We were looking at what we had been doing. My mom had homeschooled me for six years before that, and it looked like more of the same. Not that getting an education while wearing boxers is a bad thing, mind you. But then Dad was immediately hired to teach at Westminster, and they offered us everything we needed academically and financially, so I ended up going there and graduating. So I'm a proud Wildcat."

Stubblefield nodded his silent assent. Ballack raised his eyebrow slightly toward Tori, signaling her to begin.

155

"You primarily handle real estate law and collections?" she asked.

"That's right," he replied. "I had a professor at Webster who had dabbled in it before, and I picked up an interest in it back then. You could say that was my concentration in law school. I went to the University of Arkansas for that. Met my wife there, also. I started at a firm in Nashville, but that ended about ten years back. Since I moved us back here, I handle the accounts and cases for THF Realty."

"The folks with all the shops at Boone's Crossing?"

"That's them," he beamed. "Definitely a consistent amount to keep me busy. It's amazing how much can accumulate. Plus, I like the confidence of a happy, ongoing client."

"So what got you working for Pat Fishwick and the 10:21 Alliance?"

"That's a combination of Pat's doggedness and my insane need to take on one 'Boy Scout' case per year. I know, it sounds strange. Once a year, I do a major pro bono case, just to remind people—and myself—that justice is not primarily for the money you earn. The 10:21 Alliance put out their feelers and, seeing this as an area of expertise and knowing I was acting all saintly to work for free, contracted me to do so. Pat was insistent on paying me, though. He was convinced he had a definite victory; I wasn't sure, but I thought with decent cross-examination we'd win. I knew that with the Archdiocese on the other side of the aisle, Toby and I would be opposing each other."

"That didn't bother you?"

"I couldn't avoid it. The more I looked at the money flow, the more I was convinced something wasn't right. Look, it had nothing to do with Toby. He was my friend. He was just doing his job, to provide reasonable doubt. I don't even think he believed his side was innocent."

"Are you a Catholic, Mr. Stubblefield?"

"As in 'would a case like this cause me regrettable pain'? No, I grew up as Protestant as the day is long. Got away from church for some time but over the last five years we've been going to Windsor Crossing. We live in Jefferson County, so it's just a quick hike up Highway 109."

"Was there ever any indication that Toby Zweig was being targeted as the case went along?"

"That's difficult to say. The case lasted only a few days. Not much time to notice a build-up of animosity. Pat Fishwick was steamed the whole time, but then that doesn't take much, and his perspective from the outset was targeting the Archdiocese, not Toby."

"That was pretty much what he told us, too."

"Toby seemed to get frustrated with Jerome McPadden. He was the last witness called by the defense. But I couldn't tell if that aggravation was reciprocated."

Ballack broke his considerable silence. "What was Toby Zweig's role for the upcoming trial that could involve Father Joseph Quinn?"

And now Stubblefield's blue eyes narrowed as his mouth curved into a smile. "So you know about that. How interesting."

"You should know we came directly from some interesting breakfast banter with your buddy Pat Fishwick."

Stubblefield leaned forward and held out his hands, palms down, in front of him, allowing them to hover unmovingly above his desk. He seemed to stare at his reflection in his wedding band when he said, "Okay, what I'm about to tell you is pretty explosive stuff. This whole thing about Father Joseph is something that can bring the Archdiocese down like a deck of cards. I don't know if it plays in to whoever murdered Toby, but I wouldn't be the least bit surprised."

Ballack coughed, straightened up, and gestured for Stubblefield to continue.

"There's something creepy about the Father Joseph equation," he said. "He's been in the area for three years, and from what I know his arrival and entire tenure have been contentious. Were you aware that he got moved from Santa Maria Academy to a position within the Archdiocese?"

"Fishwick told us something about him being a chaplain," said Tori. "And now he's working more closely with the Archdiocese. But he never connected the two for us." She kept Crabolli's insider information to herself.

Stubblefield nodded. "Santa Maria went from grades seven through twelve. It was run by the Barons of St. Paul, a group of which I'm horrifically ignorant, but the rumor is it's a group awash in controversy. While looking over the evidence and following the money trail for this case against the Archdiocese and Harvest Capital & Mortgage, I noticed some interesting things."

"Which were?" asked Ballack, and Stubblefield went through his cross-examination of Jerome McPadden step by step. Ballack groaned and Tori whistled as he described the financial maneuvering and how it lined up with schools and churches aligned with those who were potentially suing the Archdiocese and Father Joseph.

"How does this relate to Toby?" Tori asked.

Stubblefield exhaled slowly. "You have to understand. Normally, if any attorney would do what I'm about to describe, I'd never speak to him again. We're talking shame to the profession. I wasn't even thrilled with Toby when he told me about it. My view is, if you're a prosecutor, you seek justice; if you're a defense attorney, you seek vindication for your client to the best of your ability. You don't do anything half-ass."

"Any chance you could speed this up, Counselor?" asked Ballack with a trace of impatience.

Lance Stubblefield paused to heighten the drama. "He was going to be a defense attorney who wanted justice for the plaintiff. He was going to throw the case because he was convinced Father Joseph was guilty as sin."

"How do you know this?"

"The night before he died, we met at Smaugala's Pizza on Watson Road. It was the first we'd talked since the trial and we had bet dinner on the outcome. He'd come from his secretary's place and I guess he'd just barely avoided her entangling clutches again. That's when he told me about his plan about tanking a Father Joseph trial. But he was visibly upset. Not about the decision, but because he felt someone had smelled out his intentions and was trying to cut him loose. Or perhaps he was in even worse danger than that."

"You said you weren't thrilled about his decision." Tori said. "Did you see any merit in his worry about being in danger?"

Stubblefield looked down at his hands. "Now I do, although it's too late."

"And did he mention anyone who might target him?"

"Three people, in fact. He was quite edgy about Jerome McPadden, Harvest's CEO. But he didn't have a good feeling about either Monsignor Grenier or Father Joseph. He said that when they had met earlier that day, McPadden was dead set against his further representation. He didn't think Grenier had his back as he should, and Father Joseph sat there enjoying the whole affair."

Ballack's cell phone buzzed and he saw a text from Hull asking him to call back.

"Is there anything else you think might be relevant to Mr. Zweig's murder?" he asked the attorney.

Stubblefield had turned in his chair and was looking out the picture window. "I would say that if Toby was coming off one of the biggest legal victories of his life and heading into another case that anguished him to no end, and he's murdered at the crossroads of those events, then you're dealing with someone who is protecting some powerful secrets. I knew a little of this through Toby. Religion wasn't always an area of agreement between us, but we both knew this: A group that large, that rich and that powerful can use stealth force in the name of God, and you wouldn't know it. What that looks like, I don't always know, but it can't be pretty."

160

"You think the Church is behind this, Mr. Stubblefield?"

"I'll stop short of blaming the Church as an institution, but I will say this: In my profession, in the financial sector, in a lot of places, the dollar is the Holy Grail and at least everybody knows it. And your ambition gets funneled in that direction. I try to be an honorable enough guy where I can rise above that, but it's hard. Yet at least everyone knows those are the rules of the game. But if men who speak for God fill their coffers and slit someone's throat as if they're doing God a favor, then I would have no respect for that. It doesn't matter which denomination it is. It makes me want to spit nails. It's bad enough it happens anyway. But if it robs you of a friend, well ... you catch his killer and I'll be eternally grateful."

24

While Tori looked for a gas station to replenish the Sprinter's tank, Ballack took out his cell phone and dialed Hull, who answered on the first ring.

"Thanks to Missy's knack for hidden spaces we could have some details to go on, C.B.," said Hull.

"C.B.?" asked Ballack. "Did you just call me C.B.?"

"Less formal than boss and still defers to you as lead guy," replied Hull. "They're your initials. You don't like it?"

Ballack hesitated and then heard Hull whisper into the phone, "Please say you like it. I've got a dinner bet with Missy on this one."

"Love … it!" said Ballack loudly, and he knew from Crabolli's muffled groan in the background that she had heard him.

"Now," he asked Hull, "What *have* you found?"

"Some fairly earnest love letters that, from their elaboration, seem to be after Zweig told little Tabitha that they couldn't be an item any more. That plus a few pictures of our tawny little kitten trying to make her man purr. Nothing racy, quite classy. But she was pouring it on and trying to get him to crack."

"Keeping them as mementos or stockpiling evidence of harassment?" asked Ballack.

"The man side of him might opt for the former, the attorney side to the latter. We're going to head to the Cathedral and see if we can corner Grenier and Behringer. And from there we go to speak with Monica Zweig."

"Call us when you're done there. We'll be up in Alton with our lunch interview, but at the very least leave a message. And, Zane?"

"Yeah, C.B."

"Both of you gang-tackle each priest, one at a time. Start with Father Behringer first. You haven't dealt with him yet, but he might be more forthcoming and less cagey about Father Joseph. We'll update the plan after we leave Alton." He signed off as Tori started the car and pulled out into traffic toward the highway.

25

The town of Alton, Illinois rises from limestone bluffs overlooking the Mississippi River. Large silos at the ConAgra Mill stand near the Argosy Casino on the waterfront, graced by water level marks from the Flood of 1993. Although a popular destination for bird watchers, the migration season had not yet come to the area, so Ballack knew the south side of the river would be free of the graceful clusters of bald eagles. Tori flew over the Clark Bridge, turned right on Landmarks Boulevard, and then angled left on Broadway.

"Haven't been here in forever," she mused aloud.

"I recall coming here for my twenty-first birthday," smiled Ballack.

"I doubt you remember that much of it."

"I said I remember coming here, not that I remember much of the rest of the night," Ballack laughed.

Tori got into the left hand lane. "Good thing we're meeting a priest. I have no clue what this guy looks like. Thank goodness the clerical collar is a big giveaway."

"Unless he brings the entire staff for lunch," Ballack said, looking up at their destination. "At least we get to do this in burger-and-beer heaven."

"The Best Bar in the Midwest, maybe the world," Fast Eddie's Bon-Air is arguably the most popular grill in the greater St. Louis metropolitan area. Boasting an outdoor patio that has increased total seating capacity to nearly five hundred, Fast Eddie's fills to overflowing most evenings. The prices for all items on its limited menu have remained the same for several decades, evidence of the ownership's dedication to the local community and good cheap food. The popular Big Elwood marinated steak tenderloin with peppers on a stick is the most expensive item there, at one penny less than three dollars. Most nights will find one or two bands running though their usual set of songs or covering the classics from groups of yore. Such bands are saddled with names like Sable, Hoosier Daddy's, Radio Star and the Ultraviolets. Ballack was thankful for coming up during the day. The crowd might be thinner and since musical entertainment wasn't a lunch thing on weekdays, it meant no disruption to his focus.

Hoping that Father Doyle would have the sense to refuse inside seating on this beautiful, brisk afternoon, Ballack was overjoyed to see the priest sitting at a table on the outdoor patio. He was a short, cheery man over sixty years of age, with closely cropped, bristly gray hair. He returned the detectives' waves with one of his own, his right hand clenched firmly around a beer, which Ballack saw was a Killian's Irish Red.

"You must be Cameron," Father Doyle rasped, grinning widely and extending a firm handshake. "You look somewhat like your dad. Good to finally meet you."

"Thank you, Father," Ballack replied, "This is my partner in justice, Tori Vaughan. Tor, meet Father William Doyle."

"He's too formal, Ms. Vaughan," said the priest, "Call me Billy. That goes for both of you. I already got my refreshment here. If one of us goes in and orders for all of us, we can start. I'm about to pass out from hunger." He peeled a twenty-dollar bill from his wallet.

"I'll do it," said Tori. "You two get acclimated. What'll you have?" She grabbed her pocket-sized notebook out of her jeans.

Father Doyle had his mind made up. "Basket of fries and a Big Elwood for me."

Ballack thought for a second. "Let's get a couple dozen shrimp to go around, plus a bratwurst for me. And fries for you and I to share, partner."

Tori put her pen away. "Perfect. A cheeseburger for me should just about take care of this twenty. When the waitress drops by while I'm gone, order me a Dr. Pepper."

"I'll get a diet drink myself," said Ballack.

"You don't want a beer, Detective?" asked the slightly incredulous Doyle. "Either of you? It's my treat."

"We can't drink," frowned Ballack. "We're on the job."

"And you're in uniform, too, Father," chuckled Tori as she left, "so you're technically on the job, too."

"Why do you think I'm drinking?" called Father Doyle as he let out a belly laugh. He turned to Ballack and said, "Well, this is certainly a surprise, son. I can't tell you how shocked—and glad—I was that your dad thought of sending you my way. How is he? And your mom?"

"Both doing well. Dad sends his regards."

"Holy Mary, they were both so nice to me three years ago when everything went down at the Cathedral. They were always available to listen. It was just nice to be able to vent to someone who'd been hamstrung before. Not that I'm complaining about my present

166

charge. Great people here. Nice town. And I eat here three times a week. What's not to like?"

"Dad had mentioned you'd been on staff at the Cathedral until just about three years back," began Ballack. "As I told you, we're investigating Toby Zweig's murder at the Cathedral from yesterday."

Doyle shook his head. "That was a shame. I knew I wouldn't be in any shape to work today when I heard that from you last night. Toby was not the easiest soul to get along with, but he was one of the good guys."

"At first, this was just going to be a background talk regarding the last few years at the Cathedral. But then we found out about Zweig's cases and the upcoming one with Father Joseph Quinn. I crunched the dates when Quinn came and when you left and wondered if there was some coming-and-going relationship there."

"Plus," said Doyle, "your dad has probably told you my ministry there didn't end well at all."

"He did mention you were the gadfly of the staff, the resident conscience, and that the anti-establishment rub might have been more than the Archdiocese could bear."

"Your dad always has been a diplomat when he wants to be. I should probably save most of this until Tori comes back with our food, but it's true. Father Joseph's arrival was the powder keg that set off my dismissal."

Before Ballack could reply, a waitress sidled up to their table. Doyle introduced her as Connie, and Ballack gave her their drink orders. Doyle ordered another beer for himself and waved off any attempt Ballack made to pay for the drinks. "You don't get it, son. This is my pleasure. See you in a few, Connie."

"So what happened? I guess the first question is how did Father Joseph arrive on the scene."

"You weren't told?"

"Priests not only hear plenty of confessions," said Ballack, "but they're probably experts at guarding their own."

"You're more right than you know. And now I can tell you everything without having to repeat myself later. Welcome back, Ms. Vaughan."

Tori placed a pile of food on their table and distributed it appropriately as Connie returned with their drinks. They began their meal as Doyle held court.

"Okay, here's the saga. I was at the Cathedral as a resident priest. Eventually associate pastor, but I had no desire to climb the ranks further. Just a shepherd and his sheep. Three years ago March, we got notice that Santa Maria Academy would be getting a new chaplain. Santa Maria is, or rather was, a school out in Wildwood, and it had been a sticking point for some time. The Archdiocese technically oversees it, but the school itself was founded and run by the Barons of St. Paul. Have you ever heard of them?"

Ballack felt he could trust the priest with the details. "The attorney who opposed Toby Zweig told us some bare details about the school, that the Barons ran it, but nothing about the Barons itself."

Doyle cleared his throat. "I'll try to give you the short version. The Barons were founded by one Antoine Levesque back in the early seventies in Buffalo, New York, and he ruled it with an iron fist for over thirty-five years. He was a French Canadian originally, a gifted communicator, the Vatican's golden boy because he was a charismatic recruiter for the order, and—more importantly—a peerless fundraiser. We're talking millions upon millions of dollars here, guys. These successes were front and center, and Levesque's public aura overshadowed a lot of the rot that was happening underneath. But he brought the Vatican a ton of *lira*."

"What sort of rot?" asked Tori, although she knew what Father Doyle meant.

"The Barons focused on education and evangelism, and what has exploded over much of Levesque's direction has been their dedication to youth ministry. They have been especially successful at recruiting young men to consider the priesthood in their tender years. Like thirteen, fourteen. They have several seminaries for young boys, a university in Sacramento, and numerous youth centers and retreats across the country. On the surface, it looks like a well oiled and substantially financed machine. But that's a cover for a lot of perversion under the radar."

"I imagine that crap is fairly critical if you wanted to meet," said Ballack.

Doyle nodded, then continued. "Levesque was a financial crook and an abusive predator. He also had a major alcohol problem, for which the Church raked him over the coals in the mid-eighties. But for most of his ministry, complaints and allegations of all stripes dogged him. Unfortunate, because whether you believe me or not, the Catholic priesthood is not packed with people like Levesque. Young men, some who were ordained to the priesthood and others who left, begged the Church to look into these matters. Everything fell on deaf ears, mainly because the Curia—the inner circle—kept John Paul II from significant information. His Holiness really could have done some good on this one if not for the Curia. At least Benedict had enough and knocked Levesque out of the ministry a few years back."

"You mean for decades he had his little creeper station set up and no one was able to stop him?" Tori asked, stunned. Her rage meter had passed the dangerous zone.

"Oh, his predilections were all over the map. He went after women and fathered at least four—possibly seven children—with God knows how many partners. Levesque died in Colorado over three years ago, but the Church is still cleaning up his garbage."

"Okay, we get that the Barons have skeletons in their closet," said Ballack, taking a bite of his bratwurst. "I know that Father Joseph Quinn ran a Baron school here. Are you saying he's the second coming of Levesque?"

"I don't know about second coming," said Doyle, "but he's no one I'd entrust my children to, if I had any. He ran Santa Maria into the ground. But he's been in the Barons forever. Rumors—which tend to be more true than any Catholic news you get in the media—floated that when he was dean of discipline at the Barons seminary in Connecticut, he would drive boys into Hartford and take them near some questionable parts of town. Never in, just near—or so the court documents said, but the appearance was bad enough. After a state senator—the father of a friend of one of the students—set up a sting on Quinn, he was toast and out of New England."

"So how'd he end up here?"

"What I didn't mention was that, about 1984 or so, Levesque started an adult lay member movement within the Barons called Corpus Sancti—the Holy Body. Rather than training priests, Corpus Sancti would disciple and mentor people to serve God in their everyday vocations, whenever they ended up getting one, in many cases. They have a variety of Corpus Sancti communities around the world. Many are set up somewhat like a monastery, with daily tasks, worship, prayers and communal living. The goal is to get young people fresh out of high school and equip them spiritually to either go on to other vocations or perhaps consider the ministry. One such community is located in Lake Zurich, Illinois. It's northwest of Chicago, about thirty minutes south of the Wisconsin line. Anyhow, Quinn was never disciplined, demoted, or defrocked for his offenses. In typical fashion, the folks in New England quietly shipped him to a new charge, as the chaplain in Lake Zurich."

"And did he go back to the steamy underbelly of life there?" asked Tori angrily.

"Not according to my sources."

"Your sources?" Ballack asked skeptically.

"Yeah, I have sources. Names like Fatty McGurk and Wotjek Posnack. Over thirty years in the priesthood, ten of them in Chicago. I've had enough time to build up a good network of trusted confidants. But I digress. Quinn was the chaplain in Lake Zurich for ten years. A major headache. Now you had adults trying to get out of Dodge. Seems that he targeted a few of them, rather strategically, as objects of his attention."

"Strategically?"

171

"Yes, he tended to pick on those who were smaller in frame, more vulnerable in how they could defend themselves, and more timid in spirit. A few of them got off the campus, but here it is—they were almost always caught and returned."

"Returned?" The question shot out of Tori's mouth with such force that people at other tables turned and looked at her.

"That's right, Miss. Caught and returned. Courtesy of the stealthiest Mob guys the Archdiocese of Chicago could buy. All Quinn had to do was put out the word. Chicago. I loved the pizza but now wouldn't go near the place. Eighty percent of that city is employed. The other twenty percent turn up to watch the White Sox. This went on for years, until some five years ago when something happened even the boys in Chi-town couldn't make go away."

"Which was?"

"A suicide. Someone about twenty years old. The word was he was one of the most respected members of the group, but he was also being targeted regularly by Quinn, who had sunk his hooks into this one badly. Apparently the victim confronted him at some point and told him to stop the harassment or he was leaving. Quinn told him there was no chance."

"No chance?"

Evidently, the other guy—now that I remember, his name was Philippe—wasn't the most powerfully built person, sort of along prototypical lines for this sort of thing. I mean, they're all practically eighteen and over, so legally Corpus Sancti couldn't keep them, but you'd better believe they know all manner of psychological buttons they can push. So when Philippe realized his path was blocked, he sneaked into the chapel tower and hung himself. Caused a huge stir, and the Chicago Archdiocese nobly and belatedly said there needed to be a housecleaning. The usual political garbage. That's why Quinn was eventually transferred here."

Ballack had already connected the dots but pressed the next question. "And is that what brought on your dismissal?"

"You have no idea. I raised a massive stink over that. Of course, there's only so much you can take into battle when your sources have to remain nameless. I won't give you the blow-by-blow but it was a nasty situation. It wasn't the archbishop who nailed me. This was a year before he arrived. It was his predecessor who was archbishop then, before Pope Benedict brought him to Rome to serve on the Curia and be named a cardinal. He and Grenier didn't like my stance, that we should refuse Quinn's installation at Santa Maria. They dug in. Reluctantly, I might add. They privately told me they were against it but there was little or nothing they could do against the hierarchical machine. I knew I was in a bind. I couldn't continue in that position and look at myself in the mirror. By my vows, I had promised to obey my leaders and yet the vision and leadership—at least, those above my immediate staff—were far from what I could follow."

"So they had to fire you, or redirect you?" asked Ballack.

"They never got the chance. I tendered my resignation effective when they found another place for me to minister. I just asked it be within five hours away from here—I have a sister in the area with early onset dementia. That's how I ended up here."

"You didn't force them to fire you?"

173

Doyle looked nonplussed. "I knew it was wise to continue in ministry by finishing well at each juncture. How you say goodbye is important. Need I say more?"

He paused and looked out toward the river. "I've obviously taken you a long way from where you intended. My big point is that even if Father Joseph isn't your perpetrator, his presence in the Archdiocese is what has led to that poor lawyer's murder. I just hope it's the only one. I have to get to the hospital and make some post-surgical visits. Ms. Vaughan, good to meet you. Cameron, likewise. And tell your dad hello for me. Someday I need to take him out for a beer."

"He just received a huge bottle of Jim Beam for a birthday gift. He can't drink it all by himself and he never drinks alone," Ballack said, shaking the priest's hand.

"Then maybe I'll pop by if I'm out that way," replied Doyle, "if he doesn't mind me getting absolutely plastered. I'll let you get the tip."

As Father Doyle sauntered off, Tori said, "Well, that's a bonanza that just got dropped in our laps. Quinn's got plenty of dirt on his hands and he was going to get shafted by Zweig."

"If he knew about that, it could make a juicy motive for murder," replied Ballack. "However, I think there'd need to be a stronger reason. For example, if Zweig was going to spill the beans about Quinn, then a murder to squelch that could make sense. Yet ..."

"I know. It seems like Quinn's dalliances were about as close to public knowledge without going public. We'll need to get out the pickaxes and dig some more."

"And it seems the only one who knew about Zweig's turnabout was Lance Stubblefield." Ballack threw a five-dollar bill on the table and backed away. "Let's start, Tor. I'll call Zane and Missy on the way and pray they've found something."

26

Ballack's plans to connect with their fellow detectives came to naught. Either Hull's cell phone was out of coverage or he had turned it off. Ballack tried seven times before quitting in disgust. He took his Bluetooth out of his ear and rubbed his eyes before suctioning himself. Fast Eddie's might have been a decent lunch, but it had been no smoke-free environment.

"No luck?" asked Tori.

"Not yet," said Ballack, who had been remarkably pensive ever since they left Alton. They had turned south on Interstate 170, had just reached Overland, and were coming up on Delmar Boulevard. "It would help if we got something from them, a text, anything. We need to check out the Harvest personnel and it would be good to know what they heard from the Cathedral."

As if on cue, Ballack's phone rang. His heart sank as he didn't recognize the number on his caller ID. Clicking his Bluetooth, he answered, "Ballack."

"C.B.?" A female voice.

"Missy?"

"Yeah. Sorry about the delay. We went a long time at the Cathedral and just now got out. Are you wanting us to meet you at Harvest's offices or do you want us to go by Zweig's home?"

Ballack thought for a few seconds. "Why don't we tie up the loose end we know is there? Go to his house. Do you still have Monica Zweig's cell number?"

"Got it in my card file."

"Give her a ring and let her know you want in. I know there's a possibility she might be using the time to clear stuff out, but we have no choice. We're going to the Harvest Capital offices and we hope to find McPadden and Webber there."

"Which office?" asked Crabolli.

"I told you. Harvest."

"I know, but which branch? They have four. The main two are in Clayton and Creve Coeur, but they have one in Maplewood and one in Lake St. Louis."

"Well, we're almost to the Clayton branch," said Ballack, "because we thought it was the only one. If they're not there, we'll find out where. What did you learn from Behringer and Grenier?"

"Behringer is straightforward, not because he's eloquent, but because he's so young and naïve that he doesn't know any better. Told us more than Grenier did."

"I figured so. What's the scoop on Father Joseph?"

"Doing fundraising for the Archdiocese while serving in what seems to be a phony role for Santa Maria. That's our estimation, not the direct words of the priests."

"Santa Maria closed recently," said Ballack, "so he no longer has that direct role."

"Yeah, neither mentioned that," replied Crabolli. "They said he's been here for three years, is facing the upcoming case on abuse, and they are going back to the drawing board on representation. When we asked to speak to him, they referred us to Santa Maria. The school referred us back to the Archdiocese. Typical runaround. It smells bad. We told both priests we wanted to speak to him. Behringer said when he saw or heard from him, he'd call us. The first thing Grenier did was ask why, and then he promptly gave us an alibi for Father Joseph."

"Which was?"

"He was scheduled for evening prayer at …" she fumbled for the information, "… Ascension Church out in Chesterfield. We'll check with them if that was even the case. Of course, once we left, Grenier could have gotten on the horn and sent out a flare."

"Which still leaves us nowhere with Father Joseph," Ballack heard Hull call out in the background.

"Which means we might have to wait until that bird comes back to nest at the Drury tonight," said Ballack. "We could check phone records at the rectory and see if there was a call out to Ascension. Well, for now, carry on. Go to Zweig's, and then call or text us afterward. And, Missy?"

"Yeah?"

"I actually didn't care for Zane calling me 'C.B.' Calling me 'Ballack' is fine. Tell your partner he owes you a dinner."

What sounded like a cross between a purr and a growl escaped Crabolli's lips. "I knew it. Talk to you later."

"Next?" asked Tori, when Ballack signed off.

"Go to Harvest," he said, as his phone rang again. And this time, he recognized the number.

"You're a lying cheat," laughed Zane Hull. "Just for that, I'm calling you C.B."

27

Neither executive was present at the Clayton office, although a loan associate was kind enough to call ahead to the Creve Coeur branch and confirm Julian Webber was present there. It took twenty-five minutes for Tori to weave through westbound traffic before reaching the sparkling glass structure of Harvest Capital & Mortgage at Olive and 270. A black BMW and a Lexus sat side by side in the lot. The Lexus' tungsten pearl finish was spotless, but what Ballack noticed was the bumper sticker, which blared in yellow letters on a black background: DEBT IS NORMAL. BE WEIRD!

"Tell that to Washington D.C.," grumbled Ballack.

A sylphlike redhead, who served as receptionist for the Harvest executives at the Creve Coeur office, informed the detectives that Mr. McPadden was not present and would not be expected until the next afternoon.

"Family emergency," she said, almost apologetically. "Mr. Webber has been here all day, and you are welcome to speak with him as you need." She led them back to a door marked "Julian Webber. Chief Financial Officer."

The individual who came out from behind his desk gave them a warm greeting, yet one that Ballack judged to be overworked. Probably from years of glad-handing others and closing the deals, likely intoning a mantra of "win-win." It was a world utterly alien to the forthright Ballack. He caught a whiff of what seemed to be cocoa butter lotion and Stetson cologne. Not the best combination.

Webber motioned for them to get comfortable. Tori took the chair facing his desk and Ballack wheeled himself next to his partner.

Several volumes by Steven Covey graced the dual level bookshelf behind the desk. A framed montage of photos on the east wall showed Webber shaking hands with former Senators Jim Talent, Jack Danforth and John Ashcroft. A Catholic Bible rested on the desk.

"I am sorry to have to meet and speak with you under such sad circumstances," Webber began. "Toby was a diligent worker who gave everything he had for us. It's tragic that his life should come to this. I'm sorry. I assume you came to discuss his death. I didn't mean to blurt out like that. It's just difficult to imagine him being gone. And at the Cathedral no less. Monsignor Grenier is absolutely devastated!"

"You knew him for some time, then?" asked Tori. She knew Ballack would jump in when he was good and ready.

"Harvest Capital has assisted the Archdiocese of St. Louis regarding many property issues. In many cases, we've come alongside them on matters of contracts, acquisitions, running interference on financing. Even putting on fundraising benefit functions. Because of our long history with the Archdiocese, and because Gillette, Wales, & Alexander handle their legal issues, a number of us here got to know Toby personally as well as professionally."

"So he was well known by people at Harvest?"

"More so by myself, Jerome McPadden and Colin Dwyer. Jerome is the president and CEO, and Colin is our operations coordinator. He's been out of town for two weeks; his mother lives in Sioux Falls and is going through a brutal round of chemotherapy, so he is up there taking care of her affairs. However, everybody in this branch knew of Toby and—I believe—were quite impressed with him."

"It would have been helpful to hear that as well from Jerome McPadden, but we understand he's not here."

"Yes, a family emergency, if I'm not mistaken. But he returns tomorrow, so you can catch up with him then."

"Would you say he was well liked? I mean Toby Zweig."

"It's one of the chief reasons why his death is so shocking. I can't imagine a soul wanting to harm him."

"You said Harvest has a long history with the Archdiocese. How far back does that go?

"Oh, let's see. The company started in 1974 with Jerome's father heading it up until Jerome could finish college—he was a late starter, GI Bill after Vietnam and all—and take it over. It was 1986 that Harvest began handling a lot of financing details for the Archdiocese. That would be the middle of John May's time as archbishop. We continued through the Justin Rigali and Raymond Burke years and we have kept going through to the present."

"And how long have you been with the company?"

"Oh, I came on about ten years ago. I knew Jerome from church. We both attend Saint Anselm just up the road at Priory School. After I graduated from Southeast Missouri, I worked for Sysco for three years. I got bored with that line of sales and so got busy working on my real estate license. My father died soon after and he left me a good chunk of change. I used it to finance my own company, Life Properties, when I was thirty-two. It was a combination of good business, great timing and serendipitous locations for my sites. The rent-to-own market was becoming more and more of a possibility. I selected Wildwood and St. Charles County to buy up. My properties were somehow untouched by the Flood of 1993 and we've continued to do well. I've scaled down but I continued to run Life on the side."

"You said 'We've done well.' Do you mean the company or your family?"

"The company mostly. It's hard to get the family together. My wife Tracy works different hours from me, and we don't see that much of each other. My daughter Margaret lives in Chippewa Falls, Wisconsin with her husband and kids, and I'm afraid she's gotten quite comfortable with the distance. It's …" he paused, "… yes, it's hard."

Ballack finally spoke up. "Mr. Webber, was Toby Zweig hard at work on any future cases or deals that linked the Archdiocese and Harvest Capital?"

Webber's eyes assessed Ballack directly, and his voice took on a cautious yet conciliatory tone. "Well, he had just helped us win the big trial against the 10:21 Alliance. I assume you knew about that from last week."

"Yes, both from the newspapers and from speaking directly to those involved."

Webber smiled kindly. "Of course you would. That is your job, after all. That was his most recent body of work."

"Okay," said Ballack, wanting to move things along, "Let me rephrase. Were there any matters of a generally legal, direct courtroom or contractural nature that Toby Zweig was going to head up?"

"Head up?"

"Yes, you know, represent the Archdiocese legally while Harvest was involved on the financial side of things."

"There was talk of more cases coming up. Nothing had been finalized."

"Had there been talk of his involvement with Harvest matters coming to an end?"

"Excuse me, Detective? That's a remarkable question."

"Let me clarify it. Had he assumed he'd work on successive cases that were on the horizon, only to be told not to bother?"

For the first time, Webber hesitated, and Ballack began to suspect he was hiding something for either Harvest or the Archdiocese. The question was why.

"Seems like you've done your share of checking the facts, sir," he said, "And of course, I can hardly fault you. Yes, there was … shall we say, spirited discussion of Toby's ability to handle upcoming contractual details, as well as anything that followed that whether it be for us or the Archdiocese."

"Like the Father Joseph defense?"

"Again, Detective, you've certainly done your homework. Of course that case was on the horizon. I am sure Jerome could speak more specifically to this if he were here. Toby had just led us through a brutal case when the 10:21 Alliance sued us. I was elated by how well Toby did, but Jerome was concerned that perhaps he was getting burned out. It wasn't personal; at least I never saw any evidence it was. It's just that Jerome wasn't confident Toby could give us his all when he was physically and mentally ragged. We met with members of the Cathedral clergy at Toby's firm, and those were some of the concerns brought up. Even I thought there was nothing wrong with

Toby taking a sabbatical. The time off would certainly cure what was ailing him."

"Which was?"

"He didn't seem to be sleeping well. Over the last three weeks he was especially haggard. My philosophy is if you're working yourself to the bone then you need to find way to revive yourself, and this was a point when more of the same work would not be Toby's savior."

Ballack bunched his left ear in his hand, signaling Tori to ask the next question.

"Regarding his death," she said, "What were you doing yesterday between four and five in the afternoon?"

"My alibi, you mean? As it would happen, I can account for my whereabouts, Detective. I was at Ballwin Golf Club playing nine holes with a college buddy of mine." He fished into the skinny drawer of his desk and pulled out a slip of paper. "Here's my receipt for paying the greens fee. We had a three o'clock tee time and you'll see that the time on the receipt is two-fifty and the date is yesterday afternoon. Given that we did all nine holes, you can clearly see I was nowhere in the area of the Cathedral when Toby died."

"And your college buddy?" Ballack joined in again. "He can vouch for this?"

"Absolutely. His name is Chuck Wilbur, a frat buddy from my days at Southeast. He's living in Memphis now. Bigwig for FedEx. He was in town Monday through this morning. Since Thursday was the one chance we had for some face time, I invited him to go golfing.

Would have tried for Wednesday, but my car needed a new serpentine belt. It's the BMW by the front door where you came in."

"I would have pegged you for that nice Lexus."

Webber laughed. "Actually, the Lexus is the Archdiocese's car. Monsignor Grenier was just here. You probably just missed him. Ships passing in the night and all that, or in this case, the elevator. It used to be Jerome's car, but he thought it might be nice for the Archidocese to have something dependable. It's a sweet ride, but I'm more comfortable in my Beamer."

Indeed, thought Ballack. *The clergy and their buddies seem to enjoy a pretty good life. So much for the hardships of following Jesus.* However, McPadden being the car's original owner caused the bumper sticker to make more sense.

"He's not in town anymore? Your friend, I mean," asked Tori.

"Left to drive back to Memphis today. If you want, I can give you his cell number." Webber pulled out his phone, waded through his contacts, and then showed Ballack a screen with Wilbur's name and a 901 area code, which Ballack promptly recognized as a Memphis number." ·

"One second," he told Webber and Tori, and he quickly dialed the number. After five rings, the voice mail engaged, announcing that Chuck Wilbur could not come to the phone. Ballack left a message to return his call and clicked off. He turned to Webber.

"We'll follow up with your friend to confirm things, but we have others to see as part of this investigation. Is it likely Mr. McPadden will be at this branch tomorrow?"

Webber smiled and handed Ballack a business card with his picture on it. "I believe he might. Possibly late afternoon. I forget when his flight gets in. Call before you come. And regarding Chuck, he's hard to connect with. Always got his hands in some deal or project, so he's not the best at picking up the phone or returning calls. But keep trying. And please keep us informed on the progress of the investigation. As a matter of justice, as well as interest, I'd like to see you stop the monster that caused all this heartache."

They bade him goodbye and took the elevator down. Neither spoke a word, as Tori knew her partner wanted to gather his thoughts on how everything unfolded. Once they were outside, Tori broke the silence. "What next? Join the others?" asked Tori, but Ballack was already getting a text from Hull. He shook his head at the incoming message. TOUGH AFTERNOON AT ZWEIGS. TOO MUCH ALCOHOL.

"Okay," he said. "I'm sure there's a story behind that drinking reference. They're climbing uphill. They found some correspondence from Miss Stowe earlier that might give us some insight, but little else. At least they haven't had to drive all over creation."

"I still don't think we should eliminate that little fox from our list of suspects, even if she didn't seem to have any idea how her man got iced. Head back into the city?"

The mention of Zweig's personal assistant caused something to swirl in Ballack's heart. "Not yet, Tor. Let's get in the Sprinter, zip over to Mason Road, and head south."

"Why that direction?"

"We're going to stop at a soccer game."

28

The Whitfield School is situated at the corner of Mason and Ladue Roads in the affluent area of Creve Coeur. The stately Kirk of the Hills Presbyterian Church sits west of the school, and Bellerive Country Club, a PGA championship-level course, lies across the street. Tori parked the Sprinter in the lot next to Whitfield's soccer field and pushed the button to lower the ramp before unlatching Ballack's wheelchair.

"You could have called, you know," she told him. "Something normal. This white knight stuff might be a bit much."

"It's just for a few minutes. We can also try to reach our compatriots and see what the deal is at the Zweig residence. You do that, Tor, and I'll try Webber's friend again. Also, confirm Fishwick's alibi with Mark Erwine and Father Riordan. You still have that card with the numbers? Good."

Ballack got nowhere with his call. Tori reached Hull, who asked if they could call back in ten minutes, and then continued with her other calls. Ballack continued on toward the bleachers and cast a glance at the scoreboard. Whitfield was in good position at halftime, tied with Westminster at one goal apiece. As Ballack zoomed toward the conglomeration of humanity in the stands, he swept past the Westminster bench as the Wildcats broke their huddle. The head coach looked up and, with a glimmer of recognition, called out, "Cameron? Cameron Ballack?"

Ballack glanced in his direction. "Derek Lyons! Good to see you, man. Congratulations on making a game out of it."

"More than you know," the coach said. "We have three starters out with injuries. Gave up a cheap goal and we've had a couple good chances. What're you doing here? Your caseload hasn't expanded to crimes in the athletic world, has it?"

"I am on a case, but that's not the reason for my appearance. I need to say hi to someone who works at Whitfield. You doing okay?"

"I'll be doing better once we pull out the win. Second half's due up. See you later, buddy."

"New suspect?" asked Tori as she caught up with Ballack.

"The Westminster coach? He goes to the same church as Mom and Dad. I'll make this quick. Just spotted Dana." And he shot forward in a burst of speed.

Wheeling behind the grandstand, he could see her conversing with a couple of students. Unwilling to call loudly, he pulled out his cell phone, knowing she always kept her ringer on the loudest level when outdoors. He typed in three words, "LOOK BEHIND YOU", and then sent the text message to her phone. He smiled when he saw her react to her phone's alert and pulled it from her front jeans' pocket. She peered at the message, turned completely around, and with a shout and a smile jumped down from the stands.

"Nice leap," said Ballack.

"I can't believe you showed up!" Dana exclaimed, her eyes dancing. "I thought you'd be on the case right now."

"Came straight from interviewing someone who knew the victim. We're still in the early stages and it's hard getting used to a larger team. There are multiple lines of communication and we're going all over the place."

"Is it the one where that lawyer got stabbed in the Cathedral?" she asked. She saw Tori standing at a distance and lowered her voice, not accustomed to speaking with him about specific cases. "Sorry. I heard it on the news. I didn't mean to assume or intrude. It's not so much the case itself. I'm just worried about you while you're working."

Ballack knew it was more than formal concern. The case at St. Basil's had culminated in a nasty arrest scene that went beyond mere danger; it nearly cost Ballack his life. It was due to this he sensed fear behind her eyes now that he was working another murder case.

"It's okay. And yes, it is what you're thinking. But I will be careful. I'm not going to be involved in a chase around a frozen pond this time." He paused then looked up into her face, arrested once more by her shiny gray eyes. She smoothed her hair and flicked an imaginary piece of fuzz from her slate blue sweater. Her earrings, shaped like Celtic crosses, shimmered in the late afternoon sun.

He continued. "I don't know when we'll get our next night free, but I do know I don't want to miss it. I'm sorry I couldn't explain things in such a rush yesterday."

Dana ran the point of her tongue along her lower lip and shook her head. "You don't have anything to apologize for. I'm just glad— and surprised—that you swung by here." She winked. "Just so you're not stringing me along."

Even though he knew she was joking, Ballack felt the need to remind her otherwise. "Dana, if I wanted to string you along on this, I would have stuck to the phone, not see you in person."

His comment seemed to hit a little more strongly than he intended, and for a second he wondered if Dana had taken it harshly, but she looked down and then in his face, saying, "I'm sorry. I shouldn't have said that. It's … oh, you know."

Given her late husband's infidelity, Ballack could guess at quite a bit. He couldn't help thinking there was more hidden behind those stunning eyes. And if there was, what of it could he bear? She suddenly looked much older than her twenty-seven years.

"Listen," she said, her voice calling him back to reality, "I have a bereavement support group tomorrow morning at St. John's, but that's over by noon. Mom and I are going to Soulard Market early afternoon, but I've got the evening free in case something opens up or the case slows down. Just let me know. It doesn't have to be anything ostentatious. We can just have some time alone together."

Her hand was resting on the back of his neck, and he felt the light touch of her fingernail against his hairline.

"I will. I'll call. I promise," he said. After a moment's hesitation he said, "We need to get going and meet with the rest of our crew." He pointed to the students in the grandstand and continued, "Don't want to keep them waiting."

"Have fun. Oh, by the way, have you heard from Timothy or Jennifer?"

"Haven't," Ballack shook his head. Father Timothy Birchall, a professor from Ballack's previous investigation at St. Basil's Seminary, had become good friends with the two of them. He and his wife Jennifer were expecting their first child any day. "Maybe they'll schedule an induction." He saw Tori waving him over. "Sorry, Dana. We really need to get going."

She smiled and then, before he knew what was happening, she leaned down and hugged him tightly. Shocked but pleased, he lifted his normally enervated arms and held on as close as he could before she straightened up. She gently stroked his cheek with her hand before she made her way back into the stands.

29

Fifteen minutes after the detectives left the game, a grim-faced figure meandered through the pharmacy area at Walmart on Brentwood Boulevard. Finding the products needed, the individual dropped two packages in to the shopping cart before continuing on toward an efficient checkout lane. The girl working the register noticed the two packages and thought it strange to purchase them both together, not to mention the third item that this person placed upon the conveyor belt. How these three items went together, the cashier would never know.

"So the notes from Tabitha Stowe ran all the way up to the present?" asked Tori as the four detectives sat around a table munching on sandwiches Hull had purchased from a nearby deli. They were deep within the bowels of the Metro Police Department's Central Patrol Division on North Jefferson Street. The red brick building was attractively graced with a white stone façade which took the architectural sting out of the aqua A-frame over the front entry.

"They did," answered Missy Crabolli, "and it's not a pretty picture. Most of the stuff was wildly romantic up until Christmas of last year … "

"That was the time Zweig's daughter was in the car wreck and he went limping back to his wife," interrupted Tori.

"Right. It was then that the correspondence changed. Not perceptibly at first, but she really got more forceful as the months went on. Kept getting more demanding that he leave his wife. And the more he resisted—I got that from reading between the lines of her responses—the more desperate she got. Even sent him pictures of herself. Nothing racy but definitely meant to make his heart quicken. But like I said, from the tone of the letters, she got rebuffed time after time. Looks like he meant business. I think the miracle is that he was even able to keep her as a loyal PA and maintain a working relationship."

"Woman's a psycho," put in Hull between mouthfuls of a turkey club. "The pictures, the letters. You see them, Coach. What's your take?"

Ballack had been half-listening, half-reading in silence every since they sat down to eat. He was waiting for the others to get their assessments out of their systems before speaking himself. He marked the final letters on a Jumble puzzle in front of him before tossing the letters into the center of the table. Grabbing his egg salad on wheat, he chewed on a bite before taking down a swig of water.

"Psycho, maybe," he began. "Okay, that might not be the proper label. But there's something missing, something that snapped inside our little Tabitha. She's obviously attached to Zweig even now. I tend to agree. Zweig was half satisfying his male hormones by keeping her attentiveness close at hand, but like a sharp attorney he could use that collection as evidence of harassment if the situation arose. I have to admit, I never thought someone could be both a shmuck and noble at the same time."

"Hey, you agreed she's a psycho," replied Hull.

"The question is how much of this amounts to a murder motive. Let's lay out what we've got on everybody so far, one by one. Start with Tabitha Stowe. Let's hear it."

"She's angry she couldn't have her boss all to herself," said Crabolli.

"She knew Zweig's movements on Thursday afternoons," said Hull. "That's clear from a couple of the notes and what you've shared."

"She did claim to be home at the time and never went back out," responded Ballack. "Tori, did you ever confirm with that Mrs. Dorfmann about if she noticed her come in and stay. That was the neighbor Tabitha mentioned who could verify her story."

"Yeah, I called her while you were star-struck earlier," Tori said, prompting a glare from Ballack that she would bring up any details about Dana. "Sorry that I forgot to tell you. She said she noticed Tabitha come home. But then Mrs. Dorfmann had to feed her cats and the stuff she lays out for them gets put on her back porch. She was out there having her dinner since it was a nice evening, so she couldn't say one way or another regarding Tabitha's movements."

"But you said," uttered Crabolli to Ballack, "that she seemed clueless about how Zweig died. Your phony accusation made that clear."

"That's true," said Ballack, "and here's another thing. If she's upset over the end of the affair, that's a *possible* motive for murder. But is it a strongly *probable* motive? She could have taken out Monica Zweig and she'd still have a chance at her man. If she did kill Zweig, then why now? And despite the fact she was infatuated with him, her

194

notes have almost a desperate monotony to them. There's nothing in them that makes me think she's drawing a line in the sand, saying 'This far, and no farther, or else.' There's no build-up, no sense of gaining steam, no gathering crescendo from what I can tell. It would make far more sense for her to try to hurt him—if she felt she could—by going after his wife. Or hurting herself."

"Nice image," groused Tori.

"It's been known to happen. I'm just saying there are a multitude of avenues for her to go. If she's the killer, I'm not seeing it. Maybe there's something there. I don't know. But then I'd be blind as well as lame."

"What about Grenier and Behringer?" asked Tori.

"Grenier, of course, has the more solid alibi," said Hull, "but he is the more suspicious of the two regarding knowing who else could be in on this. It was obvious he didn't want to talk about Father Joseph. He was also reticent to speak about Jerome McPadden of Harvest Capital."

"McPadden was gone today when we tried to get with him," said Ballack. "The operative phrase was *family emergency.* Evidently he is supposed to be getting back tomorrow afternoon. We can nab him for a few minutes then, and we'll probably have to go back to the office to do so. We did, however, just miss Monsignor Grenier. We must've been going up the elevator while he dashed down the stairs. When exactly did you get done speaking to him?"

"Just about two-thirty," said Hull.

"Then he must have left right after you were done with him in order to get out there. I wonder what he was doing face-to-face with Webber that had to be done in the privacy of the Harvest office?"

"Especially when he could have just called," remarked Crabolli. "Maybe he's paranoid that we're tapping his line, which might not be a bad idea."

"Then Grenier is at least acting guilty. The question is why. His alibi has to be the cleanest one out there. Behringer was in the Cathedral. Webber produced a receipt from golfing, as well as a phone number of the guy who was with him, but we haven't confirmed if that holds up."

"You did reach his friend's voice mail," reminded Tori.

"Which counts, but isn't enough." Ballack rubbed his temples again. "We'll confirm it, however. Was Monica Zweig present as you went through her husband's stuff?"

"She was," replied Crabolli, "but she didn't intrude much. Just asked how long we'd be and then went into the den to toss down a few glasses of wine."

"In the middle of the afternoon?" asked Tori.

"People do unexplainable things when loved ones die," Ballack cautioned a bit more sharply than he intended. "I can only imagine what I was like when Christopher died." He paused, looking away briefly. Returning to the subject, he pored over his notes. "Did you get a chance to ask her about the notes, about any possible threats Tabitha Stowe might have made toward her or her husband?"

"No, we never asked her. She was … sort of out of it. Not engaged," Hull said. "Really detached."

196

"Sometimes those are the best times for interrogations, folks," said Ballack, stifling a grunt. "I say you need to re-check that. It may come to nothing, and I still think Tabitha Stowe is an unlikely candidate to be Henry. But just make sure. Go back there as soon as we leave here."

"Why else," asked Tori, "do you think we can call her 'unlikely'?"

"For all the reasons before, as well as one more. Sure, Tabitha would know where the weapon was and where he would be Thursday afternoon. If she and Zweig were an item, then she knows a lot of other things. But are we seriously going to propose that—even if she wanted to murder him—she would take a dagger with a blade at least a foot long and stab him from the front? A sneak attack, perhaps. That's her only way of getting on top of the situation. Plus, that dagger went through a significant amount of muscle and slammed through the heart and danced around bone. She would have needed a tremendous amount of strength to jam it through his upper torso. Based on those realities, I'm just not convinced she's Henry."

"Which means we are looking at McPadden, who hasn't been interviewed; Webber, especially if his alibi is false; and Behringer, who was there," said Crabolli.

"What about Fishwick?" asked Hull.

"I checked out the names he gave us," replied Tori. "Both the radio guy and the professor swear Fishwick was with them during the times in question."

"Let's not forget Father Joseph. So far all he has is an alibi given us by someone else," reminded Tori.

"Or Monica Zweig," said Hull, who immediately shook his head. "I'm sorry. Didn't you say that she was elsewhere at the time of the murder?"

Ballack pointed to Tori with his index and middle finger, a potato chip poised in between them. "Didn't you check out her alibi and was it legit?"

Tori nodded. "I called her billing manager at her clinic. She could be lying, too, but she confirmed Monica was there. Said she could fax the list of appointments that day if we wanted to take a lot at it."

"What about doctor notes that would solidify that the good doctor was there?" wondered Crabolli in between slurps of her drink.

"I'd think HIPPA regulations would forbid that unless we found a major loophole," responded Ballack. "Now let's think about tonight. We're not done yet. Zane and Missy, you scoot over to the Zweig residence and finish up where you left off with Monica Zweig. Tori and I will head over to the Drury and camp out there until we get an audience with Father Joseph. In some way, he's the key to all this."

The four of them, as if intuitively sensing their meeting was over, stretched, and as Ballack pulled out from behind the table, the other three rose from their chairs. Tori thanked them for dinner before she and Ballack headed out toward the parking lot and the Sprinter.

At that exact moment, well west of the police station, a solitary figure entered the familiar environs of the Cathedral Basilica. Moving quickly from the west door near the Blessed Virgin Chapel, the individual approached the sanctuary altar and laid a single envelope on it.

30

For the second time in eleven hours, Detectives Ballack and Vaughan swept through the lobby of the Drury Plaza Hotel at the Arch. Their timing was fortuitous; having waited until after the start of the Cardinals' game against the rival Chicago Cubs. They purposefully gobbled up the distance from the sliding front doors and approached the front desk. Nyah was gone, but a tall, imposing woman with a nametag that read PETRINA stood behind the computer. Tori showed her identification while Ballack fumbled for his. Petrina looked at them with a bored visage, as if cops always descended on the Drury and this was nothing out of the ordinary.

"Detective Tori Vaughan, and this is my partner, Detective Cameron Ballack. We would like to speak with Father Joseph Quinn. We understand he is a guest at the hotel. We can meet him down here or in his room."

An efficient if plainspoken sort, Petrina responded, "I can't give you his room number, but I can call his room and have you speak to him. He is welcome to give you his location if he desires."

"That would be helpful."

Petrina's digits danced around the computer keyboard, bringing up the information she needed. She pressed three buttons on the concierge phone, cocked her head to hold it firmly to her left shoulder, and waited. Three rings were all it took.

"Father Joseph," she began, "This is Petrina at the front desk. Sorry to disturb you … oh, good. Well, there are two police detectives here in the lobby asking to speak with you. They said they'd be willing to come up, unless you wanted to met with them down here … Yes, I understand. Yes, I'll send them right up. You have a blessed day as well, Father. Bye now."

Ballack rolled his eyes. If Billy Doyle's reports were anywhere close to accurate, the idea of accepting any blessing from Father Joseph almost made him want to upchuck his dinner. Petrina handed the phone to Ballack.

"Room seven hundred nine," said Father Joseph with the hint of a song in his voice. "Take these elevators to the seventh floor. Upon getting off, take a left, then another left. It'll be the last room on the right at the end of the hall."

Although it took some time to wait for an elevator with enough room, eventually they found themselves in front of Father Joseph's door. Tori rapped four times and waited, losing patience when the cleric did not immediately appear. She was about to knock again when the latch turned and the door opened. A man in his late forties stood before them wearing a white T-shirt and navy slacks, his carefully styled blond hair combed in place. He had a powerful upper body that seemed mismatched with his slender waist and thin legs. His blue eyes were pale yet piercing, as if they could see into the recesses of the heart. Ballack and Tori both could well see in an instant how those eyes could manipulate and destroy. Ballack decided to address the priest first.

"Father Joseph? We are the detectives that the concierge mentioned earlier on the phone. I am Detective Cameron Ballack; this is my partner, Detective Tori Vaughan. May we come in? We have a few questions to ask of you. It's about the murder of Toby Zweig last night, which I'm sure you've heard about."

Father Joseph looked briefly at Ballack's identification before turning to Vaughan's. His laserlike eyes grew more trusting and welcoming and he smiled broadly. "Of course. Please come in. Yes, it was horrible. Toby was both an excellent advocate for us, and a compassionate friend. Come in. This way, please. Let me make sure there's enough room for you to maneuver around, Detective."

The room itself was serviceable enough for a priest's quarters. The true luxury was the view. Father Joseph could pull back all the curtains at the windows and have a fabulous view of the Gateway Arch. A big screen television dominated one side of the room, and a functional table was serving as Father Joseph's desk in the corner. The covers of the king size bed were partially pulled back, and a notepad and pen lay close to the pillow, though nothing had yet been written. Ballack noticed the closet next to the bathroom had four large plastic storage bins. Whatever lay inside them was anyone's guess, as the bins were anything but transparent.

Father Joseph asked Tori to take the chair in the corner. Already she was apprising him, looking for a clue based on his body language. Ballack watched the priest carefully as he sat in the other chair, scooting it away from the table. Rarely had he gotten such a strong impression of guilt from someone. Father Joseph's eyes darted back and forth between the detectives. Ballack recalled their conversations earlier in the day with Lance Stubblefield and Father Billy Doyle. While he knew little of both men, he felt no suspicions that either of them had lied when giving unprodded details. In particular, Father Doyle had left the Cathedral staff due to Father Joseph's arrival, but that had been his call. Doyle's demeanor had been more even-handed than he expected for those past battles. Ballack took a deep breath before he began. He decided they would go for the jugular.

Tori began with the token questions about his age, training, vocational background. Father Joseph was direct but not particularly detailed in his answers. Of course, neither detective expected the priest to volunteer information about any of his more salacious activities. Ballack kept a languorous, almost bored, look on his face. The more Father Joseph thought this interview was a mere formality, the better. While the initial questions went on, Ballack pulled out his portable Cricket modem and notched it into his laptop.

"You came here to St. Louis in 2008 and by direct invitation?" asked Tori, looking down at her notes.

"I did. I had been looking for a new challenge. I had done chaplaincy for adults in the Corpus Sancti movement. I also had experience as a director of discipline at the seminary level. I liked the chaplaincy bit, but I wanted to get back in the school environment. The opportunity here at Santa Maria came up and I took it. The archbishop didn't have to ask twice."

"My father is a chaplain. Hospital chaplain," said Ballack.

"It's a great profession. I've been here three years and have transitioned into a new role as director of development. It's likely to be temporary, as Santa Maria is facing closure."

"I had heard there were some financial issues," replied Tori.

"Yes, due to the flagging economy," said Father Joseph.

203

Tori hesitated. Ballack wanted her to take the lead with the questioning, but he knew it would take a superhuman effort for her to keep from letting this get personal. If indeed they were facing off with a deviant, they had the additional challenge of remaining patient through a maze of deception and cover-ups. Out of the corner of his eye, he saw Tori bunch her left ear with her hand. She knew she couldn't remain detached. Ballack glanced at his computer screen and then back at Father Joseph.

"Let's go through your early years again," he said evenly. "Seminary. Director of discipline. Where was that?"

"It was in Cheshire, Connecticut actually. I taught humanities at the novitiate center there."

It was a term with which Ballack was unfamiliar. "And what's a novitiate center? I thought you said you were at a seminary."

"I apologize," said Father Joseph with a grin that tripled Ballack's uneasiness. "I would guess that outside of our tradition, that would require some explaining. Protestant seminaries take in adult students, but a novitiate is a specialized term for educational and spiritual formation centers in several orders of the Catholic Church. Our novices—that's the term we use for our students—at the seminary in Connecticut were considerably younger. Late high school, early college age."

Ballack could tell Tori was ready to throw up her dinner. "You said 'in several orders.' In which order are you pledged?"

"I have been a member of the Barons of St. Paul since I was seventeen years of age. We are called a 'congregational of pontifical right.' Long story short is that we are a Catholic community blessed and recognized by the Pope, in this case Pope Paul VI in 1973. Yes, our roots run way back. We take vows of obedience, poverty and chastity. We train young men for the priesthood, and if they sense this call to the ministry from an early age, then it is our duty and privilege to nurture their gifts."

Ballack wanted to get back to the point. "And this novitiate … seminary … whatever. Was it part of this tradition as a Baron school? How long were you there?"

"About six years," the priest said, leaning back in his chair and looking out the window. "Those were good days, but I needed a new challenge. An opportunity opened up near Chicago, and I requested to go there."

The lie rolled easily off Father Joseph's tongue. Ballack had difficulty suppressing a grin, knowing the priest had no clue he was placing a noose around his own neck. He tapped a few keystrokes on his laptop. "I'm sorry. Did you say you needed a new challenge? If those were good days, why the need to move on?"

Father Joseph smiled. "Oh, when God directs you, there are several options. But the least painful and most glorious is to follow his clearly revealed will. That's why I went to Illinois."

Ballack, barely but successfully holding back a triumphant tone of voice, replied, "Yes, God's will. The wastebasket catch phrase of the man of God. You're sure it had nothing to do with a certain discovery made by Larry Hughes, state senator from New Britain, Connecticut?"

The shock on Father Joseph's face took over his features. The priest would have done better to say nothing, but he began to spout off a quick denial. Ballack held up a hand to stop him.

"Father Joseph, don't even begin with me. It would be best if you would look here on my laptop and confirm this story for me."

With his hands clearly trembling, Father Joseph slowly rose to his feet and circled around Ballack's wheelchair. There on the computer screen was a news story screaming guilt in all its sadly vibrant color. The online home of *The Hartford Courant* displayed the results of a sting operation. Senator Hughes' suspicions and the pleas of several Baron novitiates were verified. Father Joseph Quinn was front and center in a photo, being led to a police car by Hartford detectives.

"My, my, Father. What were you and six minors doing in the southern West End neighborhood of Hartford? I can't imagine that you were there for a book club discussion of Thomas Aquinas' works."

Father Joseph was attempting to save face, putting his hands out as if he could ward off Ballack's verbal blows. "Now … wait. Please, wait …"

"For what? Are you telling me that there were two Joseph Quinns at the Chesire seminary and that this article is about the other one? Enlighten me, please!"

"Now wait! There was never anything that went to court! And if it had …"

"Forget it, Father. The reason it never got that far was because the seminary settled out of court! I had plenty of time on the way over to Google your name and check out how often you appeared on the

SNAP network of Catholic abuse survivors. My laptop nearly blew up! The average amount was a million per novitiate. Pretty hefty pill to swallow. Yeah, God's will and all. What a joke."

"What I don't get," Tori broke in, "is how you got another position in the first place. Unless the settlement occurred well after you left."

Before Father Joseph could respond, Ballack waved his left hand. "I'll save us all some time and point out that's exactly what happened, Tori. But let's move on to Illinois. What was that situation? It was a chaplaincy, correct?"

Father Joseph's jaw tightened with anger but he kept his voice quiet. "It was. I provided spiritual counsel for the adult members of the Corpus Sancti community there in Lake Zurich. That was a different environment."

"Why?" asked Tori. "Small town had little to offer? Had to go into Chicago for some entertainment?"

Ballack slowly and auspiciously drew his palm across his throat in a back-and-forth motion. They had Father Joseph on the ropes. In no way did he want Tori losing her composure.

The flustered Father Joseph glowered back and forth at each detective. "No! What I was going to say … before you, Detective Vaughan, interrupted me was this: Corpus Sancti isn't a seminary. The adults who come there are part of the largest lay member religious movement worldwide. They come, learn in community with each other and resident priests, go out and evangelize, and think about how the Gospel applies to their individual vocations when they return to everyday life one day."

Ballack knew his next angle didn't have the same light of day as the Connecticut case. But he knew Billy Doyle had been right so far and saw no reason to distrust the man's reports. He leaned closer and said, "What about those who never return to their everyday life?"

"I'm sorry?"

"What if someone thought, 'You know, I've learned enough. I've got this spiritual life thing down. I'm out of here.' Or if the person said, 'This isn't for me. It sucks.' Or ..." Ballack paused for suspense, "what if there were events going on that forced a member of the community to seek a way out?"

"Events?" snapped Father Joseph. "What events?"

"Perhaps the tragic death of a member who wanted to leave but was told he couldn't?" asked Ballack.

"Someone who was the latest in the sad history of your victims," declared Tori.

"Stop it! What are you saying?" demanded Father Joseph.

"Ever hear of, or mentor, someone at Lake Zurich named Philippe?" asked Ballack. "It would have been about five years ago. The Chicago papers reported there was a tragic death and a cover-up, but they—the *Tribune* specifically—said it was one of those dramas where the more they dug, the more dirt piled on top of everything. People at the place were running scared. The article even said ..." Ballack pointed to his laptop to show off the Web page, "that no two stories coming out of the Corpus Sancti staff were alike. Some said Philippe was the guy's real name, others not." He looked straight at Father Joseph. "Care to enlighten us?"

"Gladly," replied the priest, eager to scrape out of his defensive position. "Philippe was a bright, sensitive young man who was quite tortured. He seemed to be running away from something more than running toward God. I mentored him, spiritually and academically as it turns out. We read many of the classics of the faith. Augustine, Anselm, and others were in that mix. But Philippe was prone to depression. He felt he was under a massive weight of guilt for his many sins. He was a young man, after all, and his afflictions were so typical of many his age. He believed he couldn't reconcile his passions and his service for Christ. I believed he could with counsel and prayer. One morning we found him on the quadrangle of our campus, face down and unmoving. He had hung himself from the chapel tower and the weight of his body must have eventually caused the rope to give way. He could not justify why he continued on there. It was a tragic loss for our community and of course, the public outcry in its aftermath was overwhelming. Although I was not technically to blame, the perception was that Philippe's death seriously undercut my ministry potential there. Once again, I needed a clean slate, and I found it here, thank God."

Ballack sat quietly, never taking his eyes off the man. It was obviously a different account than what Father Doyle had given them, and no contradictory report had occurred in the online articles he had read from the *Tribune* on the drive over to the hotel. But if Father Doyle was correct about the influence of the Mafia working in conjunction with Corpus Sancti and Father Joseph, then there was no telling how much reporting had been suppressed in the process. He tucked that thought away as a strong likelihood even though he could never prove it.

Tori's question broke the silence. "And you've been here for three years as chaplain at Santa Maria Academy in Wildwood?"

"I have," said Father Joseph, who was exhibiting a strong dislike to being interrogated by a woman. "Santa Maria is a school with oversight by the Barons, so I was remaining within my network. The archdiocese here has been very welcoming, even though the school has endured a severe financial run of bad luck. I shifted into director of development to use my Baron connections to raise some desperately needed capital. But it was too little, too late. Santa Maria will close at the end of this school year. Still, we've managed to be a blessing to others. Another school has negotiated to purchase our property and move there in time for the fall semester next year. Perhaps you saw that story in the papers recently."

They hadn't, but Ballack was already moving ahead and ready to shock. He got on another Internet site and asked, "Father Joseph, one other thing. How was your lawsuit going?"

The priest shrank in his chair, as if hit in the chest with an invisible cannonball. "What are you talking about?"

"And before you try to be a rotten liar yet again," reminded Ballack. "I have the page here on my screen. SNAP—the Survivors Network of those Abused by Priests—and Pat Fishwick's 10:21 Alliance, whom I am sure you're familiar with … both groups mention they are intending to file suit against the Archdiocese of St. Louis for financial restitution in a multitude of counts for abuse of minors. The person mentioned most frequently in cases involving the alleged victims was Father Joseph Quinn of Santa Maria Academy." Again, Ballack paused for effect. "Now again: That's not a different Joseph Quinn, is it? If not, I think you're out of options on this one."

"For once, can't you be completely honest?" asked Tori, the edge back in her voice.

"Might I ask—and this is no admission of wrongdoing—what this has to do with the murder of my friend Toby Zweig?" snapped the red-faced Father Joseph.

"Father, when this whole line of questioning reveals that you've been less than forthcoming with the truth and been involved in several past indiscretions," responded Ballack, "that leaves me little confidence in your character. You might not automatically be a suspect, but you haven't necessarily come out of the last few minutes smelling like a rose. That alone is a serious matter. But while we're on the subject of Toby Zweig, it would be nice to know where you were yesterday afternoon between four and five o'clock."

As if some cosmic force had arranged it, Ballack's cell phone vibrated, indicating a text message coming in from Hull. He looked at it while Father Joseph began his alibi. His reason the same one Monsignor Grenier had given on his behalf, that Father Joseph had been scheduled to say Evening Prayer at Ascension Church in Chesterfield. As he crisply stated his defense, Ballack smiled and shook his head.

"I'm afraid this is strike three, Father. One of the detectives on my team just spoke to the associate pastor out there. Father Michael Carter said he was the one who oversaw the service. He said you were nowhere in the building." Ballack's eyes were darts of fire. "You'd

211

better set the story straight, because you're moving more and more into suspect territory by now. Not to mention you have dragged the monsignor along with you."

And now Ballack saw a complete and utter shutdown behind the eyes of one Father Joseph Quinn. The priest jumped to his feet with both hands raised and his face betraying fear and rage.

"Enough!" he thundered. "I will not put up with your badgering one minute longer! If you must speak with me further, it will be in the presence of an attorney. Until then, you can stay away!" He pointed toward the door.

Ballack shrugged, cocking his head to one side. "Completely understandable, Father. It would be better to gather whatever sheaves of truth you can now and stop your flood of lies. We'll be going, but I think it's fair to say we'll be crossing paths again soon. Good night, Father. I hope you can sleep well after this."

Father Joseph said nothing but started toward the door. The nightly glow of the lights off the Arch glimmered in the windows. Before they reached the door, Tori turned toward the small closet next to the bathroom. "And what's in those boxes, Father, if you don't mind me asking?" she queried.

"I do mind you asking, Detective Vaughan," Father Joseph bellowed as he interposed himself between Tori and the closet, "because it has nothing to do with Toby's death and because it's none of your business! Good-bye to both of you, and rest assured I will lodge a complaint to your superior officer. You both have been less than professional and your department will hear about it from me on behalf of the entire Archdiocese."

"Ah, less than professional," replied the sarcastic Ballack. "As contrasted with your obvious saintlike aura." He whirred over the threshold and turned left toward the elevators as Tori trotted to catch up.

"Speaking of our superior officers," he said when she drew abreast, "I'll report in to Krieger and Scotty as we head out."

"Yeah, beat Father Joseph to the punch," Tori replied, "because I'd like to at least have a job when I wake up tomorrow."

31

Ballack dictated into his Dragon software as he and Tori made their way out of the Drury, his laptop automatically typing out the words as he said them. He saved the report in a document and immediately emailed it to Bosco and Krieger, adding that the final interview with Father Joseph got slightly terse and to expect, in Ballack's words, "some whining cherry bombs coming your way." That duty done, he got set to dial Hull's cell phone for a final checkup when he stopped himself and turned to his partner. "So where does this leave us, Tor? Give me your take."

Tori gave the attendant a ten-dollar bill for the valet service and drew back against a post near the front door. "Of course, Father Joseph is a scumbag. How he keeps finding work baffles me. However, that doesn't make him Henry. We have to keep lying and sexual perversion distinct from murder. One doesn't necessarily lead to the other."

"Tor, you've grown up since this morning when you were ready to pin Fishwick to the wall because he seemed vaguely suspicious. Okay, Father Joseph wins the Arthur Andersen award for lack of ethical character. Another question: What motive would he have had to rub out Toby Zweig?"

"None that we can see. As a team, we've talked to Monsignor Grenier, Father Behringer, the wife, Tabitha Stowe, Lance Stubblefield, Julian Webber and Father Joseph Quinn. The only one who remotely has a shot at a decent motive is Tabitha Stowe."

"And there are a number of reasons why she can't be a suspect. Monica Zweig could have motive, too, if she's harboring bitterness for

Toby's past philandering. But nothing seems to be fomenting there. And of course, the way he was murdered doesn't seem like a woman's work. It was too clinical. No frenzy in the attack. And that note. 'To protect the innocent.' Henry is doing this in a way where he or she is playing the role of God. The question is how this deed of murder protects the innocent."

Tori gritted her teeth and closed her eyes. The Cardinals must have just scored a run, thought Ballack, given the roar that just erupted from Busch Stadium. The valet pulled up in the Sprinter and Tori went to the side, flipping the toggle switch to open the door and lower the ramp.

"I have nothing, partner," she said as he rolled into the van. "I … I just can't think anymore."

Something was wrong, thought Ballack. It couldn't be her home life, her daughter, worrying about the zigzag romantic life of a teenage girl. He knew it was more complex than he was willing to get into now. Yesterday's visceral thrill of starting a new murder case had given way to the grinding nature of this day's work. There were moments when they instinctively understood that to overanalyze the investigation could bring on as many potential errors as lazy, slipshod efforts. This was one of those times. He allowed Tori to latch his wheelchair into place in the front passenger area. He pulled out his cell phone and punched in Hull's number, which he had memorized as if it was his own.

"Oh," snickered Hull upon answering, "Isn't this the double-dealing weasel who lost me a dinner bet today?"

"Love you too, sir. How did things go with Monica Zweig?"

215

"Two things of note. The widow was more lucid. Maybe she took some uppers. Anyhow, she did mention that her husband had never confided to her that he was going to sack Tabitha. I'm sure he might have had he lived."

"He needed to," said Ballack. "I've seen the woman. She's a ... well, let's say she has many qualities prized by the superficial man."

"Yeah, but that was only part of it. Evidently, he was upset that she passed on a confidential letter drafted by Julian Webber and signed by Webber and Jerome McPadden. Passed it on to Pat Fishwick of 10:21, who told Lance Stubblefield, who used it in court. Pretty damning stuff, it exposed that they were planning to move assets around so they'd have a hardship case in case Father Joseph got nailed on sex abuse charges."

"Well, that makes sense about Zweig's move. I'd fire her too. But the prosecution would necessarily have to share with the defense they had that document. We all know that. It couldn't have caught Zweig and company with their pants down."

"We also had time to go by the rectory and speak with Grenier. He didn't blink. Said he was out in that direction to visit some parishioners in the hospital at St. John's, St. Luke's and Missouri Baptist. Checked in to see how Webber was doing at the office. Not very detailed. But he wasn't lying."

"Except for offering a crappy alibi for Father Joseph."

"Yeah, that's true. But when was it impossible for a priest to lie? Well, that leaves us little more to go on. Anything else? How are things with Father Joseph?"

"That was one of the most miserable hours of my life. We can talk more tomorrow. I can barely keep my eyes open."

"Not even a small taste? A smidgen? Tell me one thing."

"Just that if God strikes him dead tonight by any means, I won't be shedding any tears. He got Tori so upset I thought she was going to kill him herself."

"What's the story? Is he gay?"

"Being a homosexual isn't the issue. If it's your thing, it's your thing. I have a problem with those who twist their cravings into psychological control of others. That's what it seemed to be."

"Okay, sounds like a sermon coming on. I'll bail. Should we meet back at the station tomorrow? The one on Jefferson?"

"Aim for there unless you hear from me. Sleep well."

Ballack hung up and noticed Tori drumming her fingers on the wheel. "Connecting dots, are we?" he asked.

"Fishwick had a son named Phil who died tragically. There's a Philippe who dies on Father Joseph's watch at Corpus Sancti under suspicious circumstances. Yeah, despite his alibi, I'm connecting the dots, all right."

"Make sure there's a puzzle on the board first, Tor. Stop thinking about the case now so we can have a clear head tomorrow." And with that, Ballack tilted his wheelchair back, shutting his eyes for the remainder of the trip home.

32

Ninety minutes after Ballack and Vaughan left room seven hundred nine, a door leading from the Drury parking garage into the hotel opened from the inside. Father Joseph flinched at the sight of the visitor before recognizing his friend.

"Well, this is a surprise," he said. "I didn't recognize you at first, for obvious reasons. Come on down to the room."

His friend nodded, lifting a bottle of wine into view. "I thought you might enjoy a drink while we discuss what we need. Didn't want to open it by myself."

Father Joseph smiled broadly and stepped aside to allow his guest to enter the hallway. "Now is the best time to open a new bottle, when there are things to be said."

The two figures ambled down the carpeted corridor, their muffled steps marking time and the soft radiance of the Arch making up for the lack of moonlight seeping through the hallway window. Father Joseph took out his key card while his companion patted his left pant pocket, making certain the packet was still there.

"Have a seat," Father Joseph directed his visitor, "and here's a corkscrew. There's some tiramisu in the fridge if you're hungry. I'll grab some glasses if you don't mind the cheap plastic cups provided by the hotel. Hold on. Nature calls."

Without waiting for a reply, Father Joseph stumbled into the bathroom. And without delaying further, his friend poured a glass of wine for the journeyman priest and tore open the packet over the synthetic goblet. Two pills slid into the Merlot and dissolved before Father Joseph reappeared from his bathroom excursion.

33

Ballack scooted across the basement floor, positioning himself so that Karen Calabria, his long-time nurse, could set him up for the lift and he could be gently deposited in his bed for a solid night's sleep. Karen set up his vent and attached another bag of inhalation water to the apparatus while Ballack checked his cell phone before recharging it for the night. No messages from the rest of his team, or Scotty Bosco, or even Commander Stu Krieger. But there was a text from Dana, and Ballack wasted no time opening it.

It read: *Those are the surprises I love. I know it couldn't be more than a few minutes but it's better than none at all. Maybe a full evening together will be closer than we think. Miss you already. Love, Dana.*

The smile on his face lasted until the tidal wave of sleep washed over him.

Father Joseph leaned into his friend as they lurched down the hallway. The wine had been heavy but even one glass should not have done this much damage. He suggested he was feeling ill and should perhaps go to the hospital as a precaution. Five steps down the hallway, his friend announced a change of plans.

"We're taking the stairs."

The stairs don't make any sense when your car is right outside in the lot on this level, thought Father Joseph, but his brain was too clouded and his tongue too burdened to object. Nor could he ward off the blows when the friend became his attacker. He would have had difficulty defending himself as it was. Drugged, he had nary a prayer. He felt a hand firmly grip the back of his head and slam his skull against the railing of the stairwell. Father Joseph's unconscious form collapsed on the landing without a whimper, and his assailant pulled something from a small satchel before retrieving a sheet of paper and another object from a torn breast pocket.

BOOK THREE
"And of the Holy Spirit"

(September 24-25)

LUKE H. DAVIS

34

The glory of freedom was that she was in a nation free from bombs and ethnic cleansing. The price she paid, thought Smentijlana Tukakovic, was that she still needed to walk twelve city blocks to make it on time for her morning shift. For the last four years, she had faithfully worked in the housekeeping department at the Drury Plaza Hotel at the Arch; her personal kingdom, the one no madman dictator could take from her, was the seventh floor. She felt the pain running through her feet and calves as she trotted northward on 4th Street. Some day, she swore, all this would be worth it. Years of saving money, living in a one-bedroom apartment with husband Kamal and their two children, and the other sacrifices would bear fruit in the future. Their time in St. Louis amongst its burgeoning refugee population had been lean and marked by giving up much. Meals were more boiled onions—the *sogan-dolma*—and the *popara*, bread soaked in thin, boiling milk, than the *cevapi* Smentijlana remembered from the kebab shops in her native Bosnia. Her mouth watered with the memories. She resolved to trudge on and clock in on time. Thankfully, Kamal didn't have to walk as far to reach his laundromat in northeast Soulard.

Reaching the employee entrance at three minutes before eight o'clock, she clocked in and placed her sweater in the locker she shared with Anya, who handled the eighth floor. Taking a swig from a bottle of Coke she left there the day before, Smentijlana headed out into the hallway. One minute to go. It would be best, she thought, to hurry up the stairs and be on the floor on time in case her supervisor was looming around. No sense taking a chance on the temperamental elevators. Head down, Smentijlana worked her way up the stairwell, groaning amidst the shooting pain in her leg. It was when she reached the landing for the sixth floor that she noticed reddish drops on the steps. Wondering if they were stray blotches of paint, Smentijlana climbed on, grabbing the railing to ascend one more floor.

Then she looked up for the first time and was struck by the dangling extremities of the hideous terror directly above. Overcome with shock and repulsed by the spectacle suspended in midair, she lurched to the side and slammed against the concrete wall, her right hip crashing against the metal rail. She tried to walk and couldn't; she tried to breathe and failed; she attempted to scream and found her voice unwilling. The head, held firmly in place by the thick noose, was cocked to the side, and the lifeless eyes fixated on the far wall. The face was pale except for the swollen, dried tongue extended sideways from the mouth, hanging there like a slice of salmon-colored sandpaper. But what overwhelmed Smentijlana the most was the stench. The bulge and stain in the trousers was doubtless a pungent mixture of waste, and the closer she stumbled upward, the less control she maintained, and she vomited onto the landing.

Still devastated by the sight of death before her, Smentijlana knew she couldn't handle this alone. Scrambling to her feet, she yanked herself up the stairs and plunged into the seventh floor hallway. She half-crawled, half-ran to the housekeeping closet where, thank God, she knew there would be a phone. It was when she finally reached her nook of solitude that she recalled perhaps the most frightening detail of that theater of mortality: the clerical collar on the man dangling from the rail.

35

Ballack had managed only four hours of sleep, tossing and turning as he awaited the jangling noise of his alarm. His throat hurt from the volume of interrogation the day before. He had slept wrong on his left shoulder and the joint throbbed periodically. He prayed to no one in particular that today would be one of a slower pace. When his cell phone went off, he knew his plea had been rejected. He looked at the familiar number on his caller ID and answered the phone, signaling Karen to raise the head of his bed and get ready to move quickly.

For the third time in twenty-four hours, Tori parked the Sprinter in front of the Drury. After Ballack descended, she handed over the keys and a ten-dollar bill once more to the valet, who refused the cash. "No, you not pay," he said kindly in broken English, "You police. We not charge you."

"Fat chance of getting the other bill back," mumbled Tori as they walked through the glass doors yet again. Bosco and Krieger were waiting for them at the front desk.

"Who knows?" asked Ballack as they approached their superiors.

Krieger looked at Bosco, who replied, "So far, the hotel concierge staff on site. The supervisor of housekeeping let them know. She in turn heard about it from the person who discovered the body, and the maid's name was …" He read slowly to avoid mangling the name any more than he felt he was, "… Smentijlana Tukakovic. She discovered him in the stairwell hanging from the landing at the seventh floor."

"And the reason we're called in on this is because this death is deemed connected to Toby Zweig's?" responded Ballack.

"That would be correct."

"And given that there is a connection, I'm guessing this involves an individual of interest who was staying at the hotel. In which case, it has to be either Pat Fishwick or Father Joseph Quinn …" he paused as he saw the incredulous looks come over the faces of Bosco and Krieger, "… and given that it happened on the seventh floor, I'm going out on a limb and saying …" and he swept his arm toward his partner for the *coup de grace*.

"It's Father Joseph, isn't it?" asked Tori.

"I guess I know what you were discussing on the way over," sputtered Krieger, "but how did you manage to guess that quickly when we hadn't told you who it was?"

"Didn't you read my report from last night?" asked Ballack. "I told both of you that Father Joseph was staying on the seventh floor. Room seven-oh-niner to be exact. Seems reasonable that if someone is hanging from there, it would be him. Is the rest of the team here?"

"Hull and Crabolli are around the corner ready to go up," the commander replied. "We'll take the elevator. Broadnax and Grimshaw are already in the stairwell, and after they're done, they'll check his room. Stairwell is sealed. We have the maid in an empty room on the eighth floor which we'll use for any interviews."

"Pat Fishwick around?" Ballack asked, craning his neck toward the breakfast area.

"You think he did it?" responded Bosco.

"I think we need to ask him. Let's go."

The detectives exchanged silent nods with Hull and Crabolli and then filed into the elevator. On the way up, Crabolli said, "The front desk offered us breakfast on the house."

"Buying our silence and discretion?" asked Tori. "Not like they have to worry about it. But I'm not complaining. I doubt we'll have time, though."

The doors opened and the team headed down the hall as directed by Bosco and Krieger. Ballack found it surreal that he and Tori were here just last night. The stairwell door appeared before them, plastered with yellow tape and just a few yards away from Father Joseph's room. Whoever did this, thought Ballack, didn't have far to go. This murder wasn't the result of haphazard planning. Bosco directed the team into a nearby empty room where they—excepting Ballack—could change into their observation gear. Once that was done, they were back in the hall. Krieger opened the stairwell door.

There was little room on the landing, so to accomodate Ballack's wheelchair, Bosco and Krieger descended a few steps. After a few seconds, all present could both see the corpse and smell the odor. The undignified, still form of Father Joseph dangled from a rope well tied together. The other end had been looped through a manacle attached to a hook, which in turn had been fastened to the rail. From below, Marcus Broadnax and Sheila Grimshaw stepped into view. Both were obviously glad the team was here to view things as they stood. Now they could remove the body and get to work.

227

As if anticipating their purpose, Krieger asked, "This is exactly how he was found?"

"According to the maid," replied Grimshaw. "We tried speaking with her, but it was like talking to a lunatic. Maybe you'll have more luck. We're cleaning up this vomit. Apparently it was the maid's but we're taking a sample to make sure."

Satisfied with her reponse, Krieger said, "Okay, get him down. We're going to the front desk. Lieutenant Bosco and I will interview the key staff members there. You decide who does what here."

When the commanders left, Hull turned to Ballack and said quietly, "I know this is your call, but seeing how there is no room in here for all of us, Missy and I can interview the maid and find out what she knows. After we're done with her, we can check in here."

Ballack nodded. "Thanks. Do that. I'll let you know if you're needed back here." And they left. Tori got out her camera and descended to the next landing. Grimshaw came up and said, "Okay, Marcus. I'll get him loose. You have him secure?"

Broadnax answered in the affirmative and after a few seconds of struggle he managed to place the body on the landing between the sixth and seventh floors. Ballack pulled forward as far as he could and looked down the stairwell shaft. Given the fecal odor coming from Father Joseph, he knew Broadnax would eschew a rectal temperature to determine the time of death. The autopsy could provide those details later.

"What do you have?" asked Ballack after several minutes. He didn't want to rush Broadnax, but was anxious to get going. He liked the medical examiner yet couldn't help wondering how Evan

Holbrook—who had worked on previous cases, including the St. Basil's murders—would have approached this scene.

"Well, time of death is probably one in the morning, give or take an hour," began Broadnax. "The rigor mortis makes that fairly cut and dry. Looking at his tongue, there is residue of something colored and I'm getting a whiff of wine. I wonder if he got drunk or was drugged when this happened, but we won't get tox screen results for weeks. No way it's an elaborate suicide. There are few signs of struggle. No blood. Few marks other than this head contusion. Given the size and shape of it, the bruise is probably from the metal railing. No skin under the fingernails to ward off an assailant, if there was one. There are rope fibers under the nails, though, suggesting he was trying to get himself loose. The brutal thing is what he might have suffered. It wasn't a particularly long piece of rope, so that means a short drop. It didn't break his neck, so it could take upwards of ten minutes or longer for him to die. The short drop, the likely anguish, and the rope fibers under the nails all point toward murder rather than suicide."

Ballack winced. Even though he had no love for Father Joseph and found him to be reprehensible, the idea of suffering for that long before expiring was too much. "No man of the cloth should have to go that way," he said out loud before he could stop himself.

"Did you know him?" asked Grimshaw.

"Bosco and Krieger didn't tell you?" replied Ballack, shaking his head at the lack of shared information.

"We were here last night interviewing him in his room," Tori told them. "His room was not far from this stairwell. His name is Father Joseph Quinn and he was a rather controversial addition to the

229

archdiocesan staff. We had a few questions for him regarding the Toby Zweig murder."

"Given this is murder," asked Broadnax, "do you believe they're connected?"

Ballack looked down the shaft once more. "I know they're connected. It's murder. Whoever did this intended for him to suffer."

"Don't jump to conclusions yet, Detective," said Grimshaw, popping her jaw, her nervous tick. "Why do you think that?"

"Several reasons," said Ballack.

"Here we go," Tori rolled her eyes, snapping several photographs of Father Joseph's neck area.

"First, as mentioned, we spoke with him last night. Father Joseph was an utter pain in the rear end and struck me as someone who might be a lightning rod for another's rage. Obviously, the specifics of why and how go unanswered. Secondly, random killing is not out of the question, but if you've got that much space below you, why use a short length of rope and cause the person to suffer when you can use a greater length and the force of the drop breaks your neck and ends it? And thirdly, why do it in the stairwell when his room would do just as well? The question is why here and why this way? Why so public? More people could see this here than in his room. Is there a significance to the exposure of death?"

"You're saying someone lured him in here or met him, and then killed him?" The question was from Grimshaw. Broadnax was intrigued by Ballack's reasoning and remained silent.

"Or met him in his room," replied Ballack. "This place has to have security cameras. Maybe we'll get lucky and find out who came in. But Marcus, you said there was wine residue and smell …"

"That ain't all we're smelling," said Broadnax, ready to retch from the pungent aroma. "It's like I'm back in Lynchburg again."

"Hang on there. Perhaps someone met him in the room, had a glass of wine and drugged him. Or beat him up, although this doesn't look to be that. It's only a short walk-and-drag to the stairwell. It may not be probable, but the dominos could line up that way. It's at least theoretically possible."

"The guy have any enemies?" asked Grimshaw.

"More than we can count," said Tori. "He had a bunch of people lining up to nail him for molestation."

"Oh, my …" Grimshaw looked as if she was going to hurl her dinner from the night before. She was trying to efficiently fingerprint the railing area.

"Back to connecting this with Zweig. Father Joseph's abuse lawsuit, which appeared to be upcoming, was going to be handled by Zweig." Ballack hesitated. He ruled against telling them the attorney was going to intentionally lose the case. The information might complicate the thought process. "We have Zweig killed Thursday afternoon and Father Joseph dead this morning. If both are murders, I'm inclined to think the same person did both."

"Different methods," cautioned Broadnax, still checking out the body.

"Okay, check the pants," said Ballack.

"What?" exclaimed Broadnax. "Have you smelled this stiff? I'm not going there!"

"I'm not saying rummage around! Just go in the front pants area and see what's in there!"

Broadnax was unsure, but did as requested. His gloved hands pulled out a quart-sized Ziploc bag with another paper in it.

"Doubt me now?" Ballack asked.

Tori was stunned. "How the did you know to look there?"

"I didn't," muttered Ballack. "Total guess. But I had my suspicions. What does the note say?"

Broadnax handed the bag to Tori, who opened it with her own gloved hands and brought it up the steps to Ballack. He looked at the document, written in block printing, and made sure his Dragon software was on. He began to read aloud.

"It says, 'The reason is close at hand: the human mind, distracted by cares, does not enter into itself through memory; clouded by sense images, it does not turn back to itself through intelligence; allured away by concupiscence, it does not turn back to itself through desire for inner sweetness and spiritual joy.' That's either the most philosophically damning threat I've ever read or else it's the strangest suicide note on record."

"I was about to say," said Broadnax, holding his nose. "What does it mean?"

"One second," replied Ballack, who quickly highlighted the text on his Talk 'n Type program, Googled it, and then waited a few seconds. "Aha, it happens to be a quote from St. John Bonaventure, the medieval Catholic philosopher. It's from his essay called 'The Mind's Ascent to God.' I have no clue why this choice of words."

"I'm clueless too," chimed in Tori.

"But the fact we have this note connects the deaths. Zweig had one, albeit a shorter note, in his pants as well."

"No cross, though," said Broadnax.

"Excuse me?"

"No cross on his person. Zweig had the crucifix on his entry wound. We don't have one here. We didn't even see one on him when we arrived."

"Because you didn't look hard enough."

"What?" Both Broadnax and Grimshaw practically screamed the word. Tori stood completely still, shocked at her partner's bluster. This seemed insensitive even for him.

"Let me ask you this. Did you enter this stairwell down below, or did you come in here from the seventh floor after taking the elevator?"

"The elevator," answered Grimshaw.

"Uh-huh. Okay. Well, if you came in from below, you might have seen the crucifix. Granted, it's so small anyone could've bypassed it. I barely saw it from here."

He leaned forward, placing his head on the vertical rails, and pointed downward, his compatriots following his finger's trajectory. There, resting on a step down near the fifth floor, was a small olive-colored wooden crucifix. Except for the glint from the gold paint of the Christ figure, it was barely perceptible against the grayish steps. Broadnax donned new gloves and descended the stairs to procure it.

"How the devil did you see that?" asked Tori. "You have X-ray vision or something? There's no way anyone could've noticed it!"

"Don't you think the maid might have noticed it?" asked Grimshaw. "I heard she came up through the stairwell."

"Not necessarily," said Ballack.

"And why?"

"Her name. Krieger said it was something like Smentijlana Tukakovic."

"How do you keep these details straight?" yelled Broadnax in equal parts admiration and exasperation.

"Dude, don't get me started," muttered Tori. "When his Asperger's syndrome and his photographic memory collide, scary things happen."

"I've never been tested, so the Asperger's thing is heresay," retorted Ballack. "The point is her name could be Serbian or Croatian. Or Bosnian, as many as we have in St. Louis. If it's the last category, she could very well be Muslim. A crucifix lying on the ground wouldn't arouse much clean-up compassion."

"She's a maid! Cleaning up is what she does! " rasped Tori. "Hey! Now what are you doing?"

Ballack had pulled out his cell phone and dialed a number. In no time, Hull answered.

"Zane, do me a favor. Ask the maid what country she's from and what religion she happens to be … No, I'm not insane. Trust me. Just do it. And if she noticed anything unusual on the stairs, say around the fifth floor."

Tori turned around and buried her face against the wall.

"Stay away from the wall, Tor," joked Ballack. "That can compromise the search for prints … Yeah? Okay, thank you. Nah, that's all, Zane. Later."

He pocketed his cell phone and looked at them with a triumphant smile.

"Bosnian. Muslim. Sunni, if you're interested. Never saw the cross. My guess is it fell off Father Joseph." He watched as Broadnax came up the stairs and showed him the crucifix.

"Well, sir," the medical examiner gushed. "It has a ripped cord attached to it. Maybe it fell or was torn from him. Or he struggled and tried to get loose and that's when it happened. Who knows? I have to say I'm impressed for one additional reason."

He turned the cross over. They all gathered around. The figure of Jesus was once again intact, but in an eerie repeat visual, the upright beam had been cut.

Grimshaw was first to speak. Her voice was husky with emotion. "Another broken cross."

36

The security office of the Drury Plaza Hotel was normally a quiet place. Head supervisor Nick Perry had been enjoying an easy Saturday morning until two police officers entered and demanded to see the security tapes from the past night. At first, Perry resisted, but upon seeing their identification he relented and told his associate to give Lieutenant Scotty Bosco and Commander Stu Krieger maximum cooperation.

The associate, one Chip Vinson, invited both officers to sit down with him as they began the meticulous process of combing through the videos beginning at nine-thirty the previous evening. Twenty minutes of searching brought no progress, so Bosco suggested fast-forwarding an hour ahead and focusing on the seventh floor. The prospects for success seemed bleak until Vinson uploaded a sequence around midnight from the seventh floor corridor.

Two men were walking down the hallway toward a window that revealed the Arch's haunting glow against a sky that was black as pitch. Behind them, a door swung shut, and Krieger could see cars in the sliver between the slowly closing door and its frame. One person was clearly Father Joseph Quinn, laughing and gesturing to the man on his left. The mystery guest raised his hand to reveal a large bottle of some sort. Bosco looked more closely and saw there was no way they could make out any features from the shoulders upward. Quinn's visitor was wearing a black baseball hat and covered his body with a black trenchcoat. His other noticeable feature was the light—if not downright blond— hair sticking out from under the hat.

"Scotty, take a look at this."

Bosco followed Krieger's gesture to the screen on Vinson's left. Vinson had rewound it to the frame in question. It showed the same person, ready to take the elevator from the lobby. Still nothing discernible, other than the blond hair. Father Joseph's interloper had obviously planned this out; whoever this was either got extremely lucky or else knew exactly where the cameras would be. Bosco looked at the time on the video. It read thirty minutes after the clip from the seventh floor.

Krieger punched a number on his phone. Several moments later he said, "Missy, we've got video. Affirmative. Someone came by here for the deceased. Sketchy, except for the fact we can probably judge his height. Once you're done with the maid, let me know."

37

Ballack, Tori, Broadnax, and Grimshaw had all finished in the stairwell and were set to secure the area for good. Broadnax's friends at the morgue had arrived for the body, and as they worked the corpse up for transmission, the foursome moved to Father Joseph's room. They went about the business of sweeping the room for details, Ballack waiting near the bathroom while Grimshaw dusted for prints. Broadnax, intent on hanging around for a few more minutes, walked over toward the closet and peeked in. His very act of doing so reminded Ballack of when Father Joseph ejected them the night before. "Hey, Marcus. Let's glove up and see what's in these bins."

"Don't know how it'll help, but here goes nothing," said Broadnax as the ladies scoped out the body of the hotel room. Gloves on, Broadnax lifted a bin and opened it up. A set of Bibles lay on the top layer of supplies.

"Nothing spectacular," said Broadnax.

"I'm not buying it," replied Ballack, leaning forward and nearly toppling out of his wheelchair. He righted himself and said, "In 1948, the Israeli army would smuggle rifles in from Czechoslovakia by ship. The customs agents who detained the cargo found only onions, which was exactly the point. The tons of onions in those boxes obscured the weapons underneath."

"You think God's boy was hiding something?" asked Broadnax as he lifted the Bibles in one fluid motion. "It's possible, but … oh, God help us!" His voice had gone from even tone to primal scream.

Underneath the Bibles and several feet of rosary beads was just what Ballack dreaded and suspected. Tori came over and immediately doubled over. Grimshaw looked up at the chaos and asked, "What? What?!"

The bin held over seventy issues of various magazines and booklets. Some had more mainstream material. Others were more esoteric. The common thread was the variety of pictorial filth. Tori's knees buckled at the sight, and she stumbled into the middle of the room, crawling toward the wastebasket underneath the desk. In sheer anger, she violently emptied the contents of her stomach into the metal canister, again and again.

A spine-chilling hush drenched the room. Broadnax had fallen onto his rear end into the bathroom. Grimshaw clenched her jaw and tried to go back to the job of forensics but was having difficulty. Tori sprawled on the floor, crying tears of rage, completely undone. She could sense her faith beginning to fritter away. Ballack, his face set as stone, snapped his fingers and addressed Broadnax.

"Marcus?"

"Yeah?"

"We're going to need to seal all this stuff and hand it over to the FBI."

"We? What 'we'? Just let Stu know and he has the proper contacts."

"That's disgusting," Grimshaw scoffed.

"No wonder he barred us from looking at them last night," said Ballack, keeping an eye on Tori. He took out his cell phone and dialed Hull's number. *Perhaps he needed to put it on speed dial*, he thought. Hull answered and Ballack asked him to report to the room if he was done with Smentijlana Tukakovic. Hull seemed glad for the change of pace.

"This is going to be a heck of a job for the FBI," Ballack remarked.

Broadnax nodded. "Just one man, as far as we know. To be fair, you can't assume anyone in the Archdiocese knew."

Grimshaw approached them and sat on the edge of the bed, trying to change the subject from the bins of Father Joseph's secrets. "Cameron, what's your best guess? We've got two deaths. Two notes, both of which could be elaborate threats, warnings, whatever. But why the crosses? Quinn was a priest and a flawed one, and I don't know whether or not Zweig was exactly of devout stock. Two crosses, crucifixes in which Jesus' form is left alone, but the cross itself is carefully broken. Why? Does anyone else get it?" She glanced around, but received no direct looks. Tori pulled herself from her prone position and sat Indian-style, breathing deeply. She looked sorry that a priest of her faith had besmirched everything her Church stood for, thought Ballack. She looked heartbroken, gloomy, guilty.

Guilty, thought Ballack suddenly. That's it.

"He feels guilty," the words exploded from Ballack's lips. "Henry ... the murderer. It's because he feels bad that he's doing this. He's murdered Zweig and Quinn for reasons known to him, but they are connected in that both are bound in a way that Henry feels guilt over for some reason. He feels badly that he must commit the murders."

"I'm sorry," said Broadnax, confused but in truth happy for any distraction from their recent discovery. "What makes you think guilt?"

"It's a version of Chris Benoit."

"Chris Benoit? What are you talking about?" The response came from Tori, who had miraculously recovered from her vicious purge. "Who are you talking about?"

"A few years ago," said Ballack. "Double murder-suicide outside of Atlanta. I remember it like it was yesterday. Chris Benoit was a world-famous professional wrestler. He missed a major event, in Houston I think it was, one weekend. The next day, Atlanta area police entered Benoit's home and discovered he had killed both his wife and his son, then hanged himself with his weightlifting machine pulley. A lot of people blamed it on steroids … you know, 'roid rage and all that. But Benoit had placed Bibles, one next to his wife and one by his son, after he killed them. It was as if he was hoping for their salvation and, some felt, that he felt a strong sense of guilt or tragic awareness of his responsibility. Now we have a crucifix—different religious object, but in the same family—at the site of each death within a few days. A broken cross."

"Why the brokenness?" asked Broadnax.

"That's where the twist is," said Ballack.

"The brokenness of life, that things don't always work out?" asked Grimshaw.

"I considered that," said Ballack. "It's interesting that Henry snipped the cross itself but not Jesus' figurine. I think he feels badly about something, maybe something he caused in the past that is connected with both Zweig and Father Joseph. He blames them for something, but he still feels somewhat responsible. The question is what, and when. That could be the key. I'm just thinking out loud. But we're nowhere close to that right now. I know it could be a stretch. The correlation might be tenuous, but I think it's there."

The other three were quiet. "C'mon," Ballack continued. "I'm just taking my best stab at it. Let's get out of here. We can talk to Zane in the hallway."

Tori especially needed no encouragement to leave the room. Grimshaw kindly took the wastebasket and tossed the putrid melange down the toilet, rinsing the bucket time and again in the bathtub. The entire group gathered in the hall just as Hull rounded the corner.

"Missy said you guys are to go down to the security office," he said. "Big video break to check out. What's going on here?" he asked, a little too cheerily for them to tolerate.

"I'll brief you in full later," Ballack replied. "Right now, can you see if Pat Fishwick is in the house? Given what's gone down here, it'd be prudent to question him."

"Can do. I'll check with the front desk about his room number."

"I'll save you the trouble. Five-oh-five. He wrote it on his card for Tori alongside some other details we needed. Then again, he might be out on one of his recruiting escapades. I wouldn't interview him in his room, if he's there. Find something downstairs."

Ballack began to say more but was interrupted by his cell phone. He looked at Tori, who took Hull aside and began to explain the situation in low, earnest tones. Ballack looked at the caller ID on his phone, not recognizing the number. Perhaps it was Krieger demanding an audience. He steered his wheelchair several yards away and put the phone to his ear.

"Ballack here."

"Detective Ballack?" The voice was throaty, emotional, and undeniably feminine.

"Yes," he said, his brow crinkling with renewed anxiety.

"Sir, trust me when I tell you this: I need to speak with you as soon as possible."

The rest of the crew was heading toward the elevator. Broadnax waved for Ballack to join them. He put up a finger to signal them to wait. His caller told him who she was and why she needed him.

"Ma'am," he said quietly. "Can you give me just ten minutes? I have to view a critical piece of evidence. I have your number on my cell here. Don't go anywhere or speak to anyone else … What? Yes, ten minutes. You have my word."

38

Missy Crabolli led them into the security office, where Chip Vinson was waiting with Bosco and Krieger. The SID commander apprised Ballack warily, as if he wondered how much the detective brought to the case. For his part, Ballack sensed this afresh and refused to smile or nod in Krieger's direction. The commander exuded a frostiness that went well beyond reserve. Even in his young career, Ballack had figured out when cops were using aloofness in an attempt to intimidate. He ignored Krieger and swept past the desk, coming alongside Tori Vaughan and Missy Crabolli. The video monitor was on pause. Vinson looked around and made sure everyone was ready.

"Here's your buried treasure," he said, and he hit the play button. Two minutes later, Tori stretched forward, wide-eyed.

"Looks like we've got someone in our sights. Too bad his face never shows."

"It does show it's a male," said Ballack. "No doubt there. Henry is definitely a 'he.' Gauge for me, would you, where his head crests when he walks into the elevator. Then we go there ourselves. Bring a tape measure, somebody. We can at least check his height within an inch or two."

Crabolli led them out and started toward the lobby elevators. Tori followed, but Ballack stopped in front of Krieger. He waited until the females had left and he kept his voice low enough so that Vinson and Bosco couldn't overhear as they were discussing the video sequence.

"Commander, is there some sort of an issue you have with my being on this case? That's not an accusation per se, but I sure am picking up a vibe from you."

Krieger appeared confused at first, his bewilderment giving way to a look of irritation before his face assumed a sense of calm. "An issue? That's a rather interesting way of putting it."

"Then how would you put it, sir?" Ballack replied quickly.

The commander stood to his full height, swept his hair across the crown of his head, and said, "Ballack, I welcome others on this case. I need other eyes and ears on this case. I couldn't be SID Commander and believe otherwise. What I think you're reading into this is your idea that I've got something against you because you're from St. Charles County."

"No, that's the original pushback I got from Hull and Crabolli on Thursday night, yet we worked through that. In fact, as of now our team is an absolute love-fest. Think Woodstock before the heroin took control. But let's do get serious. I don't think the issue is my original jurisdiction. I think you feel iffy about me because I'm in this!" And with the final word, Ballack slapped the wheelchair.

Krieger shook his head. "Don't put words in my mouth, Detective. Scotty Bosco raved about you up one side and down the other and said you and Vaughan would be a dynamite addition to the SID. He said you never quit and you were willing to put yourself in danger's way to get the job done. That you had a photographic memory and could connect the dots and see patterns that no one else did. There's not a doubt in my mind that sort of drive and talent can open a lot of doors for us. The fear I had was the jagged edge you

245

bring with you. You've got a real chip on your shoulder, and trust me—I really understand. I just want you to put it aside so you don't forfeit your composure."

"Do you? Understand, that is?"

"As a matter of fact, yes. My wife developed a tumor on her spinal cord eight years ago. Andi went from zooming around full speed and managing a Hallmark store to facing the rest of her life in a wheelchair. So yeah, not my own way, but through the eyes of another, I get it. I know a bit of how someone reacts when potential might be taken away. In truth, I don't mind the attitude in general. It's when you take the sneer and the attitude and the frustration and the sarcasm into a sensitive case like this one that needs to be handled with discretion. Our department doesn't need a ton of blowback on this. You need to be at your absolute best. So whatever vibe you got from me, it was out of concern for how you're progressing on the case. Can you accept that?"

"You make a good point there, Commander," replied Ballack. "All right, I accept."

"Do you really think this murder is connected to Zweig's death?"

Ballack nodded.

"Then, detective," replied Krieger, "I'd expect you understand we've stepped into some powerful stuff here. You just don't work through the landscape of the Archdiocese of Saint Louis without circumspection. Whoever did this could just as soon do it to you. And we don't need you rooting in too far and finding stuff on our priest friends and bringing it to light. That's for the press, if it comes to it, not you. Understand me?"

Ballack understood, but he wasn't listening much. He was looking past Krieger to Vinson's workstation. The tapes from the night before were rotating through, and something had caught Ballack's eye.

Krieger followed his gaze, then looked at him. "Ballack, you got me?"

Ballack, startled by the question, said, "Yeah. Yeah, sorry. Um, hang on a second. Hey, you there. Can you rewind that video there on the far left? The clips of the parking garage. Is that from last night?"

Vinson turned to Ballack, then back to the screen. "Yeah, I believe it is."

"Can you go back about thirty seconds on that video clip and hit play again?"

"Yeah, one second."

Krieger stood transfixed along with Bosco, wondering what Ballack was seeing. At that moment, Tori burst into the room.

"Cameron, you have to come quickly!"

"In a sec, Tor. Busy with some garage video, and then I have to keep a promise and return a phone call."

"We detained Pat Fishwick for some questioning and he's hopping mad."

"Tori, later."

"Why?"

Ballack watched the scene he wanted come into view. "Because of this," he said.

He pointed to the screen, which showed a blinking time of 23:38 from the previous night. Tori was wondering what Ballack was doing looking at a parking garage scene just short of midnight, but her uncertainty evaporated when she saw the item Ballack had noticed.

There, in the lot which led onto the seventh floor, sat a shiny Lexus with a flawless tungsten pearl finish. Tori leaned in to check the detail on the rear bumper, but Ballack had already discerned what the words were on that sticker. Black sticker. Yellow letters. No mistaking them.

DEBT IS NORMAL. BE WEIRD.

The driver side door of the Lexus opened, and out stepped the same figure from the elevator video. Clad in the same black baseball cap and trenchcoat, now he was slightly hunched, walking as if limping, or suffering from a heel spur.

"What's the time on the elevator video? I'd like to see which one is first," asked Ballack, his mind already whirring with the potential connections.

Vinson checked both tapes. "Less than an hour apart. If you're talking chronology, the parking garage one is first. The elevator video is twenty-three minutes after midnight this morning."

"Which means," said Ballack, "that Henry might've gone down the stairwell, come out on the first level, and then gotten back up to his parking level via the elevator."

"What a nutcase," replied Tori. "Who does that?"

"I can tell you of plenty of nut jobs who did the craziest garbage in the wake of a murder, Miss Vaughan," Krieger broke in. "But he is taking a risk."

248

"Calculated one," agreed Ballack, "but if he's killed Father Joseph in the stairwell, he's got to figure we're going to check the priest's room immediately, and we might pick up some traces if Henry had attempted to clean up in the room itself."

"How many restrooms down here?" Krieger asked Vinson.

"A couple for each gender."

Krieger looked knowingly at the other detectives.

"Still a nut job," Tori sniffed.

"Yeah," Ballack said, his eyes back on the video screens, "and he's the same crackpot who was willing to shish-ka-bob Mr. Zweig in broad daylight at the Cathedral. Given that, don't you think he'd be willing to go from St. Louis to Chicago through New Orleans if it might throw us off?"

"And if he's cleaned up down here in a public bathroom," Krieger concurred, wagging his left index finger, "then enough guests have been through there this morning and unwittingly contaminated that scene."

"Smartest screwball one can imagine in a situation like this," said Ballack. "And keep in mind he's well known by Father Joseph. He sure didn't look surprised to see his midnight guest."

"Hang on. Wouldn't there be a clip of him leaving the garage?" asked Tori.

Vinson diligently scrolled through the security videos until he found one of the same figure ducking into the Lexus. "There he is."

Krieger looked closely. "Dipping his head just enough so we can't see his face. He knows exactly where the cameras are, both in the garage and in the lobby. That took some advance scouting."

249

Ballack nodded. "Meaning it's someone familiar with the Drury and who would have had access here along with familiarity with Father Joseph." He clapped his hands together. "If there's a way to hate this guy severely and yet admire his chutzpah, I'm in."

"Now, wait. You can't get up there through the elevator unless you have a room key card," said Vinson. "Let's look again at the elevator clip and see how this guy gets in."

The four policemen gathered around Vinson. After a minute of viewing, Bosco spoke for the first time. "He used a card. Right there."

"Can I ask what that means?" asked Vinson. "Are we saying this is someone who is staying at the hotel?"

"No," said Tori. "We recognized the car in question from the garage. The obvious issue is how this person got the key card."

"Only way you can access the garage," said Vinson, "is if you have an activated key card. No other way in."

"Still, if this guy was chummy enough with Father Joseph, he might have one. Which likely tells us," said Ballack, "that Henry had access to him at some point previously. The question is when and how he got it."

"That's a mystery for the ages," said Bosco.

"Actually," replied Ballack, "it might not be. How many key cards do guests get here at the Drury?"

"Usually two," Vinson answered.

"And if Father Joseph had handed one of the cards over to someone else?" Ballack looked around at everyone in the room. "Then you have an outside person having access to the Drury *and* to Father Joseph."

Ballack, who had been leaning forward, straightened up and wheeled around, looking at his partner and then at Krieger and Bosco.

"One thing we do know is this: That's Grenier's car," Ballack declared. "Call him up. Tell him we're coming his way."

39

Before he could join Tori for the upcoming interview with Monsignor Grenier, Ballack faced the more pressing issue of keeping his promise and returning the mystery phone call from earlier. He whipped out his phone and called the number right back. He wasn't kept waiting.

"Is this Detective Ballack?" said the voice.

"It is, and out of courtesy you should inform me how you got this number." Ballack guarded his privacy jealously.

"It's relatively easy," the speaker purred. "My father spoke to me about the lawyer's murder once he got out of town. I called in to Mr. Webber and found out you were the lead detective. I asked for your number and he was very accommodating. How's that anywhere out of the ordinary? You haven't come upon anything disturbing."

"What I have come upon is for me to assess. All I know is that your name is Ashleigh McPadden Collins and you claim to be the daughter of Jerome McPadden. And Harvest Capital & Mortgage has been part of this stew since Toby Zweig assumed room temperature two days ago. Now you tell me your dad has skipped town. That makes him look suspect from where I stand."

"Well, you're wrong. My father didn't murder that lawyer."

"Really? That hasn't been the only murder."

"What do you mean?"

"I'm downtown dealing with another victim right now."

"Who?"

"As of now, I neither can nor will tell you that. But what I can say is that it was a person who was in your father's circle of acquaintances."

He heard a gasp on the other end of the line, what sounded like a rustling of papers, and finally Ashleigh Collins spoke. Her voice quavered. Her formerly confident air was gone.

"Detective Ballack, I need to speak with you right now."

"Reason being?"

"Because I want you to know that my dad is innocent. Because there's more stuff you don't know about the people who surround him. There's a reason why he is out of town. It's a good reason, but it can't be shared publicly, because it would get him in trouble on a separate matter. And because if you hear this from me, I want you to hear it in person so that you can trust it is coming from me."

"Believe you me," chimed Ballack, "I don't think of your father's circle of friends as clones of the Apostles. Whatever you have to say would likely confirm my suspicions, not overturn them. All right, I'll come to you. But before we set this up, I'd like to know something of why your father is out of town. Something to chew on before I see you."

"I swear, I can't tell you that right now. I thought I just covered that. But I bet it'll prove that he was nowhere in the area relative to whatever new murder you've dug up."

"You're causing my patience to wither away, Mrs. Collins. You have no idea what we've exhumed, and I wouldn't turn up the heat any more than you already have."

"I mean I want to tell you, but I'm going to make sure I'm speaking with you face to face. There's a reason and it'll clear my dad, but all I want is for you and your team to listen to me. I'm putting myself in the open for my father. Is that so difficult to trust?"

"I can't speak for my colleagues, and you have a lot of nerve talking about trust during a murder investigation. Is there a crime of passion you want knocked off his record in exchange for his testimony to identify the murderer? Because you'd better have the bases loaded on this one."

"Just that you'll hear me out. That's all I want. And if you hear his story from another source, maybe you'll trust him. Detective, I'm not saying my father is a good man, but he is an innocent man with respect to this crime."

Ballack cupped his phone in his hand and rubbed his eyes. He could see Crabolli ushering a bewildered and angry Pat Fishwick into a side room down the hall, and Hull following them. Tori approached him, holding up an open hand and whispering, "Grenier will be here in five minutes. He said he'd save us the trip and come down here. Wants to see the body, though."

"He can't."

"I told him that, but maybe he'll believe the news if it comes from a male."

He nodded, thinking back to this mysterious young lady on the other end of the phone line. She had already passed his credibility test. She didn't negotiate or haggle the terms. In fact, she had lowballed herself. Whatever she had, it seemed to be authentic. He had no idea where this would lead, but at this stage eliminating a suspect could prove as valuable as chasing down a potential perpetrator.

"Mrs. Collins, you've got my full attention. I'll meet with you. It'll take me some time because my partner and I have to interview someone else here, but I should be free by at least one o'clock." His stomach rumbled, and he cursed himself for not grabbing some breakfast there at the hotel.

"Okay. Well, we won't be at home, but if you're downtown, that will actually turn out well. It beats driving out to Lake St. Louis where we are. My husband plays in a Gaelic football league and the games are played at St. Vincent's Park off Rock Road. Do you know where I'm talking about?"

Ballack shut his eyes, flipping through his mental atlas. "Is that the one near Incarnate Word Academy? That's just west of Normandy. I think the fields are a ways back from the main drag."

"That's the one," Ashleigh Collins replied. "My husband's game is at one-thirty. It's early in the season, so we're expecting a decent crowd. I'll try to stay on the fringe so you can spot me better. I'm wearing a green long sleeve T-shirt and white cargo shorts."

"It's Gaelic football, Mrs. Collins," grumbled Ballack. "I would think everybody with an Irish last name would be there wearing green. Got any more suggestions? Do I look for the one person who's not playing football or passed out drunk?"

"Ha-ha, Detective. I'll make it easy for you. I've got a Cardinals ball cap but it's bright pink. I'll wear it. It'll give me a chance of standing out."

"One-thirty at St. Vincent's Park it is," said Ballack. "See you then." And then with a motion as clipped and sharp as his tone, he turned his wheelchair around quickly and scooted down the hall towards Tori.

40

The advantage of a police investigation at the Drury on the weekend was the abject lack of businesses using the hotel for meetings. The detectives had their pick of spacious conference rooms to use as interrogation chambers. Before setting out to confront the monsignor, Ballack reached into a small tube-shaped duffel bag attached to the left arm of the wheelchair and pulled out a chewy granola bar. It was not the scrumptious breakfast he had yesterday morning when they conversed with Pat Fishwick, but it was better than going hungry. As he headed down the hall looking for Tori, his teeth draped themselves around and then plunged through the textured bites of satisfaction. He allowed the oats, granola, peanut butter and dark chocolate chunks to coalesce in his mouth before taking them down his throat with as firm a swallow as he could muster.

Speeding past a smaller, well-lit conference room on the east side of the building, Ballack caught a glimpse of Tori, seated with her back to the door and facing a visibly upset Peter Grenier. Ballack accelerated into the area and sidled up next to his partner.

"Monsignor Grenier, I have not yet met you, although you've obviously encountered the other members of my team. I am Cameron Ballack, the lead detective for the Special Investigative Division on this inquiry. I'm sorry our meeting comes under such tragic circumstances."

The final words seemed wooden and phony, dredged from a weak liturgy of platitudes. Yet Grenier's response didn't help Ballack's mood. It was bad enough he was dealing with a murder suspect, thought Ballack, but the monsignor's reply made him want to vomit.

"Thank you, Detective Ballack. This is a despicable tragedy. Father Joseph was a good man who gave his life over to the ministry of the Church. To murder someone like him was not only wicked, it was the lowest depths of cowardice."

Ballack exchanged glances with Tori. Either the monsignor was covering the late priest's sordid legacy on purpose, or the man was more ignorant than was humanly possible. Or perhaps he knew better and was playing the politically correct game, thankful Father Joseph's infamy had met its end. Ballack knew it couldn't be all three.

Tori had already gotten the basic details from Grenier: name, schooling, work. Although born in Quebec City, he had been in the United States for close to forty years and retained very little of his French accent. Ballack studied him closely, especially the slightly windblown white hair. Broad shouldered yet lean, he had eyes that were bright green. When he squinted, they seemed to turn bronze. The white hair and physical build reminded Ballack of one of his great-uncles, but that's where the comparisons ended.

"Monsignor," began Tori, "what was your relationship with Father Joseph like?"

Grenier look pensive, then said, "It was a good working relationship. We didn't have as much contact together as, say, Father Joseph did with the archbishop. That was mainly because of the way things worked, Father Joseph reported directly to His Excellency. We certainly never had an argument."

"Ever have a reason to?" asked Tori.

"No, absolutely not. Then again, we didn't have many opportunities. I should say that Father Joseph would bend over backward to help anyone. It was a remarkable characteristic for anyone, priest or not. He came here to help out a school in dire need. Santa Maria Academy. It will close, but not for lack of him trying."

"Did anyone in the archdiocese have issues with Father Joseph?"

"I would say not. We were happy with his work and felt he was a good addition to the team, so to speak. We would be happy to recommend him for any task and defend his ministry at any point."

Indeed you would, thought Ballack, and that's your big mistake as a church.

"Monsignor," said Tori, more gently than she felt, "you should know that ..."

"I'm sorry," interrupted Grenier. "But my friend and fellow pastor has been murdered. He had no time to receive the last rites of extreme unction to bless him before entering eternal life. No child of God should receive a savage death like this without the consecration of God. I would like to see him, please."

"I'm afraid that is not possible," said Ballack.

Grenier turned his glinted gaze toward him. "What is that supposed to mean?"

"Father Joseph was murdered last night and thus his body is evidence in an ongoing murder investigation. His corpse is off-limits and we will make sure that policy is respected. To give him last rites would compromise our inquiry."

"It is our tradition!"

259

"Then your tradition will have to take a rain check!" snapped Ballack, who managed to keep his voice somewhat low and even. For a second, he could have sworn he was back at St. Basil's, squaring off with the bishop over tainted Communion bread and wine after another death. He continued, "I realize you might want to do this for the sake of your tradition, but you would be negating our work so far, not to mention you'd be covering the tracks of the murderer!"

"Excuse me, detective?" exploded Grenier. "What are you trying to imply?"

"Trying, nothing. I came out and said it. But let's leave behind this traditional dance and try another tack. Where were you from ten o'clock last night until one o'clock this morning?"

"Again, what are you trying to imply?"

"Can't you answer the question directly, Monsignor? I hope your sermons aren't this circuitous," said a clearly irritated Ballack.

"I was at the rectory all night. After your detectives spoke with me, I went over to the hospital to see Mrs. Tinordi. She's the one who had the stroke Thursday afternoon and the reason why I was away when Toby Zweig was killed. Another terrible death. After the hospital, I went back to the rectory for a late dinner. Afterwards, I worked on my sermon for today's Mass and then I was in bed before ten-thirty after writing some emails. You are most welcome, by the way, to come to the rectory right now and check my computer to see if the time and date stamps on the emails prove what I'm saying is true. After I got done writing, I had a small glass of brandy and got in bed. I read for a bit but was asleep by eleven."

"And you're saying there's no way you were here last night" asked Tori, "and then attacked Father Joseph?"

"In God's name, how can you even ask that?" bawled the monsignor, crossing himself. "I told you I was in bed. Father Joseph was a friend! How can you possibly draw those conclusions?"

Tori scribbled something in her notebook, and her sideways look at her partner was imperceptible to Grenier. But Ballack intuitively got what her softened features were meant to communicate: *I don't think this is our guy.* Ballack was leaning in that direction as well, but first they needed to address the car situation. And to do that, they would need to return to the security office.

"Monsignor," he said, "what follows may seem strange at first, but just hang with me and it'll become clear why I ask. You've said you weren't here last night. I'm assuming you're not a sleepwalker or a sleep-driver …"

"You're right, detective," replied Grenier. "I am wondering where you're going with this."

Ballack smiled slightly and forced a chuckle, trying to put the cleric at ease. "Is there a chance someone else has access to your car?"

"My car?"

"The Lexus which I saw outside of Harvest Capital & Mortgage when we went to visit with Julian Webber. He said you had just been there for heaven knows what reason, and we must've just missed you. That is your car?"

"The Archdiocese of St. Louis was given that car for pastoral and business use. It was a gift from Jerome McPadden. As for usage, I tend to be the primary user of that car, but it's rare to do so. We have drivers who take us around in other vehicles."

Wow, thought Ballack sardonically, *the hazards of ministry. What an incredible personal sacrifice for the sake of the ministry.*

"And where was this car parked last night?" asked Tori.

"In the parking lot at the Cathedral. The side lot, between the Cathedral School and the church itself. Do you know where that is? The car is still there. Our driver brought me over here today in a Pontiac Bonneville, if you're interested."

"Yes," replied Ballack. "I know the west lot, considering it's the only place I can park when I go there. Monsignor, there's something you need to see. And then there is something else, relatively minor, that we'll require from you right afterward. Come with us, please."

The monsignor had no trouble keeping up with the pace of Ballack's wheelchair. Tori followed from the rear, anxious to see Grenier's reaction to the video. In no time, they were back in the security office. Bosco and Krieger had gone, said Vinson, to report to other separate cases. But he didn't mind queuing the parking garage tape in question.

The group watched the tape twice. Grenier looked aghast. Ballack turned to him and asked, "Is that your car?"

"That's the one, Detective, but the person getting out isn't me."

"I know the video is in black and white, but that is light colored hair under that hat, though. You sure?"

"I told you where I was."

"Can others confirm that?"

Grenier looked glum. "Father Behringer lives in a room in the rectory, but to be honest, neither he nor I saw each other after five o'clock yesterday."

"So there is no one who can verify your movements from last night?"

"Other than my computer emails, no. Not after I saw Mrs. Tinordi at Barnes."

Ballack looked thoughtful. There was one way to clinch this. "All right, Monsignor. Follow me. Mr. Vinson, thanks for your patience with us this long morning."

"No problem," said the security officer. "It never gets this exciting around here. I should be thanking you." It was a comment that brought a frown to the detectives' faces. It had been an unnecessary and insensitive statement. But rather than letting Vinson have it, Ballack decided to get out of the room.

Ballack signaled Tori to come alongside him as they swept out into the hallway. "Get him next to the elevator, the center one. You remember the spot where you and Missy measured? This is the moment of truth."

The three of them stopped at the elevator in the middle. Grenier looked genuinely puzzled, as if he was in some labyrinthian complex. Ballack motioned toward the elevator doors. At just past midday, there were few people milling around except for Cubs fans from out of town for the game which was due to start in forty minutes.

"Monsignor, if you could be so kind as to stand next to the right frame of the elevator. Just relax. Stand as you normally would.

Now you see someone is coming down. When the doors open, walk into the car and then exit in one fell swoop. Do you understand?"

"I understand, Detective." The monsignor managed a slight smile. "I'm completely confused as to your reasons, but I understand your instructions."

The doors opened and a family of six, bedecked in the blue colors with white and red trim, came out, shouting "Go Cubs!"

"You were eliminated from the postseason in August, people. At least we still have a shot at the playoffs," muttered Grenier with a grin. Ballack smiled back and motioned him to step in and out. The monsignor did so.

Ballack look at Tori and nodded. He said, "Thank you, Monsignor. That helps a lot, even though I think we should refrain from mentioning why. One more cluster of questions, though. Did you take the Lexus over to Barnes to visit Mrs. Tinordi?"

"I did. Our regular driver was ill, so rather than contact the other one, I just took the Lexus myself."

"Thank you. And you specifically remember parking the Lexus in the west lot last night before you returned to the rectory?"

"There is no doubt about that. I parked there, yes."

"This may be a stretch, but I'll ask. Did you happen to check the odometer last night before you turned off the car?"

Grenier seemed apologetic. "No, I didn't. It's not my habit to do so. I'm sorry. I know that could be somewhat helpful in determining if it was actually used, but I can't help you there."

"Just so you're honest," said Tori. "I don't suppose you have security cameras for the outside of the Cathedral, do you?"

"I can't help you there, either," replied the monsignor.

"Well, then I believe this is all we need for the moment. Here's my card, Monsignor. If you remember anything else, no matter how unusual, I'd appreciate you calling me immediately."

"You have my word on it."

"Good," said Ballack. "And one more thing. I would like you, to the best of your ability, to ensure that no one uses that Lexus today until we've had a chance to examine it. I'm going to call our forensics chief and have her come to the Cathedral. I would be very pleased if you could meet her there in the lot and allow her to open up the car and check it out from top to bottom. If the killer used this car, then perhaps there is a trace or clue left behind."

"Again, you have my word I'll make it so."

As the monsignor stepped aside, Ballack looked at Tori, who said, "At least four inches' difference. Not our guy."

Ballack looked past his partner and saw Hull and Crabolli coming out of the other conference room with an obviously upset Pat Fishwick. The 10:21 director headed in the direction of the bathroom while the detectives came over to Ballack.

"Next stop?" Hull asked.

Ballack nodded. "You guys know Monsignor Grenier. He is headed back to the Cathedral and I would like you two to join him there in the west lot."

He signaled them to draw closer and he lowered his voice. "And here's why …"

41

Ballack suctioned himself as Tori stopped at a McDonald's in the Central West End. He placed the Neo-sucker plastic catheter back in its sheath and waited for his partner to return to the van with their lunch. On the way over, he had called Sheila Grimshaw with the news she was needed at the Cathedral to comb through a Lexus, and that Hull and Crabolli would be making sure Grenier didn't interfere ahead of time. Ballack checked the time on his cell phone and saw they were running late on their dash to St. Vincent's Park. The pre-game traffic around the stadium hadn't helped their rate of speed. He thought of calling Ashleigh Collins to let her know they'd be tardy, but then he thought better of it. Why apologize for eating one's first meal of the day? It wasn't as if they'd miss the whole game.

Tori returned with her chicken wrap and a large Coke. Making a face, she tossed a large bag in Ballack's lap. "You knuckle-dragger. It was embarrassing walking in there solo and ordering this much food. You owe me a lot for my loss of public dignity."

"I guess saying thank you is a start," said Ballack. "You know how to get there by darting up through Normandy? Let's do it then."

In the next ten minutes, Ballack proceeded to demolish a Filet-o-Fish sandwich, an order of large fries, a large iced tea and two apple pies. His hunger conclusively banished, he leaned back and closed his eyes while he could spare a few fleeting moments. He might have fallen asleep if Tori had not chosen to suspend his blissful respite.

"So what did Zane say about Fishwick?"

Ballack swore under his breath. Getting on to the next phase of the investigation had so dominated everyone's thoughts that the four detectives hadn't compared notes on their morning interrogations. He once more pulled out his cell phone and dialed Hull's number for what seemed like the thousandth time in the past two days.

"Don't kick yourself, Cam," said Tori kindly. "I forgot, too." Ballack ignored her comfort.

"C.B. calling in," Hull answered in a deliberately gravelly voice.

"You sound like you smoked eight packs of cigarettes," Ballack said. "Forgot to ask you how things went with Fishwick."

"He had his alibi ready, that's for sure. He gave the names of several people involved in the upcoming case against Father Joseph. Said he was having dinner with them last night at the Dubliner, so he didn't go far. Just a few blocks west of the Dome on Washington. Then he was invited to the home of one of the alleged victims for a dessert reception with several others in the same lawsuit. He claimed he wasn't dropped off at the Drury until two in the morning."

"Seems to have his tracks covered again."

"It's spooky how he does this. We asked for the names of those he was with, especially the guy who drove him back to the hotel. He wrote out the list quickly and gave it to us, so he either ripped stuff off the top of his head or he's got an incredibly razor-sharp memory. Also, Missy had him stand next to the elevator. She said it looked like he was an inch or two taller than what Henry appeared to be on film, but it was hard to say."

"Be sure you mention to her that I'm impressed she remembered that. Tell you what, Zane. Lance Stubblefield was Fishwick's lawyer in the recent case against Harvest and the

267

Archdiocese. I'll text you his number. He might be able to confirm if those names are among the ones in what would have been the upcoming suit. It might still go through. Not like Father Joseph's death can prevent the Archdiocese getting sued."

"Will do. If these check out, it looks like Fishwick's clean."

"I think he was anyway. His Thursday alibi checked out, and these murders seem committed by the same pair of hands."

"Yeah, what similarities were there about today? We've been going full speed and haven't had many moments to discuss the finds."

"Sorry. I should have slowed things down and at least brought you up to speed. A note, this time a quote from St. Bonaventure. Plus, a crucifix with Jesus intact and the cross broken. Just like Zweig. The rope was short and failed to break Father Joseph's neck. He likely suffered pretty badly."

"A stabbing and a hanging. Someone's got a serious axe to grind. Okay, we're here at the Cathedral. Grimshaw's already here, so Grenier can't wax down the car if he wanted to. We'll call you when we're done here, but it might take a bit."

"No problem. We've got to meet with McPadden's daughter who is maintaining her dad's innocence. If you get a chance, try to find Father Behringer and see if he can confirm that the esteemed monsignor never left the spiritual compound last night."

"Got it. Anything else?"

"Nope, except Grenier's too short to be Henry. Call me when you're done."

St. Vincent Park sits on the north side of St. Charles Rock Road in the small community of Greendale. Valhalla, St. Peter's and Bethany Cemeteries are all within walking distance. A bit further east, stingy shoppers can happen upon the Normandy flea market to find a bevy of cheap clothes, jewelry, shoes and pirated movies among the daily wares. The Gaelic Athletic Club of St. Louis runs their sports leagues at the park, with hurling teams taking the field during the spring. In the fall, the pitch transforms into the home of a six-team Gaelic football league for a ten-game season, plus a championship game just before Thanksgiving. Tori guided the Sprinter into a handicapped parking spot not far from the cheering crowd.

It didn't take them long to locate Ashleigh Collins. She had deliberately stayed close to the edge of the lot while still having a decent sightline of the football pitch. Ballack had kept the word of his disability a secret from her, and so she nearly jumped out of her shoes when he drew alongside her and said, "Ashleigh, you're taller than I expected for the daughter of a murder suspect."

He flashed both his St. Charles and SID identification. When her heart dropped back from her throat and her breathing returned to normal, she said, "You could at least have described what you look like. It could have saved me the spike in my pulse."

"I prefer the joy of seeing the shock on the faces of those I meet," Ballack replied. "This is my partner, Tori Vaughan. I've briefed her on what's going on."

Tori shook hands with Ashleigh, whom Ballack judged to be about thirty years old. Her silky blond hair was tied in a neat ponytail and threaded through her baseball cap. She had completed her green-shirt-and-cargo-shorts ensemble with open-toed sandals on her feet and a four-leaf clover painted on each cheek.

"Hopefully, I can introduce you to the rest of the family," Ashleigh said. "My boys are around here somewhere. Stephen—that's my husband—is in the game now. Just kicked off. He's the one over there. Number twenty-four. White jersey with the red cross on the front."

"Okay, Mrs. Collins, before we get into what your dad is doing or not doing, who's playing who?"

"Have you ever seen Gaelic football before?"

"I'd be surprised if he hasn't," said Tori. "He probably knows who the Irish champions would be."

"It was Dublin beating Kerry. Championship game was last weekend," said Ballack as Tori threw up her hands in vexation. "Don't get so huffy, Tor. I looked it up online on the way over. Settle down!"

"I'll bet less than half this crowd knows that fact," said Ashleigh. "Stephen plays for Tower Pub McBride and they're playing against Tigin Pub Kerry Patch. As you watch the action, you can sort of pick up on the rules. The best way to describe it to most people is that it's kind of part rugby, part soccer and all mayhem. Three points for getting the ball in the lower goal, one point for kicking it above the crossbar. You pass that round ball by kicking it or punching it with a closed fist."

"Seems like they're doing a bit of that," remarked Tori. "Why can't they just run with it?"

"Rules against it," said Ashleigh. "They can't go more than three steps without releasing, bouncing or kicking the ball up to themselves. Watch this guy." And as if on cue, a Tower Pub player took off with the ball at full speed, and in fluid motions he would drop the ball in full flight and toe it gently back up into his hands, never breaking stride.

Easily distracted and quite impressed, Ballack watched the game for several minutes while Tori asked Ashleigh about some rudimentary matters, and Ashleigh spoke at length about her childhood, schooling, and present family and location. She had lived in Ladue for most of her life, graduating from John Burroughs before earning her degree in creative writing at Truman State. She managed to do some freelance work here and there, but Stephen made more than enough money as a regional executive at Milton Transport Solutions, a company based out of Indianapolis. As a result, Ballack divined, she could focus on the soccer mom scene in Lake St. Louis, grooming their two sons for future achievements at St. Dominic High School or, if they dared the commute, Christian Brothers College High School. Always the school, the big deal was always which school, he sighed. Oh well, there could be worse idolatries.

After she finished her biographical blitz, Ballack decided he'd enjoyed enough of the game, in which Tower Pub McBride held a slight lead. He spun around and took the verbal baton from Tori.

"Ashleigh, I'll be direct. Where has your dad been?"

Her eyes dropped, clouds rolling in behind her pupils. "He's innocent."

Ballack looked back at the game in time to see one player slammed to the ground and scream in pain, his elbow bent at an unnatural angle. Turning back, he said, "That's no answer. I'm going

271

to assume you will maintain his innocence, so to prevent broken record mode, just stick to my question. Where has your dad been?"

"He was due back in town yesterday evening. He called and said he wouldn't be back until about three o'clock today."

"From where?" asked Tori.

Ashleigh stared straight ahead, her jaw tight.

"Mrs. Collins," said Ballack with the hint of a growl, "as much as I can appreciate the affection of a daughter for her father, this is a murder investigation. What possible reason do you have for delaying your answer? I'm going to start believing the scenario marked 'guilty' if you can't be honest."

She blinked, her eyes growing moist. "He called from Dallas. His flight is coming in today on American Airlines. I forget the flight number."

"And the reason he was in Dallas?"

"I want assurances that he won't get in trouble for this."

"For what? Was he selling cocaine to the Dallas Cowboy cheerleaders? Raiding a hedge fund? Making a massive donation to Rick Perry's presidential campaign?"

"I said I want assurances."

Ballack sensed an impasse and wanted to forge a compromise so that they could either pursue or eliminate McPadden as a suspect. "If it's a minor violation, I can overlook it unless it impinges on our case. Anything worse, I can't make any promises."

Caught between a rock and a hard place, Ashleigh Collins relented. "He was visiting his son from a previous marriage. The marriage had ended badly. He had been less than faithful to his first

272

wife when he was on his tour of duty in Vietnam. They had married out of high school and it was a mess regardless of what he did over there. But Terry was their honeymoon surprise before he went over there. Anyhow, when he found out she had remarried later, he got drunk and assaulted her. No judge has relented on the original restraining order which stated he couldn't be within five hundred feet of either her, the husband or Terry. From the perspective of many, he gave up on trying to overturn it. But he and Terry somehow reconnected. He hasn't been clear how. Every so often, he flies to Dallas for an overnight trip and manages to see Terry. About twice a year, but it's something. It's also an utter violation of the order, and he'd get in real trouble if it came to light."

She wiped her eyes. Clearly, sharing the secret revealed the weight upon her heart. "I'm the only one he's ever told. Mom found out on her own. He always tells the office that it's a family emergency or that he needs to go to his uncle's place in Texas for some real estate matters that are important to the family. The reasons alternate and he tells us which one he's using before he goes."

"What was the family emergency this time?" asked Ballack.

"Niece having brain surgery."

"I'm surprised that everyone can keep these lies straight."

Ashleigh shrugged. Her eyes were on the football pitch, but she clearly hadn't been following the game.

Ballack looked at Tori, who pulled out her phone and jumped on the Web, looking for flight details on American Airlines flights from Dallas to St. Louis. He turned back to the anxiety-riddled Mrs. Collins.

"Ashleigh, I'm trying to put this all together and what I come up with is irony on steroids. You're trying to convince me that it's true your father is innocent because he's providing a lie to cover how he's guilty of something else." He chuckled. "It's really quite an exquisite web if you think about it."

She said nothing. In that second, he moved from delicious irony to controlled rage. He moved in front of her and turned his wheels hard around, looking up at her. And then he flared.

"If you're lying to me, Mrs. Collins, I hope you know what obstruction of justice looks like in the court system. What I told you was that Toby Zweig's murder Thursday night hasn't been the only death. Now you'd better cooperate fully and you'd better pray everything you've said is the truth and nothing but."

She looked at him, a single tear sliding off her chin. "Anything else?"

He saw Tori signal him to start moving toward the van. "Yeah. Here's my card. We're probably too late to catch him, but if you call his cell, find out where he's headed. And don't mention that I've spoken to you. I'm sure he knows by now that we've been throwing a net over everyone associated with the conspiracy case against Harvest. Just don't even breathe a word that we're coming to see him. Don't even let him know we've spoken to you. Call me and let me know where he's going. If you say to anything to him beyond that, I'll be able to tell once I see him."

At that point, Ballack's phone buzzed, giving evidence of a new text message. It was from Tori, waiting impatiently at the Sprinter. *Flight has landed. McPadden on the move.*

"What is it?" Ashleigh Collins asked. She had gained back some of her control.

Ballack looked up at her. "Okay, your dad has come in, Ashleigh. Change of plans. I'm parking myself here until you get hold of him on his cell. Just tell me his destination. And again, don't give away a syllable to him that we're on our way."

42

"I'll call the others and find out where Grimshaw is on the Lexus," Ballack gasped, reaching for the portable suction pump between them in the van. A nasty coughing fit, however, prevented him from accessing it, and so Tori nimbly hooked up the Neo-sucker to the tubing before turning on the motor. Once Ballack cleared his airway, she turned the key in the ignition and eased the van out of the lot.

"We're at least ten minutes away from the airport. I'm assuming his head start being what it is, we'll be playing catch up," she said. "But the most direct route he can take will be 70 to 270 to 40. A white Audi A8, right? And you are certain this address is the place he's headed?"

"I didn't tap her phone, if that's what you're asking, but no," responded Ballack, whose watery eyes hadn't cleared after he'd nearly hacked up his windpipe. "They'll need to spread out if they want to win."

Tori was lost. "What? What are you talking about?"

"Tower Pub McBride. The team Ashleigh Collins' husband plays for. During those first few minutes, they had a couple chances, but their ballhandler didn't notice his teammate streaking down the sideline just to the right of him."

Tori didn't know whether to scream or laugh. Here they were chasing potential murder suspects into the wind for the past two days, and he was fixated on blown opportunities in a Gaelic football game. Sometimes she felt her partner moved seamlessly back and forth amongst several worlds and only he truly understood the logic behind the transitions.

Ballack looked out the window. "Either that guy has horrible peripheral vision or he's a selfish player." Then after a moment's reflection he shifted gears. "Right. I was going to call about the Lexus."

But there was nothing yet to report. Hull said that Grimshaw was taking her time dusting the interior. Nothing had come up for fingerprints. The driver's seat had been swept clean and was bereft of hairs or fibers of any kind. Whoever had used the vehicle, Grimshaw had remarked, must have known they'd be tearing it apart the next day for any shreds of evidence.

"Sorry, C.B.," said Hull. "We might find something yet. Stay tuned."

Ballack didn't believe him. He knew somebody's alibi had to be a lie. There was one explanation that wasn't completely airtight. As of now, the most likely reason was that Henry had asked others to lie on his behalf.

Tori's question shocked him, as if she had been reading his thoughts. "You think Fishwick had everyone play along so he could do all this?"

Ballack scrunched his hands as firmly as his muscles would allow, turned his knuckles toward his face, and began massaging his forehead with them. "The advantage of having Fishwick as Henry is that he fits the Occam's Razor guidelines on many fronts. Let's go through those."

"He knew where Zweig was going to be Thursday afternoon," said Tori.

"He's staying in the same location as Father Joseph," replied Ballack. "So there's accessibility to both victims. Doesn't prove it, but it's something to take into account."

"Where we're weak is motive. Maybe he was angry with Zweig and furious with Father Joseph. I don't know if that was at the level for murder."

"Quotes on paper at both scenes. I can understand the first one on Zweig about protecting the innocent, it being a court case and all, plus the upcoming sex abuse trial," Ballack mused. He stopped rubbing his forehead. "What baffles me is that Bonaventure quote in Father Joseph's pants. I've been turning it over in my head all day, and it still doesn't make sense. *'The human mind, distracted by cares, does not enter into itself through memory; clouded by sense images, it does not turn back to itself through intelligence; allured away by concupiscence, it does not turn back to itself through desire for inner sweetness and spiritual joy.'* It's a critique of humanity's failure to redirect their desires back to God. Yeah, Henry is applying that to Father Joseph. For crying out loud, even from last night's talk, we know enough about that priest to say amen to Henry's quote. But why? There's an edge, an anger specifically applied to Father Joseph. He's failed Henry at some point, in some way."

"I thought you said you weren't a profiler, Cameron."

"Just thinking out loud. What else?"

"The one possible motive that comes up with me is Fishwick's dead son Phil and this person Philippe who committed suicide in Lake Zurich under the Father Joseph regime. That's a possible connection."

"Remember the fallacy of modality, Tor," rejoined Ballack, who had thoroughly enjoyed his logic and philosophy classes in college. "Because something is possible doesn't mean it's true, or even that there's abundant proof."

In a few minutes, they were far west of the city, coming up on and then past Boone's Crossing. Tori sped the van into the right hand lane with Exit 16 in her sights. Ballack dialed Dana's number and waited for her to pick up. They had just gone through the intersection of Long Road and Chesterfield Airport Road when Ballack heard a weary "Hello?"

"It's me," he said, "bustling about chasing down hardened criminals. I didn't wake you up, did I?"

"I took a nap after my support group this morning," Dana replied. "Still shaking off the cobwebs. What's up?"

"No end in sight. We're going to have to push this until next week. You know the first seventy-two hours are the most critical."

"It'd be nice if you could solve this within a three-day span."

"Not likely. And plus I'll be so zonked from this it might take me a while to recover. At least this gives you a chance to finish your lesson plans for next week."

"You should stop in sometime. Next week it's a seminar discussion on *The Children of Men.* Right up your alley."

Ballack smiled. Her understanding of what made him tick always warmed his spirit. "The way things are going now, that's a big if. Support group went okay?"

She hesitated. "For the most part. Some drama from others, some legitimate grief and me trying to figure out if I belong. I'll tell you about it later. I need to get moving. Call me tonight when you get home."

"Why's that?" Ballack asked, although he knew well enough.

"I just like to know you got through your day in one piece, Cameron. I mean it. Call me."

"I will, Dana. Bye."

Tori continued south on Long Road and before long the detectives saw the stoplight for Kehrs Mill Road. Tori gunned the van forward, screeching through the intersection in a sharp left hand turn, barely beating the yellow light.

"What's the problem?" Ballack barked. "You afraid we'll get to the house and McPadden won't be there?"

"I'm taking no chances," she replied, checking the fuel level and—evidently satisfied—continuing on, making another left and heading east on Wild Horse Creek Road. "Now this is where he was headed? Ashleigh Collins was absolutely sure?"

"As sure as she could be. One way or another, we're getting answers. Eliminate or validate, as our boss would say. Slow down. Here's the turn to the right."

Tori ably swung the van southward into a neighborhood of newer homes belonging to the upper middle class. Stealing a look at the index card upon which the address and directions were written, she peered ahead to their endpoint. Creeping closer, they stared into the driveway area.

"Got to hand it to Ashleigh Collins," said Ballack. "She wasn't deceiving us."

There in the driveway was Jerome McPadden's Audi A8, still warm from its long drive from the airport. And in the open garage, next to a functional tan Toyota Avalon, sat the black BMW M3 coupe of Julian Webber.

43

The surprise on the face of Julian Webber dissipated almost as soon as it appeared. Yes, Jerome McPadden had just arrived, but the two of them were having a private business chat. Webber stood in the doorway wearing khaki shorts, a navy polo, Docksiders and a painter's cap.

"We're not here on business and have no interest in refinancing anything," Ballack intoned firmly. "This is part of the murder investigation of Toby Zweig and—as of six hours ago—Father Joseph Quinn."

"I'm well aware of Father Joseph's death," replied Webber just as strongly. "I doubt if you understand how we feel like we are under attack. With our attorney dead, as well as a member of the Archdiocese, we're incredibly frightened as to who could be next."

"What's not frightening is the height of these steps out front, Mr. Webber. They certainly hug the ground enough so that my portable ramp can provide easy access to your domicile. We need to speak with Mr. McPadden, and we need to do so now. As he's allegedly come back into town, we need to speak with him."

"And why's that?" Jerome McPadden said as he appeared in the foyer.

"Because we had a nice chat with your lovely daughter, sir. It would help if you come clean about a few things."

McPadden glared at Ballack but, knowing he had little choice, drew near to Webber. "Julian, I know it's your house and I'm just a guest. But it would really help if you let them in."

Webber looked at his friend, down into his glass of ginger ale, and then said, "Seems like the votes are in your favor, Detective. I assume you'll have no problem laying down your portable ramp to enter?"

The fan was running at medium speed from the high ceiling of the living room. Webber offered drinks for both detectives, but they refused. Ballack in particular felt he ate and drank too much and too quickly at McDonald's. Webber sat on his sofa, McPadden took a leather armchair, and Tori selected the matching recliner on the other side. Ballack rolled into the middle of the room and faced McPadden.

"How was the flight?" he asked.

"I don't see how a flight is relevant to your investigation," said McPadden, "but it was as pleasant as airline travel can get."

"And the reason you were out of town? Again …" Ballack trailed off, feigning interest in his notes but remembering the secretary's statement from the day before. "Family emergency? That's the reason we were given when we stopped by Harvest to speak yesterday."

"If they gave that as the reason, I can't very well prevent them from their statement."

"Is that an affirmation or denial of that being accurate?"

"What?"

"Their statement."

McPadden gave his most menacing look possible. "You said you spoke with my daughter. What's your take?"

283

"That's interesting. We're usually the ones who ask the questions. What if I told you what she said in full?"

McPadden went from menacing to slightly more thoughtful. He waited a few seconds and then turned to Webber. "Julian, again I hate to ask this of you, but can I speak to these folks in private?"

Webber looked aghast. "Last time I checked my name was on the deed of this house, and yet I'm being asked to take myself out so these guys can set up an interrogation chamber?"

"Julian ..."

"I don't have a problem with it in principle. You need to be interrogated. The rest of us have had our backs to the wall for you. I just expected more tact in my house."

"Then I'm not asking you as a friend. I'm urging you as a colleague and your boss. Does that help?"

Webber stood up, hands on hips, and relented. "If that's the way these guys get you to sing their tune, I can't stop you. I hope you know what you're doing. If either of you detectives needs to see me, I'll be in the back room." And he walked away.

Ballack looked at McPadden. "Was that necessarily a wise thing to do?"

"You needed to speak to me, and you mentioned my daughter," McPadden said in a hushed voice. "Julian doesn't need to know about the details. Only three people in my life know about these trips, or at least *knew* about them until today. My son, my wife and my daughter—that's all. And while I would have preferred it remain just those three, I guess Ashleigh must have freaked out and figured I needed rock-solid evidence that I was nowhere around at the time of the murder."

"How long have you known about Father Joseph's death?"

"Julian called me about it this morning on my cell, after he was made aware. He's ..." He dropped his voice even lower, where both detectives had to strain to hear him. "He's still under the impression I was in Dallas to see my niece."

Tori spoke for the first time. "We got that detail, too. Something about brain surgery. Did you have a hospital in mind?"

"Methodist Medical Center."

"Covered your tracks pretty well unless someone in the office decides to call and send flowers. Do you even have a niece?"

"Let's not even go there. The point is I have a son and that's the reason I go. He's the reason I was gone Thursday evening until this afternoon. My boarding passes are in my briefcase in the car if you want to see them."

"We'll be wanting to," said Ballack. "Is this son the only one you have?"

"What are you implying by that?" snapped McPadden.

"Just a question. Sorry if that struck an infidelity nerve."

"Were you and Mr. Webber meeting today to discuss the blowback of the Father Joseph murder?" asked Tori.

"I was concerned about this, especially given the fact that our company and the Archdiocese of St. Louis were the co-defendants in the recent conspiracy trial. Our attorney has been murdered. A priest whom that attorney was to defend at a future date has now been murdered. So excuse us if we feel a little threatened right now!"

"What were your feelings toward either one?"

"What do my feelings ..."

"Save it," Ballack interrupted. "Long experience, my friend. Just answer the question."

"Toby Zweig was our attorney. He did excellent work for the Archdiocese and reasonably successful work for us. There were some items I felt were out of his league, but then isn't that the case for us all? Father Joseph was a relatively new addition to the Archdiocese and I know less about him. But any death is hard, even if it's a mere acquaintance of yours."

"You were wanting to keep Toby Zweig on for future cases involving Harvest?"

McPadden once again grew wary. "Future cases have nothing to do with it. Toby worked on stuff assigned by the Archdiocese." He looked pleadingly at Tori, trying to gain some leverage. "Why is he asking this?"

"Possibly because of the way you answered that question," she said. "Calling his work 'reasonably successful.' Hardly a ringing endorsement."

"Plus it would go hand-in-hand with what everyone else has told us," Ballack added with a smile.

"Who's been telling you that?" hissed McPadden.

"Is that an admittance?"

McPadden opened his mouth to say something, then thought better of it.

"Tell you what," said Ballack. "Just answer me this: First, at what time Thursday did your flight leave?"

"Six-fifteen in the evening. American Airlines flight 2211. Got to Dallas at five minutes after eight."

Ballack thought fast. Given that McPadden was liable to pack light, he wouldn't need a check-in. He could have been at the Cathedral when Zweig went down. That wouldn't help with the second murder, though, and Ballack was convinced one person had committed both.

As if inside Ballack's head, McPadden said, "You could always request the manifest from my return flight to confirm if I was on it."

Ballack ignored that challenge, not wanting a suspect to have any control on the investigation's steering wheel. He said, "Mr. McPadden, one final question. You realize that running out of town casts some doubt on your innocence. Significant doubt. I realize that you wanted to be circumspect about your son, but why the secrecy? I'm just curious."

"Because I've lived long enough out of my son's life that I didn't want to risk having anyone else know. Being a father is a difficult enough job and I've come to realize that. I've accepted that based on my own experience. I've also seen the wisdom of redeeming the time because of what others have gone through, friends and enemies. Julian's son has gone on his own path and Julian hasn't heard from him at all, nor does he contact his boy."

"I didn't know he had a son."

"Maybe you didn't ask enough questions, Detective."

"Watch yourself, Mr. McPadden, before you continue."

"My apologies. Moving on, speaking of children, as much as I can't stand Pat Fishwick, I know enough of his story to know he lost a son, although I've never gotten the details straight as to how. We were on opposing sides in the trial and I think he's an overbearing, obnoxious whistleblower, but I don't believe for one second that he deserved that tragedy in his life. No one does."

Ballack held up his hand to stop the head of Harvest Capital & Mortgage right there. "Thank you, Mr. McPadden. We'll check on some other matters connected with what you've shared, but for now we're done."

McPadden relaxed noticeably and rose from his chair. Tori was confused but rose as well. McPadden then said, "I guess I should stop acting like the host and see if Julian would like to see you to the door. One second, Detective."

"Not so fast," Ballack replied crisply. "I said we're done, meaning you and us. But now I'd like to speak with Mr. Webber."

44

The normally unflappable Julian Webber gave a start when Ballack entered the doorway in the studio at the rear of the house. He had been sitting on a stool looking at a recent copy of *Field and Stream.* He had added a well-used painter's apron to his clothing ensemble. A rather large artist easel stood in the corner with a watercolor painting mounted on it. On closer inspection, it was a landscape depiction of an equestrian outing in a pastoral locale. The colors were vivid without being grandiose, the background tones subtle yet not sacrificing detail.

Webber followed Ballack's gaze. "My latest project," he said. "It's due to a highly inspiring moment I spent out at Babler State Park, just down the road a few miles. It almost seems like a fox hunt from the sheer numbers, but truth is they have a six-mile equestrian trail and the folks were out in droves that day." He held up his fingers, which were tinged with black, and nodded back at the painting. "From the border and the trim on their red coats. Being intricate can get messy at times."

Ballack nodded, not wanting to get sidetracked. "Mr. Webber, we've finished with Jerome, but as it turns out we have a few additional questions for you. Do you mind joining us in the living room? I'm sure that would be more space for you."

"If it doesn't take too long," said Webber getting to his feet.

Ballack followed him back into the center of the house. Tori had just put her glass back on the island in the kitchen and was returning to her recliner. McPadden was on the sofa. Webber chose to stand.

He said, "Well, is anyone go to say what this is about?"

Ballack decided to plunge on. "When we spoke yesterday, you mentioned your family network. Your wife Tracy and your daughter Margaret. Interestingly enough, I don't see any pictures of family members around this place. Is there a reason for this?"

Webber seemed confused by this line of questioning. "This is what you're asking about when a murderer is loose?"

"Answer the question, please, Mr. Webber. Just play along and assume there's a reason for this."

Webber breathed in slowly as McPadden got up off the sofa, heading into the kitchen. Ballack decided that Webber's hair had to be the strangest mix of fibers he'd ever seen. It was mostly coarse black, and Ballack could have sworn there had been salt-and-pepper streaks in the back from their meeting the day before. My mistake, thought Ballack, remembering the Harvest office had been dimly lit. The living room's effulgence was positively dazzling, given the abundance of natural light from the many windows and skylights. Webber sat down slowly and looked warily at Ballack. Clearly, the question about the family had chipped away a portion of his confident exterior.

"The reason for my reaction was for relevance, Detective, and also because questions about my family are somewhat unnerving anyway. When you asked yesterday, I resolved to give you the bare facts. Tracy and I are married, technically, but years of my work here and her work on the evening shift at Channel 2 mean that we see little of each other. We separated eight months ago. She moved out. This home is one of the issues in an impending divorce. I'd likely sell it if we split up. That's why the minimal decorations, including the lack of framed photographs. It isn't due to any hatred of my loved ones."

"You didn't tell us about a potential divorce when we spoke to you yesterday."

"Because it wasn't relevant to your case, Detective."

"Mr. Webber, I decide on those merits. You told us about your daughter in Wisconsin, that you never see her, and it's hard. You told us about your friend, Chuck Wilbur, and that you played golf with him during the time when Zweig was murdered. Speaking of which …" Ballack pulled out his cell phone and dialed Wilbur's number.

"Julian?" called McPadden from the kitchen. "Is there a leak in the gas stove? Started going on and off, hiss, hiss, more like a hum."

"I had it checked three months back. You must be hearing things," Webber called back. "The refrigerator hums and hisses when it's making more ice." He turned to the detectives. "He'll tell you himself that he hears things that aren't there. He'll even come back here and say how he's being paranoid again."

"Anything?" asked Tori to Ballack. He shook his head. Failure to reach one Chuck Wilbur dimmed his patience. He faced Webber again.

"Then perhaps you can clear something up for us, Mr. Webber," Ballack said slowly. "Aside from your wife and daughter, and any grandkids, my question is why don't you have any of your son up anywhere?"

"Son?"

"Mr. Webber," said Tori, "We have a strict no-BS rule. We suggest you tell the truth."

"And how would you know if something like that is true?"

"Well," said Ballack, "you obviously don't have good ears, because your friend let it slip to us. Now you'd better own up to it."

Jerome McPadden had stepped into the room when Ballack spoke those words. Julian Webber looked at his colleague blankly. McPadden stood still, paralyzed by the discomfort of the moment.

Tori jumped in, not wanting Webber to get off the hook. "It's obviously somewhat public knowledge. You felt like you had to tell your friend. It should be no problem for us to know."

"No, Ms. Vaughan. I had to tell my friend. My friend didn't have to tell you," said Webber. "And again, I'd like to know what the point of this is, because it sure isn't relevant to your inquiry."

"Did you murder Toby Zweig?" asked Ballack.

"No," replied Webber. "I've been very clear about …"

"Did you murder Father Joseph?"

"Officer Ballack, if you want an answer, perhaps you'd let me finish my sentence. I've been very clear that I was playing golf with Chuck Wilbur at the time of Toby Zweig's death."

"Did you murder Father Joseph?"

"Refer to my answer for Toby Zweig."

"Do you know who killed them?"

"No."

"Then you are in no position to decide what is relevant and what is not. I am, so leave those matters to me. Now, where were you between ten o'clock last night and two o'clock this morning?"

"Here, at this house. In this room. Reading a book, a novel. Anne Rice's *Of Love and Evil*."

"So no one can vouch for your movements last night?"

"I can. Because there were no movements. I sat in that chair where Officer Vaughan is and stared at the book for ninety minutes. I went to bed around eleven-fifteen. I'm sorry to disappoint you, Detective."

Ballack smirked. "Let's talk about your son, Mr. Webber."

"Is this necessary?" pleaded McPadden. "This has caused Julian a good deal of pain and I'm sure revisiting it won't help him or you!"

"And why don't you let us draw that conclusion, if it comes to that?" rejoined Ballack. He turned back to Webber. "Well?"

Webber took a sip of his drink and began. "Jacob was a good kid. Jerome remembers him somewhat. Graduated from DeSmet a few years back. Accepted into Mizzou. Very promising in what he was interested, and that's what led to him leaving. He was into drama and acting. I leaned toward wanting him to go into business or IT or engineering. Something that would pay the bills and free him up for the times he wanted to dedicate himself to those other things. Jacob didn't want to listen, and so things culminated in an argument soon after graduation. He packed his things and left for New York City, to take a stab at acting, making it into any play or production possible. The parting, shall we say, was less than amicable. That was when Tracy and I started having problems and Margaret refused to speak with me anymore. They circled the wagons and defended Jacob, which on several levels they were completely right to do. He and I have drifted apart so much that we never have any contact anymore."

"Does he ever communicate with your wife or daughter?"

293

"It's hard to say. I certainly have no idea, but then again, I never ask. In truth, I am my father writ smaller. If I'm guilty of anything, it's that."

"What do you mean?"

"I grew up in Kirkwood. Dad spent a lot of time outside the home. Law practice. He never did anything immoral or cruel, but the warm fuzzies were never there. Mom was the one who practically raised my older brother Timmy and myself. Tim was eight years older than me. He doesn't live around here anymore. Tim's in Boise, Idaho now and is the lead accountant for a petroleum engineering conglomerate. He has five kids—proof of good Catholic roots running deep—and he sees his wife and kids every night. The antithesis of our father. He probably knows his son Robbie's soccer stats backward and forward.

"You went to Kirkwood High?" asked Tori.

"We both did, excelling in different ways. Timmy was baseball captain, while I played basketball and tennis. He went off to SLU, while I attended Southeast. I told you the rest of the story yesterday."

The room was silent, as if everyone assembled was awaiting a postscript to the tale. Finally, Ballack said, "And this is something you couldn't have shared yesterday when we met? How much damage would that cause?"

Webber replied, "It's not a matter of damage to the relationship between Jacob and I, nor a matter of sidetracking your investigation. It has to do with leaving the pain and mistakes of my past as far behind as possible. The only hope I have now is to seize chances to make things right in life whenever they come up."

"Meaning that if Jacob seeks reconciliation, you'd apologize to him for the past expectations you had for him?"

"I doubt that will occur," said Webber. "I don't think Jacob is capable of that, much to my sadness. I believe we've passed the point of no return."

"Is that why you paint?" asked Tori, pointing at his black fingertips.

"That's one of the reasons. It's a very peaceful activity. I can block everything else out. Probably why I didn't hear your conversation with Jerome here. Total focus while I was working on the painting."

With the conversation beginning to spin away from the point, Ballack said firmly but quietly, "You are saying you were here all last night during the time in question? Is there anyone who can state they saw you here? Someone across the street or next door who would see a light on?"

"None, although you're welcome to check around the neighborhood and ask. Maybe someone can provide an answer where I'm lacking."

The previous rancor in the conversation seemed to have vaporized, and the present cooling down period was as good a time to leave as any. Ballack thanked both men for their time and patience. He and Tori left the house and after several minutes were headed back up Long Road toward the interstate. Neither spoke a word until they turned right on Chesterfield Airport Road and made straight for Boone's Crossing.

"Still slamming against the wall," remarked Tori.

"Eventually someone will crack," said Ballack, "because there is a lie out there somewhere. We've heard all the alibis, we've connected plenty of strings together. The principle, since this morning, remains the same: Whoever did this had something against both Toby Zweig and Father Joseph. Some sort of axe to grind. And someone is lying. The moment we figure all that out, we'll be on our way to solving this case."

"Figuring that out is going to take strength, and for strength we need food. How about if you call our comrades and find out if they're done detailing Grenier's holy roller. See if they want to go somewhere to eat. I'd like to just sit somewhere and process the whole day."

Ballack admitted the idea made sense. It might even be a good time to eat outside, and he had just the place in mind. He dialed Hull's number and waited. Like clockwork, Hull answered.

"Got done twenty minutes ago. Sheila was thorough. The interior got a good look-over. Still no prints. Still no hair or any defining marks. Two things of note, however. There was a slight spot of diluted peroxide in between the driver's seat and the passenger seat. Plus, there was a dry residue of what Sheila thought to be a soapy solution. We just checked it out with her lab kit. In short, Henry used this car and he made quite sure he blitzed it down good. We're talking military academy inspection-worthy."

"Peroxide, huh?" said Ballack. "He either used it as part of the cleaning solution or it was for another reason, maybe a product that had peroxide in it."

"Whitening formula for teeth?"

"Don't confuse me, Zane. Did you manage to speak with Stubblefield? I know it's Saturday, but I was hoping he might have been at the office to do some work."

"Voice mail. Left message. It was a longshot, but worth taking a chance. Should we meet up somewhere and debrief?"

"Actually, we were going to take you and Missy out for dinner tonight. Our treat. We can hash out the whole day over a meal. How fast can you guys get to the corner of Ballas and Manchester?"

"Twenty minutes, maybe, if post-game traffic isn't a problem. Where do you want to eat?"

"Oh, we'll meet where we're picking it up. But I've got an idea about where we'll eat it. I hate to waste such a lovely evening." His call waiting throbbed in his ear. "Got a call coming in. Meet us at Five Guys at Ballas and Manchester." He pressed the talk button. "Ballack."

"Cameron, it's Krieger. Got some homework for you guys."

45

Several locations of the burger franchise Five Guys' Burgers and Fries dot the St. Louis landscape. One in particular stands just south of the Ballas and Manchester junction in the West County setting of Des Peres. Just west of Five Guys is the imposing complex of West County Center mall. It towers over Interstate 270, aided by its most famous feature, a gigantic figure of a dove on a high sign, which encouraged local seminarians and churchgoers to tag the shopping center "Holy Spirit Mall." Ballack looked at the dove which stood outside the Nordstrom store as Tori passed over the highway on Manchester Road, made a right on Ballas, and then pulled left to get to Five Guys. In an astonishing show of efficiency and good timing, Hull and Crabolli pulled in less than a minute later as Ballack rolled down the Sprinter's ramp.

"Get out only if you need to see the menu," Ballack said through Hull's open driver's side window. "We're doing carry-out."

"Now that's a change of pace," said Crabolli, peering over. "Where are we headed? Local station?"

"Over there," Ballack pointed northward across Manchester Road. "Let's find a place to munch at Des Peres Park. What'll ya have?"

Twenty minutes later, all four detectives had settled down on a slope facing the small lake in Des Peres Park. Tori had pulled an oversized blanket from the van and she, Hull, and Crabolli reclined on it while Ballack rolled his chair to an acceptably level position. The two bacon cheeseburgers, two regular cheeseburgers, and the avalanche of fries were sufficient fuel. Crabolli lay back and stretched out, sighing contentedly. Hull popped two pieces of bubble gum in his mouth and blew a couple of sugary spheres. Tori leaned forward to touch her toes and let out a satisfied belch. The group exploded into laughter. The aggravations of their initial day together had evaporated, replaced by a collegial bond of mutual respect. Ballack snickered with the rest of them and then brought his hands up, palms facing down, and said, "Okay, everybody. Let's get to work and see where we are."

Tori got her notebook out to review her observations. "Grenier claims he was at the rectory all night and never touched the car. Did you guys confirm that with Father Behringer?"

"I asked him," said Crabolli, "and he said that he saw the monsignor enter the rectory when Grenier said he did. They have their own separate apartments on opposite sides of the rectory. But when I asked if he had seen him the rest of the night, he said no."

"Unless he was wearing lifts in his shoes, I'd say Grenier isn't Henry," said Ballack. "We checked his height against the dark intruder's at the elevator, and in all likelihood he was a good three inches shorter."

"Behringer would be several inches taller than Grenier," replied Hull. "What was his alibi for this one, Missy?"

"Just that he was in bed."

"Behringer is one guy who fits the height description and he was in the Cathedral when Zweig was murdered," Tori thought out loud. "He knew Zweig's movements. He'd have to know Father Joseph was at the Drury."

"His hair is certainly light enough where it might be the shade on that video," said Ballack. "We at least have to consider him, although we'd be incredibly weak on motive."

"Nothing else about this is making much sense," said Hull. "The motive might not, either."

"No," replied Ballack more sharply than he intended. "Sorry, I didn't mean to sound like you were wrong. You could be right. But I think there's a huge interconnected puzzle that fits together the pieces we've got so far. What we're missing is how to link them up."

"No offense taken," said the easygoing Hull. "By the way, the word is you guys found a haul of illegal stuff in Father Joseph's room."

"Yeah," said Ballack. "The final count was four bins. Only one, as Stu discovered when he met with the FBI rep, had the 'stuff' in question. He called on our way over here and said there were a lot of records in the others from the late priest's past. Three bins, one each fully stocked with papers from Father Joseph's days at Santa Maria, at that Corpus Sancti joint in Illinois, and at the place in Connecticut. I asked Krieger if we could keep those to leaf through for any details, and he was only too happy to negotiate possession of them as evidence. He said he'll bring them out to us."

"Like a house call?" asked Crabolli.

"Something like that," replied Ballack. "Now back to suspects. We already talked about Fishwick and that he appeared to be taller than Henry, or whom we assume to be Henry. Alibis check for the most part. We're still drawing a connection between the death of his son Phil and this Philippe character that committed suicide during

Father Joseph's time at Lake Zurich. It may be a link, but did Fishwick open up at all about his son's death? When we had breakfast with him, he said 'tragically.' But he said no more. Either of you crack open that clam?"

"He wouldn't speak about it," said Crabolli. "Any effort we made just got him more incensed. Said it was too much sadness and he didn't want to return to it."

"And yet if we knew how, we could eliminate him as a suspect, if the manners of death were different." Ballack felt the pressure headache beginning again. Information overload. He had to get home earlier tonight and do something active, even if it was playing tennis on his Nintendo Wii.

"How'd it go with McPadden and Webber this afternoon?" asked Hull, and Tori quickly went to her notes and gave them a summary. She was detailed but concise. Nothing needed to be repeated. At the end of the monologue, Crabolli sat up and rubbed her hands.

"Okay," she said. "So we have one person—Fishwick—who's lost a son. McPadden has illegally—although touchingly— reconnected with a formerly estranged son. Webber's son is gone and never is in contact anymore. Three men, three sons, all strange situations."

"That's an odd confluence of circumstances," said Ballack, who knew that Tori would be able to drain his pregnant statement of its intention.

"You think one of them's lying?" she asked. Ballack nodded slightly.

"I think that to discover the deceiver," he said, "we might have to wait for that person to tip his hand. I just don't want to wait that long"

"And we can't discount Behringer," reminded Hull. "If he's got the hair color, the height, and—most critically—the strength to flip Father Joseph over that railing, we've got to put him in the circle of suspects."

"So we're looking at Father Behringer, Pat Fishwick, Jerome McPadden, and maybe Julian Webber. The last two are soft possibilities as it stands, but that could change. For Behringer, we'd need to know other details such as motive. What about Zweig and Father Joseph would have clicked and made him want to murder them?"

"Grenier is out?"

"We can safely assume the monsignor is not Henry."

"Are we safe in assuming that Henry is Catholic?" asked Crabolli. "It's someone who knows how to quote Catholic sources and use crucifixes, but hear me out on this. Anyone can Google a quote from a Catholic authority. It's not impossible. And why the broken crosses? Is snipping a crucifix evidence of Henry being Catholic? Or is the desecration of it evidence to the contrary?"

"I see what you're saying. I really do," said Ballack. He had discovered he was almost too kind when Crabolli said something he would usually reject outright. "I wouldn't say these crucifixes are desecrated, however. 'Strategically cut with precision' would be how I'd say it. This is someone who knew the Cathedral, in order to murder Zweig. And it's someone familiar with Father Joseph. I would say the odds tilt toward Rome more than anywhere else. Now, let's talk about the next steps."

"I'm guessing you want us with Behringer first thing tomorrow?" asked Hull.

"If he can spare the time. Tomorrow's Sunday. He'll have a full slate of masses if nothing else."

"That reminds me," put in Crabolli, "that when I spoke with Father Behringer earlier, he said there was going to be a special procession at the ten o'clock mass tomorrow. The archbishop will be back leading it and the Cathedral Choir will be involved. It'll go from the front of the church, from the outside, up the steps, and inside."

"What's the occasion?" asked Tori.

"Education Sunday, according to Behringer," said Crabolli.

"Sounds to me like they're celebrating the trial victory a bit early, the Zweig case that loosened up the money control to the schools," grumbled Ballack.

"You saying there's an ulterior motive, partner?" Tori inquired.

Ballack covered his eyes, his ears, and then his mouth in three fluid motions.

"We could at least set something up again with Fishwick, if you think he's worth pursuing," said Hull.

"Call him now and find out when tomorrow he'll be available," replied Ballack. As Hull dialed the number for the Drury, Ballack turned to the women. "Let's split up the duties on the Father Joseph papers. Tori, you look through the bin that has the documents on Santa Maria Academy here. There might be a lot of stuff that connects

Father Joseph and Toby Zweig and we'll find who might have had motive to ice them both."

"Yes, put me through to Pat Fishwick's room," said Hull into his cell phone. "Even if I get his voice mail, that'll be fine."

Ballack continued, "Missy, can you and Zane divide the Connecticut bin? You never know. We could be dealing with someone from way back that is acting now. The one difficulty ..."

"... is why would someone also murder Zweig," said Crabolli.

"Right. There's something between the two. I can smell it. The murder scenes bear that out. The question is why and how. I doubt we'll find it in Connecticut, but split the pile between you."

"You're kidding me!" screamed Hull to who obviously had to be a very flustered operator or associate. "There's no way!"

Ballack looked at both women. He knew they were getting the same uneasy feeling he had, but he wanted to button up this assignment. "And I'll take the file on Lake Zurich. Let's snare them and get going on this, but now I've got a suspicion we're not going to receive good news here."

Hull gripped his cell phone so hard and angrily that Ballack was shocked it didn't break in half. He turned to face the others with a ghostly look on his face that barely disguised his boiling wrath.

"Fishwick's not there. He's gone! Checked out an hour ago. No one knows where he is or where he's gone!"

46

"Okay, okay!" exploded Ballack after they had feverishly discussed the Fishwick disappearance for the past two minutes. "We're getting nowhere on this by talking. Let's make the calls we need to. Call the airport to see if he's trying to skip town by air. The question would be how he got there, if the Drury has a shuttle service, and if so, who took him to Lambert. That's not the only possibility, however. What if he took a car?"

"A rental car? One way?" asked Tori. "That's not the most economically feasible thing. Where would he be going?"

"Home, maybe. A one-day shot from here to Omaha is not out of the question. Those are the two most natural possibilities, air and car. The first is easy to quash. Just stop him at the airport. But a car means an APB and especially checking the major highways and finding out if he nabbed a rental car and, if so, from which company."

"Not to mention he might not be Henry," said Tori.

"Oh, come on!" exclaimed Hull. "You don't think he is?"

"We have to prepare in case he is," said Ballack. "But first call the Drury about the shuttle."

A now-gloomy Zane Hull called the hotel and, as expected, got through to the front desk in no time.

"Checked out at eight minutes before six. Said an out-of-town emergency came up and had to go. They asked if he needed a lift to the airport. He said he had transportation, but they couldn't discern— when I pressed them on it—if he meant that he had a car to go to his next destination or that someone was taking him to the airport."

"So they can't tell us anything?" asked Ballack, popping one last French fry into his mouth.

"Sorry," Crabolli offered meekly.

"What a jackass!" barked Hull, causing the others to flinch. It was the first time they had heard him explode so vociferously.

"Forget it," said Ballack, as if that reminder could erase Fishwick's vanishing act. "Contact the airport. Better yet, go to the airport and if he's there, nail him. If he's not there, then we've got a long road ahead of checking rental car companies, combing what could be the whole state of Missouri and adjoining states, and … and …" before his words died away into a veil of choked silence. If he hadn't been buckled in, he would have fallen headfirst out of his wheelchair.

"What's going on?" asked Crabolli in a strident, worried voice.

Ballack slowed his breathing. Having the fish sandwich for lunch and the burger and fries for dinner was a higher caloric intake than his accustomed total. He felt as if he was going to throw up. After a few moments, the queasiness passed and he began to breathe normally.

"You okay?" Tori asked.

"Yeah. Thanks," Ballack wiped his mouth. Despite his recovery, he wore a clearly fatigued look on his face. His heart burned and his body scrambled to regain its normal vigor. "Where were we?" He tried to reinforce a sense of normalcy.

"Okay, as you were saying, we could be chasing too many rabbit holes if we try to nab Fishwick. For all intents and purposes on our work this evening, that should be just about it," declared Hull.

"There's no shame in calling it a night. You're obviously exhausted. Your body's taking a beating at this pace. Don't let your pride get in the way. Go home and rest. We can take care of checking at the airport for Fishwick."

"Someone needs to double-check Behringer, if we're putting him on the list," said Crabolli. "We can do that, too."

"No," demanded Ballack, who had suddenly found his voice and seemed determined to use it for all he was worth. "You're not about to cut us out of the action like that."

"And you clearly need rest," Crabolli's imperative crackled in the gathering dusk.

Tori stood to the side, knowing where this was headed.

Ballack waved them off. "We all do. We've had a couple of brutal days and we need to recharge before going into the next twenty-four hours. But we split up the duties. You two go to the airport to see if Fishwick is trying to take a puddlejumper to Omaha, a Boeing to Seattle, or an Airbus to Helsinki. Then divide between you the calls to all the rental companies you can think of. If Fishwick's guilty as sin, he may try to pay cash and not leave as noticeable a trail. I don't know. I never rent cars, for obvious reasons." And he smacked the side of his wheelchair.

"Every self-respecting rental car company would demand to see his driver's license," said Tori. "There would be something in someone's system."

"What did I tell you guys? I don't know," said Ballack. "That world is alien to someone like me. So call around and see where you get. Some places may call your bluff and demand to speak to you face-

307

to-face. If so, we may have to drop this angle and alert other authorities. I'd just like to do as much as possible under the radar."

"What about Behringer?" asked Hull.

"Tori and I will see him," said Ballack. "Then we and you two are calling it a night. Call me whether you succeed or not, so I can make a note of it in my report. Are we all clear?"

They nodded and broke up wordlessly. In a few minutes, both vehicles were streaming toward separate appointments.

47

The increasingly familiar parking lot of the Cathedral welcomed Detectives Ballack and Vaughan once more. Ballack's throat was scratchy and irritated from his digestive incident after dinner, although his ego had sustained considerably more damage. It wasn't anything Tori hadn't seen before, but having two fellow detectives as eyewitnesses to even a minor issue was a humiliating embarrassment to Ballack. He was thankful to Tori for being willing to remain silent the entire trip to the Cathedral and leave him alone in his thoughts. Facing this reminder of his weakness afresh made him angry, and anger steered him toward silence. Tori hated his noiseless stretches. Even if he was ruminating out loud and losing her with his outlandish paucity of conversational transitions, she found that preferable to an icy calm.

Ballack rolled down the ramp once more, turning toward the rectory when Tori said, "How do you expect to interrogate Behringer when I don't hear a peep out of you? Maybe I'd better take this over and …"

"Shut up or I'll run over your toes with this wheelchair," snapped Ballack.

Tori grinned. "Good to have you back, partner," she said as she strolled toward the rectory, but when she turned back, she saw Ballack rooted to the spot, staring at a car in the north parking lot as if it was the key to the whole mystery.

"Cameron? Aren't we going to find Behringer in the rectory?"

Ballack wheeled around and pointed toward the church. "We won't find him in the rectory. I'm sure there's something more interesting brewing in the Cathedral."

"What do you …?"

"The car," Ballack jerked his thumb backward toward the north lot. "Where have you seen that one before?" It was a bright yellow Honda Fit with a pink license plate frame.

Tori had absorbed a landslide of images overt the past two days, so many that she had trouble keeping them distinct. She was on overload. "To be honest, I can't recall, so why don't you tell me?"

"Two days ago, we saw that overgrown canary in Tabitha Stowe's detached garage. Now it's here. Let's see if little Miss Muffet is eating her curds and whey in the confession booth with the good Father now." He bolted for the side entrance and hit the automatic disabled door opener button.

They didn't have long to wait. When the door opened, Father Behringer stood before them, his hand placed tenderly on the shoulder of the pouty-lipped Tabitha Stowe. The unlikely twosome flinched at the sight of the detectives, and before they could speak Ballack held up his hand.

"Now this is a coincidence! Miss Stowe, Father Behringer, whatever are you two doing here? Another reconciliation by private appointment?"

Without missing a beat, Father Behringer shook his head. "Detective, despite your pessimistic view of this sight, I can tell you truthfully that Miss Stowe and I were not in the confession booth. Nor were we doing anything suspicious. She came by because there were matters about which she needed advice and reassurance, and she would only speak to me."

"I'll bet those matters are smoking at nuclear level if it means you have to meet in the Cathedral well after evening Mass has run its course," said Ballack. "We were going to speak with you, Father, but as Miss Stowe is here, perhaps we could have an audience with you both. Separately."

Father Behringer's face pulsated a worried look, but Tabitha remained calm, as if a police intrusion was just what she had been expecting. "If you would like to speak with them first, Father, I'll remain near the back of the church." Without waiting for a reply, she turned and walked down the west wall.

When she had put some distance between them, Ballack noticed for the first time they were the only ones in the entire place. His voice seemed to carry with greater depth in the emptiness even though he was barely above a whisper.

"This should be a brief conversation, Father, but it pertains to last night. Monsignor Grenier made it to the Drury today where we found Father Joseph's body. I am sure you've been told about this. But as we haven't seen you at all today, I thought it best to ask you this directly: Where were you during the hours of ten o'clock last night and one o'clock this morning?"

"I was here, Detective. At the rectory."

"Can anyone vouch for that?" asked Tori.

"The archbishop called me at eleven-thirty last night. He was letting me know that he was still scheduled to return at eight-thirty this evening from San Antonio. He was also confirming our processional at tomorrow's ten o'clock Mass was still scheduled as planned, despite the difficulties of the past few days. I assured him it was."

"What about after that time up until one a.m?" asked Ballack.

"I was asleep at midnight and stayed that way until seven-thirty this morning. The monsignor told me that Father Joseph had been killed before he headed off to the hotel, presumably to meet with the two of you."

"And did you leave your rectory apartment at all during the night?"

"No, Detective. I was asleep the whole time. Although, as you can guess, no one could verify that."

"You didn't happen to drive over to the Drury last night in the archidocese's Lexus?"

"For what? Why would I do that?"

"That's what I'm asking you, Father."

"Not that. I'm sorry. I'm used to people being in the know about this. I wear contacts because I'm blind as a bat. So bad that even with contacts, it's not safe for me to be on the road at night. From sundown onward my depth perception is gone. I never drive anywhere at night."

Ballack thought back to the video. The mystery figure that entered the elevator, and before that exited the Lexus in the garage, was most likely not this priest who stood before him. Henry had made his exodus from the driver side of the vehicle, and if what Father Behringer said could be verified, here was one more person they could eliminate.

"Father," said Tori. "We have two dead people, friends of the Archdiocese, both murdered. Is there anything you can tell us? Has anything strange gone on here the last couple days? Anything out of sorts? Any new revelations of detail?"

The priest hesitated, looking down the aisle as if verbal assistance would emanate from thin air. He took a deep breath before what was sure to be a non-committal response when all of a sudden Tabitha Stowe appeared from the shadows and said, "Father, it's okay. I've told you, I can explain to them. It's high time they knew anyway."

"I'm all ears," said the increasingly intrigued Ballack.

The four souls decided on All Saints Chapel for their clandestine encounter. Tori had not laid eyes on this precinct of prayer yet, and it brought Ballack back to his interview with Greg Varner. Stowe waited quietly, stroking her hair while Father Behringer directed the two ladies to sit on the bench. Obviously, the cleric preferred to stand.

"Miss Stowe," said Tori once they were all situated, "why were you meeting with Father Behringer just now?"

"It wasn't for confession," she responded. "Although I felt I had sinned. That seems odd to label it that. I'm not a particularly religious person, but I was thrown about in the middle of what I felt were pretty rough waters. And I also want to apologize to you, Detective Ballack and Detective Vaughan. By the time I digested everything I'm about to share with you, two men were murdered. The

313

fact that Toby was one of them is something for which I can't forgive myself. I can't bring him back, but I can at least make sure other things are made clear. Maybe then you can catch the killer."

"And perhaps we'll catch him sooner if we don't run around in circles," replied a clearly impetuous Ballack. "What were you discussing with Father Behringer? I assume that since you weren't getting assigned ten Hail Marys for telling him that it can be public domain."

Tabitha's eyes were shifty, and she exchanged the briefest of looks with the priest. Father Behringer nodded for her to continue and she began.

"I should have mentioned it sooner, but I was in shock over Toby's death. It will raise suspicions that I never told you this when you first came to my house, but I truly had not connected it to Toby. Last Wednesday, I took off work, and that's when Toby came to my house to ask if anyone was trying to screw him over at work. On Thursday, I had gone back into the office and was playing catch-up. In the middle of the day, I checked my voice mail and ran across a message from Jerome McPadden of Harvest Capital & Mortgage. He said he had an offer that I should heavily consider. In essence, he was asking me to sucker-punch Toby for him. I called him back after Toby left the office that afternoon, for what turned out to be the last time." She paused, her eyes growing wet yet again. Ballack tapped his pen on his right wheel and Tori glared at him for his impatience.

Tabitha continued. "McPadden said he was in a rush because there was a family emergency and he'd have to fly out of town, but he had no desire that Toby assist them in their future mortgage matters and contracts. I think it's no secret he didn't care for Toby, although Toby told me that McPadden was a disaster on the witness stand and nearly lost the trial against the 10:21 Alliance single-handedly. Anyhow, McPadden said what he was about to ask me, I needed to keep confidential. He had the backing of the executives at Harvest on this. He wanted me to cause a problem for Toby, one that would take him out of the picture, where Harvest could justify saying, 'Look, no way we can have you represent us now.' He wanted me in on the plan."

"And what was the plan?" asked Tori.

"It's so humiliating," replied Tabitha, her eyes flashing with anger at the memory. "Apparently the affair that Toby and I had was less a secret than I imagined. And our breakup was more public than I thought possible. McPadden must have figured I'd still want Toby so badly, or that I'd want to get revenge on him in the worst way. He said he wanted me to go completely public with the affair."

"He actually laid that scenario into your lap?" The question flew out of Ballack's mouth.

"Yeah, he did. I understand that he hated Toby, but that was a little too creatively hateful."

"I would understand that anyone putting that idea out there is a cold-hearted jackass," growled Ballack. Then remembering their company, he nodded apologetically to Behringer. "Sorry, Father."

Behringer graciously waved it off.

Tabitha went on. "He assured me that I wouldn't be left out to dry. He said he was restructuring things at Harvest and that there would be a position there for me if I chose to go with his plan for

Toby. He even asked me what I was making at Gillette, Wales, and Alexander, and when I told him, he upped it ten percent with full benefits."

"And did you accept?" It was Tori's turn to express astonishment.

"I'm so ashamed. I actually told him I'd have to consider it, that I wanted to see his offer in writing, and that to request it wasn't a commitment to going through with the plan. He told me he'd work up the initial contract and put it in an attachment. He asked for my email and I told him. He said he'd be in touch after he got back."

"That phone call was what time?" asked Ballack.

"Quarter till four on Thursday afternoon."

Tori checked her notes from that day. "Fifteen minutes later, Toby Zweig was here in confession. Soon after that, he was dead. What happened after that, I mean, with McPadden?"

"Obviously, the deal was off with Toby dead. McPadden didn't need me anymore."

"Would you have taken his offer?" asked Ballack.

Tabitha looked at him with such venom that Tori thought she might try to strangle him. "What are you insinuating?"

"You told McPadden you'd have to think about it. That says enough to me that you were at least somewhat drawn toward his offer, whether by frustration, revenge or the desire to put a part of your life behind you."

"I loved Toby!" Tabitha hissed. "Sure I was angry that he didn't love me anymore, but sooner or later I'd have to come to grips with that. I see that now. Last week I didn't. But that should at least show you that since I had the offer of a job waiting for me at Harvest, any motive for murder due to Toby firing me is a moot point now."

That was true, thought Ballack, on paper. He still didn't believe the ravishing Tabitha Stowe was a candidate to be Henry. But this wrinkle complicated things and he was getting weary of new evidence and conjecture and heresay cluttering up his mind. What he needed was to get away on his own, to clinically assess the details he had. And he desperately needed time to go through the treasure trove of Father Joseph's collection from Illinois. Staying here wasn't helping him piece things together.

"So you came here to tell Father Behringer all this?" he said. "Why?"

"I needed to get everything off my chest. I might not be guilty of murder, but my obsession with Toby has been part of a chain of events that led to his death. Someone out there wanted him dead. I was going to be fired, true. But I'd give anything for Toby to be alive and for his family to have him back, even if that meant me finding another job and never seeing him again. That would be the right thing. That's what I feel horrible about. I never made things right. Even now, after having admitted everything to you, Father, I still don't feel forgiven."

There was little left to be said, but Ballack had to ask one more question. "Would anybody else at the office or outside the office know how access Mr. Zweig's desk?"

"Not to my knowledge."

"One more thing. Can you remember anyone at all snooping around Mr. Zweig's office, noticing where his grandfather's dagger would be?"

"No, not snooping around," said Tabitha. "But he noticed it was gone after everyone come over to celebrate the victory against 10:21 and plan for the next cases. He had people like McPadden and Webber from Harvest there, and Father Joseph along with Monsignor Grenier. And you were there too, Father Behringer."

"I was," said the priest, "However, I think my fellow priests could account for the fact I was with them in the room the whole time and never went anywhere near Mr. Zweig's office."

"Only one of them can account for it now, Father," remarked Ballack. "Whatever Father Joseph saw or did is between he and his God now. And if there is no God, he's got nothing to worry about."

48

Tori had pulled out of the parking lot and made two right turns to get to Maryland Avenue when Ballack's phone rang one more time. He put it on speaker.

"Update time, C.B.," said Hull, "but it's not pretty."

"Well, nothing else is clearing up," said Ballack. "This case is about as logical as a road map of West Virginia. What do you have?"

"We stopped by Lambert and spent most of our time there inquiring every airline about departures in the last few hours. Only one plane had a Fishwick on it, but it was a Brian Fishwick who went to Philadelphia on a US Air flight just before two o'clock."

"It couldn't have been Pat Fishwick? I have no idea what his middle name is."

"Nor do I. We asked for manifests of all flights today. Also checked with TSA guys and gave them Fishwick's physical description. No one remembers having seen him."

"I wouldn't put much stock in their collective memory, Zane," replied Ballack. "So the manifests showed nothing?"

"Nothing. Missy saw there were only two flights at all leaving Lambert today for Omaha, in case Fishwick was going directly home. Both Southwest flights, which is why we had to go all the way to the east terminal. One flight left at five-ten, the other is going out at eight-fifty. We checked both lists. Fishwick isn't on either."

Ballack rubbed his eyes fiercely and gazed out at the gathering darkness.

"C.B.?"

"I'm still here."

319

"What do you want from us? Call rental car companies and see if Fishwick has skipped town and put out the APB to others?"

"I'd vote against that, if you want my opinion," said Tori loudly, who wanted to rescue her partner from his frustration. "I say if Fishwick is our guy, then less is more. Don't go looking for him. Wait until he surfaces. We can get out the word to others and nail him that way. Besides, if anyone wants my opinion, we're beat. We are dog-tired. I'm saying that about everyone. We've had two murders in the last fifty-three hours, we've run all over town trying to play Connect Four with who did it, and we still know two things. One, everyone seems to have a decent alibi. And two, somebody is lying."

"And three," said Ballack, "We still have to look where we haven't looked. That means wherever the lie is, we might unlock everything in Father Joseph's past. Go home, everyone. Get a hot drink or something. Watch a movie on TV. Clear your head. Then we go through our bins of stuff."

"Do you want to meet somewhere tomorrow?" asked Hull. "Missy's wondering."

"How about going to First Watch or something like that. Sit down, have breakfast, redraw the lines. You know where the First Watch is at Olive and Ballas in Creve Coeur? About a half-mile east of 270?"

"Got it. Sorry this day wasn't better. Feels like we're running in mud."

"That's what I get for having high expectations. We're not going to solve this case immediately. Don't rule out the solution finding us, either. But don't beat yourself up. Excellence isn't perfection. It's being better than we once were. Let's aim to have a better day tomorrow."

He signed off as Tori continued west toward St. Charles. With nothing more to be said, he closed his eyes and drifted off for a fitful nap, the pictures of the day still pricking at his soul.

49

Forty miles northwest of St. Louis, a honey beige Chevrolet Impala eased to a stop in the darkened parking lot next to eastbound Interstate 70. The rental car agreement lay on the front passenger seat and shivered slightly as the driver opened the door on his side. Other people were filing out of the Rural King market and the army-navy surplus store that shared the same shopping center. Looking each way to ensure he wasn't being watched, he circled around to the trunk, which he opened to reveal a suitcase packed with several nights' worth of clothes. Unzipping the case, he felt through the layers of material and pulled out three items, staring at each one in turn.

He gazed first at the Beretta M9, which he held lovingly in his grasp, alternating it between his left and right hands. It had been cleaned so well he could even see his face clearly in it in the gathering evening gloom. This weapon, he knew, would be sufficient for the task. He had spent enough time at the firing range over the years to be confident that he'd finish his job tomorrow. Then, and only then, would his soul be at peace. At that moment, his heart would know he had made atonement and would be fully forgiven.

He looked next at the book that he slid gradually out of the slipcase. It was well worn, so small it qualified more as a booklet, and he often wondered how often both students and teachers had flipped through this classic. Despite the wear and tear, there was no mistaking the title. There it was in clear relief on the front cover: *The Mind's Ascent to God*, by St. John Bonaventure.

And with tears forming in his eyes, he stared longingly at the third item. It was a photograph, in full color. The image was unmistakable, even though the picture had been torn. He knew the child in that photograph. He loved him, even though now was too late, and it had taken many years for him to realize he truly cared for his child. Steeling himself for the next day's duty, he decided to pack everything up and head to the hotel one exit away. As he put the photograph back in his suitcase, his gaze fell on the name written in elegant, flowing script below the child's face.

Phil.

50

Having said goodbye to Tori, Ballack rolled into the den of his family's St. Charles home. Tired and stiff as he was, he was in no mood to go to bed. In moments like these, he knew exercise was the best way to get the blood flowing to his brain. Rhoda, his nurse for the night, had not yet checked in, but Ballack didn't need any help to seek out his weights. He grabbed a pair of five-pound dumbbells from the end table and wheeled into the center of the den, turning on the television before going through the discipline of bicep curls. To an outside observer, the activity might look minimal, but given his muscle disorder, five pounds to Ballack would feel like a fifty-pound curl to someone else.

Marie Ballack appeared out of the shadows of the hallway and sat down on the love seat. "Long day?"

"It's about to get longer," replied Ballack. "If you don't mind, Commander Krieger will be stopping by with a bin full of evidence that I need to go through. Papers and what not. I need to go through all that crap tonight, all for the sake of hoping a clue will jump out of the pile and slap me across the face. One of those 'hold my calls' kinds of nights."

"Speaking of telephones, Graham had called earlier. He wanted to know if dinner next week sometime was a possibility with he and Leah."

"He'll have to get in line behind Dana. She's been waiting this one out for some time."

"I think he meant the four of you."

"What's this?" A voice from the front door called out. Martin Ballack had just made his way into the foyer, a bag of groceries in his hands. "Someone just rob Storage Solutions?" He was followed by Stu Krieger, and Martin jerked his thumb toward the SID Commander. "He with you?"

Ballack nodded, pointing toward the dining room table. "Thank you, Commander. You can leave it there. These are my parents, by the way. Martin and Marie."

Krieger shook hands with both of them. "Sorry to be flying away immediately," he said, "but I have one more delivery to make." He waved goodbye and headed out the door.

"Stay away from that, Pop. It's evidence," said Ballack, knowing full well his father had no problem restraining his curiosity.

"Rough day?" asked the elder Ballack, seating himself on the love seat next to his beloved.

Ballack gave a half-rub, half-swat to his forehead above his right eye. It was a nervous tick he claimed he never knew about until Tori proved it one day on her cell phone video recorder. "Just a matter of running hard all day only to find out your opponent keeps moving the goalposts." He placed the dumbbells on the larger sofa and scooted toward the television stand, opening a door to retrieve his Nintendo Wii game controller.

"Tennis?" asked Marie. "You're not going to play all night, are you?"

"However long it takes to get the frustration out," said Ballack, as the images for Grand Slam Tennis appeared on the screen. "I'm surprised to see you two up and around, rather than winding down."

"Too much to do," said Martin as he got up and walked into the kitchen. "I'm speaking to the adult Christian education classes tomorrow at Covenant Presbyterian. They're combining for this Sunday only and I'm presenting the idea of an intentional sequence of assimilation and spiritual nurture, plus talk about the new study center the church is establishing down the road."

Ballack heard the sound of clinking glasses, the refrigerator ice dispenser engaging, and the pouring of drinks.

"Are you all ready for that?" asked Ballack, thinking of little else to say.

His father re-appeared. "As ready as I can be. Here's your Pelligrino, sweetheart," he said, handing a glass of water to Marie before sitting down with his own glass of much darker fluid.

"Owen's Jim Beam?" asked Ballack.

Martin nodded. "A quick nightcap of God's gift to wretched sinners like myself."

"Father Doyle said he wants to come by and get snockered one night. His eyes lit up like a rabbit's in a carrot patch when I told him about the bourbon."

His father laughed. "Billy Doyle may talk a good game, but he's all restraint when it comes down to brass tacks. He knows where the line is and makes sure he ends up well short of it. He called today, by the way."

"Father Doyle did? What'd he want?" Ballack asked as he selected Boris Becker for his video player. Further honoring his German heritage, he chose Michael Stich as his opponent.

"Just passed along how much he enjoyed having lunch with you and Tori yesterday. It gave him a break from the usual crowd and he hopes that whatever he told you might come in handy on your case."

"It has to. I just don't know how it all unlocks. The answer's out there, but I can't find it."

"Remember what I said at Easter?" said Marie.

"About what?" said Ballack. "You said a lot of stuff."

"At the cemetery. That you might not have to find faith, but that maybe faith will find you. Maybe this is along those same lines. You might not find the answer, but it might chase you down."

"From a detective's point of view, that's rather humiliating," responded Ballack as he swiped a forehand winner for a fifteen-love lead in the opening game. "I hate that my intellect would get outsourced to the whims of the *zeitgeist*."

At that moment, the front door opened and Rhoda, complete with her usual array of Spongebob Squarepants attire and paraphernalia, burst into the Ballacks' residence.

"Good evening, all!" she called out.

"Rhoda's in the house," smiled Martin, swallowing the last of his bourbon and rising to his feet. "I assume you'll be okay, son?"

"Just need time and space to go through that box of less-than-sacred memories," replied Ballack as his drop shot handed him the opening game of the match. "You two can go off to bed now."

"So nice to get your permission, your majesty," said Marie, rolling her eyes. "We're out the door early tomorrow for the eight-thirty service."

"Try not to get too excited," deadpanned Ballack as his parents shuffled off.

After finishing his tennis match, which took an energetic—yet not brutal—forty-five minutes, Ballack rolled into the dining room to tackle the collection of Father Joseph's past. Krieger had set it in a chair by the table where he could reach in and take what was needed. Rhoda had kindly brought him some chocolate chip cookies, and the treats were laid out on a plate, arranged as if this was a five-star restaurant. Ballack had managed to open the refrigerator himself and pulled a diet soda from the door shelf. Rhoda opened it for him as he grabbed a pile of papers from the bin. Before anything else, he called Dana to let her know he got home okay. She didn't answer and he was forced to leave a message on her voice mail.

Many of the initial documents were admissions files. Ballack didn't expect a sudden bonanza of insight such as what befell them when they went through the files at St. Basil's in February. No incidental notes of interest brought anything to light. Father Joseph was an organized soul, having categorized all entrants by year of admittance, then subcategorizing each year by gender, and then again by alphabetical order of last name. There were photos attached to each application, standard shots, all with the same background, hearkening back to the picture days scheduled early each school year. Looking through names, addresses and ages, nothing seemed to betray anyone. Ballack was about to give up and take a break when he saw a photograph lodged in the bin between the side and several books.

He reached in and took it out, staring at it intently. A young man in his early twenties, if that old. Nothing attached with it, but that didn't mean it wasn't in the bin. Ballack leaned over as far as possible and used all his remaining strength to cast extraneous papers aside. It took several minutes but he finally ran across a folded collection of papers, bound by a rubber band. The giveaway was the torn staple location in the upper left hand corner, an exact match with the tear in the picture.

Ballack looked at the name space on the application, disappointed at first because there was nothing listed. There had been a name once before, but it had been obscured with permanent black magic marker. His brow creased in frustration and he took another sip of soda to mollify his sore throat. It was when his eyes returned to the page that he saw it.

In the lower right hand corner.

In green ink.

The name.

Philippe Xavier.

It has to be a dream, Ballack thought. No way it was this cut-and-dried.

But he interfaced the picture and the papers together. The tear location looked to be a spot-on match. Whoever was in the picture had to be Philippe.

A door opened off the hallway, and Ballack heard his father's footsteps in the den.

"Everything okay, Dad?" he called out.

There was a rustling of paper and then Martin responded. "Yeah, just forgot a few things, and Mom wanted to read today's paper. That's all."

Ballack froze.

More rustling, then his father's footsteps heading back the way they came.

Ballack sped into the den. His father had just turned the bedroom knob.

"What did you say?"

Martin looked at his son. "Just getting a few things. I'm sorry if I disturbed you."

Ballack shook his head. "Not that. About Mom."

Martin displayed the copy of the *St. Louis Post-Dispatch* in his hand. "She wanted to read the newspaper."

And everything became clear. Crystal clear.

51

Ballack knew now was not the time to jump the gun. Verify first, and then cross the line. Even Rhoda got involved, taking everything out of the bin and arranging the piles on the table as Ballack directed. Papers in one area, books in another, photographs elsewhere. It took Ballack another hour and an additional can of soda, but he finally found what he needed. Father Joseph might not have believed in flash drives, but he had some CD-ROMs in the rear pocket of a red binder. Ballack inserted the first one—labeled ACCOUNTS— into his laptop and opened one file after another. There was enough information to hang Father Joseph and the Corpus Sancti community for misappropriation of funds. Even a casual glance at the ledgers bore that out. But there was nothing about a Philippe Xavier in any folder, any file, any document. Ballack took the final bite of Rhoda's cookies, ejected the first disc, and then loaded the second one. Nothing seemed promising from the list of files, but he noticed one title in particular that stood out from the rest. It was marked SECOND CONFIRMATIONS.

Second confirmations? Ballack thought. Was Father Joseph doing some sort of ceremony for the members of the community? And if so, what was it? Was it done in secret? He opened the file to a list of names, dates, and remarks about various confirmation services over the years Father Joseph was at Corpus Sancti. The document was one hundred pages long. Ballack frowned. This would take time. And, he thought, it wouldn't hurt to get a knowledgable source to fill in the gaps.

"Rhoda," he said, his eyes still on his laptop screen, "I saw my dad's cell phone in the den on the glass table. He was charging it. Can you grab it for me, please?"

"Running low on minutes?" she asked. "Or checking out what he's got on his photos?"

"Neither. There's a phone number I need to look up."

Rhoda did as requested and Ballack quickly got into his father's contacts. He found the numbers he was seeking, both land line and mobile, and dialed the home number.

"Peter and Paul rectory," answered a raspy voice. "If you're looking for Mary also, you missed the Sixties."

"Father Doyle, it's good to know your humor is razor sharp at ten o'clock on a Saturday night before a slew of Masses the next day."

"But not my voice recognition," the priest said. "Who is this?"

"I'm frankly shocked you're not at Fast Eddie's, sir. This is Cameron Ballack."

"Cameron! How are you? Why didn't you call my cell? I've got your dad's number banked in my contacts."

"Well, I've got you now, Father. I have a question for you. I'm sifting through some evidence regarding Father Joseph's Illinois days, and while I can't tell you which way the case is leaning, I've run across something that our esteemed cleric must've been doing there. And I was calling you to find out if this is a legit thing or if it's some renegade Romanist ceremony."

"He wasn't sacrificing goats, was he?"

"Maybe worse than that, Father. Can you tell me what the purpose of a second confirmation would be?"

"What in the ever-loving, locust-eating, honey-dripping name of St. John the Baptist is a *second* confirmation?"

"I'm asking you, Father."

"You know what a confirmation is, right?"

"Yeah. The initiation rite for entry into the Church, accompanied—in the Catholic tradition, at least—by the laying on of hands to signify reception of the Holy Spirit."

"You know, for being a gloomy young pagan you sure know a lot about our most sacred traditions."

"I'm not that bad of a pagan. I just like turning a lot of sacred cows into digestible burgers. But what's the deal with *second* confirmation?"

"I'm telling you, Cameron, I don't have a clue. What are you looking at that has this 'second' garbage on it? Is this Father Joseph?"

Ballack's instinct told him Father Doyle could be trusted, even if revealing these details of the case was not ideal. "I'm looking at a document labeled 'second confirmation' and it lists people names, dates and some liturgical details about different services."

"But these people, if they're in Corpus Sancti, would already be confirmed members of the Church," said Father Doyle. "I'm confused. Why are they being confirmed again? It doesn't … oh, oh … oh no!"

"What?" asked Ballack.

"That's it. Mother of mercy, that's got to be it."

"What, Father?"

Father Doyle paused before speaking again. "Cameron, look carefully. Are there any comments about the first ceremony listed on that document?"

"Yeah, like a whole paragraph."

"Look at all the details."

"Okay, it'd help if you told me what I was looking for."

"What's the name of the confirmand?"

"The what?"

"The person who is being confirmed."

"Ah, okay. First one I'm looking at here is Paul Francis."

"Date?"

"November the fourteenth, six years ago."

"Tell me everything Father Joseph said."

"Like I said, it's a healthy paragraph. Here goes," said Ballack, and he dove into the maze of vocabulary describing the liturgy of the confirmation service. Father Doyle had to assist him on the pronunciation of a few words, but other than that Ballack handled most everything with ease. It was at the end of the paragraph that Ballack ran across the words, "And so, invoking the blessing of our Lord and Savior Jesus Christ, who gives us a new identity through his precious blood, we sanctify your servant William Barkley and christen him anew, giving him a new designation, that of the name of your Holy Apostle and Great Missionary with the name of your saint from Assisi. With the laying on of hands, we bind unto a second confirmation your servant, Paul Francis."

There was a stunned pause on the line, and then finally Father Doyle exploded. "What was all that?!"

"The whole changing of the name? It's creepy is what."

"The service itself. The only people in the Church who take on a new name would be the men who are elected Pope. Albino Luciani became John Paul I. Karol Wotylja became John Paul II. Joseph Ratzinger is now Benedict XVI. What did Joseph think he was doing? Ordaining priests? That's what I was worried about. Still, I don't know how this fits in your case."

Something snapped within Ballack. "That's it!"

"What's it?"

"He's ordaining them."

"To the priesthood?" screamed Father Doyle. "He can't do that! Only a bishop can do that."

"Not the priesthood. Something else," said Ballack. "He had to know he couldn't do any of that. But what if he was setting people apart for some purpose?"

Father Doyle didn't know what to think. "You've lost me, Detective. Start making sense quick."

"You yourself said Father Joseph targeted people, and at the very least he used his position as a springboard to lure students into relationships that we can hardly qualify as being truly consensual. What if was using these services as a bridge to that?"

"Still not making sense, Cameron. You think he would bless them and then corner them in the vestry afterward?"

"I'm saying what if Father Joseph affirmed many things about novitiates, students, and young adults over the years—definitely in Lake Zurich—in order to give them confidence they were future leaders, movers and shakers in the Catholic church? He provides a means for that by re-christening them to another name and some sort of life path. Each one of them is head over heels devoted to the man, and the mentor-student relationship continues blissfully unabated for months afterward. And then, he strikes."

"You mean the re-christening was a ploy to begin and maintain manipulative, subversive and abusive connections all over the campus?"

Ballack let his silence speak for itself.

"That's probably the tidiest explanation you'll get without an insider investigation, but there's got to be more," said Doyle. "All who were re-christened were males?"

"More male than female, a ninety-to-ten ratio. But women can't hold leadership in the Catholic Church anyway, so the female ceremonies must be something else. Here's one … hang on. Says for this one girl that they were opening God's door in her life for sacred purposeful singleness and chastity."

"If she wants to do that, she can do so outside the Church."

"Can't say for sure," said Ballack. "It could mean something, or it could just be a red herring."

"Okay. At the very least it seems like you're on to something. You have any more questions for me? Because if you do I'll have to call in sick for the eight o'clock Mass tomorrow."

"I think we're done. Go to sleep. And, Father Doyle?"

"Yeah?"

"Thanks. For everything. We wouldn't be at this stage in the game unless you helped us along."

"Whatever you need, Detective. Have a good night."

Ballack warded off two attempts from Rhoda, who was trying to convince him sleep was paramount. The clock ticked past eleven. He had sifted through more material in the bin but came back to the laptop, plowing through more details of the re-christening services. It hit him after a few minutes of this that scanning the names of the Corpus Sancti members might be more helpful. He rubbed his eyes and flipped ahead several pages in the file, alighting on one service that took place less than six years before. The date did not immediately catch his eye. The name, however, did.

There it was, in black and white, as clear as the Ten Commandments were to Moses. Unmistakable.

Philippe Xavier.

Here was the one who allegedly scaled a church tower in the dark of night, encumbered with guilt and despondency, casting aside his misery with a leap from the bell window. And with that misery, he cast aside his life. Ballack scanned several lines upward reading the words of the Father Joseph-penned liturgy.

"And so, invoking the blessing of our Lord and Savior Jesus Christ, who gives us a new identity through his precious blood, we sanctify your servant ..."

And he saw the words that followed, the name that had been thrown by the wayside for a new identity that would be soiled and destroyed in eighteen months.

The name.

Leaning across the table as far as possible, he grabbed the picture of Philippe.

Of course. Those eyes. The cheekbones. The forehead. And the wariness of his whole persona. Ballack wondered why he didn't see the resemblance before. He looked back at the screen and smiled at the sight of the young man's name.

In his heart, ever since his father had mentioned the newspaper, he believed this name might be there.

And now it was time to act.

52

Zane Hull opened the refrigerator in the kitchen of his one-bedroom apartment at the corner of McKnight and Manchester. He had lugged a box of Father Joseph's mementos up the stairs and tossed them on his sofa. He and Crabolli had gone over much of their division of labor at her house, but his critical eye had at least an hour left to spare. Looking over the sparse choices of lunchmeat, pizza and condiments, Hull opted for a Bud Light and swiftly twisted the cap off a twelve-ounce longneck. He tilted his head back for a long swig, savoring these moments of winding down at the end of a mentally bruising day. Still, there was more work to be done with these documents from the past. He drew a deep breath and listened to the silence. There was no listening ear within these walls, not that he required one. He had no wife or girlfriend to speak of. In his honest moments, if he had his druthers, he'd want to retreat into the waves of Missy Crabolli's soft blond hair. For the sake of their working relationship, he knew he couldn't. Because she was coming off a bad breakup, he knew she wouldn't. He thrust his head back and slammed down the remainder of the beer, tossing the empty bottle in the trash.

As he walked into the living room, he could vaguely make out the sound of his buzzing phone. He had deliberately turned it down. Was it too much to expect a few spare moments of solitude? The phone stopped buzzing as he approached it, and as it did, the mobile number of Detective Cameron Ballack appeared as a missed call. His eyes now slits and his body screaming for rest, he turned away.

"If it's absolutely important," said Hull, "and if he's solved the case, he'll call again."

And no sooner had that sentence launched from his vocal cords than the phone hummed again. Simultaneously cursing and admiring such persistence, Hull decided Father Joseph's papers could wait another quarter-hour. He answered the phone.

"How soon," shouted Ballack into the phone, "can you get a warrant?"

"Excuse me?" replied Hull, trying to unseat both his weariness and the initial effects of the alcohol. "Did you say a warrant?"

"Yeah, how soon can we get one? Forget First Watch tomorrow. More like today, given the time now. Warrant. When can we get one?"

"Where is this coming from? If you want a warrant on this case, then we have to track down Krieger, have him produce one, and then find a judge to sign the thing. And you haven't yet answered why we need one."

Ballack wasted no time telling him the whole story. Five minutes later, Hull was grabbing his car keys and racing down the stairs to his car below.

"You want regular search warrant or does it need to be no-knock?" he asked Ballack.

"Either one. Henry doesn't need to know we're coming. I think we've got a good case for one."

"I'd agree," replied Hull as he started his car.

"Is it possible to have a SWAT team on this one?" asked Ballack.

"In St. Louis County, it's part of the package deal with any warrant. Let me call Krieger and find out where he is, then I'll let you know what our progress looks like."

"Thanks, Zane. When I hear from you, I'll call Tori, depending on the word. I'm sure she'll hate me for this."

Thirty minutes minutes later, Hull called Ballack with the good news.

"We couldn't be luckier if we tried," Hull exulted.

"Luck is the residue of design. We're meant to catch Henry. It's our destiny. Whatchya got?"

"I'm headed to Llywelyn's Pub. Almost there, in fact."

"Don't drink until we've got Henry, man. Why are you going to Llywelyn's? Is this the one in Soulard or the Central West End? I can't imagine you're coming all the way up to Llywelyn's St. Charles."

"Missed on all three. Moody Avenue in Webster Groves. Krieger's there and I'm having him verify the warrant for the judge."

"And how far," asked Ballack, "will you have to go to run down a judge for this?"

"Three feet to Krieger's left."

Ballack shook his head, not believing this surprise. "What?"

"You heard me. Of all nights to need a clear path for a no-knock warrant, and we hit the heaven-blessed bonanza."

"You're kidding!"

"It's a godsend," whooped Hull. "Sergeant Krieger is throwing down shots with none other than the man who oversaw Zweig's last case. Judge Dave Valle."

"Hallelujah."

"It'll take a few hours to assemble the SWAT team and plan our moves, but be ready to roll."

53

Sunday morning arrived with an overcast sky gracing the greater St. Louis area, along with a temperature hovering near fifty. Tori had placed the Sprinter in the parking lot at the local Exxon station, which also housed a Blimpie sub shop. As a blurry sun tried to break through the tenacious clouds, Hull and Crabolli pulled up beside them.

"Bear claw?" offered Hull, getting out of the car and extending a white cardboard box toward Tori's open window.

"You're a dear," said Tori, who wrapped her fingers around one and drew it to her mouth. She passed the other one on to Ballack, who took a bite of it before having another sip of apple juice. He peered into the distance as his cell rang.

"Ballack," he answered without delay. "Yes sir … Okay … Yeah, we'll meet you at the address I gave you …We're just a quarter-mile away. We'll park in front of the house and slightly to the right … Five minutes."

He hung up and looked to his left. Hull and Crabolli were huddled next to the window behind Tori. The four of them drew deep breaths.

"This is it," said Ballack. "Let's go. We'll follow the SWAT team and Krieger. Zane and Missy enter, and then we'll set up the ramp for me. Scotty will be along in another hour and a half. He'll join us in progress wherever we are."

"You're absolutely sure this is going to shake out okay?" The words were those of SID Commander Stu Krieger. It was one thing to grant carte blanche entrance when having drinks with a friend the night before; it was something else to execute that permission in the light of day.

"No disrespect, sir," whispered Ballack, leaning in so that only Krieger could hear, "but I have a feeling you thought this was a good idea for reasons other than a few tequilas floating through the bloodstream."

"And you know this is a good idea? When did you realize that?"

"Remembering the lack of newspaper. And I brought along the file for us to look at whether he is or isn't here."

Krieger shook his head as his radio crackled. "Chief, we are in position. Waiting for the go ahead from you, sir."

"Does it look like anyone's at home?" asked the commander. He and Ballack were behind the Sprinter with the other detectives, out of view from any vantage point within the house.

"From our perimeter setup, there are no lights on. But both cars are in the garage. He might be here."

Krieger nodded. "I'll make sure the detectives are ready for entry. Three of four are wearing vests from what I've been told."

He turned to Ballack. "Everyone set?" He looked at the others, who nodded in the affirmative.

"How's your wife, Commander?" asked Ballack.

Krieger blanched. "My what?"

"Your wife, sir. How is she doing today?"

"You're asking about my wife when we're about to gun our way into the house of a murder suspect? Why?" His radio crackled something incoherent.

"Well," said Ballack in an uncharacteristically compassionate tone, "After our talk yesterday in the security office, I thought I should ask you about her the next time I thought about it."

Krieger was baffled. "Right now?" He nonetheless had the hint of a smile tugging at the corners of his mouth.

"Yeah, well, I just thought of it."

Krieger shook his head, the tension of this morning's activity draining out of him. "She's fine, Detective. Extremely tired. Didn't sleep well last night. But she's happy to be alive."

"There you go, sir," smiled Ballack. "We're ready to go. Shock and awe."

Krieger looked around the van, fingered his gun in its holster, and spoke into his radio. "I'm heading up. Be ready, guys." He moved with a resolute stride and made a beeline to the front door. Two SWAT team members edged closer around either corner of the house, crouching low, toward the entry. Krieger pounded the door with several vigorous knocks.

"Mr. Webber. Julian Webber. This is Commander Stu Krieger of the Special Investigative Division of Metro St. Louis with a warrant to search your premises."

54

The initial sweep through the house by the SWAT team ended in a few seconds. Hull and Crabolli jumped into the foyer and spread into opposite rooms, the dining room on the left and an office on the right. Crabolli re-emerged from the house to help Tori put the ramp up for Ballack, who wasted no time zipping into the heart of Webber's domicile.

"Can't you wait, you reckless fool?" Tori voiced in an anxious susurration.

"Tor, the SWAT guys have come through here," said Ballack. "Krieger's in. Do you really think they've missed something and Webber's hiding up in this chandelier?"

The detectives converged in the kitchen with Krieger.

"Okay," said Ballack. "We're here for several reasons. Let's go over them now while the SWATs confirm if he's here or not. Last night it clicked that when I spoke with Webber in his studio just yesterday, he told me he had just been working on a painting. His fingertips were black so I passed that off as some of the paint he was using in his artwork."

"What's the point?" asked Krieger, decidedly impatient.

"I'm walking you through it. Last night, it came to me that in re-creating that scene in my mind, there was no drop cloth or newspaper on the ground to catch any drips or spatters." Ballack chuckled, thinking how it was his father's innocent comment about getting the newspaper for Mom that triggered the whole inquiry. "He couldn't have been just working on it. So I thought, if he's lying about that, what else is he hiding?"

"To be fair," said Crabolli, "We don't know if everyone's been above board with us. And given that Fishwick skipped town, shouldn't we include him?"

"What if the stuff on Webber's fingernails wasn't paint from his horse picture?"

"What else would it be?" The question was from Krieger.

"Sorry I didn't have time to go into this last night because I gave you guys a ton of other reasons to come here, but hear me out. Webber was wearing a painter's cap yesterday when we spoke to him. The whole time. Never, ever took it off. You could see his hair where it was sticking out from under the cap. But what if there was a reason he had the cap on the whole time? Like, to cover his hair?"

"You mean the dark stuff was from re-dyeing his hair back from a lighter dye, if he had dyed it differently," said Hull, remembering their conversation from the previous night. "Like if he had dyed it blond."

"Which could explain the blond hair on the security video from Friday night," answered Krieger. "But what does this Webber guy look like, height-wise?"

"That's where we can't verify an exact match with the elevator, since we only interviewed Fishwick and Grenier at the hotel," said Tori, "but I would ballpark him at the same height of the person from that video."

"So what we need to do is check the trash here in case he was stupid enough to do the darker dye at home and throw away the box in the garbage here," said Crabolli.

"Let's do that, plus check any file cabinet for letters, notes, anything about his son," ordered Ballack. "I'm not betting we'll find any dye box here, but it's worth a try. About his son. His name was Jacob, and his name—just to make sure we're all on the same page here—was changed by Father Joseph to Philippe Xavier. There was a Philippe who committed suicide several months later at the same community. Later, Father Joseph was shuffled over here. I'm betting that Webber bided his time toward revenge and now was the time to strike. I think he's a grade A liar. Heck, I haven't been able to confirm his alibi about playing golf with this Chuck Wilbur guy." And with that he pulled out his cell and tapped in the number once more for good measure.

"We don't have much time, then," said Tori. "We need to tear this place apart."

"Shut up, Tor! Listen!" barked Ballack. Everyone paused. "Do you hear that?"

"It's a buzzing noise," said Krieger.

"And it's coming from above the gas stove!" exclaimed Ballack.

"Gas leak?"

"No," said Ballack, remembering McPadden's remarks from the day before and Webber's counter-excuse. "Open those cabinets above the stove!"

Hull and Krieger, being the taller individuals, did so, removing cookbooks and binders galore until Hull swept his hand on the bottom of the cabinet, retrieving a mobile phone.

"Tracfone," he said, handing it to Ballack, "and it looks like it just missed a call from you."

"That conniving fraud," muttered Ballack. "And I bet all these voice mails are from me."

"He had planned this out," remarked Tori, through clenched teeth. "He buys another cell phone, gets a new number for a Memphis code, and then sets up this whole charade to draw us off track."

"One devil of a swerve," growled Ballack, slamming his fist down on his armrest in frustration. "It wasn't the gas from the stove, as McPadden thought it was when we visited. And it sure wasn't the water line in the fridge, which was Webber's little deception. It was this phone! I just should have called FedEx and asked if they had ever heard of a Chuck Wilbur and we could have avoided this whole goose chase!"

"Don't beat yourself up over that, C.B. Any of us could have done this," said Hull. "However, there's one issue you never conclusively solved for me. As far as Webber doing all this. Why now? Why this time?"

Ballack looked at him as Tori handed him the Philippe file. "Just so you can confirm, there's the picture. This photo was in the file. Look at this photo business card of Webber," and here he pulled out one of Webber's cards. "Doesn't that look like Philippe? And as far as why now, because it coincides with the anniversary of Philippe's—or Jacob's—death five years ago. Same date, in fact. And with hanging, he ensures Father Joseph goes the same way."

"But why Zweig?" said Tori. "That's the part of the puzzle that doesn't fit. What had Zweig done against Webber? He had just defended them in court!"

"He was going to defend Father Joseph in the future, though," said Hull.

"But Lance Stubblefield said Zweig was going to throw the case and toss Father Joseph to the dogs."

"Okay, Detective Vaughan," interrupted Krieger, anticipating what Ballack himself would have said in response. "But did Webber know that?"

"Thank you, Commander," said Ballack. "I couldn't have expressed it more perfectly."

One of the SWAT team members came into the kitchen. "Commander?"

"Yes, Cramer?"

"Searched the entire house. No sign of the suspect. Bed made. Studio emptied. But we went into the basement. I think you'd better see this."

"Coming," replied Krieger. He turned to the detectives. "While I'm checking this out, fan out and find what you can. Start with his office, but check endtables, file cabinets everywhere. Any place that might have a scrap of information about his son." And off he went.

"Let's go guys," said Ballack, signaling Hull and Crabolli to take the office and that he and Tori would begin in the bedroom. They didn't get very far when Krieger came running up the stairs with wide eyes.

"The money man has a whole cache of weapons down there. One of the guys managed to pop a door open in the finished basement and discovered an arsenal of automatic pistols and ammunition!"

"How much stuff?" asked Hull.

"About twenty different guns and plenty of bullets. The crazy thing is there was a slot for one more gun and it's missing."

"Meaning he's on the move with it toward his next destination and victim," snapped Ballack. "Come on, let's kick it in gear and find something!"

"No worries!" screamed Crabolli from the front office. "Found it!"

"That quickly?" called out Tori in amazement. "Where?"

At that moment, a SWAT member entered the room with a small cardboard box in his hand. "Sir," he said to Krieger, "is this what you guys were talking about?"

Krieger took the box. "Thanks, Baron," he said, peering at it with a look that said they were one step closer. He showed it to the team.

"Unbelievable," said Hull. "Black hair dye. You didn't find any blond?"

"No sir," said Baron. "I went through that trash bin until I nearly passed out."

"Could've bought both en route to killing Father Joseph and might have done the blond dye elsewhere," mused Ballack. "I can't believe he was stupid enough to dye it black here and throw it away in his own trash."

351

Crabolli came into the main atrium waving a letter aloft. "File cabinet in the office."

"It wasn't locked?" asked Ballack.

"It was, but the trick in that situation is to tilt up the front of the cabinet and feel around the right side of the bottom, toward the front. There's usually a hole there, and if you poke your finger in the hole, you should normally feel the end of a metal rod. So what I did was push up on the end of that rod and it released the locking mechanism. From there, it was a snap."

"But you found that in two seconds!" exclaimed Hull.

"I figured it wouldn't be in a regular file, but hidden somewhere near the back or underneath all the folders would be a more likely probability. What can I say? We won the lottery on this. I've already given it a quick scan, but I think everyone should hear it out. It seems like a must read."

"Rather than gathering around, how about if I read it aloud?" said Krieger, taking the letter from her. He found the beginning of the note, written in perfect print on gray stationery, and began to read the sad, broken tale of a voice beyond the grave.

55

Jacob Webber's final musings floated audibly in the room, the detectives absorbing the pain in their private thoughts.

Dear Julian,

Try as I will to call you 'Father', it doesn't seem right. Not because you were a horrible parent, though you and I know there was room for better attempts on your part. It is because I don't know what a good father is, and I never will. I know you didn't respect my choice of going to Corpus Sancti, of running away from home, from a chance to go to college and move beyond all that. I wish we had a more open relationship for me to tell you that your fears were accurate.

Even though I felt you had failed me, I always believed I would have a chance to vindicate myself. I thought God would help you to see that my forays into drama and art rather than athletics were for a purpose. I wasn't built physically for the latter. And so I prayed that God would provide divinely appointed alternatives to you for my new life path, and I believed I had found one in Father Joseph Quinn. I had long wanted to tell you of the months of assisting Father Joseph in the celebration of the Mass, of engaging in mission projects in inner-city Chicago, feeding and ministering to the homeless, and long dialogues about what God was teaching me. I was thrilled when—so soon after my arrival—Father Joseph told me that he had never encountered someone in whom the Holy

Spirit burned so brightly. I'll never forget his words, 'The potential in you for the outworking of our Savior's brilliance is overwhelming.' It appeared so sincere that I never imagined it could be a sales pitch to feed his own selfishness. He capitalized on our community's vow of silence—no correspondence with the world that we had left—and to ensure that vow was kept, he had his strict eye fastened on the mailroom there. The outward reason for this vow was so we could dedicate ourselves to our new path. I now realize it was because we were cursed to this life, and correspondence is verboten so that word doesn't get out.

But I believed Father Joseph. His dedication to me was inspiring at first, and his public warmth and carefully groomed image is attractively astounding, especially given the rot that is underneath that façade. Because of the possibilities he said he saw within me, he wanted to re-christen me for this new life of service to God. A number of Corpus Sancti individuals had received this blessing, but not all were chosen. During vespers one evening, he included in the liturgy a time of dedication, of new blessing, where I would be christened with a new name. He selected the name Philippe Xavier. The first name was in honor of the apostle who preached in Samaria; the surname honored the founder of the Jesuits. I blushed with embarrassment and a twinge of pride when Father Joseph's hands, heavy with oil and water, fell lovingly upon my head, sealing me to a life serving Christ with all my heart. One thing I do remember about that service. When I looked up and gazed at my friends in the chapel, I expected to find joy resplendent etched on their faces. Yet for the most part, I saw fear. Within months, I discovered why.

My life came apart. The man overpowered me both physically and psychologically. I had no chance. I cannot speak in detail of what I endured. I was a pure heart when I entered Corpus Sancti and I will leave it as a ravaged soul.

This pattern repeated itself for several months. I wanted to leave, to cry out, to ask others if this was the case for their existence as well. But the vows of silence and obedience were overpowering. It didn't help me that Father Joseph majored in psychology during his college years at DePaul. Ever since then, this brutality and twistedness has buffeted me more than I can count. The cadence of 'Hail Mary, full of grace ... The Lord is with thee' brings only sadness. I cannot escape this monster. That is what he is. Not a man of God, not a servant of Christ. A monster. No matter what the public image is of the man, the reality is that he is a liar, a fount of evil.

The good news is that I have called him on it. The bad news is he is unrepentant and I know there is no way out. The Mob has assisted in apprehending runaways from our community before, and the word in the hallways here is that what awaited those brave souls upon their return was even worse. There is no way out, except one, and it is the road that I have chosen to take. And by the time you receive this, I will have carried out that solution.

Right now, you might be wondering why couldn't I slow down, find a way to reach out to you, to think rationally even for one second. And that is the problem. Slowing down and thinking rationally doesn't help. It just causes the reality to come crashing down again like the walls of an ancient city. There is no way out but one. But it can at least come with an attempt on my part to call out to you one last, desperate time.

I know we have disappointed each other. What has happened in history cannot be reversed. I ran away from a father who never was 'Dad' to me and went looking for that true manifestation and example somewhere else. And there I found it to be even more horrifying than I could have imagined. A man who represented God to me managed to tear apart my soul. Saying the Lord's Prayer makes me want to vomit ferociously. I cannot even audibly get past the words 'Our Father' without silently retching. Whether out of disappointment, violence or manipulation, I hear other voices label me, and the monikers stick. I can't prevent them from doing that. I can neither stop believing them nor break beyond these voices by trusting that something in life will make it all better. I can only run to God on the sole avenue remaining. I can only have peace from evil by removing myself as a target. I am sure others will privately call it a scandal, yet the word won't get out in the media. Many honest ones here will weep that I had nothing left to live for. The leadership will shake their heads and quote the traditional dogma that suicide is the most wicked and selfish of all sins, and because of it I have no hope of eternal life. I see it as the ultimate chance to fall into God's embrace in heaven, because I'm sure not sensing His adoring smile on earth. It is the only move left on the board.

I am passing this letter on to a friend. I am hoping that—due to the official stationery and envelope that I stole from Father Bourque's office—this has a chance of reaching you. I wanted you to know these things because you are my birth father. And even if there has been little, if any, love, you still deserve to know what has been done to me, your son. Perhaps one day you can seek peace and justice in your own way, although for your sake I hope it is a different method than mine. Through it, maybe you will find forgiveness for what you have done. For what it's worth, you have my full blessing to do so. It is the last thing that I can give.

Your son,

Jacob

56

The entire team had shot out of the subdivision and eventually hit the interstate without slowing down. They were all in a race against time, still with no conclusive idea where Webber would strike next.

"The positive thing is we can bank on Webber being Henry. Of that, there's no doubt," said Tori. "So we're heading back into town. I assume you want to stop at Harvest first and see if he's there?"

"Quiet, Tor," said Ballack, planning the next several moves of this chess match in his head. "Head for St. Anselm Church on Mason Road." He called Krieger on his cell phone, hoping that the commander was keeping up with Tori's eighty-mile-per-hour pace. "Change of plans, sir. Don't go to Harvest. Let's stop at St. Anselm and check it out."

"The church at Priory School on Mason?" Krieger was incredulous. "Are you drawing up plays in the dirt?"

"Julian Webber said he attends St. Anselm. That's his home parish. I think Mass is at nine o'clock. It's on the way, so let's stop in there. He might be getting the slate cleaned before he dirties it again with his next victim! Call Hull on his cell and let him know. Scotty, too. I need to suction myself."

"Fine," responded Krieger, "but if we do this, we're getting vested up."

Father David McReynolds made the short trip from the steps to the altar, reverently picking up the book of the Gospel that lay on its beautifully carved wooden stand. He turned to face the congregation spread throughout the church. From the outside, St. Anselm looked like a white mushroom with vertical slashes equidistant from each other running down its sides. But the inside was a well-lit hallowed space of prayer and worship. Father McReynolds truly could not imagine anywhere else he would rather be today.

Looking out upon his fellow celebrants of the sacrifice of the Mass, the priest continued the liturgy in his sonorous voice that seemed out of place with his skinny frame and owl-like face, chanting "The Gospel of the Lord."

The congregation, dutifully responding, offered words well-carved into their religion's history. "Praise be to you, Lord Christ."

Father McReynolds, having found the passage from St. Mark that would be the focus of the sermon that morning, opened his mouth to read the familiar story of Jesus calming both the storm on the sea and the disciples' nerves. However, he never got to that point. At that moment, the doors at the rear of the church opened with such force that he swore they would fall off their hinges. Four people—two men and two women—carrying firearms, as well as a young unarmed man in a power wheelchair, came into the heart of the sanctuary. The parishioners gasped at the sight of the guns and scrambled away from the aisle the five people entered. McReynolds, for his part, was so stunned he fell sideways against the altar, knocking over a plate of Eucharistic wafers already blessed for that day's Holy Communion.

Recovering somewhat, McReynolds called out, "What in heaven's name is going on here? Why are you interrupting our service?"

Krieger slowed to a stop in front of the priest, holstering his pistol and raising his empty hands in an apologetic fashion, showing his identification. "We are deeply sorry to interrupt, Father, but our reason for doing so is absolutely essential. We are seeing if one Julian Webber is in attendance here right now."

Ballack motioned to Hull, who crept toward him.

"What is it?"

"Just quietly tell these people that we're detectives," said Ballack. "I'm not sure how many of them saw Krieger's badge in his hand."

Hull whispered to Tori, then to Crabolli. In the meantime, Ballack joined Krieger and Father McReynolds near the altar. They were already engaged in quiet, yet vigorous, conversation, and it didn't take one to be a genius to recognize the priest was upset.

"He's not here, Commander!" whispered Father McReynolds.

"You haven't seen him all day?" asked Krieger.

"Of course not! This is our only Mass today. We are a small parish for the community and school. I would know! Now if you don't mind, I'd like to pick up where I left off in the Mass. It's bad enough you interrupted Education Sunday!"

Krieger didn't get it, but Ballack scooted up toward the priest. "I thought the Cathedral was celebrating it today, Father," he said.

McReynolds shook his head. "We are among some of the schools in the Archdiocese of St. Louis celebrating this today. Why do you ask?"

Ballack looked at the priest, at Krieger, and then all around the church. His gamble that Webber would be here had been a colossal failure. That meant there was only one possibility remaining.

"Commander, we need to go," he said quietly to Krieger.

"What?"

"Trust me. This was a gamble that turned into a goose chase. I think I know now where he's headed. Just get the crew outside and I'll explain."

"You've got a lot of explaining to do! This better be good."

They passed the rest of their team in the aisle, waving them to join them outside. As they made for the rear of the church, Ballack could hear Father McReynolds begin his Gospel reading. Knowing there was no point waiting any longer, Ballack dialed the rectory's phone number on his cell as they walked out into a morning now suddenly drenched in sunshine.

58

"Hello. Archdiocesan rectory. This is Father Jim Behringer speaking."

"Father Behringer!" Ballack practically bellowed into the phone as the others gathered nearby as he maneuvered up the now-lowered ramp of the Sprinter. "Listen! It's Detective Ballack. When did you say the procession for Education Sunday was taking place?"

"I have to get over there soon," said Behringer. "It's at the ten o'clock Mass with the Cathedral Choir. The archbishop is leading the procession into the Cathedral from the outside steps."

"No!" screamed Ballack as loud as he could while Tori strapped his wheelchair down in the front seat area. "Father, you have to stop the processional. His Excellency's life could be in danger. Is anyone else on staff going to be with him?"

"Yes, of course. Myself and Monsignor Grenier."

"For crying out loud, cancel the processional!" Ballack shouted as Krieger signaled everyone to get in the respective cars and leave. "You're going to get killed! Julian Webber is possibly coming your way."

"Detective, you're not making much sense."

"Nothing is making sense this weekend."

"My previous statement stands, Detective. Perhaps …"

"Father Behringer," Ballack pleaded as Tori swung out of the parking lot, "have you not being paying any attention to what's been going on around your church the last few days?"

"I know you are involved in a murder investigation, but our faith and traditions must go on!"

Ballack was absolutely livid. He couldn't understand why this priest was being a brick wall. Think, he told himself. Keep the line open. He was overwhelmed with anger and confusion when he heard himself saying, "Father, has anything strange occurred since we spoke last night?"

Behringer was silent for several seconds, making Ballack think he'd lost the connection. Suddenly he said, "Actually, Detective, I noticed one thing at the rectory last night. Not so much strange as much as slightly odd. The archbishop had opened some mail and left some of it on a hallway table. Monsignor Grenier said one note had been addressed, not to the rectory itself, but in care of the entire clergy."

"What was it?" asked Ballack ominously as Tori turned eastward onto Highway 40. "Was it a letter?"

"A card, actually. The archbishop said he had found it on the altar in the Cathedral. Looked to be hand-painted and crafted nicely. It had a rendering of the archbishop, the monsignor, and myself on the front flap of the card, with us outside of the Cathedral. A cross—a crucifix, actually—was coming from the left side of the Cathedral and was tipped toward us."

"What?"

"And the inside, if I remember reading it correctly, said 'To eternal life. May God forgive.' That's what I mean by odd."

Ballack's blood ran ice cold. "Father, the cross. Was Jesus' body intact?"

"Detective, I can't take any more time. I have to get over to the church and put on my robe for the processional. I'm late enough as …"

"Was Jesus' body intact?!" shouted Ballack.

"Yes, it was, Detective. And now I really must ..."

"Don't hang up that phone! Don't you dare hang up that phone unless you want me to clobber you in front of God and everybody! The cross itself. The cross! The upright beam in the card painting. Was it broken?"

"Broken? I ... Yes, yes. Come to think of it, I'm sure it was. I at least seem to remember there were wooden splinters everywhere. Now that was odd, too."

A broken cross, thought Ballack. A sloppily broken cross. End game.

"Detective, I'm sorry but I really must go."

"No, Father. Stay on! You said the cross was broken, Jesus was intact, and it was coming out of the bushes. Was someone holding the cross? Can you remember if ..." The dial tone engaged and he realized he'd been talking to dead air for a few seconds. He exploded with rage.

"What's the matter with you people?!" he shouted at the windshield. "You're a priest! You deal with evil every day! Is it so hard to believe that someone wants to murder you?" He slammed his fist on his armrest for the second time that morning.

"Krieger's calling me," said Tori. "Settle down. Where do you want me to tell him we're going?"

Ballack swallowed hard. "The Cathedral. Tell him we need to drop a blanket of cops around that place so hard it looks like we're running a drug bust on St. Peter himself. We have no clue what car

Webber has, so we can't bank on identifying his ride. But we need to do all this fast. And I think I know where he's hiding."

Tori relayed the message to Krieger. She signed off and pressed her foot down on the accelerator. "Scotty's coming, too. He's on 270, coming from an arrest at Frontier Park and we might run into him on the way. When does the processional start?"

"Twelve minutes," Ballack shot back.

"How far is it to the Cathedral again?"

"Probably fifteen minutes, Tor," Ballack said, biting down on the knuckle of his right middle finger. "You've got ten."

59

The detectives were not expecting the streets to be blocked off on Lindell from Euclid Avenue onward. Tori had to slam on the brakes to avoid a collision with a barricade, and Ballack's neck snapped back from the sudden stop. Krieger had decided to go the back way a few blocks previously.

"The least he could have done is tell us about the block-off," groused Tori as she undid Ballack's wheelchair straps and pushed down the toggle switch, releasing the ramp and allowing Ballack to exit the vehicle. A policeman approached them.

"You'll have to stay out. There's a processional into the church and we've had this area blocked off for the last thirty minutes to accommodate the parishioners. We also can't allow anyone to come inside the perimeter due to a mild threat!" he said.

Tori showed her identification, and Ballack displayed his as well, saying, "Hardly a mild threat. Officer, this is our ticket in. This 'mild' threat to the processional? You heard that from Commander Krieger of the Special Investigative Division? Because there's going to be some dead priests lying around unless we get moving."

The cop, named Jansen according to his nameplate, nodded. "Detectives Ballack and Vaughan? Krieger said you had clearance to head in and kick ass, if needed."

"Good. Trust me, we need to," shouted Tori. "Look out for any suspicious approach and dial in to let me know. I'm on channel three."

They turned to race down Lindell Boulevard when Scotty Bosco screeched to a halt, nearly blindsiding them with his Toyota Tundra.

"How many times," Ballack yelled at him when the lieutenant dropped to the ground, "are you going to try to kill me with that truck whenever we're trying to make an arrest?"

"Easy, compadre," replied Bosco. "At least Tori's not at the bottom of a lake this time. We headed directly to the church?"

"On a dead run!" Tori called as she took off. She pulled out her cell phone and dialed Krieger. "Commander," she called into it, "Where are you guys? You remember Cam's report on the way over about the card and everything? ...What? You'll never get through! You'll run right into the ... Oh, okay. Did you give everyone a description of Webber? ... Yeah, about six-two, dark hair, with a mustache. Likely carrying an automatic pistol. You got it. We're on our way, about two blocks out."

Bosco caught her after nearly twenty yards. Ballack had started slowly, needing to readjust the speed on his wheelchair, but with his renewed speed he was closing the gap at full throttle. They were a block away from the Cathedral when they both saw and heard the choir's lilting praises begin the service outdoors. Staring ahead, he saw Monsignor Grenier and Father Behringer follow another priest, who could only be the archbishop. Fresh from his time in San Antonio, he was unwittingly walking into another Alamo. Ballack slowed as the crowd had swelled around the celebrants, starting to form two lines to enter the Cathedral. The human chain cut off most of their visibility of the east grounds in front of the church. They were within twenty yards of the processional.

"I can't see anyone," gasped Tori to both Ballack and Bosco. "Where is he?"

Ballack, keeping his head about him, never forgot Father Behringer's description of the peculiar—no, insidious—card. Leaning to his left, he scanned the cathedral grounds to the left of the clergy. Instinctively, he knew there was no reason to distrust the disturbing notecard sent to the priests. The choir had begun the first stanza of "Come, Christians, Join to Sing." The archbishop had just ascended from the street to the curb and was headed toward the outdoor steps when Ballack saw the shadowy image of a dark-haired creature leaning slightly out of the bushes by the southwest corner of the church. From the left side. It was their broken cross.

"Tori!" he screamed as loud as he could, pointing with his left index finger. "It's Henry! In the bushes! Over there!" Both Tori and Scotty Bosco followed his finger and broke for the line.

"Oh, God help us!" snapped Tori as she realized Webber was crouching for the clearest shot he would have. She couldn't shoot across the processional and endanger the parishioners. But in that moment, Scotty Bosco solved her problem for her, brandishing his gun and screaming "Get down!" as they bore down on the worshipers. Shrieks and cries rent the air as chaos ensued. Ballack sighted an area of the curb that was open for his wheelchair and shot toward it.

In those precious seconds, the entire drama unfolded. Two men, oblivious to Bosco's policeman status and playing hero for their clergy, leveled the lieutenant with a crushing tackle and pinned him to the ground. The maneuver eliminated Bosco from being any more help than he was, but it opened a chink in the line, and Tori leapt through it. In that moment she saw Webber, having taken aim, hesitating because of the commotion. The unforgiving father saw Tori break through into

369

the open, raising her own gun toward him, with an all-too-familiar face rushing behind her, low to the ground in an electric chariot. Webber had taken his eye off the triumvirate of Carlson, Grenier and Behringer and had to swing his vision back toward them for the shots he wanted. As he did so, Tori fired.

The bullet clipped him in the knee, going cleanly through several ligaments and throwing Webber to the ground. As the gathered throng screamed in fright, Tori never broke stride but kept going at full pelt, closing the distance fast and heading straight toward Webber, who was reaching for his pistol that had fallen out of his grip. Tori closed the gap to fifteen yards and had jumped the ledge onto the grass when Webber grasped it and fired from his knees—three quick shots into her chest, knocking her to the ground.

Ballack knew Tori would be okay because of her bulletproof vest, but that still wouldn't stop the shooter from aiming for her head, and besides—Webber now had a clear shot at *him.* The financial officer struggled for his balance, pushing off on his arms and attempting to stand, attempting to finish his quest, reaching desperately to make a final blood atonement for the sins of his past.

But Webber never got the chance. Quickly rounding the west side of the church was Missy Crabolli, followed by Zane Hull and Stu Krieger at full speed. Crabolli was the first one to Webber and went to tackle him. Webber guessed her strategy, though, and used the breakneck pursuit against her, flipping her tail over teakettle onto the grass at Tori's side. Yet the tactic had put Webber himself off-balance, and as he endeavored to right himself, Zane Hull flew at him like an Olympic sprinter and knee-lifted him in full stride in the face.

Webber's nose disintegrated like a sodden pomegranate, and his eyes rolled in the back of his head before he hit the earth with a soft thud.

Only then did Ballack realize he had been holding his breath all along, had broken into the open as a sitting duck for Webber, and had been partly responsible for the screaming around him that was just now beginning to subside. Hull and Krieger were situating Webber and placing the handcuffs on him. Ballack rolled down the sidewalk toward the females, who were visibly shaken and pulling themselves together near the retaining wall that hovered above the pavement. Ballack stopped in front of Crabolli and looked at Tori, who had picked herself up off the ground, three holes perforating her Fort Zumwalt South sweatshirt.

"You okay?" he asked.

She nodded. "You owe me, partner. He just ruined my favorite shirt."

"Better that than these classy threads," Ballack replied, touching his navy long-sleeve polo. He gritted his teeth in a superhuman—and successful—attempt at holding back the tears. The adrenaline from the chase and capture had finally hit the wall, giving way to a flood of emotion.

Missy Crabolli slid over toward Tori, gripping her shoulder. "Was that your fire? That was a shot for the ages."

Zane Hull was pulling the handcuffed Webber up from a prone position and maneuvered him toward the sidewalk. Ballack drove over to Krieger, who had been joined by Bosco. The lieutenant had apparently broken free of his tacklers, but he was wincing in pain and holding the back of his head. "Trying to get yourself killed again, cubbie?" he asked Ballack.

"One of these days I might just succeed," Ballack replied.

Krieger gestured toward the church steps. "Looks like the fathers have picked up the scent and are coming over here to give us a big wet sloppy kiss." Ballack and Bosco followed his line of sight. Behringer and Grenier were approaching with unsteady gaits, behind the obviously appreciative and bug-eyed archbishop.

"Before they do, there's something I need to say," said Ballack, and he whisked past Krieger. He scooted ten feet to his left toward Hull and their captured Henry. Ballack came face to face with a kneeling and glowering Julian Webber, no more than a foot away from his nose.

"Julian Webber, you lying, pathetic vengeance whore. You've gained the right to remain silent."

EPILOGUE
"Amen"

(September 26-27)

60

No matter if you were in a hospital rightly judged to be among the nation's elite, thought Ballack, the same core sensations were undeniably palpable. The sour whiff of disinfectant; the constant hum and footfalls of food service workers or those involved in supply, processing and distribution of linen; the cookie-cutter look of the patient rooms; and what seemed to be at least one flickering ceiling light on every floor. Submerged in his thoughts, he took the elevator to the sixth floor with Tori at his side. It was time for their final confrontation with Henry.

The policewoman at the door checked their identification and stood aside.

"Has he been quiet today?" asked Tori.

"No trouble from him," said the guard. "But we are making sure. We even have a security camera in there in case he tries any funny business. Still, he'd be stupid to try. Until about an hour ago, he was still incoherent because of the pain meds. Doctors have lessened the dosage, so maybe you'll get him to sing."

"Thank you, Officer," said Ballack, and the detectives entered the room.

The space that Julian Webber inhabited for his recovery was more pleasant than the garden-variety medical center fare. The walls had the right combination of almond-colored paint with green trim. The windows opened to a towering view of Highway 40, and he enjoyed a decent sight of the Science Center and St. Louis University High School. Tori took the recliner on the far side of Webber's bed while Ballack positioned himself between the bed and the sink area. Tori unsnapped her holster should she need her gun one more time.

Webber stirred from his nap and awoke to find two familiar detectives in a much different environment. He sat up with some difficulty. Tori made no move to help him.

"I guess you've both come to question me yet again," declared Webber.

"Actually," replied Ballack, "We figured you might want to do the questioning and find out how we landed on your space in this game. If you're expecting us to return the favor, wouldn't you want your lawyer present?"

"Well, we haven't had much time to slow down over some hot dogs and beer, so I'll play along. And I don't need a lawyer. I've done what I intended to do. Why admit shame to that? When did you know?"

"When the loose ends keep getting more and more that way," said Tori, "you just follow the threads."

"I have to hand it to you," said Ballack. "You stitched together a fairly compelling alibi."

"Not good enough," replied Webber. "At what point did you know it was me?"

"Two nights ago. It was a chance statement by someone else, a mention of a newspaper, that triggered our conversation from Saturday."

"Newspaper triggered something?"

"You said you had been painting and you even showed me your fingertips as proof. The problem was there was no newspaper, no drop cloth, or anything underneath your easel in the studio. Had you just finished painting, I would expect it to be glistening wet. You were, after all, using oils. That was clear even from a cursory glance across the room. That meant the stuff on your hands might not have been paint, but hair dye."

"And how did you get from there to here?"

"Father Joseph's collection bin of memories. That's where I ran across Jacob's picture. We knew about the Philippe suicide from another source. I found some digital documents in Father Joseph's stuff that connected me the rest of the way."

He nodded to Tori, who tossed an envelope on Webber's lap.

"We made a copy of it for evidence," continued Ballack. "But I thought—despite your actions—you deserved to have the original."

Webber slid the picture of his son out of the envelope. For several fleeting moments, his eyes grew soft and moist.

"Thank you," he said.

"There's no need to thank us," said Ballack. "However, I do believe you owe us an explanation of several things, beginning with Toby Zweig's murder."

Webber looked down at his son's picture, a rueful stare pouring from his eyes. "All those years ago, ages they were. I was a happier man and a worse person then."

"Mr. Webber," said Ballack in a voice pregnant with hurriedness. "About Toby Zweig, please."

"Of course. He was part of the equation. Wrong place, wrong time, wrong ideas. He insisted on defending Father Joseph on all those abuse cases. Typical defense attorney. Never worry about the facts as they are. Just change them into what they can become. We met as a group two days before his death and he kept at it. He wanted to be the kingpin on that case. Setting a man free to ruin the lives of more of God's children. That made him part of the game. Defending the man who destroyed my son. It was more than I could bear."

"Is that why you stole his dagger, then put the case back?" asked Ballack.

"To that," replied Webber, "I plead guilty, although it's not theft if you need it. And besides, Toby Zweig would make sure Father Joseph walked free."

"You're absolutely sure of that, that he had committed to defending Father Joseph to the death?" asked Tori.

"I am," replied Webber, "only it turned out to be his death. To do so protected the innocent. I can't bring back Jacob, or repair my marriage, or have a connection with my daughter anymore. But I can keep that from happening in the lives of others. I can be their redeemer."

"Redeemer?" asked Ballack. The prospect of Webber having a Christ complex was bad enough, he thought. What if he discovered that he had murdered in vain, that he had snuffed the life out of a principled counselor who was determined to throw that very case because he and Webber had something in common, seeing Father Joseph as a murderer? Ballack suddenly thought better of it and decided not to tell Webber that explosive bit of detail.

"The phone call from your boss to Tabitha Stowe. Your idea?"

"What a bright young man you are, Detective! What a worthy adversary!" Webber's voice was lost in the deep ravine between the cliffs of civility and sarcasm. "Jerome didn't think it would work, but I mentioned that hitting him in the romantic nerve would be more subtle yet effective. Of course, I was banking on the likelihood Miss Stowe would go for it. She was already under duress because of the letter implicating us in the conspiracy trial. But she was more loyal to Toby than I imagined she'd be."

"But it wasn't her fault, about the letter, that is. She was more conscientious than that. Someone else would have placed that in there, someone who had an axe to grind with the Archdiocese of St. Louis. You had done that to gain victory in the upcoming trial."

"Is that a crime to add to the list of charges, Detective?"

"Just a piece to the puzzle. I think you'll have trouble enough with what we've already scraped together. Two counts of murder, three of attempted murder, and you shot my partner here."

Webber sneered at Tori, who gave her own evil eye in return. "Don't you dare," she seethed, "give me a chance to return the favor."

Ballack put up his hand to quell her fomenting temper. "So you couldn't budge Tabitha Stowe?"

"When she delayed, I couldn't take any chances."

"The only way was murder?"

"As I am guessing from your ringless finger, Detective, you are neither married nor have you had the joy or responsibility of having children. It must be an alien universe to you. I doubt you've ever known the sadness and tragedy of loss. I knew when she delayed her response that it would never come to my advantage. And besides, I felt some relief when she said no. This was not to be her restitution, but mine."

Webber's comment caused Ballack to seethe internally. He saw his late brother's image in his mind and wished with all his heart he could throttle Webber for that statement. "You believe that murdering Toby Zweig and Father Joseph was an offering so that you'd be forgiven?"

"A complex matter, but yes, Detective. I have suffered egregiously since Jacob left our home. I have come to see that it was my arrogance and improper expectations that pushed him away. How I wish … how I wish to God it had not fallen out this way! I had placed him in the path of danger, had shoved him into the valley of the shadow of death. I was responsible for causing him to encounter the man who destroyed him. The only way I could forgive myself was to destroy the destroyer, but it soon became more than that."

"Father Joseph's death would never be full satisfaction, would it?"

"Over the past year, as our case moved toward trial, I came to believe that anyone who aligned himself with my enemy became my enemy. You might label this as a complete break from reality, but it is only a few moves from the desire for forgiveness to the utter, driving passion to take a life. To see the surprise in Toby Zweig's eyes was not enough. For me to be cleansed, I needed to see the light leave those eyes, and I had to be the one who took it from him."

"There's little point asking about Father Joseph," said Tori. "The anniversary of Jacob's death coincides with the date, hour, and method of Father Joseph's death. And I'm guessing you made sure you scored access to his extra entry card to the hotel, from a previous visit."

"As I've said before, Detectives, you have done your homework."

"And the broken crosses?" said Ballack. "A nice touch. Your way of declaring forgiveness for your sin in advance or admittance of guilt for your failure and brokenness as a father?"

Webber said nothing.

"Tell you what, forget that. It's obvious that's the case. But it never crossed your mind," asked Ballack, "to see that murder is hardly the benchmark for absolution? That what your Church calls a mortal sin cannot truly make a right? That your actions show no respect toward the laws of mankind or the laws of the God of your religion? That your choice would hardly qualify you, in the eyes of many, as a good Catholic?"

"I have nothing to apologize for, Detective Ballack, no matter what you might think. The world is safer today for innocent children and young adults because of what I did. I am still a faithful Catholic because I sought to clear the earth of those who were faithless. And before you even try, you have no right to judge me as evil. My son was a victim of that evil. Others who defended Father Joseph and gave him a position and vocation in time of need were perpetuating and maintaining that evil. So don't think for one second you can roll in here, gloat in this arrest, and judge me for what I did!"

Ballack decided the lovefest was over. He reversed himself toward the door, but before he turned to leave, he decided the time was right for one last salvo.

"Mr. Webber, I am just here to investigate the evidence and make an arrest. The trial is up to a jury and judge, and God, if he exists. For the record, I am truly sorry for the death of your son, if for no other reason than this: that you would not have turned into the creature you are, and so others might be spared your need to play the roles of both savior and saved."

61

Tori decided to make a pit stop in the restroom by the waiting area, so Ballack waited by the elevators in the interim. Nurses and other hospital staff strolled past him while he finalized his official report for Krieger and Bosco. Suddenly, the elevator doors opened, revealing someone whose presence was as strangely pleasing as it was ironic.

"Detective Ballack?" said the scrub-adorned employee upon disembarking the elevator. He was pushing a small cart of tubes, labels, needles and other materials.

Ballack looked up at his spontaneous visitor and extended his hand. "Well, Greg Varner, how odd it is to see you outside the Cathedral's walls. How are you doing, sir?"

"Meeting post-surgical deadlines before the morning shift ends in an hour, then it's off to pray, as usual. What are you doing here? Visiting someone? How has the case gone?"

"Well," smiled Ballack. "You'd be shocked at how closely those three questions are linked. That's all I can say right now, but suffice it that we got our man."

"That's a relief. The last thing I want is to know my spiritual home is stained by an unsolved crime."

"I think there are more 'last things' you'd want than that, Greg."

"True. True." He looked thoughtful, and then he drew closer to Ballack. "Detective, I want to thank you."

"Thank me? I should at least be thanking you for being part of this."

"Not about the murder," said Varner. "About what we talked about in the chapel last week. What I told you about my life story and the painful stuff of my past. I wanted to thank you for listening."

"I asked you a question about your religious commitment. I was intrigued. You answered. I hardly thought you or I went above and beyond the call of duty there."

"Maybe you thought that, Detective Ballack, but what you didn't know is that you're the first person—aside from my coach—with whom I shared those memories. They were painful enough as they were, but what was even more painful was the feeling that perhaps I wasn't truly forgiven for what I did. And the more I thought of it lately, before the murder, was that maybe I felt that way because I had never shared it with anyone else. That was what I was thinking about the day you first bumped into my pew. When I saw you again and you said you wanted to question me, I took that as a sign."

"A sign?"

"From God. That there was a reason you were speaking to me, so that I could eventually get the memory of my past story off my chest to someone else. Righting my life's ship is one thing. Moving toward a better position elsewhere is another. But I felt God was showing me that I needed to understand his forgiveness by speaking to another person, and God's pardon would become real through that individual's reaction."

"My listening to you was an answer to prayer?"

"You asked, I spoke, you listened, and you accepted my story, never condemning me, Detective Ballack. Because of that, I can say this: Perhaps you consider yourself a lousy pilgrim, or no pilgrim at all. Yet you overlooked my wrong, and because of that, you gave me a picture of God. So that's what I meant when I said I wanted to thank you."

There was a long pause, and then Varner said, "Well, I've been chatting way too much on the clock. I've got to draw blood from a patient down this hallway."

"New patient?"

"Apparently came in yesterday around noon. Now post-surgery. Someone shot him in the knee and the clip zapped his ligaments. Hope he's in a good mood."

Ballack could hardly stifle a cackle as he saw Tori approaching from the other direction. "Well, Greg, good luck with that. Just one word of advice. Don't expect him to be in a good mood. I'll see you." And with the irony invoking further chuckles, he left Greg Varner standing there with a dumbfounded look on his face.

62

The next day brought abundant sunshine and a high temperature in the low seventies. Ballack had called Dana the night before and the two of them agreed their date could be delayed no longer. She suggested dinner out and an evening by the lake, to which Ballack readily agreed. But first there was the nasty business of returning to the scene of the crime, seeking closure in more ways than one.

The Cathedral Basilica was the site of an enormous crowd for the funeral of Tobias Stefan Zweig. The archbishop gave a powerful eulogy, a veritable litany of Zweig's most worthy qualities. The requiem Mass was complemented by shared memories, with Monsignor Grenier, Andra Alexander and Monica Zweig giving testimony of the man's character and honor. Even daughter Serena read a poem she had written for the occasion, moving several in the nave to tears when she laid the copy of those tender stanzas on her father's coffin, tucking them within the spray of flowers.

Ballack hung back from the receiving line afterward, not wanting to give either of the Zweig females any memory of the murder investigation than was absolutely necessary. He looked around and saw Tabitha Stowe was in attendance. Brazen, thought Ballack, but understandable.

One notable absence was that of Jerome McPadden, but Ballack thought it would have been in considerably poor taste. He was about to signal Tori that they should make their exit when he felt a tap on his shoulder. He turned around to find the archbishop towering over him.

"Detective Ballack," he said, "and you, Detective Vaughan. I want to convey our deepest thanks and relief to both of you for your work. You have saved our lives in the process and brought a murderer to justice."

"We arrested him, Your Excellency," said Tori, "Justice is up to the courts. That's the gamble we take."

"I'm sorry for the grief this has caused, Your Excellency," added Ballack. "I can only hope this brings some closure."

"We will still feel ripples of sadness for some time," said Monsignor Grenier, who had come up from behind so quietly his voice startled the detectives.

Ballack looked at the monsignor with a stony stare, nodded, then turned and rolled his way out of the Cathedral.

A quick lunch break with Tori burned the ninety minutes between the funeral and when the clergy would return from the burial service. Neither detective had any desire to traverse northward to Calvary Cemetery and see Zweig's body laid to rest. Ballack could live without contemplating such gravity.

They arrived back at the Cathedral parking lot one more time and Ballack hurried down the Sprinter's ramp. "You sure you don't need me, partner?" asked Tori.

"I'll be okay," he replied. "If I get worked up, I'll suction myself. This is something I'd like to do alone.

He rovered to the front door of the rectory and rang the bell three times in succession. The door opened, revealing a heavy-set man

387

of nearly forty with a bushy mustache, wearing a black shirt and gray trousers. Ballack judged him to be a sexton for either the rectory or Cathedral, or both.

"Detective Cameron Ballack," he said, "I would like to speak to the monsignor for a few minutes."

The sexton ushered him into Grenier's study. The monsignor was finishing an email, one that—according to him—was a report on the tragedies of the last few days, and he was sending it straight to the Vatican. He seemed reluctant to divulge how much detail was in the note.

After the sexton had left the room and shut the door, Grenier looked at Ballack with some relief mixed with trepidation. It was steaming off the priest's persona like excessive cologne from a teenage boy on prom night.

"I want to thank you personally, Detective," he began.

"Details, Monsignor. You're thanking me for what?"

"For justice, for diligence, for discretion, for everything you provided throughout the course of this investigation."

Ballack ground his teeth. "That sounds," he replied, "like the sort of relieved answer someone gives when they've dodged a major bullet."

"I don't understand."

"This justice, this case, it wasn't cut and dry. We might have caught a murderer, that's true. And Julian Webber is guilty as sin. But mightn't there be considerable guilt on the hands of the Church which allowed this disaster?"

"Guilt? On us?"

388

"Yes. Because no matter how well you tried to work things out, no matter how noble your intentions were in giving Father Joseph a chance, there was a deviant in a position of religious authority, representing your God to others. His police record in Connecticut was a matter of public record, his dalliances and Jacob Webber's suicide were major blots on his ledger. Yet you shuttled him here …"

"Now wait, Detective, and get your facts straight. We did not shuttle him here …"

"Well, you accepted him and the stained reputation he brought with him …"

"He was re-directed here! I don't know what your expertise might be in the field of ecclesiastical maneuvers, but it wasn't like we had much choice."

"I don't follow, Monsignor. I hope there's a story behind those maneuvers."

"Simply put, Father Joseph came from the Archbishop of Chicago, and in the superstructure of Catholicism, Chicago outranks St. Louis any day of the week and twice on Sunday."

"And yet in terms of statesmanship and recent favoritism from the Vatican, it could be argued St. Louis has the upper hand."

Grenier raised his eyebrows. "You're quick on the draw."

Ballack shrugged, "Even an agnostic like me does some reading to know which way the wind is blowing."

"So," replied Grenier, "should we receive blame for doing the best possible thing we could with damaged goods when handed a bad card? Don't you have to battle against the unreasonableness of bureaucracy at times?"

"I'm not saying that, Monsignor. I get the whole political thing. But try seeing it from my side of things, having been through a dangerous weekend. My partner and I handled a murder case with discretion and tact. I think that calls for courtesy. Doubtless that calls for transparency and answers. Given all the garbage and filth we ran across in this inquiry over the past few days, one could argue that you should be willing to give us gold medals before a packed house at Scottrade Center."

"Father Joseph's indiscretions followed him here. They did not originate here, Detective."

"That's true, and I agree with you there, Monsignor. But what if others contend that all you have done is fence and contain what your Church calls evil, not eradicate it? From where I sit, that's not good enough."

"Then let me put forth the facts. We removed him from Santa Maria. That's a line in the sand."

"Your response to his wrongdoing was to re-assign him to a post as remote director of development, overseeing the demise of a school as part of a re-distribution of hush money. And he did that from the relative comfort of a plush room at the Drury Plaza, where he could enjoy free breakfast and dinner."

Again, Greneier fell silent at Ballack's onslaught.

Ballack continued, "I'll bet the indoor swimming pool and weight room reminded him of how Jesus championed the cause of the poor and oppressed."

Grenier looked immeasurably sad. "Detective Ballack, I'll let you get that out of your system. But now allow me to respond. We in

390

the Archdiocese fought against Quinn's transfer every step of the way. God knows we have enough problems of our own without tossing any more fuel on the fire. And God gives us the grace to meet every challenge. But neither do we have the right as His shepherds to accept wolves in our midst."

"Quinn got in anyway."

"Forced in over our protests. I can show you enough correspondence between His Excellency and the Vatican to prove that."

"Private correspondence?" asked Ballack.

"The archbishop was furious about the appointment," said Grenier, "but he was just as much a churchman. He wasn't going to do this in an open forum and drag the Church's name through the mud. If Christ loved the Church and gave himself up for her, then we shouldn't shoot one another in broad daylight."

"Admirable," said Ballack quietly, "but Quinn was still here."

"Is that a sin on the part of our superiors, to put a priest in a more limited role?" asked Grenier. "To believe that he should not have the authority he once did, but still believing in the remnants of God's vocational call still upon the man, flawed though he was? I would answer their decision was wrong. Unfortunately, I was not in position to make that call."

"Flawed? That's not the card I'd play when he had a bin full of horrific porn in his hotel room the night of his death. Then again, given the plug-our-finger-in-the-hole-of-the-dike mentality typical of much of America's religion, I shouldn't be surprised they felt this was one of the few remaining options."

Grenier shifted in his chair, positioning himself so he was sitting up more erect. "Whether that decision was sinful or not," he said to Ballack, "Julian Webber committed the two murders."

"Again, I concur. But, Monsignor, is it so difficult for you to see here what some people would label hypocrisy?"

"Where?"

"Why does the Church—Catholic, Episcopal, Presbyterian, Baptist, whatever— command her rank-and-file to come before their leaders, begging for scraps of hope while their salvation hangs by a thread? Why demand such an approach, when there's such obstinate refusal on the part of many leaders to say 'I'm sorry. Please forgive me'?"

"The sin of the clergy of this Church is to our sadness and shame. My only prayer is that—speaking for our tradition—people would see the Catholic Church is greater than the sum of the failures of its leaders. For every Joseph Quinn, there are scores of monks and nuns living in willing, loving fidelity to their vows. For every Toby Zweig who follows his roving eye toward other women—and yes, it's not like that was a secret—there are priests who faithfully preach the Gospel and serve the poor, the indigent and the oppressed all over the world. For every dubious organization within our expansive reach, there are dozens that clothe the naked, feed the hungry and shelter the homeless."

He leaned toward the detective, peering over the desk, and added, "You would wound and denigrate all that good by emphasizing the existing evil, all in pursuit of truth?"

Ballack swallowed hard. "Monsignor, seeking purity is hardly denigrating a faith community. I don't doubt the Catholic Church does a world of good. You'd have to be an idiot to deny that. But that's not my point. Your Church has a billion followers scattered over this planet. It would be not only irresponsible, but also arrogant to assume a whitewashed global monolith of devotion. My problem is with wherever that assembly refuses to stand in the light of day, because if any part of any church or religion willfully chooses mass secrecy, it cannot claim to speak the truth honestly. If Christians are content with wearing masks and cloaking the past, why should anyone set their faces to follow their God?"

"A noble black-and-white view of religion," replied Grenier, "but reality forces us to live in shades of gray."

"Don't be so sure, Monsignor. Your gray can't exist unless you have two things."

"What are they?"

"The existence of my black and white combined together, Father. You can live in stained glass comfort for the remainder of your days. And I'm not upset by that. If there is a God, I think he should be worshipped in majestic cathedrals and in the beauty and tradition that he deserves if he is all that Christendom has professed him to be. But I tremble at the thought of kowtowing to the enemy of honest belief."

"And what is that, Detective? The Catholic Church herself?"

"No, Monsignor. If anything, the Catholic Church kept knowledge alive throughout history at times most needed. I'm not saying the enemy is Catholicism, Orthodoxy, Protestantism or any religion outside those bounds. It's simply the bad, poisonous faith that accounts neither for human flaws nor the need to be open about them."

Grenier looked extremely thoughtful as he adjusted his eyeglasses. "What if you could look past the public persona of religion and look at what honest priests, leaders and laypeople are doing day after day? I'll be honest, Detective. The bureaucracy tires me out. Do you think I have to agree with everything that arises in the Church? I know that I can't overcome all the flaws of my spiritual home. My Church has deep faults, egregious blemishes and devastating failures. For heaven's sake, I do as an individual priest. But what would you expect from the Church when it is made up of flawed humans? Do you look upon the errors with indignation or do you marvel with joy at what good comes out of our honest efforts? Or do you try to strike a balance? And if so, how?"

Ballack could have sworn he saw a soft glow of honest confession in Greneier's eyes. "Monsignor, all I'm asking for is transparency. And I think that's all anyone would want."

The monsignor rubbed the ring on his right hand, smiled and said, "That is indeed a view of religion that any of us would aspire to, and I wish God would give all of us the grace to pull that off. However, less charitable folk would label it primitive. I hope we get closer to your goals in my lifetime. As for me, my way of doing that now is to make sure the victims of abuse in our churches are cared for and restored as much as possible. That might cost me much, but it's what truth demands. Perhaps your call is to be the type of person to hold the faithful accountable. I would just caution you that despite your best intentions, remember you are just one man."

Ballack turned his wheelchair power on and set himself to leave the room. Before gliding away from the monsignor's desk, he looked Grenier dead in the eye.

"One man. Determination. And hope. Victory has occurred with fewer resources. But thank you for at least being direct. Whatever has happened within this past week, I can say that I honor you and I respect you. Good day, Monsignor. Walk in faith." And he headed out into a gorgeous late September afternoon.

63

Scotty Bosco drummed his fingers on the top of the Ballacks'
dining room table. Three glasses of iced tea rested on coasters, one
each in front of him, Cameron Ballack and Tori Vaughan. Their post-
investigation roundtable discussion had been free of bureaucratic
bleating; both detectives knew they would never get the politically
correct runaround from their boss. Bosco knew Tori wanted to get
home and catch the sleep that had eluded her the last week. He felt
rather than realized a strange reluctance within Ballack to speak out
about the travails of the past week. Finally he said point blank, "You
two, what are you hiding? It's me. Speak up."

Tori looked at Ballack, who reached for his glass of tea,
content to speak second. She began, "Look, Scotty. We know that this
new opportunity could feel more like pain than promise at times. No
one doubts there were some less-than-ideal moments. I'm just
wondering if the exhaustion and the puttering around these land mines
are going to be par for the course from here on out."

"Only in cases involving the Archdiocese, Tor," said Ballack.

"I know it was a new experience, guys," said Bosco. "You
were going around a larger area than what you're used to. For crying
out loud, your previous case was centered on a twenty-acre plot of
land. Plus, you're used to working together and getting by with one of
Ballack's reports to me. Things spread out more on the SID. You get
the feeling of being thinned out more. My question is, can you handle
it?"

Ballack didn't hesitate this time. "We're not quitting, Boss. We
just had to get used to the way the wind was blowing."

"We're sticking it out, Scotty, if for no other reason than to say we're a couple of good cops who can get things done."

"That, I'm glad to hear," said Bosco. "One other thing that's been eluding me. It has to do with knowing it was Webber but eliminating Pat Fishwick at the same time. How did you know it wasn't the latter?"

"Things happened so fast Saturday night that my brain was working ahead of what I could share," said Ballack, "When I called Tori then to tell her we were going after Webber the next morning, she said 'That explains a lot.'"

"I had gotten off the phone with Fishwick not one minute before," said Tori. "He had called me to resolve his guilty complex. He explained that he had left the Drury earlier that day because there were several folks wanting to meet with him in Jefferson City. Some more potential lawsuits for 10:21 and all that. They heard he was in the area and offered to put him up at the Truman Hotel there if he could meet with them from Saturday night through Monday. He was so caught up in getting another lead that he forgot how bad it would look if he left the area."

"What an idiot," said Bosco, shaking his head.

"I think he sees that now," replied Ballack. "Being a scatterbrain in that respect doesn't make you guilty."

"And he was quite gracious," said Tori. "He completely understood why we were up in arms about it. And given what's coming out about Father Joseph and 'Philippe' he could see why we'd keep an eye on him. He had never been straightforward about how his son Phil died."

"Did he clear that up for you?" Bosco asked.

"Evidently, Phil did die in the company of a priest, but the cleric wasn't at fault," said Ballack. "It was a rafting trip with the youth group in their Omaha church. They went out to eastern Colorado and were going down the Arkansas River. One of the flumes got unwieldly and, unbeknownst to the other kids in the raft, Phil tumbled out and hit his head on a rock. Knocked unconscious and somehow he didn't have his life jacket on properly."

Bosco shut his eyes, shaking his head slowly as Tori concluded. "The jacket came off, and Phil was never that good of a swimmer to begin with. He had drowned before the priest and the kids knew what had happened. To his credit, Pat and his family have remained members of that parish since then. Can't say they haven't been faithful despite the fact it is a painful memory."

Bosco nodded and pulled himself together, as if he was preparing to leave. "Anything else?"

"Just try to grant us one thing, boss," added Ballack.

"What's that?"

"The next SID case we take, we want Zane Hull and Missy Crabolli at our side."

"You want a reunion?" a shocked Bosco exclaimed.

"Absolutely, Boss," said Tori. "I know we had our battles and all, but we grew to respect each other quickly."

"What we discovered was there's a synergy there," added Ballack. "We may have different ideas of how to reach our goal, but we want the same thing, and that mutual purpose fills in the gaps rather than magnifies them."

Bosco shrugged his shoulders. "You're completely sure?"

Ballack nodded. "We're not asking you, sir. We're telling you."

64

With the sun setting beyond Creve Coeur Lake, Ballack leaned back in his wheelchair, a serene and delighted expression flooding his face. Dana sat on the bench next to him, a midnight black fleece blanket covering the two of them, protection from the evening's dropping temperatures. Dinner at Shogun Steak House had left both pleasantly full. Dana fidgeted with the keys in her pocket. She had borrowed the Ballacks' Honda Odyssey for the evening to ensure he had a vehicle for transport. Ballack had complained about sitting in the back, separated from Dana while she drove, but in retrospect he was glad for any time they could have now. The evening was well nigh perfect, and he drew a blast of autumn air into his nostrils.

"A thermos of hot chocolate would be just the thing now," whispered Dana.

Ballack nodded. "Possibly when the temps dip into the thirties. I'd drink some, but I don't know if it's the thing to mix around with the scallops I just ate."

Dana leaned in, pressing her body into Ballack's left side, brushing her hair back as the breeze made it difficult for the light brown locks to stay in place. She looked at him, taking in his stony brown eyes that had seen too much of a difficult life and observed additional hardship in a difficult job. It had been his duty that had brought them together at first; would there be more than that to sustain a matched journey?

Stroking a miniscule chip on her left middle fingernail, she asked him directly, "Cameron? Why did you come by school on Friday? I know you say that you were showing you meant business and all, but I know your work is crazy. You knew I'd be happy with a phone call at night before bed. So why come by?"

Ballack grinned, remembering the delight and shock on her face when she turned around in the stands upon receiving his text message. "You getting a phone call wasn't the issue. I didn't want to be one of those guys who will find time when it's convenient, yet stay at arms' length. Too many people have admired the uphill battles I've had, spoken of whatever courage they say has been there and even prayed for me. But when it comes down to it, the idea of really getting to know me, listening, and having patience with me being very slow to accept and trust others ... well, people often interpret that as a wall. Or others like to build those walls and keep me at a distance. I don't blame them. I sometimes wonder what it's like for you to be you and be here with me. I'm not sure I'd know what to do with me. It's just that once we left Harvest that day after we interviewed Julian Webber, I had a moment of clarity. I at least wanted to show you I wasn't someone who hid. I might not be much more than that. Maybe I've had the challenges and down points of life, not to withdraw from pain, but to rise above it. And even for those few moments, I wanted to rise above a comfort zone of distance and just see you."

The sun continued its descent behind the soccer fields that bordered the west side of the lake. Dana said, "You thought of all that on the way over to Whitfield?"

Ballack smiled. "Not bad, huh?"

She looked out at the glimmering, shadowy water. "When I saw you there, I knew something was afoot. I know we've compared life notes and relationship ledgers, and my stories are different from yours, but I often think we're at the same place together."

"Which is what?"

"We want something, with each other, that is more than what happened as a result of February, more than a reaction to tragedy. Even if that's a mystery for now, if you believe what you just told me, then I am willing to reach for it."

"I'd like to think it's possible," said Ballack, and as he did so, he took his index finger and stroked her cheek. "Even if it means more challenges."

"I hope we've put the lion's share of them behind us," Dana replied, looking somewhat pensive as the words crossed her lips.

"At least …" began Ballack, but before he could fashion any more of his thought, his cell phone rang. He groaned, wanting to kick himself for not turning it off during his few quiet moments with Dana. "I don't believe this."

"It's not another murder, is it?" laughed Dana, trying to wish away any work-related crises. "What does the caller ID say? It's not your boss or Tori, is it?"

"Whatever it is," Ballack said, staring at the screen of his phone, "it's not a murder, unless something has happened at St. Luke's Hospital." He thought hard. "That's odd. Dad's not on call tonight. I wonder who this could be."

He pushed the talk button and spoke as clearly as he could. "Good evening. This is Cameron Ballack having the time of his life right now, so this had better be good."

Dana rolled her eyes.

A deep voice on the other end of the line erupted in side-splitting laughter. "Oh, trust me, Detective Ballack, this will only add to the time of your life, my friend!"

"Excuse me?" replied Ballack. He shrugged to Dana, drawing a complete blank. The voice was somewhat familiar, but he couldn't make a positive ID. "Um, I'm not sure how you'll do that, but can you identify yourself and we can take it from there?"

"Well, I can identify myself or the lovely lady next to me, but I think you might like to hear from someone else."

And as the caller paused, a baby cried in the background, a sweet call of life so clear and loud that Dana heard it perfectly. "It's not …" she began.

"Oh, my word," Ballack finally got it. "Father Timothy! You had your baby!"

The strictest professor Ballack had ever known, one who brought back vivid memories of the St. Basil's Seminary case, now chortled at high volume into the phone. "Well, technically Jennifer did all the work. I just held the cup of ice chips. She delivered just twenty minutes ago. A son. God Most High be praised! We have a son!"

For the first time since those bitterly cold days that February, Ballack eyes pooled with tears, this time for joy. He mouthed to Dana, "They had their baby. A son."

Without asking, Dana took the phone. "Father Timothy! Oh, my gosh, congratulations!"

The silence on the other end of the line gave way to recognition. "Dana? This is a surprise! What a wonderful blessing to catch the two of you together!"

"Saves him a phone call," guffawed Ballack. "Put it on speaker so we can both hear."

Dana did so, then asked, "Now the typical female questions. Name, weight and length."

"I'll gladly give you the first two, as long as you respect the fact that, as a former basketball player, I prefer to call the third item 'height.' But here you are: Linus Gregory Birchall. Nine pounds, twelve ounces. Twenty-three inches."

Ballack cringed. "Holy smokes. I don't even want to think how brutal that was. Welcome to childbirth."

"My womb hurts just thinking about it," said Dana, who stopped in mid-sentence, again looking thoughtful, and for a second Ballack thought he could see a fleeting trace of pain behind her eyes.

"I have one request of each of you," said Father Timothy. "Please hear me out. I know it's been awhile since you were at St. Basil's. But if we are out prior to the weekend, as we should be, we are planning on Linus receiving the mystery of baptism this coming Sunday in the chapel at the seminary. I know this is on short notice, but it would mean the world to us if you could attend."

The Orthodox priest didn't have to ask again. Dana nodded to Ballack with tears forming in the corners of her eyes, and he took the phone and said, "Father Timothy, we'll be there. You can count on it."

"Thank you, Cameron. Dana, thank you as well. It is so good to hear your voices. Now I need to make some more calls."

"You do that, Father. And congratulations again."

"We have a son. A son! Glory to God."

Ballack closed his eyes, and the response was out of his mouth before he realized what he was saying, "Glory to God indeed."

How long they sat there, leaning into each other—he in his wheelchair, she on the bench—Ballack didn't know. The sun had disappeared and the new moon was hanging in the heavens above. The night was full of bliss, of thanksgiving for the birth of a child, of warmth for the hope that symbolized, and of joy for the young lady pressed against him.

"Anything is possible," he heard Dana say. "Even this."

He turned toward her and saw she was already leaning in closer. Her lips, soft and inviting, intersected his in a gentle kiss. He opened his eyes afterward and saw she was still looking at him.

"Even this," he said, and they both turned westward, looking out over the lake as its waves shimmered on the surface.

LUKE HERRON DAVIS is the author of the Cameron Ballack Mystery Series, of which *The Broken Cross* is the second volume, following his debut novel *Litany of Secrets.* Born in Kansas, he has taught in the religion departments at private schools in Louisiana, Virginia, Florida, and Missouri. He presently teaches Ethics at Westminster Christian Academy in St. Louis. Luke, his wife Christy, and their children make their home in St. Charles, Missouri.

www.ingramcontent.com/pod-product-compliance
Lightning Source LLC
Chambersburg PA
CBHW020928020726
47495CB00002B/399